Praise for the Neil Gulliver and Stevie
Marriner Novels by Robert S. Levinson

"It's a quick read, a glib insider tour of Hollywood, a fun book
for a James Dean Fan."
　　　　—*The Florida Times-Union* on *The James Dean Affair*

"A smart, sassy, fast-paced crime read that is funny, inventive,
and hard to put down. . . .Levinson's debut should leave many
ardently hoping that it just begins what ought to be a most en-
tertaining series."
　　　　—*Booklist* (starred review) on *The Elvis and Marilyn Affair*

"Did Elvis Presley and Marilyn Monroe have a secret love affair? Finding out is half the fun. The other half is reading one of
the funniest, sexiest, and best-written novels to come along in
years; the words dance and sing on the page, the dialogue is often side-splitting. Robert S. Levinson has written a great read."
　　　　—Nelson DeMille, best-selling author
　　　　of *Spencerville* and *Plum Island*

"A deliciously twisted story with an offbeat sense of humor and
an edge of cynicism towards showbiz. . . . An unexpected find."
　　　　—*Romantic Times* on *The Elvis and Marilyn Affair*

"Stylish and droll. . . . A glorious assortment of characters. . . .
The hunt for the real murderer and the chase for the letters
doesn't stop until the last page. Levinson knows this Tinsel-
town and its myths, and uses them both to smart effect."
　　　　—*Publishers Weekly* on *The Elvis and Marilyn Affair*

"Take *The Aspern Papers*, add plenty of sex talk about Marilyn
and Elvis, sprinkle in some dead bodies, and you get a first
novel brimming with brio, self-confidence, and nostalgia for
vanished idols of Hollywood's various Golden Ages."
　　　　—*Kirkus Reviews* on *The Elvis and Marilyn Affair*

Forge Books by Robert S. Levinson

NEIL GULLIVER AND STEVIE MARRINER NOVELS

The Elvis and Marilyn Affair
The James Dean Affair
The John Lennon Affair

The
James Dean
AFFAIR

A NEIL GULLIVER AND
STEVIE MARRINER NOVEL

Robert S. Levinson

A TOM DOHERTY ASSOCIATES BOOK
NEW YORK

This is a work of fiction. All the characters and events portrayed in this book are either products of the author's imagination or are used fictitiously.

THE JAMES DEAN AFFAIR

A Forge Book
Published by Tom Doherty Associates, LLC
175 Fifth Avenue
New York, NY 10010

www.tor.com

Forge® is a registered trademark of Tom Doherty Associates, LLC.

ISBN: 0-812-57246-7
Library of Congress Catalog Card Number: 00-023937

First edition: August 2000
First mass market edition: August 2001

Printed in the United States of America

0   9   8   7   6   5   4   3   2   1

FOR SANDRA, OF COURSE,
and also for
DEBORAH AND DAVID
with all the love that life allows (and more).

1

SLUG LINE: THE LITTLE BASTARD

By Neil Gulliver

*He caught the old guy studying him from down the row
of sinks in the airport terminal men's room. Checking
the mirror again, he saw nothing to give him away for the
killer he was, not in his melancholy blue eyes or in the
boyish, drifting smile that always made women want
to mother him and men comfortable in his presence.*

*He turned toward the old guy and answered his
stare with a nod and a friendly grin.*

*The old guy took it as his opening and announced in
a voice as gaudy as his emerald green blazer,
"Couldn't help but to notice . . . You know who you remind me of?"*

*He knew, but shook his head. It was always more fun
to play along and watch their faces light up like a lottery winner as the inevitable name sailed past their lips.*

"James Dean," the old guy said, followed by a noisy smile. "The actor? Anyway, like a older version, I suppose like what Jimmy would of been looking like only he lived long enough."

"Thank you. I take it for a compliment."

"Really something," the old guy said, nodding in agreement with himself, "like maybe you could of even been a relation or something. I don't suppose though?"

He shook his head. Telling the old guy the truth was out of the question, of course. Especially today.

He didn't need anyone looking up from tomorrow's headline, remembering him and going to the police knowing more than, "Hey, I saw him, that guy. Yeah. James Dean."

Yeah.

James Dean.

Some people are naturally stupid.

Others have stupidity thrust upon them.

I had no reason to suspect it would be me the morning my ex, Stevie—Stephanie Marriner, the undisputed "Sex Queen of the Soaps"—called to ask me to escort her to the Hollywood branch of the post office for a VIP ceremony celebrating the first day of issue of a commemorative stamp honoring a long-gone icon of the silver screen, James Dean.

Dean, whose early, tragic death in a car crash helped make him an enduring symbol of teenager rebellion, was following Presley and Monroe in the grossly successful "Legends of Hollywood" series. He had been selected by the U.S. Postal Service ahead of Bogart, Hitchcock, and Cagney, which on its face speaks to the power of youth, living or dead.

Stevie's appearance would speak, of course, to the power of her special celebrity.

Her presence guaranteed a media turnout none of

the civic movers and shakers on the dais could inspire by themselves, given none were capable of moving and shaking the way Stevie can move and shake whenever a camera turns her way. Including my best friend and mentor, Augie Fowler, who'd received a gilt-edged Postal Service invitation in a wedding-sized envelope, meter-stamped, and would be on the dais because of some early connection to Dean.

I had already turned down an invitation to cover the event from a Postal Service PR rep in Washington, whose phone pitch pleaded the stamp story as perfect for "On the Go," the general interest column I do for a living for the *Los Angeles Daily* Community section, pieces that observe and comment upon the drama of everyday life and sometimes death and rarely anything as fluffy as a new stamp.

Stevie also recognized it for what it was.

"The usual routine, honey," she explained into the phone, letting me hear her boredom at having to play the body beautiful one more time. "Speeches that go on too long, some other famous faces who've been invited, then I get introduced, and—"

"Let me guess. You sashay to the podium, give a succulent lick to the first James Dean stamp and apply it to a first-day–cover envelope featuring James Dean's sulky likeness, employing a chest-heaving precision that possibly only Pamela Anderson Lee could hope to match."

"Mine have always been real," Stevie said, her temper springing to attention as it always did at any hint of competition.

"I wasn't taking anything away from you."

"Ha. Ha. Ha."

"Given the opportunity, we both know your adoring public would also love you for your mind."

"From your lips, honey," she said, recognizing I meant it as a compliment, for the truth it was, although

I also knew as strongly how she feared Stephanie Marriner was victimized by the stereotypical dumb blonde image few stars have ever escaped.

Not Harlow.

Not Turner.

Not Monroe.

Not Stevie, notwithstanding her two Emmys or the gaggle of good reviews she had accumulated earlier in the year, after I helped untangle her from a murder one charge and then handheld her through the trauma of a failed one-woman show about Monroe, her idol.

Stevie had hoped to take *Marilyn Remembers* to Broadway, but it limped along in a series of small-town tryouts before she decided the script would never come together to her demanding standards. Ignoring the positive reviews from critics who'd marveled over how good she was breathing new life into the Monroe legend, Stevie gave her final performance at the historic Dietrich Theater in San Francisco.

"You resent this tits and ass stuff so much, why do you keep putting yourself through it?" I challenged my former child bride, not for the first time.

"Because, honey, that's how smart I am," Stevie shot back.

"And modest. Don't forget modest."

As if she hadn't heard me, another trait that taints our relationship: "Give them what *they* want until you've positioned yourself to get what *you* want. Outsmart them at their own game."

"I hear more than that in your voice, babe," I said, suddenly on guard.

A modest squeak of acknowledgment. "A favor for my producers," Stevie said offhandedly. "*Bedrooms and Board Rooms* is in a tiny ratings slump right now and the show can use the exposure."

At once, I felt had.

When the phone rang, I'd answered sensing it was

Stevie, interpreting the call even before I heard her voice as her signal the current strain in our tangled relationship was over.

We had not spoken for two weeks, waging silent war over what I couldn't say and probably she couldn't either. She and I argue too much and too often for simple answers. It's like disagreement is our mutual lifeline to each other.

She had found a painless excuse, I'd unilaterally decided, a way to make up without apology, restore the last surviving parts of our past to our future. And about time, I told myself.

That's how Stevie and I have played our game—and it is a game—for most of the seven years since she decided only a divorce could save our marriage.

She was right about that.

In her mind, anyway.

Me? In my mind?

I love her under all circumstances, but in this moment of realization, the anger at being deceived again pinching my throat and making speech difficult, I charged, "You only invited me for my column. That's really it, isn't it? You need me to plug you and your damn soap." I felt my veins straining at my temples.

She was quiet for a moment, then, "You're not so dumb, either, honey—but maybe also for your company? You care to consider that?"

"I'll consider it, but can I believe it? What happened? Did the post office flack call, tell you your former husband couldn't make it? Did he whine a little, wondering if you might be able to persuade him otherwise?"

Nothing for a moment, then, trying to control her anger, "I'll tell you what, Mr. Ex . . . In the immortal word of Mister Robert DeNiro: 'Fugedaboudit.'"

"Al Pacino. That was his immortal word. In *Donnie Brasco*."

Stevie faked a laugh and said, "How come you know so much about the movies and so little about me?"

I said, "More about you than you know about me."

"You mean because you knew enough to marry me and I didn't know enough to say no?"

"I know everything there is to know about you, except how to understand you."

"I'll say," she said—

And hung up.

Hanging up is Stevie's exclamation point.

Usually, she's back on the phone inside of a minute. Thirty-five seconds this time.

"Listen," she started, "the post office PR guy told me the Dean story is already set to play great on all the newscasts, here and on the network. On *Entertainment Tonight*. On *Extra*. The tabloids will be creepy-crawling to get at me and I have to return a call to *People*. One from Larry King. So, don't do me any favors, okay? Okay? Sure, I hoped you'd do a column, for me, but not about me. I don't need it. Okay?"

I took a deep breath.

Closed my eyes.

Counted to five.

Asked, "About who then? About what?"

"I'll tell you when I see you, honey. Okay?"

What's a fella to do?

I agreed to meet her at the studio around eleven. She expected to be through blocking her scenes and running lines by then, she said, and the studio limo could get us to the post office on Wilcox, less than a mile away, well before the scheduled noon starting time for the Dean stamp ceremony.

Stevie's soap, *Bedrooms and Board Rooms,* films on the old Columbia Studios lot, where a legendary ogre of historic Hollywood, Harry Cohn, once made movies like *It Happened One Night* and movie stars like Rita Hayworth and Kim Novak. It's been the Sunset-Gower Studios for fifteen or twenty years, but I invariably feel the magic of those golden years when I visit. She got that part right, Stevie did, the part where she accused me of knowing a lot about the movies.

I grew up loving them, studying them, and never lost the knack. It means I can be a bore to people, polite conversation often overtaken by my need to recite complete casts drawn from memory, plot summaries for pictures that played on the bottom half of double bills years before I was born, many too awful for so much as a one-shot airing on the Turner Classic Movies channel.

The original Columbia sound stages still stand guard over "Gower Gulch," where cowboys once hung out in a long-gone corner drugstore, nipping from a hip-pocket flask while waiting out the hope of a day's stunt work, maybe a line or two, the way Walter Brennan got his start, or—for those who really knew how to dream—to be discovered by one of Cohn's talent scouts in the market for the next Tom Mix or Buck Jones. Or, deep breath now: Gary Cooper, who came to Hollywood a green-behind-the-ears cowpoke who'd grown up riding and roping on his pappy's Seven-Bar-Nine six-hundred-acre spread in Helena, Montana.

The old movie posters lining the walls and halls of the reception area and the corridors immediately inside the old pedestrian entrance on Gower hint at all the great stars, directors, and writers who served at Cohn's will and whim: *Mr. Deeds Goes to Town, Mr. Smith Goes to Washington, Lost Horizon, All the King's Men, From Here to Eternity, Lawrence of Arabia, Pal Joey, Picnic.*

Nowadays, sadly, the tired carpeting leads to offices inhabited by production companies turning out TV sitcoms, low-budget-no-budget features, commercials, as well as contemporary versions of the drugstore cowboy: independent producers trying to develop properties, many hanging on by a shoestring, hoping to catch a break before the month-to-month comes due again.

See what I mean?

I'm doing it here.

The security guard at the studio's motor entrance a block east of Sunset and Gower recognized my aged Jag and waved me through. I found a spot on the second level of the four-story parking structure behind the main building and, checking my watch, angled diagonally across the enclosed cement and brick courtyard to Stevie's sound stage, where the soap's been shooting since *Days of Our Lives* moved to the NBC lot in Burbank.

The sun was beginning to burn through a layer of gray clouds that for several hours had threatened to put a damper on the post office's plans, and it was beginning to feel like Los Angeles was in for another of those scorchers that had fooled the TV weather clowns off and on all month.

I spotted Stevie at once.

She was waiting for me outside the *Bedrooms and Board Rooms* production office, perched against the front fender of the limo.

She had on a clinging black silk chemise that covered her the way a cloud covers the state of Texas. Her remarkably erect breasts half exposed between spaghetti-strap goalposts; hard nipples struggling to escape the tight material that quit eight inches above her knees in the trendy *barely there* style she swore had been stolen from her by the pencil-thin actress who plays Ally McBeal. Blonde, shoulder-length, stylishly feathered hair framed soft features accentuated with just enough makeup to hide her ample freckles and satisfy the news cameras certain to show up at the post office.

There are not many women who can carry this much sizzle at thirty, her real age, not the twenty-seven she admits to, having chipped off three years at the urging of her agent right after landing the part of resident bitch-goddess-vixen on *Bedrooms and Board Rooms*. All actors do it, he explained, insisting it would lengthen her career.

Three years worth, I suppose, but looking at Stevie and not knowing better, given the milk-and-honey complexion, a face full of childish innocence, and scarce traces of laugh lines at her eyes or commas by her lips, you figure her for even younger: twenty-three, twenty-four tops.

Me, I'm eight years older than her, for real. My job banging out seven columns a week doesn't require a lie. I look my age; possibly older. I've earned my face, which some people find good-looking in an offbeat way and others a bona fide disaster area. Every crack and crevice tells a story, not all of them pretty, but whoever was the first to say "Life is beautiful" forgot to mention that life can also get ugly.

Stevie saw me, too.

She took a last drag of her cigarette, ground it out under a three-inch Ferragamo heel, and hurried to greet me with an unusually generous hug and kiss.

"Okay, spill . . . what is it?" I said, when Stevie finally sucked back her tongue and I could squeeze out a sentence.

"What's what, honey?"

"Up. What's up?"

"Why should anything be up, unless—" Stevie pressed her aerodynamically perfect body tighter against mine until she'd caused the response she wanted. "—you mean . . . ?"

"Tell me about the column you need, only you don't

need it for yourself. That one. Is that what this delicious greeting is all about?"

Stevie applied her palms to my chest and pushed me away like I'd been the aggressor. Anger began flashing in her erotically green eyes.

"You didn't believe me, did you? When we were talking on the phone, I thought you believed me that it wasn't about me, your damn column."

We were interrupted before I could answer by a coarse, tobacco-stained voice summoning Stevie. I looked past her shoulder and saw it belonged to the small, bald-headed man in his well-preserved, elegantly attired early sixties closing in on us.

"Daughter of mine!" he called triumphantly, his outstretched arms welcoming the world before locking Stevie in a warm embrace as she wheeled around.

She returned his hug as enthusiastically as she had greeted me, and he pressed his cheek against her neck and cooed into her ear words I couldn't make out that made her laugh gleefully and insist, "Papa, stop that now. You old flatterer. I'm blushing. Look." She eased free of him.

He took a few steps backward, executed a gallant musketeer's bow, then trapped me with his coal-black eyes and insisted, "True what I tell her, Neil. A fine actress, an intelligent actress, who gives better than she gets from this by-the-numbers soap opera."

"Oh, Papa, please." Stevie urged, but you could hear agreement in her tone.

He tilted his head and tapped a temple with an index finger, insisting, "I know. Father knows best. Some day soon so will the world, so, please, don't argue with your papa. Am I right, Neil, or am I right? You tell her."

"You're right, Nico. I agree with Nico, Stevie."

He elevated a victory fist and his chin at the same time, looked around like a bullfighter acknowledging

the cheering crowd, eyes wide, lips drawn back to reveal a set of snow-bright teeth brilliant against a handsome face heavily masked in a rich, artificial tan.

It was typical, larger-than-life Nico Mercouri, the
one-time "Golden Greek" of the movies, who along
with his career had faded into obscurity until one of
the show's casting directors with a memory and a
sense of film history located him earlier this year and
set Nico to play Stevie's father on *Bedrooms and
Board Rooms*.

She'd asked me to check out their first episodes together and the instant rapport between them was evident. Maybe because her "Papa" had come back into
her character's life at a time of life-threatening crisis,
after years of an unexplained disappearance, and I recognized that Stevie had layered the make-believe onto
her reality, turning Nico Mercouri into the real father
who had disappeared when she was a kid and to this
day remained missing without a trace.

Nico sensed the special bond forming between them
and encouraged it, for whatever reasons. He became
Stevie's gentle protector, her setside confidant, her
most ardent fan. The father she longed for, filling a
role that once had been mine exclusively.

He was a good choice.

A generous, decent man as well as an extremely tal-
ented actor; happy to be working again; never showing
any of the temperament anyone in the business might
expect from someone good enough to have walked off
with a scene right out from under the great Brando's
busted nose in *On the Waterfront:* always modest, flattered, and accommodating when asked to run lines
with some of the younger players, many of whom
were getting their first chance at an acting career, not
sure who Nico had been, but certain of how fine an actor he was.

Stevie threw a "Go away" gesture at him, shot me a

look that said the same thing, then decided, "Okay, you're both right," and broke into self-deprecating laughter. She knew she was a good actress, yeah, but like so many actors she knew it with a conviction that came without confidence. Her pair of Emmys meant something, but her failure getting *Marilyn Remembers* to Broadway told her something else.

Nico glanced at his watch.

"Better flee, my pet. I'll see you there, at the post office?"

Nico going to the ceremony, too? Of course, as I remembered, the Golden Greek had played a teenaged tough in *Rebel Without a Cause*.

Stevie said, "Are you sure you don't want to ride with us, Papa? The show is paying for the limo."

He shook his head. "Thank you, my darling, but I have errands to run after the ceremony, the other side of town. Besides, better you two have this time alone, no?"

I flashed a look at Stevie that wondered exactly how much about us she confided in him. It went unnoticed.

Stevie said, "You belong on a stamp, too, Nico."

"As long as I have your stamp of approval, dear one, that's all that matters," he said, shaking his head again. "And you, dear Neil . . ." He tracked to me with small, determined steps and held out his hand. I raised mine, and he gripped it in both of his. "I know you're doing it for our precious Stevie, but I thank you very personally, for myself, from the very bottom of my heart."

Nico surrendered his hold and placed a palm over his heart, staring up at me like I had just rescued his cat from a tree. His eyes grew moist before he turned to hurry off in the direction of the parking structure.

The limo driver, his black suit overpowered by his paunch, had been holding up the building with his back and a shoe. He acknowledged Stevie's signal with a grunt, ground out his cigarette, and came around to open the rear door of the stretch Mercedes for us.

"What was that all about?" I asked Stevie, as I moved aside to let her get in first. "Exactly what is it Nico thinks I'm doing for our precious you?" At once, the answer struck me. "Wait!"

Too late.

"The column you're going to write about him, of course," she said without hesitation, like I should have known without asking. "I told you not me. Nico, my papa. That's who."

"Of course," I said, sliding in next to Stevie. "Now, tell me the rest."

"It's about saving Nico's job," Stevie said. "I know you can do it, if anyone can, honey."

The limo rolled out of the Sunset-Gower Studio lot and made a cautious left turn onto Sunset.

Stevie found the remote and silenced the music drifting in through the overhead, a hot version of the old Rodgers and Hart classic "Blue Moon" by, I'd bet, Art Blakey and his Jazz Messengers. I recognized Cedar Walton on piano and Wayne Shorter's tenor sax. Freddie Hubbard on trumpet. Their *3 Blind Mice* LP. I had it in my collection.

"You know what a focus group is, honey?"

"Of course," I said, having a vague idea, "but tell me anyway."

She gave me a knowing look and said, "Shows hire people who get people to watch the show and tell them after what they think about the various characters, their story arcs, and so on. . . . You know what a story arc is, of course."

"Of course."

"What's happening with the characters."

"I said 'of course.' I'm a writer. Writers know that sort of thing."

"Yeah, right," she said, oozing sarcasm. "So, my arc with Nico lately has not tested so strong with any of the focus groups, although I don't believe they know what they're talking about, those people."

"They don't know their arcs from a hole in the ground."

"Honey, I've told you before—you don't have to try being clever with me all the time," she said, patting my thigh. "This is serious." She stared wistfully at the brown leather upholstery. "I think they're getting ready to fire Nico at the end of our current story cycle. The scripts are starting to point in that direction." Heavy sighs. "Nico has noticed, too, and he's too dear to me for me to just sit by and let it happen, and I won't, either, damn it."

"You let them know how you feel?"

"Every chance. It helped at first, but lately I only get producer babble back. One of the reasons I said I would do this James Dean thing so fast, when they asked, was to soften them up with kindness before I hit them hard and say they'll have one pretty unhappy 'sex queen' on their hands if her papa somehow doesn't make it through his quadruple-bypass operation."

"And my column?"

"Well, him being at the Dean thing is the excuse to talk about Nico. How Nico was so big in the movies for all those years and how his millions of fans have been thrilled ever since he became a regular cast member of *Bedrooms and Board Rooms*. How much better the show is because of him et cetera, et cetera, and so forth. C'mon, honey. Do I have to write it for you, too?"

"And you mentioned the idea to Nico before you called me."

"I had to be sure Nico didn't mind. He's a proud man, honey. He has a mountain of debts he's been trying to pay off for years, where most of his salary goes, and he's been worried sick over the concept of them dropping him and falling back to square one. . . . The producers, I think they'll be influenced by what you write more than by anything those focus group people have to say."

I could hear in her voice that Stevie meant it, although I wasn't as certain as she about my influence. I said, "And you told Nico not to worry, that I'd go along with doing the column?"

She thought about her answer. "Was I wrong?"

"All you had to do was ask. You didn't need the post office or any other excuse. You know I also like Nico. Besides, I ever say no to you when it really matters?"

"There's always a first time, honey."

"This wouldn't have been it, babe."

Our limo turned north off Sunset and navigated the short block north on Wilcox to Selma Avenue and the Hollywood branch of the post office, where we were guided to a roped-off parking area reserved for the participants and welcomed by an official greeter wearing a T-shirt emblazoned with the Dean stamp; an overzealous young man about seventeen years old.

He ticked off Stevie's name on his clipboard and led us inside to the main lobby through a casually guarded side entrance.

Less than fifteen minutes later, Nico Mercouri was sprawled near death on the post-office floor, shot by James Dean, and Dean—if it was Dean—certain I was about to do something stupid, was threatening:

"You move, you die; you kill us all."

Not in *East of Eden*.

Not in *Rebel Without a Cause*.

Not in *Giant*.

In the Hollywood branch of the United States Post Office.

Threatening me.

Forty-five years after his death.

2

We heard him before we saw him. First a whistle, a long, shrill blast to get our attention, then:

"Ladies and gents. Hello. If you all would kindly look on over this way . . . ? Hello?"

His voice was sultry and sullen at the same time, clear above the hum of casual chatter among the dozen or so VIPs being organized for their orderly march outside to the broad terrace steps of the main entrance on Wilcox, where the street was fast filling with people hungry to be among the first to view the hypnotic likeness of James Dean on a postage stamp.

He seemed to emerge from nowhere, simply suddenly there, nine or ten feet away from the invited guests, near a thick glass security door connecting to the other side of the glass-enclosed service counter running the full length of the customer corridor. I noticed after a moment that the door was half ajar.

The whistle hung from a coach's cord around his

neck. He blew it again, longer, louder this time, and let it slip from his mouth. Raised his voice stepping forward, out of the shadow cast by a wall of postal boxes. "I said, 'over this way!' Okay? People, I have some business I want to share with you."

His right hand held a short-barreled .38 caliber revolver. The fingers of his left hand were tight on the the pin of the grenade tightly cinched to his outsized flak jacket, just below the heart.

He wore the jacket over a cheap brown suit with wide lapels. White shirt with a button-down collar. An out-of-fashion paisley tie. Air Jordans. Somehow it all pulled together, giving him an appearance of belonging to go with any story he might have concocted to talk his way inside.

"In case you're wondering, not just a grenade. I got enough boom-boom packed inside my flak jacket to take out a city block. Understand?"

His voice as sly as his expression.

"You fellows over there," he called to a pair of security guards who looked like they were moonlighting from a retirement home. "I need a favor, please? I need to have you lock all the doors, then go and get everyone from out back or wherever to come join our little party. Every one of them, please? Tell them no tricks or games and I won't play any on them, either."

The security guards stared a moment at the .38, the flak jacket, and assented without comment.

By the time the doors were locked and the workers had joined the VIPs, noisy conversation had dissolved into an undercurrent of murmured alarm, the belief that another disgruntled postal clerk had gone nutso and was holding us hostage likely sailing through everyone's mind.

Except Nico Mercouri's.

Nico, standing on my immediate right, had been whispering the same ID at me from the side of his mouth, like a mantra, almost from the moment this antique Looney Tune moved into the full glare of the overhead fluorescent lighting.

"Jimmy. Jimmy Dean. It's Jimmy. . . ."

Abruptly, seemingly oblivious to the danger, he stepped out and called to the grenade-toting gunman in a voice bright with recognition, "Jimmy! It's you, really, you, for the love of Christ; isn't it?! Jimmy Dean!"

"Dean" answered him by squeezing the trigger.

The shot jolted Nico backward.

He grabbed his side and bounced off a deputy mayor, a portly woman with flying-saucer eyes. Whirled around, staggered ahead four or five feet, and tumbled ahead like a drunken acrobat. Rolled over onto his back.

The hostage noises, a loud mix of surprise and fright, hit the high ceiling and caromed off the dingy, nicotine-crusted walls, drowning out Nico's cry.

Stevie was standing to my immediate left. Her hand slapped around my back, clutched my waist, and she let go a wail of pain as Nico went down.

She called his name, froze, seemed paralyzed by the sight. Stupidity clobbered my common sense. I wrenched free of Stevie and moved to help Nico. Her fingers missed a try at pulling me back before Dean riveted me to a halt by aiming the .38 at my face and commanding:

"You move, you die; you kill us all."

He smiled at me like he'd enjoy the next moment immensely, if I were now stupid enough to disobey him. "If you think I'm kidding . . ." He made like he was about to pull the grenade pin.

Stevie shouted at me, "Freeze your slinky butt!" and drew instant, frightened cries of support from the terrified hostages.

I didn't need their encouragement.

I raised my hands like a football ref validating a touchdown and shook my head and said quietly, trying to rouse sympathy, "I know you're not, but the way the man is bleeding—"

Dean cut me off with a wave of the .38.

He inquired softly, "You're a doctor?"

"No."

"He your daddy? Brother? A best friend of yours?"

I shook my head. "Not really, but you can see—"

"Then, man, don't go be some kind of dead hero," Dean said, barely raising his voice.

Stevie loudly seconded Dean's recommendation and got another wave of urgent consent from the other hostages.

Dean motioned me back with the .38.

Stevie gave my shoulder a comforting squeeze.

I leaned in closer to her, glanced sideways, and wondered under my breath, "Slinky butt?"

"I needed to be sure you knew I meant you," she said, her mouth drawn tight, the words barely escaping her lips. "I didn't invite you here to get you killed, honey, so don't you do anything else dumb."

"Miss Marriner, are you saying something you'd like to share with everyone?" Dean said, like a teacher addressing a pupil who's been caught open-mouthed.

I felt Stevie shudder at the recognition.

She said, "You didn't have to shoot him!"

"He brought it on himself, Miss Marriner."

"You are one definite creep," she said, the veins in her neck straining with anger. Her heart was ruling her head. I clapped a hand over her mouth. She ripped it away. "One definite, cold-hearted creep!"

"Cold-hearted enough to kill you all," Jimmy Dean agreed.

The other hostages responded noisily.

Dean put a warning finger to his lips.

The noises stopped at once.

"Better," he said nonchalantly. "Much better."

He surveyed our faces, as if he had a decision to make.

Just then, Nico made an eerie moaning sound.

More and more of his blood was trickling onto the linoleum, running toward us in one narrow tributary while another branched off toward the brass and glass front doors of the post office.

I understood the sound.

I've heard it often enough in my lifetime.

Too often.

Either Nico received medical help quickly or he was a dead man.

In my mind I pictured the crowd outside, people who had no way of knowing what was happening in here, not yet anyway, and wondered if there might be a doctor among them. I was thinking about how to plead the possibility to Dean when Stevie spoke up again.

"Listen, you!" Her chest heaved angrily and her jaw muscles flexed ominously. Warning signs. I clamped her upper arm, fearing she might make a tiger's lunge at Dean. It would not be the only time I've seen Stevie attack on impulse. Instead, she screamed at him, "That man needs a doctor, damn it! Now! Now!"

Dean seemed amused by her outburst.

He drafted a little grin.

He tied an index finger to the grenade pin, to keep us under control while he straight-armed the .38 at Nico and squeezed the trigger.

The shot slammed into Nico's chest and his body lifted off the linoleum in answer to the impact.

"What he needs is an undertaker," Dean said, as if it were a punch line to a joke, but his expression told another story. Now, maybe for the first time, I believed he was capable of blowing all of us into obit notices.

Abruptly, Nico called out for Jesus in a voice gurgling with the sound of blood that puddled and spilled from the corner of his mouth onto the rounded shoulder of his Armani jacket.

Dean's shot hadn't quite accomplished his aim.

My friend Augie Fowler, resplendent in a vivid blue cassock and matching eye patch that complemented the cloudless summer sky, picked this moment to push his way through the hostages, using his hands to part them like the Red Sea.

Averting Dean's ominous glare, ignoring the .38 that Dean seemed boyishly anxious to use on him, like one of those crazy school kids on a campus killing mission, he kneeled alongside Nico and made the sign of the cross and began administering last rights to the dying man in a voice too low to be overheard, making me wonder if Augie even knew the right words to use.

He wasn't actually a priest, much less Catholic, just an old newspaperman nearing septuagenarian status. My mentor of yore on the *Daily*'s crime beat, who quit to start a new religion after a personal tragedy and somehow made it work and prosper in a hacienda-style monastery overlooking Griffith Park.

I supposed Augie—"Brother Kalman" he now calls himself, but he's still Augie to me—was counting on Dean not knowing that and Nico, beyond caring, content with any pastoral blessing to mark his righteous passage to the afterlife his Lord intended for him.

"Back off, monk man," Dean ordered Augie. "Back with the pack."

Augie looked up at him like he was God's personal messenger and declared in a deep, whiskey-rotted baritone tinged with the slight wobble that comes with the decades, "Deny this man his final rites and you will rot in eternal Hell for certain."

"Been there, doing that," Dean said, and fired another shot into Nico. "Amen, over and out," he decreed, using the .38 to paint a cross in the air. "Now will you get on over with the others, and nothing fishy or I will make it so you stay where you are for good."

Augie grunted, raked Nico's eyes shut with his fingers, and eased up slowly, arms akimbo, showing Dean he meant no threat; tugged at his thighs and pulled out on the collar, adjusting the cassock, and retreated cautiously to a spot between Stevie and me.

Stevie gave him a forlorn smile and rubbed his arm appreciatively. Her eyes were wet, her cheeks stained black by rivulets of mascara. She was feeling the loss of Nico beyond any depth I might have ascribed.

Dean surveyed the room, as if he were deciding what to do next.

His attention off us momentarily, Augie said at my ear, like a ventriloquist, "We can take him."

"Tell me how," I said back, like a dummy.

"I'm thinking."

"Always dangerous."

"Hush."

Augie closed his good eye to privately review his thoughts. After a moment, he said, "You have no intention of blowing all of us up, do you, Mr. James Dean? Much less yourself?"

Dean tilted his head, pursed his lips, and aimed a squint at Augie. "And cows give coffee," he said, rigging the grenade with his index finger.

Augie shook his head left and right and threw away a hand.

Dean cautioned, "Just be a good monk man, okay? Else I'm sending you and all these other supposed big shot mucky-mucks down the last dark hole for absolute certain."

The hostages began wailing and weeping nervously among themselves. While Dean shouted for them to quiet down or else, Augie decided, "Distract him," louder than he had intended, for the words caught Dean's attention.

"Monk man, exactly what's that supposed to mean?"

"Let me tell him," Stevie declared, snapping out of her grief.

Recognizing Augie's concern, and mine, she gave us a look that said she understood what was necessary and had the situation under control. Nico had meant too much to Stevie for her to do nothing.

A moment ago, I'd had my turn to be stupid.

Now it was Stevie's turn to be stupid.

"He meant *this,* you murderous cretin!" she yelled at Dean, yanking down one of the spaghetti straps on her silk chemise and exposing her right breast, its hard pink nipple aimed at Dean like a bullet; then, the other strap, revealing its mountainous twin and the other pink bullet.

Sex, the ultimate weapon.

The act surprised, then riveted Dean. It bought Augie and me time to lunge for him, but he sprang away from us with the ease of a man half his age. In the same motion, he jerked the pin from the grenade, then the grenade from his flak jacket, and flung it overhand, over the heads of the hostages, to the far side of the post office lobby.

The grenade landed with a loud clunk and made a noise like a whirling roulette wheel.

He wrestled free of Augie's octopus grip, then slipped out of mine with amazing dexterity and did a fast back pedal, dodging and weaving away from the two of us while smacking his chest the way a smoker searches for his pack of cigarettes.

As we rushed him from two directions, our hands snaring him, the hostages crashed into us like stampeding horses. We stumbled and fell and were trapped inside their fearful flight to as far away as possible from the grenade.

We were on our knees, grappling our way to our feet, when the grenade went off. Bodies and building parts flew past Augie and me, accompanied by screams and shouts of panic and pain. Tore a hole the size of double doors in the north wall and took out a chunk of ceiling.

Two doors had blown open and another was hanging by a hinge. I spotted Dean among the hostages pushing and shoving their way outside to Wilcox—where the explosion had ignited pandemonium among the spectators—and around the makeshift stage and podium set up on the landing level of the stairway, scrambling the two rows of folding chairs that also had been set up for the ceremony.

Stevie was with Dean. He had the .38 dug into the small of her back and was using it to shove her forward. I charged after them.

Stevie caught sight of the first police cars on the scene forming a barricade wall on wheels while the cops shouted at the civilians and the TV camera crews to hurry, move it, get out of the way, get down the street. They were too busy to notice James Dean pushing and prodding her down the post-office stairs, angling them south in the direction of Sunset Boulevard.

Keep your wits, girl, find your chance, she kept telling herself.

She knew better than to give into fear, as well as she knew Dean meant to kill her if she didn't obey his demands, and gave her chemise a final tug back into place.

He spoke them to Stevie under his breath, in a whisper as menacing as the .38 digging into her underarm. Dean's words, his tone, his manner, they were so, so—

Beyond make-believe!

So, so—

Methodical!

The realization brought Stevie up short.

Dean was being so Marlon Brando, so Montgomery Clift, the two Actors Studio giants who had changed the way actors act, James Dean foremost among them, even before he left Fairmount, Indiana, and its middle-American down-home reality for the brightly-lit jungle of Broadway and a seat near the kissed-upon feet of the Studio's guru and god, Lee Strasberg.

There was a *method* to Dean's madness, *the* Method, Stevie thought, not really believing she was playing with words while her head hurt so much from the piece of thick safety glass that had flown off a clerk's station window and caught her on the temple when the grenade exploded.

As they neared Selma Avenue, Dean hissed in her ear, "We get to the corner, we turn right, and don't you make it any harder on yourself or this gun goes off again."

He poked her hard in the waist again, harder than before. Stevie knew it would leave a bruise, but a bruise was better than a bullet hole, and she wasn't going to get one of those, not the way her dear papa, her dear Nico, did from this creature.

Dean was acting.

This rotten old man was acting, and she'd caught him at it, the way she'd never caught James Dean making a single false move in *Rebel Without a Cause* or *East of Eden* or *Giant*. Dean was perfection, whether on a big screen or a cable channel, or from one of the videos Neil surprised her with when they were still honeymooning through their first years of marriage.

It was the day after they saw *Rebel* on American Movie Classics and it inspired them to a night of non-stop lovemaking, like they imagined it was or should have been for Jimmy and Natalie Wood.

Neil came home with the tape and made certain she understood it was not for some birthday or anniversary. Not that kind of gift, he said, but something to always remind her, his very own blossoming star, how dreams can come true and how his love for her would never need a holiday or any excuse in order to be celebrated.

Dean was acting.

Stevie locked her eyes onto Dean's and, her head shaking left and right, let him know, "No, you're not. You won't shoot me." She tried to pull herself loose, but his grip on her wrist got tighter.

His chin rose and he seemed to squint for sharper focus, trying to understand if he had heard correctly, then jammed the gun hard and deep into her rib cage, then twice more, each time making her flinch with pain.

"Don't do that again," Dean said, making each word a coarsely whispered threat.

There were two cops in the street, herding back gawkers who seemed to think this was another movie filming on the streets of Los Angeles and were asking the cops what the title was and who the stars were.

Still not believing Dean, Stevie started to call to the cops, but was drowned out by someone on their heels yelling, "Wait, you!"

Dean pushed her into the turn west on Selma and, without releasing his hold or losing a step, angled around to spot the caller, took swift aim, and fired the .38.

Over her shoulder, as Dean pulled at her arm like he was freeing a chicken leg, she recognized Jack Austin, head of the L.A. Film Commission, his hands gripping his bloodied sport jacket, totter backward and drop. Jack had been one of the guests on hand for the stamp ceremony.

Neil came around the corner, pumping harder than he ever did on his morning jogs, so focused on Dean and her that he'd missed seeing Jack Austin crash to the sidewalk.

Neil's left foot caught under Jack's grizzly bear of a body, breaking his stride. His hands flailed madly at the air. He tried unsuccessfully to regain his balance before flip-flopping onto the post office lawn.

The two cops, recognizing the gunshot, were now cutting diagonally across Selma, drawing their weapons and shouting for Dean to stop.

He did.

Pulled Stevie in front of him like a shield.

Must have seen the same fleeting hesitation in their eyes that she did as they halted and began to raise their weapons, because—

Dean didn't hesitate for an instant in pushing Stevie aside, taking two-handed aim, and dropping the cops, one after the other.

He swung around and sighted Stevie.

Stevie closed her eyes against the inevitable.

Thought about God as she counted to three and—

—was surprised when she reached four.

Then five.

Opened her eyes to see Dean studying her.

Appreciatively.

Grinning boyishly.

"You were right," he said. "Wouldn't shoot you, Miss Marriner." He pointed a finger at her. "You are too damn fine on that soap of yours and I'd miss you something awful, something awful happen to you."

He shot the finger gun and with a wink turned and raced down the street, about fifteen or twenty feet, to the post office parking lot behind the building, where a black Honda had just pulled into view, facing onto Selma with its motor running.

The passenger door flew open. Dean step-hopped across the hood and into the car. Even before he had the door closed, the driver was pulling a hard right.

Neil reached her.

"Babe, you okay?" He took her in his arms. "Tell me you're okay."

"He wasn't alone in this," Stevie said, refusing to acknowledge the jackhammers at her temples and fighting the need to be sick. "Dean had an accomplice, honey. That miserable cretin had an accomplice!"

She freed herself from Neil and hurried over to the row of hedges that ran alongside the building, dropped to her knees, and threw up.

3

To that question I say, 'Indeed, it was heartless murder. Absolutely cruel. Inhuman and unnecessary. But when we find and arrest this monster, we must resist our passion for revenge. An eye for an eye is not the answer. . . .' " Augie Fowler paused to locate and censure with a grimace the news reporter whose snicker doubtless was inspired by the patch covering his left eye. He took a deep breath and continued, "The answer is a fair judgment of justice in a court of law that—" He thought about it for a beat. "—that sends the miserable bastard behind bars for the rest of his natural life."

Augie had not forgotten that three of the local stations and CNN were sending out a live signal.

He didn't care anymore.

Propriety be damned.

He had reined in his emotions beyond the breaking point. The tragedy of today, beyond its horror, had touched a personal wound he knew would never heal.

Augie flashed on Wimpy Angleman, who did not need or deserve to die any more than Nico Mercouri needed to die, and he still believed, after all this time, that it should have been him, the former August Kalman Fowler, lately the Lord's humble servant, Brother Kalman, ranking member of the Order of the Spiritual Brothers of the Rhyming Heart.

Not Wimpy. The victim of a different blast in an earlier time, the poor dead kid, who—

While he, Brother Kalman, was still battling the physical and personal demons that come with almost seventy years of living.

Until the question soliciting his opinion, Augie had been able to answer most of the reporters' questions in short, monosyllabic sentences shorn of emotion, giving them the facts unadorned, without the theatrical overtones that marked so many of the stories he'd written in his previous existence, covering the police beat and then the courts for the *Daily*.

The dozen cameras were turned on him at the north end of the post office, set up so the grenade hole in the building wall served as a dramatic backdrop, a horror prop, for what was certain to play as the day's major story, here and across the country.

Augie had been pulled over after spokesmen for the LAPD, the fire department bomb squad, and the ME's office said it would be a while before they could make statements, and three or four of the invited dignitaries already deep into post-traumatic shock had muttered and stuttered out particles of what they remembered, often contradicting one another.

Vikki Gonzales of KCLA-TV, who knew him from a series of investigative reports she'd done three or four months ago on organized religion outside the mainstream, popped the first question.

"What happened, Brother Kalman? Your version."

"*My* version? What happened," he said emphatically, in a way that told them his version would be beyond dispute, at the same time daring the TV lenses with his good eye.

"The Postal Service people wanted everyone inside the building thirty minutes to an hour before the ceremony was scheduled to begin," he started, "to give us a general briefing and to set the order of speeches before they took us outside for introductions."

Augie continued slowly and calmly, as if dictating deadline copy to a city room freshman.

"They explained to us how Dean came to be included in their Legends of Hollywood series of commemorative stamp issues, which led off with Elvis Presley and Marilyn Monroe. Justifying to us why Dean was coming before Humphrey Bogart, who was set to be fourth in line. Then, after Bogie, Alfred Hitchcock and James Cagney."

A memory made him smile.

"I knew Cagney, you know? Even better than I knew Bogie. In my younger days, I spent many nights and far more bottles trading lies with Jimmy and the remains of his Irish Mafia at Dave Chasen's, the likes of Pat O'Brien and Spencer Tracy. Frank McHugh and Jimmy Gleason, you remember them? Jack Ford, of course, who always was saying how between us we shared one good pair of eyes, and—"

Vikki's voice overrode him, getting Augie back on track: "Brother Kalman, who was inside the building?"

"You had your celebrities, movie and television, whose careers somehow intersected with James Dean's. Each was expected to offer up an anecdote or two at the podium. Also, the City Hall bunch and the VIP crowd, armed with the usual proclamations and declarations."

"And the killer," Vikki said.

Augie nodded.

"The squeaky-clean director of special events for the National Postal Museum of the Smithsonian Institution was justifying Dean to us, explaining how genuine icons had to come before mere legends, when we heard what sounded like a referee's whistle. That was him, Senorita Gonzales. That was the killer among us."

Another reporter called out in a boombox voice, "Brother Kalman, how do you figure the gunman made it past security and into the building, especially wearing a flak jacket filled with explosives?"

Augie didn't hesitate in responding, "Obviously, it wasn't as difficult as it might appear at first. He was dressed like he belonged. He could have passed himself off as a cop easily, and that would explain the flak jacket. He might even have flashed a badge. . . . Listen, all of you, I see tighter security at garage sales."

By the time Augie had finished describing Nico Mercouri's murder by the man Nico believed was James Dean, he'd lost the starch in the usually heroic set of his wide shoulders. He felt knots the size of boulders in his back. He was drained, despondent, sorry he had agreed to be lured in front of the TV cameras, wanting only to be back at the Order, where he could retreat to the privacy of his office and address the sadness and guilt he felt.

The whooping of another ambulance down the street distracted him momentarily. Its whirlybird siren subsided as it glided to a stop alongside two other ambulances.

How many wounded by the blast? Augie wondered to himself. Anyone dead besides Nico? And why? How? How can I preach turning the other cheek, yet know in my heart how I would truly deal with this killer if I had him here, now?

He shut his mind to the possibility and asked the reporter to repeat the question he'd only half heard.

"You've explained to us who the people were who were invited to the ceremony, Brother Kalman, but you don't seem to fit any of those categories."

Augie nodded agreement. "Not any more, but I was an actor at one time. Years and years ago. Did some movies, and one of them was with Jimmy Dean . . . *Giant.*"

Another reporter: "Can you tell us who you played in *Giant,* sir?"

"Elizabeth Taylor," Augie responded, using humor as an antidote to his anger and remorse.

Laughter all around, broken by Vikki Gonzales's question: "So you can second Mr. Mercouri's identification of the man who held you at gunpoint as James Dean?"

Silence cloaked the media as Augie contemplated the answer he would give them.

He propped a hand over his eye patch, as if that would improve the vision of memory in the good eye that now wandered and sighted Neil behind and to his right, just out of camera range.

Neil's look said he also was anxious to hear the answer and, as if he could read his mind, Augie's question about Stevie—how was she?—he made a small circle with his right thumb and index finger.

Augie said, "No, I don't believe so."

"But he was the right age?"

"The right age, I suppose, Vikki, assuming James Dean had not been killed in a car crash. . . . How long ago was it? In 1955?" Augie did a quick count on his fingers. "Long ago," he said, raising his hands to show them four fingers on one and five on the other. Forty-five years.

"Then why—"

"I can see where Mr. Mercouri might have noticed certain similarities," Augie said. "Around the eyes and the corners of that madman's mock innocent smile, but—" Augie threw away a gesture "—you understand how the mind tricks us now and again. I fear Mr. Mercouri, poor soul, allowed the emotions of the day's event to get the best of him and his memory."

"You're certain."

"Yes, Vikki, I'm certain enough, but I can always double check with Elvis next week, when we have our regular monthly get-together."

Laughter from the news crews, a reflective shake of the head from Neil, but Vikki Gonzales clearly was not buying Augie's sidestepping response. She pressed on like the exceptional investigative reporter he had found her to be, and he wondered what Vikki thought she might have here.

She asked, "Then why do you think the man picked today to be here, a day that was bound to draw attention, crowds, the media, the police . . . increasing the possibility of his being caught in the act?"

Augie extended his arms, palms turned to catch the clouds.

"Because today would draw attention, crowds, the media, and the police? Increase the possibility of his being caught in the act, and maybe that would give him a special kind of rush? How can I know? Truthfully. Any of us know?" He challenged them with his look. "Isn't that what all the sicko crazies of society do to earn the right to be called sicko crazies? Sick and crazy things?"

He said it hoping the Lord would understand and forgive him his newest lie. He knew, all right. And it was sick and it was crazy.

I watched Augie closely, wondering if anyone else had caught him keeping something to himself. Probably not. Nobody knew him as well as me, and after he had had enough and dismissed himself from the media, I said, "Tell me what you were holding back from them."

"Nothing, amigo." Augie assumed an expression of choirboy innocence and took an oath with his right hand.

"Yeah, something. Please. No games with me."

"Did I miss the part where I invited you to hold your own private press conference with me?"

"I know all your games, remember?"

"Hardly, amigo." He examined the modest ash on his Cuban cigarillo, flicked it off with a finger tap as we headed for the ambulances, where I'd left Stevie before going off to hunt for Augie. "You only know what I taught you. Some of the best games remain my exclusive property."

He had regained the air of exalted righteousness that I'd found missing from his appearance in front of the TV news cameras. It's not that you can't argue with Augie, it's that you can't win if Augie doesn't feel like losing.

I said, "I surrender. Let's drop the subject."

After a few moments and a pause to hand over a dollar to a broken-faced bag lady pushing a Lucky's market cart, Augie said, "Take a guess."

I rolled my eyes at the sky and, just to say something, said, "It *was* James Dean."

Augie gave me one of his "Not bad, kiddo" looks. "Close . . . It *could have been* Jimmy Dean."

"Yeah, right, except he brought along a .38, a hand grenade, and a belly full of explosives instead of a couple pounds of premium pork sausage."

"You know, amigo, there are people to this day who believe the actor Jimmy Dean and the Jimmy Dean from the commercials are one and the same. I mean, you ever see the both of them in the same place at the same time?"

"Old joke, Augie."

"An oldie, but a goodie, like me."

He pursed his lips and shot an arrow of Cuban smoke at the sky.

Leaned in to tell me, "And I do have a hunch why Jimmy Dean was there. The actor Jimmy."

"Let me guess again . . . To sign autographs. Pose for pictures."

"Do I sound like I'm kidding, sonny boy?"

"No, like you got a harder clunk on the head than Stevie is how you sound, Mr. Fowler."

"Brother Kalman," he said, and left me behind as he shuffled along in his scuffed leather sandals, hopping over cracks in the sidewalk, reciting like a kid at play, "Don't step on a crack or you'll break your mother's back."

I caught up with him.

"It could have been James Dean?"

"Could have," Augie agreed, scanning the sidewalk for cracks. "Wouldn't be the first time I've seen him since he was killed."

"Augie!"

"Don't step on a crack or you'll break your mother's back. . . . Don't step on a— Look, there's Stevie."

Stevie was sitting on one of the folding chairs set up in a row between two of the ambulances, helping the young daughter of County Supervisor Ben Coleman rework the arms and straighten out the hair and clothing on her Barbie doll.

The girl wasn't more than six or seven years old, a chubby little thing who'd been brought to the post office ceremony in her Sunday best, corn-rowed braids and skin the color of fresh honey, and taken noisy delight in posing for pictures with all the celebrities and Daddy, who was up for reelection next year.

One of her eyeglass lenses was cracked and there

was a fresh cast on her arm now, but she hadn't lost any of the bubbling childish exuberance and wonder she'd delighted us with before James Dean showed up.

Even Dean had seemed captivated by her when she questioned in a singsong voice that bounced off the walls of the lobby when she was going to get her picture with him and if the gun was real.

"I know you men," she said, pointing at us. "My daddy is going to be like new, the doctor says," she said, shaking her head, her smile wide enough to reveal all her missing teeth. "That so, Stevie lady?"

"That so, Coretta angel," Stevie agreed.

Coretta reclaimed her Barbie and clutched the doll lovingly, stretched up to share a thank-you kiss on the lips with Stevie, then scampered off to find her papa, calling back at Augie, "You wear a funny dress!"

The three of us watched her race past the others waiting for medical attention, and when she'd ducked out of sight around the ambulance in front of the old Citizen-News Building that nowadays functioned mostly as a set for movie and TV productions, Stevie said, "Her daddy, the supervisor, he was hemorrhaging. They got to him barely in time."

I asked, "How about Jack Austin?"

"I heard the paramedics saying he's going to be okay, too. That SOB shot him in the chest. Another three or four inches to the left . . ." Stevie's enchanted emerald eyes stared off into space, seeming to search for more than the dust devils stirred up by the afternoon breeze. "Those two police? Also them, like it was only my sweet, precious Nico who was meant to die today."

I settled onto the chair beside her, wrapped an arm across her back, and took a finger to her tears. The gesture inspired more tears. My hand became a washcloth. She began sobbing, deep noises that started in her chest and clogged her throat, and she wrapped her arms around me like I was her security blanket, a role Stevie only rarely had let me play since our divorce.

She was too tough for that.

Too smart.

Too independent.

But, she was human, too, and she had just been through a life-threatening episode that resulted in the death of a man who had become a strong and influencing father figure to Stevie.

After a minute or two, she freed herself from me, composed herself, and pleaded quietly, "We have to catch him, Neil. We have to find him and catch him. Find him and catch him. Then I'm going to kill him."

Stevie trapped my eyes with hers, wouldn't let go until I answered.

I said delicately, "A job for the cops, babe."

She shook her head. Not good enough.

"Nico didn't deserve to die, Neil. Nico did not deserve to die."

I said, "How about two out of three?"

I shouldn't have. Humor isn't always the cure-all it's made out to be, any more than my sensitivity is always perfect. My baby was hurting badly, and it wasn't only from the head wound she'd sustained in the explosion.

Stevie closed her eyes to suppress her anger, not entirely succeeding. "Didn't you hear me? What I just said? He killed Nico, Neil. Nico! You know how I felt about Nico and you won't do anything about it?"

"That's not what I said, babe."

"Yes, it was. I heard you." She challenged Augie. "You, too. You hear him say so, Augie?" Her voice had grown strident. She was heading out of control.

Augie spoke up.

"Three out of three, child," he said, reassuring her. "Neil will help you find him and catch him so you can kill him." He aimed a palm at me to stop me from speaking. "Me, too," he said. "How does that fare with you?"

If Augie was humoring her, as I knew he was, why couldn't I find the lie on his face?

Stevie pushed out a sigh.

"Thank you, thank you, thank you, you beautiful soul," she said.

She pushed up from the chair and pressed herself lovingly against him.

He seemed embarrassed by the gesture, but didn't try to end it. He called over to me, "Three out of three, right, amigo?"

"Three out of three," I answered, desperate for her favor again, wishing she had found my arms instead of his.

Stevie nodded appreciatively and rewarded me with one of her magic smiles, like she was doling out a treat to her pet pooch.

"No serious damage," said the green-smocked LAFD paramedic who picked this moment to saunter over. He pushed back Stevie's hair, exposing a small rectangular bandage by her right temple, and lightly tamped the adhesive. Pressed two fingers against her neck and clocked her pulse. Nodded affirmatively. "You may experience some recurring headaches and even some memory loss for a brief period, and you are likely to sleep more, trying to escape the trauma that way, but you'll be good as new in no time." His voice was brisk and efficient, directed at Augie and me as well as Stevie, who found cause for alarm in the paramedic's pronouncement.

"Memory loss?"

"Uh-huh, uh-huh. Maybe not, though. Has as much to do with what you just went through as with the blow to your head, Miss Marriner. Your mind rejecting memories it would rather forget."

"What about scripts? I have to memorize fifty or more pages of dialogue every day for my show."

"Isn't most of the dialogue forgettable anyway?" I said, the words out before I could stop myself.

Stevie glowered at me and I thought, Well, maybe, she won't remember later.

What she did forget was more critical to tracking down James Dean. Finding him. Catching him. Killing him.

Killing him?

By six o'clock he was relaxing over fresh mixed nuts and black coffee in the Continental clubroom at LAX, waiting for the TV news to start. He expected to be the big story—like always—pushing aside the latest scandals in Washington, whatever crisis was tearing apart the Middle East or Europe tonight.

He was unrecognizable now, having taken pains to put on the disguise he should have worn on the trip over, he supposed: scratchy beard, silly mustache, the kind of sunglasses everyone in Los Angeles wears, even when the sun isn't shining, like some membership card in a Fake Blind Guy Club.

For next time, okay? How's that?

Right now no use crying over spilled milk.

Spilled blood, more like it.

He laughed inwardly, then let a giggle escape, looked around to see if any of the other frequent flyers had noticed. No. Good. No value in drawing attention to himself under any circumstances, definitely not after the fact.

The news started and he was not disappointed. The newscaster was talking about him and the murder in a kind of breathless way that made it sound like Los Angeles never had any homicides. Yeah, right, Jimmy, and like the saying goes, "Don't throw raisins in a shit pie."

A picture of the James Dean stamp, then a picture of the post office, followed by the usual police department spokesman describing the murder and the victim in cautious terms while the TV screen filled with a publicity photo of Nico from Bedrooms *and* Board Rooms, *how Nico looked until today; then, a still from* Rebel Without a Cause *they must have found in the files or in some movie picture book: Nico menacing Jimmy with his fist and a bad-ass expression that looked no more real in the photograph than it ever did in the movie.*

At least, Nico had learned to act some over the years, he admitted to himself, although Stephanie Marriner could blow him off the screen any time she wanted, the way Jimmy turned him invisible in Rebel *without even trying. He smiled. Ol' Jimmy made them all invisible without even trying, in* Rebel, *in* East of Eden, *in* Giant.

Eat your guts out, Brad Pitt.

You, too, Tom Cruise.

Travolta? Sean Penn? More mincemeat.

The monk man was on the screen now, telling them how it had gone down inside the post office, doing a good job of it, too, he decided, and—

What was that?

The question?

The monk man's answer?

He was so startled by what he was hearing, he almost spilled his coffee. He settled the china cup on the end table and scrutinized this "Brother Kalman" until the news report was over, then hurried across the room to the banks of courtesy phones, choosing the one that gave him the most privacy.

After four rings, "Yeah? Hello?"

"Eddie, it's me."

"You calling from the plane?"

"It doesn't leave for—" He checked his watch. "Another forty minutes. But, I can't go, Eddie. Sorry to make you drive all the way back, but you have to come and get me."

"Slow down a minute. What are you talking about?"

He swallowed a quart of air. "You see the news on the television just now?"

"Not yet. What about?"

"That monk man I told you about? Who almost got a little heavy into the hero stuff?"

"So?"

"So, he was on the TV, telling it, and—"

"You the big story, like always?"

"Yeah, Eddie, listen, that's not it. . . . He was no ordinary priest."

"Some crazy cult? You know we got them all over the damn place."

"Eddie, Eddie, listen, okay? The priest was Augie Fowler."

That stopped Eddie until he had to know, "Are you yanking my chain?"

"I didn't have time to notice then, but I'm sure now. It came out when he was talking to the news and he was asked what business he had at the James Dean commemorative stamp ceremony. Next I know, he's telling his name and how he was in Giant."

"Small fucking world."

"I knew then, at the post office, I would have killed him along with Nico."

"Damn right."

"So, come get me, please. I wouldn't feel right going home and leaving him behind."

"You so cheap, you don't want to pay for another trip out here, that it?"

"Eddie, stop your kidding. Just come and get me, okay?"

"*Better idea. Never any sense you being too close to cops looking for you, so you get on home like we always figured, and I'll personally take care of Augie Fowler.*"

4

Getting shot at was the last thing Augie or I expected when we met for breakfast at Fred 62, a trendy fifties-style coffee shop on Vermont Avenue, about a mile and a half from the hilltop mission-style hacienda across from Griffith Park that housed his Order of the Spiritual Brothers of the Rhyming Heart.

The area itself was also trendy, ever since the magazines and newspapers found out the hills and flats of Los Feliz had become a Beverly Hills lifestyle alternative for dozens of celebrities, current flavors such as Leonardo DiCaprio, Matt Damon, Brad Pitt, Madonna, and, in the last year, Stephanie Marriner.

The media made the word an official part of the geographical landscape, as in "Trendy Los Feliz," and this caused an influx of trendy restaurants, trendy boutiques, trendy night spots like a revived Brown Derby, where the customers dressed in trendy styles of the forties and live bands recreated swing in the trendsetting styles of Glenn Miller, Benny Goodman, Artie Shaw, and the Dorsey brothers. Assorted wannabe types, who aspired to trendiness, fantasized that day arriving while sipping their decorator coffees at the local Coffee Bean & Tea Leaf.

Augie, sitting across from me at one of the Fred 62 umbrella tables outside on the street, had been taking one-eyed aim at my "On the Go" column in today's *Daily.*

He finally set down the paper in his lap, rinsed with another hearty mouthful of his café au lait, swallowed, and decided, "Not bad."

"The coffee or the column?"

He knew I had to ask. After all these years and even some prizes, although they didn't come anywhere close to equaling Augie's closet full of honors, I still needed my mentor's approval.

He waited a beat before answering.

"The coffee, of course," Augie said. Another beat. "The column is better than not bad," he said, and gave me time to relish the compliment. "Your piece caught the moment, kiddo, and who could ask for more? In every graph, I felt your sweat, everyone else's panic, while we faced down Jimmy's murderous threats. Not surprising they played you on page *numero uno.*"

"Thank you," I said, savoring his words like a pat on the ass from my old Little League coach, knowing the moment wouldn't last. It wasn't in Augie's nature.

He bit into his crumb doughnut and through a mouthful said, "I would have handled it differently, of course."

"Of course."

"Better."

"Naturally."

"Tagged it with a graph about Nico Mercouri that would have had all the readers creaming tears into their corn flakes."

"Who knows that better than me?"

"Me," Augie suggested, absorbing my expression. He finished the doughnut, pasted some table crumbs to his index finger, and sucked them off. "You're much too agreeable. You're buttering me up. Spill it, amigo."

"You're so wise, I shouldn't have to."

Augie acknowledged me with a loud, crackling laugh that turned trendy heads at the other tables. He smiled at everyone and, after the attention had subsided, played with another mouthful of coffee, pushed forward and whispered at me over the table, "Yesterday . . . not the first time I saw him alive after his death—Jimmy Dean. And I'd bet the farm, if I had a farm, that Jimmy turned up yesterday specifically to reduce poor old Nico to morgue meat."

"When, Augie? When was the first time?"

He relit the Cuban stogie lingering in the ashtray. His mind seemed to follow the mouthful of smoke he sent to the post office across Vermont Avenue.

Augie said, "November the twenty-ninth, nineteen hundred and eighty-one." He considered the date. "She'd be in her early sixties now, you know?"

"Who, Augie?"

"Nat," he said, almost longingly. "Natalie Wood."

"You saw Jimmy Dean with Natalie Wood on November 29, 1981?"

"Could have, yes," he agreed, arching his thick, coarse eyebrows. "Over on Catalina Island, the night she accidentally drowned . . . *supposedly* drowned accidentally."

His granite expression seemed to be staring death in the face.

"Follow me back to the Order; I'll show and tell you the rest of it there," he said, motioning our waitress for the check. Took it from her. Studied it in a glance and decided, "Looks correct, amigo." Passed it over, decreeing, "Add a generous tip." Excused himself to go to the john, reared back and rose in a single movement, and—

—a shot sang out, missing Augie by inches.

The bullet sailed past where his head had been a fraction of a second before, past his belly, and shattered the plate glass window on its way to creating a hole in the wall next to the coffee shop cash register.

People made incoherent noises all around me and ducked for cover. I pitched sideways out of my chair. Was able to get a glimpse of the car that had brought the shooter as it sped away north up Vermont.

A black Honda.

The black Honda Stevie said she'd seen James Dean make his getaway in yesterday?

I spent an eternal minute getting my heart out of my throat. Used an overturned table to help get back onto my feet. Gripped it hard for support while my legs debated what they wanted to do. Looked for Augie.

He was frozen exactly where he had been when the shooter fired, but his mind seemed to be working full-tilt, the wheels speeding to compute the eternity that had passed in less than thirty seconds.

"No accident," Augie said, shifting his head left and right. He dropped back into his chair. Reached for the water glass. Emptied it in a swallow. Said, "Meant for me, kiddo. No question. Meant for yours truly, that bullet."

"Why?"

"*That* is the question," he said, calmly, letting his mind wander into possible answers. Then a shrug. "Obviously because somebody wants me dead."

"You have a name?"

"A whole list of names. This time it leads off with Jimmy Dean."

* * *

We gave the cops our statements, agreeing with their assessment that it was another one of those damned drive-by shootings that had become more common than spit on the sidewalks of L.A., but fell back to Augie's reality after I had trailed his red Rolls Royce out of the parking lot to the Spiritual Order of the Brothers of the Rhyming Heart, where we settled down in the privacy of his den.

He used the intercom to instruct Brother Saul not to disturb us, plucked a half-smoked stogie from a cassock pocket, and powered up en route to the French windows that afforded a clear hilltop view across Los Feliz Boulevard to Griffith Park. He spent a minute or two clogging his lungs and spray painting the wood-beamed ceiling with smoke, then straddled into a military *at ease* and launched the story he had promised me, drifting back in time to 1981 as easily as the cumulus clouds were gentling past the windows.

"I was drinking *mucho* heavy in those days, if you remember, amigo, the poster child for hangovers, waking up in places no human being ever belongs and no idea how I got there. So, once again, Colonel Bixel calls me up to his office and cracks wise about being pleased to see I could find it.

" 'August,' he says, 'the biggest crime on the crime beat is your problem.' Well, I set him straight right away, like a million times before. 'My drinking isn't the problem, Colonel Sam,' I inform him. 'It's the solution.' And like he has a million times before, he tells me how much he owes me and how he'd hate having to fire me and how it's again time for me to try climbing back on the wagon, for good this time.

"I know better than to tell the great man I have no idea where to even *find* the wagon, so I agree with him. He decides, 'August, we have the long Thanksgiving weekend coming up. Get yourself over to Catalina Island and use my place there. Come to grips with the truth, what it is you are doing to yourself, to all the people who love you, and make the decision.'

"I say, 'The decision, Colonel?' He says, 'For our Lord Jesus and for sobriety, man.' Like we haven't rounded this corner before? Where I've gone looking for God only to find another liquor store? Besides, those days I also knew certain as a Valenzuela fast ball that the only person who loved me was me, and I loved doing what I was doing, loved my liquor the way a gambler loves his long shots." Cast the good eye at me like I needed his assistance remembering my own sorry times hooked on betting the ponies.

"So, of course, I threw myself at him gratefully, like a grifter on a money belt. We stood there embracing in the middle of his office, the colonel making nice-nice on my back, me pumping tears and repeating my promise to come back a better man.

"Finally, he eases back from my grip, bookends my face with his hands, and says forlornly, 'Your returning a better man would take a miracle, August, so returning clean and sober will do for now. Clean and sober, August, or all you will discover upon your return are my sincerest regrets and a generous severance check.'

"That put the fear in me—not the threat, but the man behind it—so I head off for Catalina that Thanksgiving weekend knowing what I had to do.

"By the time I grab the Catalina Express in Long Beach, I am totally blitzed and twenty-six miles across the bay later I am blind to the beauty of quaint Avalon and all the island has to offer, in urgent need of the nearest bar to review my senses and begin searching for our Lord Jesus.

"The bar is easier to find than salvation. Bars, one right after another, as plentiful as the roaming herds of buffalo that have graced the island interior since 1924,

when fourteen bison were brought over for the filming
of a movie, *Vanishing American.*

"Now, amigo, comes the part you've been wanting,
starting at a place called El Galleon on Crescent Avenue, a mere stumble from Luau Larry's, where a
mush-mouthed stool pigeon had been broadcasting
loud as a loon that a superior margarita could be
found. My exceptional nose for news took over for his
word and off I went to El Galleon.

"The barkeep slips me gossip with my margarita, reporting, 'You look there and you'll see Nat and R. J.' I
say, 'Who?' He says, 'Nat, Natalie Wood? And Robert
Wagner? Her husband? The movie stars?' I show him I
know. He says, 'They got married here on the island in
1972, you know?' I do, but I make like it's big news
and move to have a look.

"They're just paying the tab, and a minute later
Wagner hurries past me with a guy I recognize as the
actor from *The Deer Hunter,* Christopher Walken. Like
all stars, they don't look left or right, so there's no eye
contact to invite civilians into their world, or I'd have
stopped R. J. and said hello. I knew him when he was
a kid on the Fox lot wishing he were Paul Newman.
Knew Nat before that, when she was sweet little Natalie and hanging out with Santa Claus in *Miracle on
34th Street* for Zanuck. . . .

"Nat stays behind with a guy who looks familiar, but
I can't separate his ID from the shadows. I think about
sending over a round, then wandering over myself. Before I can, they also take off, so I give life a shrug and
return to the task at hand, judging the margaritas.

"Before long, I am blitzed and ready to go home,
only I can't remember where Colonel Bixel's island
chateau is located. Not that it matters, because I can't
find the key, either. I've been generous with the barkeep, so he props me up at a wall until closing, then
carts me to a motel, the Pavilion Lodge, where I'm

roused by the smell of daybreak cracking into the room through the window blinds. No memory of where I am or where I was. Needing the dresser mirror to make sure who I am.

"I wobble outside into the half light, trying to get my bearings, and there's that guy who left last night with Nat. It appears he's just waltzed out of a room down the corridor, in enough of a hurry that he narrowly avoids crashing into me. The bump slows him down and we give each other a hard stare before he double-hustles away.

"I don't know if he recognizes me from *Giant*, but I know James Dean when I see him. The sight of him has me speechless and he's gone before I can get the name out, amigo. I mean, I'm sent packing to Santa Catalina to find Jesus and instead I find Jimmy Dean. The man has been dead for thirty-odd years, yet here he is, and now I know the truth: Santa Catalina is heaven."

Augie cracked a sharp laugh, then a pause to let the drama of the moment sink in.

"Before I could convince my legs to go after him, a motel door slams shut, and out on the corridor is Natalie Wood. She starts my way from the same direction as Jimmy a minute before.

"Am I hallucinating?

"Maybe not, but I don't need to embarrass Nat or myself.

"I retreat back into my room and get splendidly drunk—or drunker—before evening and set off again fully expecting to encounter the ghost of a Bogart. Flynn. Duke Wayne. One of the other Sunday sailor stars from those days who aimed their boats for Catalina. . . ."

I said, "And that's what your 'Maybe' is based on? A hallucination starring James Dean that's almost twenty years old?"

Augie hates being interrupted and it showed on his face as he wheeled around and folded his arms against his barrel chest.

I begged forgiveness with a gesture.

He dashed out the cigarillo and made a smug show of relenting.

"It's maybe nine, nine-thirty, when I struggle into Doug's Harbor Reef Saloon at Two Harbors, where Colonel Bixel and the money crowd have been parking their yachts forever," Augie continued.

"I push my way past some fugitive from a luau who looks like he wants to eighty-six me without inspecting for the other eighty-five. I stake out a table for one on the wooden decking and even before the waitress gets back with my margarita, a table across the deck snags my attention.

"I see it's Nat and R. J.

"One minute, it seems they're laughing, smiling; acknowledging a bottle of champagne sent over by someone who recognized them. Next minute, it seems they're arguing about something. R. J. storms out, Nat right behind; so fast she slips, falls on the dock on the way to the mooring.

"I watch them disappear into a night as black as the devil's soul before the old, trusty sixth sense swings me around, and I see inside the Harbor Reef, watching just as intently as I had been—

"—Jimmy Dean."

Augie and I said the name together.

No admonishment from him this time.

"Jimmy Dean," he said again.

"Augie Fowler still hallucinating," I said.

He waved me off. "This time, I willed myself up and across the deck to where he had just been, only he wasn't there now. I scoured the dining room. Went into the john and even got down on my hands and knees to search for signs of life under the toilet doors. Nada."

"Understood for certain you'd hallucinated."

"Only until the next morning, kiddo. Only until I heard Nat had drowned. The news sobered me up fast, took me back to 1976, when Sal Mineo was killed, and to Nick Adams' death eight years before that, in 1968; two others who had appeared with Jimmy Dean in *Rebel Without a Cause.*"

"Don't tell me you're suggesting there's a serial killer out there who's devoted a career to killing the cast of *Rebel*?"

"And now Nico Mercouri, yes. Only I'm saying off what I saw yesterday, who I saw—Jimmy Dean going on twenty years older than I remember him from Catalina—he could be the guy. And, going by this morning's incident, I could be Jimmy Dean's next intended."

"Augie, you weren't in *Rebel*. As you're fond of reminding me, you were in *Giant*. How do you explain that? Making yourself the usual exception to the rule?"

"I think Jimmy recognized me yesterday, amigo. I think he remembered me from *Giant* and from Catalina, same as I remembered him. I think he doesn't want anyone around who can connect the murders, however many, to James Dean."

"Including Natalie Wood?"

The good eye in motion. "Maybe."

"Then tell me why he would even show his face, give *anyone* the opportunity to recognize him?"

"Good question," Augie decided. "Let's ask Jimmy when we find him."

I left Augie about a half hour later and headed for my child bride of the long ago. She was home nursing a memory blackout that had hit her harder than an autumn flu yesterday, after the limo returned us to *Bedrooms and Board Rooms* from the post office.

On the ride back to the Sunset-Gower Studio lot, I'd

asked Stevie what she remembered about the car James Dean fled in; anything besides what she'd been able to tell the law?

It added up to zero.

Honda, she remembered, and black: a black Honda.

An accomplice, yes, she was certain, because Dean had climbed into the car on the passenger side, because the black Honda had its motor running and was spitting exhaust, because—

That's where the darkness set in.

I had asked her if she could describe the driver. She couldn't. I'd asked if she had managed to catch a look at the license. She thought she had, then—

Maybe not.

Then, a part of it, perhaps, but—

No.

"A Honda, honey," she said. "Black. A black Honda."

Fortunately, I knew this description, of itself, would be extremely helpful to us in trying to flag a lead on Dean, given the scant number of black Hondas trafficking the streets and freeways of Los Angeles.

When we reached the set, her coworkers at once had surrounded Stevie with concern for her and expressions of shock and remorse over Nico's death. There'd even been talk of shutting down production for the rest of the day.

Stevie wouldn't hear of it.

"I'm here and I'm ready to work. Nico would have wanted it this way," she said, resolutely, drawing from an inner strength that also had her waving off suggestions she might be better off going home and taking it easy for a few days.

They told her they could rewrite her scenes and assign them to another cast member. Not to worry. No big deal. They already were doing this with the scenes Stevie would have played with Nico.

Stevie winced at the news and told them again,

tougher this time, "I am here and I am ready to work."

I also believed she belonged home, but know better than to argue a point with her when she's made up her mind. No question Stevie believed she'd be honoring Nico's memory. She wore her attitude defiantly.

She turned to me and said, "Tell them, Neil."

"Like the lady said," I said, nodding vigorously. Thought to add, "The show must go on," like I had invented the concept, but at the same time my concern for Stevie was at a boil. Something was definitely out of kilter with her.

Stevie rarely; okay, make that hardly ever—

Make it never.

Stevie never needs me backstopping her opinions.

She's this strong and independent creature now, with a need that often appears to be insatiable, to leap the same tall buildings as Superman.

Any man.

Yet, desire and determination have limitations.

An hour later, on the set, Stevie was fine during the dress run-through, but halfway into the first take her memory began to fizzle. She blew lines she had rehearsed in the morning as well as new lines hurriedly written to cover her absent "Papa."

She did no better on the next three takes and the director, already frazzled because makeup had not entirely hidden her head wound—creating a problem matching scenes already taped—switched the shooting order and moved on to a scene where Stevie was in the background, silent plumbing to two of her costars.

She blew that scene, too, unable to remember her marks or her moves. Fighting back tears, making senseless noises, her frustration turned to demolition. She kicked a hole in the faux mahogany boardroom set of Latham, Loganno, Benton and Speer, counselors at love more than at law, so far as I've ever been able to determine watching her soap.

The director summoned the producers and, while they huddled over how to handle the crisis, as if it were Monicagate all over again, Stevie sat disconsolate in her dressing room, barely aware of my presence, wailing at her image in the mirror that her memory would never come back, fiddling with her lashes while bemoaning that she'd never again be able to memorize or remember lines.

Stephanie Marriner's career was kaput.

The "Sex Queen of the Soaps" was all washed up.

Nothing I said convinced her otherwise, not even reminding Stevie that the doctor had assured her it was a temporary, trauma-related condition.

I reminded her, "You're only human, babe."

She answered me with a growl, became more certain she'd never work again after one of the assistant directors rapped on the door and timidly poked his head in to release Stevie for the day.

He smiled anxiously, clutching his clipboard to his Marilyn Manson T-shirt, and explained, "They said to tell you the show will shoot around you for the next day or so, Stevie, or for as long as it takes you to get up for it again."

She beheaded him with her look.

"They couldn't come and tell me this themselves?" Stevie said imperiously.

The AD didn't quite know how to answer her, so he said nothing, wrenching his mouth into a taut grimace while his eyes zigzagged the room.

Stevie rose from the dressing table, reached for her Ferragamo shoulder bag, stretched her spine into a maypole, and marched out, her breasts dancing across the AD's face as she slid sideways past him and through the door.

I called after her, "Babe, I'll follow you home, make sure you get there okay. Okay?"

Stevie raised an arm and, without looking back, flung her fist around in a meaningless gesture, demanding, "Don't you dare! I can remember where I live without you!"

Well, of course.

That's how she's lived for seven going on eight years, so far.

Without me.

The drive to Stevie's from Augie's took less than ten minutes. A couple miles west on Los Feliz, then a sharp turn into the Oaks before the boulevard dead-ended into a curve and automatically became Western Avenue, followed by a series of climbing lefts and rights.

Stevie, who traded homes and boyfriends at about the same rate, had sold her sprawling estate on the other side of town and leased this fifteen-room gated hideaway after shutting down *Marilyn Remembers* and her romance with its director, Monte Berger, who at the time was also the director on *Bedrooms and Board Rooms*.

The show had not worked out for her but it had helped get Monte Berger to Broadway, where he was directing his current girlfriend, Kit Marshford, in *Babes in Tolstoy Land,* a musical based on the works of the revered Russian novelist.

"Nice boy, but it just wasn't going to endure in the long run," she'd explained to me at the time, in a way that made me wonder to myself if it was Monte Berger who had dumped her, like so many other men in Stevie's Cavalcade of Hits since our seven-year hitch evolved into her seven-year itch.

"I understand," I had responded, because it was

something Stevie had continued to need besides my presence upon command: my understanding. Because Stevie also needed my support, I'd thought to add, "And, I'll bet you're glad to be out from under him."

She looked hard at me and said, "Can that possibly be another world-famous Neil Gulliver double entendre?" She intentionally mispronounced the world *entendre,* the way we both sometimes use *ain't* for emphasis.

"Not if you have to ask," I said.

"Yeah, well, honey, be advised that with Monte I was always the one who was on top."

"You'll always be tops with me, babe."

She did a little Morse Code thing with her eyes.

"And yet another double entendre!" Stevie clucked and declared, "Ladies and gentlemen, boys and girls of all ages! Is there no stopping this madcap newspaper clown?"

"Not a double entendre," I said, going along with her pronunciation. "A promise."

A promise.

That told Stevie everything she had to know.

You give your word, but a promise is something you keep.

Stevie had watched me live and sometimes come close to dying on that moral commandment, drilled into me during my apprentice days at the *Daily* by none other than the retired dean of crime reporters, August Kalman Fowler himself. Not until years later did I find out Augie broke this rule the way he broke other electives of life anytime it happened to serve his purpose.

I was not so cavalier with my life.

Certainly never with hers.

Call me old-fashioned, but I take seriously words like "love, honor, and cherish" and "till death do us part."

One day, maybe, Stevie will, too, I was thinking as I parked the Jag on her inclined street with the front tires eating into the curb.

She buzzed me through the gate and I was hardly halfway up the cobblestone path when the front door flew open and Stevie dashed out to greet me, wearing a gaudy shower towel and matching turban, her open-backed sandals slapping the cement before she catapulted into my arms.

Blotted my face with kisses.

All the while singing exuberantly, "Honey, I remember! I remember, honey! I remember! I remember!"

"Your lines?" I said, sharing her joy.

"And the driver, honey. Also about the driver! Also about the license number! The license number, too!"

5

Stevie told Neil, "It came to me in a nightmare," and led him by the hand into the cottage, through a series of rooms decorated in an overstuffed, turn-of-the-century manner that wasn't to her taste, into the bedroom and over to the oval oak nightstand where she had left the notepad. On it she had scribbled the Honda's license plate number. She swooped it up and held it out proudly for Neil to see, anxious for his approval.

In transit, somewhere between the living room and the formal dining room, she had inadvertently lost the towel and was naked except for the turban, but she saw in his eyes he knew it was accidental. After fourteen years, he knew her body far too well to ever consider her being naked some kind of signal, like the way the ladies once dropped lace hankies to solicit attention.

Neil knew her body better than anyone, even better than she. He had composed symphonies on it, rhapsodies that began with their marriage and endured past their divorce and were still as memorable to her as a Gershwin melody.

Besides, she saw he was too intent on the notepad now to even notice, wearing his smile pasted up one cheek in the way that always reminded her of Steve McQueen. She took it as her reward for remembering the license number.

Neil was better looking than McQueen, of course. To her. Still. Even for someone getting ready to confront forty, thinning hair and reading glasses as exhibits A and B in mankind's case against eternal youth.

The laugh lines and life lines etched everywhere on his lean, sharply angled, ruggedly handsome face during the past fourteen years had only made him more attractive, more appealing than she thought he was the day he found her in the festival crowd and crowded into her life, almost a decade older, a million years wiser than her sixteen years, and—

The most loving of men.

Then. Now. Still.

She thought about all the men who had followed Neil, the one-night stands, the status screws, the affairs that had been more than that, but never as much as she had ever had with Neil, with whom she finally, in the end, had nothing at all, except a need to lose him and find herself.

She framed them in her mind, the ones she still could put faces to, and reminded herself how she had loved a few of them, and maybe a few had loved her back. Not the same few, maybe; maybe, not even the ones who after making love rolled over and cupped her breast and kissed her neck and told her, *I love you, Stevie.*

It made a difference on the days when she needed a lift and Neil wasn't around to lift her spirits, and on the nights when she even more desperately needed someone else's breath on her silk sheets.

But she never said "I love you" to any of them.

Not once.

Not ever.

And before them only to Neil, who was looking squarely at her now, as if he were reading her thoughts instead of the license plate number; scrutinizing her the way a weatherman looks at a rainbow.

He opened his mouth, thought better of what he intended to say, and seconds later said, "Let's see what this gets us."

There it was, Stevie thought, business as usual for Neil. What finally broke them up: his work, the whore of commerce.

He picked up the portable phone on the nightstand and tapped out a number, filled the wait with a smile and a wink. Identified himself by name. Asked for the Metro desk. Dropped his voice to a whisper, his free hand cupped over his mouth and the mouthpiece, keeping the truth from her as he often did, like she didn't already know, while he told the desk what it was he needed, recited her phone number, and clicked off.

"About ten minutes," he said, looking her way, examining her face, then her body again. "You put on a few pounds?"

"Go to hell!" she exploded.

"Why? You thinner there?" He crossed the room to check out a small oil painting on the wall by the door, a dark image in an old-fashioned frame.

"I haven't put on a pound in the last year."

"Carryovers from the year before?"

They sparred back and forth while he studied the oil and Stevie resisted an urge to leap across the room and put a few pounds on his back, until the portable phone rang and Neil snapped it on. He locked it to his ear, hurried to the nightstand, and used the pencil there to make notes on the page where she had written the license number.

"Thanks, Al, I'll let you know," he said, and clicked off. Ripped the top sheet off and stuffed it in a pocket. Gave her a *thumbs up,* and said, "We have us a winner, Ms. Marriner. Registered owner and an address."

He took a couple steps in her direction, his arms out like he aimed to embrace her in a victory waltz, but—

She put an arm between them.

He showed his disappointment.

Stevie said, "You're checking it out personally, right? You, not the cops?"

He nodded vigorously.

"First me, then the cops. That way less chance of me losing an exclusive."

Stevie understood all too well. "Give me five to throw some clothes on," she said. "I'm going with you."

Neil's smile disappeared. He shook his head and gestured like a conductor ending the symphony. "A scouting mission, but it could be dangerous. I'll call you later and let you know."

"Like you're Superman and faster than a speeding bullet?"

"Don't you have to be at work? What are you doing here anyway this late in the morning?"

"Getting ready to go with you," she said, already at the closet and trying to decide on an outfit. "Because I remembered a license number and what the driver of the Honda looked like doesn't mean I can remember my damn lines."

"But you can, can't you? You've already all but said so."

"How does this look, honey?" She draped a black cashmere sweater across her chest and, not waiting for his answer, not bothering with a bra, slipped it over her head. She found a pair of denims and crossed over to the dresser, grabbed a pair of red silk panties from a drawer, wriggled into them, then into the black denims. Removed the turban from her head, tossed it on the bed, threw her hair free, and announced, "I think the boots? Or, the high tops? You have a preference?"

I said, "No, Stevie."

"You remember teaching me years ago not to take no for an answer when the correct answer was yes?"

"Today's correct answer is, 'No.' "

"The high tops," Stevie said, heading back to the closet. She turned away from him, bent over to work them onto her feet, made a defiant point of wiggling her ass at him. She felt his eyes on her, and didn't mind. Had never minded.

For as long as Neil had admired her body, he had never failed to respect her mind, more than she could say about the too-many others who only saw the flesh to inspire their fantasies. He always had. Even before they married. Never talking down to her. Showing unspoken regard for the intelligence she always knew was there, only dormant inside her street smarts.

Stevie turned and modeled the outfit for him.

He said, indifferently, "They'll be thrilled to see you on the set and not bumping into walls. Describe the driver for me and I'll get out of your way."

"Tell you in the car," she said, not about to be put off.

"I said I'll call you later. Let you know what happened."

"You drive off without me and I am on the phone to the cops in a New York second, telling them what I remembered about the license plate, telling them about the driver, and so much for your stop-the-presses exclusive."

"You would, too . . ." He let out the mother of all sighs. "What is it I ever saw in you?"

"A lot of you," Stevie said. "Call it. Your gas-eater or mine?"

* * *

Stevie and I were in for a surprise when we got to the address in the Crenshaw district, a tract home from the post–World War II era that time, rehab, and landscaping had given a personality different from the dozens of cookie-cutter houses alternating on both sides of the street with two or three other gingerbread designs.

We didn't approach immediately after I had parked the Jag across the street and several doors down, under the shade of a manicured palm tree. First, we reviewed the plan we had cooked up during the half hour drive.

We were a pair of TV production company scouts, checking out possible locations for our new movie. Chatter, chatter, until Stevie signaled to me this was the man she saw at the wheel of James Dean's getaway car, then into a fast retreat. I would have my exclusive, and the cops could take it from there.

The signal was an innocuous yank on the brim of her Lakers cap, one for yes and two for no. The cap and a pair of her oversized sunglasses were Stevie's disguise. I wasn't as recognizable as Stevie, of course, but added to my pair of sunglasses the spare Lakers cap I kept in the car trunk.

"One other thing," she said, leaning over and clamping her hand on mine as I started to open the door. "What if James Dean's also there? We see him, then what?"

"Same plan, but a faster exit. He's more likely to recognize us."

"One other thing," Stevie said.

"The last one other thing?"

"The last one." She dipped into her clutch purse and pulled out a .32 caliber Colt hammerless automatic, a flat, lightweight weapon that someone who didn't know guns might mistake for a toy and not for the powerful, accurate, and utterly dependable eight-shooter it was.

"What's that about?" I said, certain I didn't want to hear her answer.

"When I was on the road with *Marilyn Remembers,* some of the spookier *Bedrooms and Board Rooms* fans got a little too close for comfort once or twice, so I and Monte, we went—" She stopped, corrected herself. "So Monte and I, we went shopping for protection."

The grammatical error is one she's been making since we met, a habit I never was able to shake loose from her and she only halfheartedly tried to break, explaining to me on several occasions, "It's a good reminder of what I learned getting kicked around so many years, honey: You put yourself first and you will never be satisfied with second best."

Stevie hefted the .32 in her hand, checked the aim. A string of sunlight bounced off its full blued finish.

She wasn't the marksman I was, but she knew how to shoot. I'd taught her myself, years ago, when I had my own bad news baggage and feared the bastards might try to get even with me through my child bride.

"Stevie, put it away in the glove."

She shook her head.

"I see James Dean there, I'm going to shoot him dead, honey, for what he did to my dear Nico, one of the sweetest, kindest, most wonderful . . ."

Hard as she tried, she was unable to spend the words and finish the thought. Through some inner sorcery, she pulled herself together and said, "Unless you're going to do it for me, in which case—"

Stevie offered me the .32.

I hesitated, then took it and stashed it under my jacket, inside my belt by my spine.

She eyed me cautiously and said, a tear tugging at her voice, "If he's in there, tell me you really will, honey. I have to hear it."

I told her I really would, not entirely certain I was telling her the truth.

Okay, knowing I was lying to both of us.

"A promise, right?"

"Why would it be anything else?" I said, hoping that would satisfy her.

I locked the Jag and we crossed the street at a casual diagonal. There was no other foot traffic, no autos wheeling by to drown out the sound of barking dogs guarding their territory behind windows and inside fenced yards. Not a black Honda to be seen, and I figured it might be behind the door of the single-car garage about thirty feet up the home's paved driveway.

The man who answered the doorbell was tall in the small way favored by stock brokers and shoe clerks, a head shaped like a mushroom, features that would be handsome on a toad, and a glare as loud as the voice complaining, "You woke me from my nap, so this better be good."

"Mr. Rawlings?" I said, repeating the name I'd gotten from Litrov on the Metro desk, putting a question mark after it.

He spit a slit-eyed look at me, less of one at Stevie. "You're here early if you're here on the unlawful detainer, so piss off, okay? You two are trespassing on my property, understand?"

I stuck my Nike in the crack before he could shut the door all the way. Quickly checked across my shoulder at Stevie. She looked uncertain. Neither of her hands was near the Lakers cap.

Stevie eased in front of me and, with a smile in her voice said, "Mr. Rawlings, we're here about your car?"

Rawlings shifted his attention and softened his tone, but not his attitude. "You people ever talk to each other? Your repo depot was already over, two nights ago, middle of the night, leaving me with no wheels to go with no job and pretty soon no more roof over my head. You ever get laid off after twenty-two years? Don't. I don't wish it on you or no one."

"Your Honda was repossessed, Mr. Rawlings?"

"Honda? Whaddaya . . . ? You're stepping on the

wrong bug here. I only ever bought strictly American, if you read me, people? My worst year, you wouldn't catch me dead in a Honda. Your fellow thieves stole back my '98 Cad, and you can all go to hell the hard way, through Idaho."

I removed my foot from the door jamb and, at once, Rawlings slammed the door shut and threw the locks. Almost as quickly, he threw back the locks, opened the door wide, and grinned at us while he drew his shabby bathrobe tighter around his distended belly.

"I just got it," he said. "It didn't sink in on me until just a minute ago." He pointed a finger at Stevie, then me. "Stephanie Marriner," he said, mispronouncing her names. "I thought you looked familiar. From the tube. Your friend I don't recognize, but lemme guess. *Candid Camera,* right? We're on *Candid Camera?*" Rawlings's eyes wandered hopefully after our hidden lenses.

I took Stevie home by way of the *Daily,* where she described James Dean's getaway driver to Ron Pipes, the art department's computer graphics guy, who used his mouse like a gunslinger putting together pieces of face until she told him, "Stop right there, darling, that's him!"

She leaned over and gave him a hug and a kiss on his peach-fuzz cheeks that almost fogged the kid's glasses while he stammered an embarrassed thanks and double-clicked for a printout.

I was just getting back from a noisy meeting with my managing editor. Ron handed the glossy copy over to me, entirely pleased with himself.

Stevie asked, "How's that, honey? Make up for the license number?"

"I don't think so," I said, studying the copy.

Stevie frowned. "What's that supposed to mean?"

Ron said, apologetically, "Gee, Mr. Gulliver, I listened to Miss Marriner very carefully, and—"

"Nothing you did or didn't do, Ron," I told him, to his relief, and gave the printout to Stevie. "You don't see anything strange about this?"

"Like what, for instance?"

"Stevie, that's James Dean. You gave Ron a near-perfect description of a young James Dean, instead of the driver."

She examined the copy like a student studying for finals. Her head began shaking up and down, left and right, emphatically, violently.

She slapped the printout on the desk.

Insisted, "That is him! That's the driver! I know what I saw."

"The driver of your nightmare, maybe? The same way your nightmare woke you up to the wrong license plate number?"

Stevie thought about it. Scowling, she picked up the printout again, buried herself with the image. Her head began the same dance as before.

"What I saw, honey," Stevie declared, although subdued this time. "What I saw. Who I saw. This is him."

I squeezed her shoulder blades sympathetically. "Your memory playing tricks, babe. Give it another couple days and—"

"No," Stevie said, "not my memory. This is him. And not near-perfect. Perfect."

As dusk settled over Los Angeles, Eddie was still at the Griffith Observatory, hanging out at his favorite spot, the planetarium steps where the knife fight between Jim and Buzz took place, watching the cars jockey for the limited parking and the loaded busses arriving for the six o'clock laserium show.

After missing the crack at that damn Fowler, the es-

cape up Vermont Avenue and into Griffith Park had taken less than ten minutes and could of been less, except for the long red traffic light at Los Feliz that might of got him snipped if any police or such happened to be on his case.

It was an easy getaway, though. Who'd expect him to be so near and yet so far? They probably figured him for the 5 or the 101 and long gone. Gone all right, free to try another day. Free to pay back Fowler right and proper.

He'd done a steady thirty past the nine-holer and the Greek Theater, eased onto the first climb up after the bird sanctuary, and pretty much had the one-lane road to himself the rest of the way, through the tunnel, on beyond Western Canyon Road and the next bends into the parking lot, where he sailed into a spot just opening up in front of the snack bar.

After all this time, Eddie could do the drive in his sleep, eyes shut tighter than a miser's purse. There were times he thought he had. He'd set off for someplace and, next thing he knew, he was here again, checking out the guard tower that reminded him of pictures he'd seen of guard towers at the Nazi concentration camps and rattling greetings to the bronzed scientists, whatever in hell they were, in the monument up front of the place. He had made a game of it, a little poem:

Henschel and Newton and Hipparchus, too
Copernicus, Galileo, and Kepler, how you?

Eddie knew it should be "How you been?," but that would of spoiled the rhyme.

Most of the day he spent just hanging out, lost in the crowd and in the knowledge of how close to Jimmy he was. A lot of his time was spent at the statue of Jimmy, of course, one of those busts done by Kendall the *artist, who did not know what he had back then in '55, when Jimmy and the one-legged girl he had picked up one night in a Strip bar walked into Kendall's studio on Melrose.*

Jimmy was lured inside the studio by a bust of Brando in the window, and he went through this Kendall's collection of Brando photos and wondered if Kendall would be willing to do one of him.

This artist Kendall had no idea who Jimmy was, that wouldn't happen until a couple weeks later, when he seen him in East of Eden, *and Kendall kind of hesitated, thinking to himself how this kid had major nerve probably thinking he was in the same class as Brando.*

So, what did he know anyway?—except, he was won over by Jimmy's shy smile, the boyish dimples, and he wound up doing a damn fine bust of Jimmy after Jimmy got killed; a lot of busts, including the one they put up back at Park Cemetery in Fairmount and the one they put up here at the observatory in '88.

Eddie drifted back and forth to the statue, most of the time when there were folks looking up that six-foot slab of concrete to Jimmy's handsome, near-beautiful face and telling each other how wonderful an actor he was, how tragic the crash was, and taking pictures of the monument, one at least with them in it, trading off the camera, or asking someone to take the picture for them.

He got asked a lot, to take them or to be in one of them, especially after they saw the resemblance, which most of them did, of course.

He'd lean against the railing directly behind Jimmy's bust, his back to the Hollywood sign and the wild growth in the untouched canyons below—pine trees and stuff in shades of brown and green; that damn sumac that, when it rose up with the wind currents, played hell with all of his allergies—and angle his head to match Jimmy's.

If that didn't work, if they didn't notice then, he'd recite the Aztec poem engraved on the plaque that told about Jimmy, pretending he wasn't aware his voice was loud enough to be heard:

It ended with his body changed to light.
A star that burns forever in that sky.

That usually got someone's attention, and they'd notice how much he looked like Jimmy, and wonder if he was any relation. And, of course, he would smile like Jimmy and lead them on, like the answer was some big, deep-down dark secret, and that always made them want him in a picture.

He'd put on a show of modesty, but give in before they could give up, and give them a squint and a smile the size of his face, and they'd want him to have something for his trouble.

"No, no, no," he would insist, but that also was for show, and he would be richer, usually by a couple of dollars, by the time they wandered away. It added up, all those dollars, and it was better than begging outside some post office.

Here at the observatory steps, Eddie didn't get asked as much. These weren't necessarily Dean people, like the ones who made a point of finding the bust. These were people aiming for the stars, the planetarium and laserium shows, classrooms brought up for the Hall of Science tours, students whose parents, even, probably were not born until decades after Jimmy breathed his last.

Here, Eddie always thought about what it was like getting ready for the scene. Slipping into the protective vest and working through his mind the artful choreography the director, Nick Ray, had commissioned, a combination of ballet and bullfight movements, with some room for Jimmy's improv, but not too much, just enough for Jimmy to inject some of the special touches that already were marking him as someone special.

He and his nemesis Corey Allen, "Buzz," would be using real knives. This was a reality Jimmy had insisted on, although he'd never been in a knife fight in his life. The edges of the switchblades were dulled, but the blade points were still there, still could kill someone.

It was something like the seventh or eighth take when Nick Ray shouted "Cut!" and for someone to get first aid for Jimmy.

Jimmy was bleeding from the neck.

But Jimmy didn't care and he let Nick Ray know so at the top of his voice.

This take had turned into something real and true and who was Nick Ray to rob him of a real moment?

"I'm the director," Nick Ray shouted back at him.

"And I'm James Dean, so fuck you!" Jimmy shouted back at Nick Ray, trying to hold on to a real moment.

Yeah, a real moment, Eddie thought, bringing his fingers to his neck, tracing an imaginary trickle of blood. He dipped into his pocket for his switchblade, gripped it lovingly, and shut his eyes to the brilliant Technicolor shades of orange and red illuminating the skyline until—

A young woman's voice dragged him out of the moment. Early to mid-twenties. Maybe his age. Small, tight features on a round face, except for blue eyes the size of saucers. Lips painted brown and outlined in a darker shade.

Running in place.

Shapely legs.

Hips deliciously flat, like ironing boards.

Tits bouncing inside her blue-and-gray jogging sweats. Auburn hair trailing down her back, held off her face by a blue sweat band.

"Excuse me, sir," she said, "but I was noticing something you must hear all the time."

"Yeah, and what would that be?" he said, fighting to be polite, suppressing the anger he felt for having been dragged out of his moment.

Eddie lowered his head and looked up at her with eyes that sent the same shy signals as his awkward smile, while his fingers anxiously rotated the switchblade in his pocket.

I was home laboring at the computer over the next column, trying to come up with something clever and new to say about corruption in government and was just about convinced it was hopeless—the something *clever* would be a cheap shot and anything *new* impossible—when the E-mail box popped up on my monitor.

It was the Metro desk, Litrov telling me where to look in the network for an update on James Dean.

The story by Clancy McPhillip, the *Daily*'s first-string crime reporter, was slotted to lead off tomorrow's section.

In his usual overwrought prose, Clancy described a young woman found beaten and barely clinging to life in the thick underbrush running alongside a jogging path near the Griffith Park Observatory.

She had "suffered a series of severe knife wounds that caused a serious loss of blood and suggested a sadist at work," he reported with breathless alliteration.

Showing how to make dozens of words do the work of a few, he explained how the woman managed to identify her attacker to police before lapsing into a coma, saying it was "James Dean."

The police were reserving further comment pending ongoing investigation, but Clancy used the ID to lead into a rehash of yesterday's attack on the post office by a Dean he now dubbed "The Post Office Poltergeist," and put a tag quote on the story that he ascribed to an unnamed resident, undoubtedly Clancy McPhillip himself, who wondered, "Do our police stand a ghost of a chance at catching this demon?"

It wasn't good journalism, but it gave me a good idea for the new column. Government corruption would have to push forward a while longer without benefit of any new and trenchant, possibly inspirational, observations from me.

I saved what I'd written to my "Futures" file and started fresh:

SLUG LINE: GUNGA DEAN?
By Neil Gulliver

Contrary to the opinion of people who love their icons more than the truth, most of them too young to have been around when an actor named James Dean was the brief candle of the silver screen, Jimmy was never much of an actor. He fancied himself the next Marlon Brando, another Montgomery Clift, but we already had Paul Newman for that.

Jimmy belonged in some Republic serial, where he could wear helmets and tights, carry a ray gun, and convince the Saturday matinee kiddies he mattered as much as their popcorn, Bon Bons, and Jujubes, although I'm not so certain his talent for make-believe stretched even that far. . . .

The column almost wrote itself. I kept putting down the kind of words that would insult Dean's ego and, hopefully, smoke him out, at no time pausing to consider how the insults could make me Dean's next target—

—until I had sent the column into the *Daily*'s production system.

Crazy is not my long suit, especially when a little *finesse* might work just as well smoking Dean out without inspiring him to snuff me out.

I scrapped the column and kick-started the new angle:

SLUG LINE: A GIANT
By Neil Gulliver

An icon doesn't just happen because someone says so. James Dean, for example, the brief candle of the silver screen, who rose to the pantheon of immortals off a trio of memorable roles that even today has movie fans not yet born when he died properly spending Jimmy's name in the same breath as Brando and Clift . . .

As it turned out, I would have been better off writing nothing.

6

Augie usually began his day at the Order of the
Spiritual Brothers of the Rhyming Heart with five
o'clock devotionals, then joined other members of the
congregation for a robust breakfast in the main sanctuary. Fresh orange juice. Eggs prepared to order, usually scrambled. Pancakes and waffles, some of each,
which Augie always drowned in hot maple syrup and
whipped cream. A mound of hash browns. A couple
slices of toast lost under a layer of butter and straw-
berry jam. Coffee. Black. Three cups.

Augie considered it the most important meal of the
day and attacked breakfast with total disregard for the
calorie count or what it might do to his cholesterol
level. "If it's breakfast going to kill me," he reasoned
whenever the question was raised, "rest assured I'll
pass on to the blessed beyond with a smile in my belly
as well as on my face."

After breakfast, Augie would meet with Brother

Saul, his cardinal assistant, on matters that required his consideration, approval, or signature. These included brief interviews with potential members of the Order, who had responded to the classified ad that ran three times a week in the *Daily*.

Today was no different, except for something that struck Augie as strange about one of the applicants, the fifth of seven, although—as good a judge of character as he knew he was—he could not figure out what, except for the eerie sensation they had met before.

So, he asked the question.

The applicant, Jared Gallagher, looked at him for a moment or two, like he could see the question on Augie's lips, and then gave his head a modest twitch.

"I don't think so, Brother Kalman. If we had, I certainly would of remembered."

Augie returned his smile and, moving down the list of questions, memorized Gallagher's California surfer looks. Not yet thirty. Maybe five-ten or eleven on a lean frame. Thick blond, sun-bleached hair on a narrow face tapering down a strong jaw line and past a slash of mustache to a prominent chin lurking inside a two or three day growth of whiskers. Penetrating blue eyes behind thick coral-colored frames.

"Brother Saul did make it clear that, if you're invited to become one of us, you're required to give up all your worldly possessions, turn them over to the Order?"

Jared nodded.

"Entrust yourself to our rules and care?"

Jared nodded again and, scanning the room in a glance, said uneasily, "Don't have much to give up and, it comes to trust, you couldn't be no worse than other people I've met up with since coming to Los Angeles." He pronounced it Laws Angle-us, with a hard G, reminding Augie of the late Mayor Sam Yorty, who never got the pronunciation right, either.

"You told Brother Saul you were living on the

streets when you happened to see our advertisement in the newspaper?"

"On the streets and—" He ran his teeth onto his lower lip and took a deep breath. "—being totally honest with you, Brother Kalman—*off* the streets, too, if you get my meaning?" Augie showed he did. "Talk about a fairyland, that West Hollywood," Jared said. "I ain't come across so many Hershey dippers since my blessed mama was reading me stories at bedtime."

"So, you're gay then?"

"A survivor is what I am, Brother Kalman. What I am is a survivor."

He looked hard at Augie, challenging him.

"The Order is full of survivors," Augie said. He stood up to signal the interview was coming to a close and pressed the buzzer underneath the desk, near his knee, that signaled Brother Saul.

Jared rose, too. "So what you're saying is there ain't room for one more?"

"What I'm saying is, there's always room for one more, Jared, but it will be about a week before we're able to tell you for certain. Always, there are more applicants than we have space for."

"I understand. . . . So, I should come back or what?"

"You have someplace to go?"

He ran a hand through his hair and down the back of his neck. "Unless they went and dug up the streets while we been talking."

He turned his head away before Augie could read his eyes and seemed to settle his interest on one of the smaller Charlie Russell oil paintings hanging on the wall.

"Then you are cordially welcome to stay with us until the final decision is made," Augie said, as the den door opened on noisy hinges and Brother Saul entered. "Ah, Brother Saul. Please find a place for Mr. Gallagher here, someplace comfortable in the guest wing."

Brother Saul frowned and said, "Every place in the guest wing is comfortable."

Augie moved around the desk to take Jared's hand.

Jared had a strong grip, equal to his own, adding to his lingering certainty they had met before.

"Why?" I asked, not unreasonably I thought, when Augie called this morning to announce we were having lunch. No morning is complete without at least a couple calls from him—more before any day is over—to sit in judgment on my column and, as often, my life. His spontaneous invitations are rarities, I reminded him. "Maybe I already have lunch plans?" I said. "Can't this wait for our regular weekly at the Press Club?"

"No. You remember my friend Manny Gelman? Manny knows something about Jimmy Dean I want you to hear straight from his ornery mouth."

Manny was a retired county medical examiner, one of Augie's old cronies and confidants from his days on the crime beat.

"Manny also saw Dean on Catalina in '81?"

"If you don't interrupt and let me finish, maybe it will keep your mouth from emulating your backside." He waited to be certain. "Remember I mentioned Nick Adams to you?"

"Manny saw Nick Adams on Catalina?"

"Please. Save your humor for your column, where it's usually in short supply. . . . Manny was one of the MEs on the Adams death, which got written off as a suicide. Only it—"

"—wasn't," I said.

Augie hated that, not having the last word.

Momentary silence. "It's what I want Manny to tell you," Augie said. "And, something else." He played the next few seconds like eternity. I could even hear the drum rolls. "Records got conveniently lost or buried that might have proved murder in the first."

"Let me guess . . . by James Dean."

"I said it's what I want you to hear from Manny."

"First let me hear it from you."

A contemplative silence before Augie lubricated my ear with several uglies and spent a reluctant grumble I elected to take as his affirmation.

I said, "What time and where?"

He decided on Jerry's Famous Deli on Beverly Boulevard, across the street from Cedars-Sinai Hospital. Manny was working part time in the hospital's basement morgue, where the unlucky patients are kept on ice until their bodies are claimed, putting in just enough monthly hours to bring his retirement benefits to a livable sum.

I arrived a few minutes early and found street parking, dashed in and out of the Mysterious Bookshop to pick up two signed firsts Shelly McArthur had on hold for me, a DeMille and a Cussler, and got to the deli as Augie's Rolls came to a brake-squeaking stop at attendant parking.

The place was already jumping, the outdoor tables filled on both sides of the entrance with smokers eating a lot of carbon monoxide with their tobacco appetizers while studying the passing traffic and the arrivals behind their Ray Bans, like some audience in a theater of the street.

The purple canvas patio roof, the green, waist-high sidewalk-divider fencing, and exterior wall paneling painted mahogany red give Jerry's the feel of a bistro on Paris's west bank, designed by some studio art director who had never been to the Carnegie or the Stage in New York and took his pastrami on white bread, slathered in mayonnaise. The smell inside was authentic, and it hit Augie and me in the face like a breath of fresh chopped chicken livers.

The crowded booths and tables hummed with a stew of undecipherable conversation as thick as Jerry's chicken soup, and it was easy to spot the tourists. They were the ones giving as much attention to the old movie posters on the walls as the menus offering combinations of sandwiches invented by the King of Heartburn.

"He's probably halfway through his meal," Augie predicted. "Manny Gelman is always hungry and never late."

Before we could ask the hostess, we saw Manny signaling to get our attention. He was a large man, about the size of Nevada, and filled his side of the far corner wall booth. He still had all his hair, dyed a curious shade of elephant gray, above the round face of an aging cherub. His green eyes struggled past folds of flab. His lips were an unnatural primary red, the same shade as Roger Ebert's.

Manny greeted us with his mouth full, put down his corned beef and pastrami combo as we slid in across from him, and said apologetically, "I got here a little early and was starved, so I took the liberty of ordering. That okay with you boys?" If pigeons could speak, they'd sound like Manny Gelman.

We assured him it was and, while we reviewed the menu and gave the waitress our orders, Manny embarked on a conversational journey, destination unknown, that almost a half hour later was still in progress.

"I know I do not have to tell you boys," he said,

winding up to tell us something else about life and death and everything in between. "Dying definitely is not what it used to be."

He picked up his bowl of chicken noodle soup with both hands and attacked it like a cup of coffee. "Dying, it was once upon a time a commitment to God, an obligation to life. Now? Now it is something people do to get this damned world over and done with, and like speedy death brings with it a bonus discount coupon from Forest Lawn or Hillside."

Manny replaced the bowl on the table and made the sign of the cross, followed it with some Yiddish words he'd already used several times.

"I believe in reincarnation," he said, "so it's not so awful as I make it sound—death. In my last life, you want to know, I was a mutt, no pedigree, no nothing, but I had it good, no stress or strain. A Beverly Hills couple. Him a stock broker and her in real estate. They made a nice living, better than nice, or they would have been a couple in Studio City or Sherman Oaks, or God forbid, North Hollywood, you know what I mean?" We waited for him to tell us. Augie had warned me to expect this from Manny and to be patient with him, although I sensed Augie's own tolerance waning. "You know what I would like to be in my next life?"

"Quiet?" Augie said, showing he had heard enough. "A mute?" He reached over the table and patted Manny's liver-spotted hand, the fingers blown up like a balloon toy. "My dear old friend, please let's get on with why I invited you to join Neil and me for lunch."

Manny reared his head so hard his wattles danced, and censured Augie with his frown.

"A mute? A mutt, you mean. A dog again, maybe a cat, just for a change, and a couple in the south of France or, if it has to be in a city, Rome. I always wanted to see Rome, but life kept getting in the way."

Manny removed his hand from underneath Augie's and reached for his toasted bagel.

Broke off a piece and piled it high with butter, cream cheese, and raspberry jam.

Saluted us with it.

Popped the whole thing into his mouth.

Augie said, "Keep eating like that, Manny, build up your cholesterol, and you'll die and see Rome quicker'n you imagine."

A smile crinkled the corners of Manny's tired mouth. He followed his swallow with a sip of hot tea and, as if Augie didn't exist for a moment, told me, "Everyone wants to be a doctor, Neil. Like I do not know? Like I do not also know the expression is 'See Rome and die,' and Augie got it backwards?"

"Neil, please advise the old coot that we either get to Topic A right now or he picks up his own tab."

"Neil, please advise the old fart sitting next to you that I am the doctor and he is the—what the hell is he now? Dressed like nobody told him Halloween is over."

Augie was wearing his black cassock and matching eye patch today, a suitable color for a meal with a retired county coroner.

"Manny, given your advancing years, do you even remember what I told you I want you to talk to Neil about?"

"Okay, okay, all right." Manny raised his arms in surrender. He squinted. For a moment his eyes disappeared entirely. "You mean the Nick Adams business?"

"Yes. The Nick Adams business."

"Tell me, who would want to be a *Nick Adams* and let everyone confuse him with the boy in all of the Ernest Hemingway stories?"

"He changed his name from *Adamshock*," I said, the movie buff in me answering Manny like I was some contestant on a quiz show. "Nick Adams was Nicholas Adamshock until he became an actor."

Manny's expression moved from not knowing to not caring. "What else do you know, *boychick?* Maybe you already know what Augie wanted me to tell, and you could have saved him the price of the lunch?"

"He doesn't, Manny. Just tell him. Please."

Manny shrugged his massive shoulders.

"Over dessert," he said, and motioned for the waitress. Asked for "the usual," which five minutes later became a thick slice of chocolate mousse pie topped with two scoops of French vanilla ice cream.

Augie and I watched him over coffee refills and, while he sank into some form of spiritual solitude waiting for Manny to finish, I reflected on what I'd learned about Adams's death in the time between Augie's call and jumping into the shower, when I logged onto the *Daily*'s reference library.

The file was thicker than I expected. He had done about thirty movies and starred in a successful TV series before his body was found in a house he rented up in Coldwater Canyon, on February 7, 1968, by a friend who was supposed to meet him for dinner that night. I marked for downloading only the clips that interested me, those dealing with Nick Adams's death. Most carried Augie's byline, and over several days blended reports from the police, the coroner's office, and various friends and acquaintances:

Nick, divorced, has custody of his children, but he is alone that night. He is barely back from a location shoot in Mexico and will be leaving for Rome in a few days, to start work on a new movie.

His dinner date, Nick's lawyer, is concerned when Nick fails to show; it's unlike him. The lawyer goes to the Coldwater Canyon home to check up on him.

Nick is dead, his body propped upright against a

bedroom wall. There's no sign of foul play. He's dressed to go out, in blue jeans, shirt, and boots.

A few months earlier, his nerves frazzled by the custody battle for his children, Nick had started taking a small daily dose of the potent drug paraldehyde, prescribed by his doctor as a sedative.

The coroner's autopsy reveals about 30 cc's of paraldehyde in Nick's system. Not enough injected to kill him, but there are traces of other sedatives and drugs that, taken in combination with the tranquilizer, could have caused a deadly chain reaction.

Nick's death is ruled a suicide.

Nick Adams, dead at 37.

RIP.

Over and out.

Cut!

Buried in the "D" matter in some of his copy was a factoid that could be the reason Augie included himself in the serial killer concept he was drumming up.

The graphs noted that Nick, one of the closest friends of the late James Dean, who had played the part of Moose in *Rebel Without a Cause,* was hired after Dean's death to loop his pal's voice in a drunk scene in *Giant,* because Dean's takes had been totally inarticulate.

Nick was in both movies.

He was an obvious link to Augie, who had only been in *Giant.*

Obvious to Augie, anyway.

I would have to ask him later, because Manny had started telling us what I already knew, slowly, polishing every sentence like a precious stone.

Finally, "And that was that," Manny said.

Augie, who had listened patiently, a smile fixed on

his face while his hands drummed nervously on his thighs below eye level, said, "Now, tell him the rest of it."

Manny didn't take to that instruction and looked around the restaurant nervously.

"Tell him, Manny."

"We couldn't figure how he got the paraldehyde into his system," Manny said reluctantly. He shrugged and wiped at the chocolate residue on his plate, sucked it off his finger.

"More, Manny."

"Augie, don't you think—?"

"More, Manny."

Another shrug.

"The cops could not find any trace of paraldehyde anywhere in the house. No pills or prescription bottle or any other kind of container, no hypodermic syringe, you see what I mean? There should have been something, because the amount of paraldehyde in his system would have knocked him out immediately. He would not have any time to dispose of anything at all."

"You're saying—"

"Adams either got fed the stuff someplace else and was brought back to his house or he took it there, was given it there, and somebody cleaned up after him and then got the hell out of there." He gave Augie a "There, are you happy now?" look.

"But you called it a suicide," I said.

A shrug.

"I called it a 'possible homicide' but I was only one vote and got over-ruled."

"What does that mean, Manny? Who overruled you?"

A long pause until, "Confidential, *boychick.* I have already said too much."

He looked to Augie for rescue.

Augie raised his eyes to the ceiling and left a frustrated look behind.

"Manny, we are talking history here, not mystery. They can't threaten you anymore, not even the ones who are still around. You got your pension."

"Easy for you to say, but all right. I die, it's going to be on your conscience. . . ." He took a deep breath.

"Some big-time Hollywood lawyer, I never learned who, got to City Hall, which got to LAPD, which got to the ME's office. The first report got tossed, the one that said a possible homicide and a new report got put into the file, one that said a suicide. Same over at Parker Center, I heard later, the original police reports. Shredded wheat. Nothing that didn't go on before. Or since. Hollywood has always been in bed with City Hall, at the highest level on the lowest of deals, you know what I mean?"

Turning to Augie, I said, "You knew this?"

"Of course."

"From when?"

"From even before it went down, amigo."

"And you didn't report it? Expose it? What was going on?"

"That bed Manny mentioned? Always been big enough to include newspapers."

"The *Daily*?"

"And the *Times* and the *Herald* and the *Examiner* and the *Mirror* and the *Hollywood Citizen-News*. Throw in the Santa Monica *Outlook* and the *Valley Green Sheet*. Even back then, there was always more than enough influence peddling and corruption to go around."

"So, you buried the truth and let some murderer off the hook?"

"It didn't get that far. It became just another abortion, one more news story that wasn't carried to full term. Favors, kiddo. The way of the word is the way of the world. How many times you have to hear it before you start to understand?"

I sent the question to center field with a left-handed gesture. "And the murderer?"

Augie looked past the disappointment in my eyes and flagged Manny's attention. "Tell him the rest of it, Manny."

"You mean about—?"

"Yeah, the *Twilight Zone* part." Turning back to me, Augie said, "Listen carefully, kiddo."

Manny said, "Okay, okay. But, it's only hearsay coming from me. . . . Meanwhile, Augie, do you think I can have another Diet Coke or something, to wash down the meal?"

Our waitress was about to pass by. Augie stopped her with a snatch at her hemline. By the time she returned with Manny's Diet Coke, he was talking about James Dean.

"You heard me, *boychick,* James Dean, risen from the dead after thirteen years. The night Adams died, Dean was there with him. The way I heard tell, he slipped Adams the fatal dose, then watched his pal die, cleaned up after himself, and shuffled off, back to the graveyard; you know what I mean?"

"You're saying a dead man killed Nick Adams?" I could not believe I was even asking the question.

Manny shrugged.

Augie said, "So maybe the cops figured they were justified in shutting down the investigation and going for a verdict of death by suicide. What were they going to do, catch Jimmy? Try him? Sentence him to the gas house? Scare the L.A. citizenry into a *Guinness Book of World Records* all-time community dump?"

"Tell me you don't believe this, Augie."

"Of course not, but I finagled my way into a fast

look at the first police report, before it died, too—after Manny whispered me an off-the-record on the subject—and it did star Jimmy Dean."

"And it said Dean was in the Coldwater house with Nick Adams that night?"

"Yes."

"And the report said Dean, James Dean, the late actor James Dean, administered the overdose to Nick Adams, then disposed of—"

"Yes," Augie said.

"I already told you that," Manny said, managing to sound hurt that I had to hear it again.

I said, "And who fed all this information to the cops? Also Dean? A little confession always being good for the eternal soul?"

Augie screwed up his face derisively. "Don't be silly, amigo."

"Then who?"

"Somebody who traded the story for his own neck."

The words eased out of his mouth as easily as the smoke from one of Augie's cigarillos. I sucked it in, along with all the air in the deli.

Manny said, "I would have told you that, too, you gave me the chance."

"Who, Augie?"

Augie held the moment for dramatic impact, then said, "The guy who knows who drowned Natalie Wood, maybe, and who knocked off others on his way through the years to the murder of Nico Mercouri and, in my humble opinion, knows who just narrowly missed with a pot shot at me?"

I saw he meant it for the truth.

"Did he have a name?"

"When I checked it out—no such animal."

"Why didn't the cops hold on to him as a material witness, maybe worse?"

"People in high places, remember? Favors?"

"And what did the people in high places tell you when you asked them for a name?"

"My neck wouldn't stretch that high, and that was before it was strongly urged upon me to toss my memory away and stay on the smart side of the street."

"But it's okay now to cross over?"

"Yes, now that those who were high are mostly six feet under and someone out there is trying to have me join them."

"Are we about through?" Manny wanted to know. "I have my own dearly departeds across the way at Cedars that need ice packing for shipment."

"For now," I said, thanking Manny for his time.

Augie also thanked him and, after Manny squeezed free of the booth, hovered over the table dripping thanks and expressing the hope we'd think about making this lunch a regular habit, shambled up the aisle and out of earshot, he turned to me and said, "I think I know where we can get the name."

"Where?"

"Sal Mineo."

"Sal Mineo is dead, Augie."

His raucous laughter shook the room.

"Isn't that what you'd been saying about Jimmy Dean, amigo?"

7

Nothing eventful happened over the next couple days, until the phone call and the death threat.

Augie had been unable to make immediate contact with whomever it was he believed could give us the name of the third man in Nick Adams's house the night Nick died, and it was not a name he was sharing yet. He was admitting only that it was not Sal Mineo and, yes, Sal Mineo was dead for keeps, *so far as he knew*. The qualification was baggage carried by any halfway-decent newspaperman past or present, who knows better than to take an unverified fact at face value.

Stevie's memory kept waffling in and out. She had managed a few hours on the set both days, but fled whenever line readings or blocking became difficult for her, usually when the scene touched on Nico Mercouri's character, who in a matter of hours had been rewritten to the farthest corner of the Brazilian jungle, desperately searching for the cure for a disease hurriedly conceived and written into the plot to explain Stevie's problem, *ex-lapsus memorexus.*

I managed to keep the James Dean business out of my mind, most of the time, and follow my everyday routines, rising automatically at the first hint of daybreak, hitting the naked streets of Westwood for a brisk jog north across Wilshire and around a chunk of the UCLA campus.

The morning sky is as monotonous at this hour as all those clusters of glass and stone office buildings that rise like monuments to the quiet college town this was as recent as the 1920s, an oasis of education in the middle of nowhere. A clue to the future among the scant few alleys of commerce and vast open dirt fields for sale dirt cheap by real estate speculators who could see beyond the Beverly Hills to the east that was barely emerging from its own sleepy town status.

There's not a lot of traffic and the air is clear and clean, free of smoke, exhaust fumes, and all those germs bound to be blown out by snorts and sneezes and coughs in a few hours, when the sidewalks thicken with people and UCLA becomes that city within a city; its student population the size of an average suburb in L.A.

I halted as usual for a caffeine booster at an old-fashioned coffee shop shaped like a railroad car, on Gayley, where the other counter regulars hide behind their morning newspapers and gear up for today's realities with overdone eggs and cremated bacon, burnt toast, and a brain-pummeling cup of coffee that makes up for all the sins of the fry cook. After that, back home, I turned to standard bachelor stuff like wondering how that much dirty laundry manages to pile up in barely a month's time.

My place is easy to clean, because there's not much to it, a little less than seven hundred square feet of a one-bedroom condo apartment south of the Federal Building on Veteran Avenue. Comfortably and inexpensively furnished and what you'd expect from someone whose main interests are movies, music, art, and literature. A bookshelf wall filled with first-edition novels past and present and nonfiction books about history, Hollywood, and Broadway. Cheaply framed county museum posters by Johns, Rauschenberg, Lichtenstein, Hockney, and Warhol. A couple cheap Picasso prints. A small original etching by Kathe Kollwitz, more scary than cheery, I like to keep around for reality checks, as a reminder of the potential for man's inhumanity to man.

My special prize is an original full-sized poster for *Casablanca,* Bogie and the incomparable Bergman framed for the ages, a reminder that Stevie and I are not the only ones who were ever pulled apart by fate. Okay, maybe there was more pulling by Stevie than by fate, but at least she left space for the beginning of the beautiful friendship that followed the final fadeout to our wedded blitz.

When she phoned to say she was home and wondered if we could meet for a late lunch or an early dinner, her voice desperate for company, confident I would oblige, I was back on the trail of James Dean.

As on the day before, I'd returned all my phone calls, answered E-mail and a pile of snail mail that had been sitting too long in the *Pending* file on my desk, paid some bills, did some shopping, and ran some errands, then hit the *Daily* files and the Internet, scouting history and piecing together background that might give me a stronger handle on Dean and his life.

Possibly his death.

Friday morning, September 30, 1955.

Jimmy, dressed in light blue pants and a white tee shirt, brown shoes, and the red windbreaker he wore in Rebel *and has since made his trademark, gets behind the wheel of his week-old pride and joy, a low-slung, two-door Porsche Spyder convertible, its sleek body silver with dark blue tail stripes.*

His racing number, 130, has been painted in black on the doors and the hood. His nickname, "Little Bastard," is scripted in large red letters across the rear cowling.

Next to him in the passenger seat of what Jimmy already is calling his most prized possession, purchased for three thousand dollars in cash and his smaller Porsche Speedster as a trade-in, is mechanic Rolf Wutherich. Their destination is Salinas, seven hours up the California coast and best known as the home of John Steinbeck, where scores of drivers will be rallying for a weekend road race.

The sky is a laundry-fresh blue, the air hot in spite of a modest breeze from the ocean. Overall, a fine day to give the Little Bastard some road break-in.

Jimmy tucks his windbreaker behind the seat and snaps sunglasses over his prescription lenses. Discards a half-smoked Chesterfield, pops a fresh one into his mouth, and waits for a light from Rolf Wutherich, who has to use Jimmy's own chrome Zippo, because the Spyder has no lighter of its own.

It's a little before one o'clock when Jimmy eases the Little Bastard onto Highway 99 and, once past the city and on the open road, eases his foot down on the pedal and jumps past the posted speed limit, indifferent to urging by Rolf to take it easy and not invite a speeding ticket.

Trailing behind them are Jimmy's friends Sanford Roth, a photographer, and Bill Hickman, a racer he's known since they played bit parts in the movie Fixed Bayonets. *They're in Jimmy's '53 white Ford station wagon, which has Jimmy's Spyder trailer hitched behind it.*

Sometime around three o'clock, the sun beating

down on them, Jimmy suffering a mighty thirst, he steers off the road, pulls into Tip's Diner in the Newhall area.

Jimmy and Rolf relax at the counter, Jimmy over a glass of cold milk, Rolf with a soda. Sanford Roth and Bill Hickman order sandwiches.

Jimmy can't stop talking about how he is going to win the race in Salinas.

Rolf, a test driver for Porsche in Germany before coming to America, urges him, "Don't try and go too fast. Don't try to win. Drive for the experience."

"Yeah, man," Jimmy says and in the next breath is describing how he plans to beat the competition.

By three-thirty, they are out of the sun-bleached hills, Jimmy doing seventy miles an hour in a fifty-mile-an-hour zone on the dusty divided highway stretch known as the "Grapevine."

A California Highway Patrolman pulls the Little Bastard over. The Ford wagon, too. He tickets Jimmy for excessive speed and cautions him to be more careful. He also tickets the Ford wagon for speeding.

Shortly, Jimmy glides the Spyder past the sleepy town of Bakersfield and onto another endless chain of road, clocking an average seventy-five miles an hour, sometimes getting the Little Bastard up to 130 miles an hour before he reaches Blackwell's Corner, at the junction of Route 466 and Highway 33, where there's a general store, a gas station, and a diner.

Jimmy finds a friend there, Lance Reventlow, the son of heiress Barbara Hutton, who is on his way to Salinas for the race in a dark blue Mercedes 300 SL Gullwing. They chat a while before Jimmy excuses himself and goes into the store, where he calls a pal in Salinas, Monty Roberts, to say he expects to pull in by early evening, so have a pot of chili cooked and waiting on the stove.

Jimmy puts on his Rebel jacket against a rising chill

and, before settling back behind the wheel, brags to Hickman about his speed. Hickman urges Jimmy to be careful about cars turning in front of him. The Spyder's hard to see, Hickman reminds him, especially in the fading light, because of the silver color and it being belly low to the road.

Jimmy accelerates hard onto the highway, his safety belt still unfastened, yelling back at Roth and Hickman, "Nonstop to Paso Robles!"

Five-thirty.

The sun is setting.

It is shining directly into Jimmy's eyes as he nears the Y intersection of Routes 466 and 41, where the highway splits east of Cholame.

Jimmy most likely doesn't know there have been a series of collisions here in the past and probably wouldn't care, anyway.

Jimmy is doing somewhere between eighty-five and 110 miles an hour as a two-tone, black-and-white Ford Tudor sedan prepares to turn left onto the highway in front of the Little Bastard.

Donald Gene Turnupseed, a twenty-three-year-old student at Cal Poly in San Luis Obispo, completes his turn at thirty miles an hour.

"That guy's gotta stop," Jimmy shouts at Rolf. "He'll see us."

Turnupseed sees the Spyder.

Slams down on the brake pedal.

The Ford's rear wheels lock and the car slides thirty feet. Jimmy swerves the Spyder. Too late.

The Little Bastard crashes into the left side of the bigger, heavier sedan. Spins off the road, wraps around a telegraph pole, the left side ripped apart and the engine pushed almost all the way into the drivers seat.

Totaled in the blink of an eye.

Spectators from passing cars are gathering by the time Roth and Hickman drive up to the scene.

Rolf Wutherich, thrown clear of the Porsche and into a ditch, has suffered a broken jaw and other injuries he will survive after a series of operations.

Donald Turnupseed is dazed and bruised, otherwise uninjured; his Ford sedan damaged only where it was struck by the Little Bastard, above the left front wheel.

Jimmy Dean?

What happened to Jimmy Dean in the fraction of time after impact depends on whose account you choose to believe. The electronic clips I pulled down told a lot of the same story most of the time, but cautious reading put me in touch with inconsistencies.

They were the kind of inconsistencies that always result from confused statements made at the incident scene and careless accidents of reconstructed history and faulty memory found in biographies written long after the fact:

Trapped behind the wheel of the Little Bastard, Jimmy's neck is twisted and broken. He suffers multiple broken bones, fractures of his jaw and arms, lacerations over his entire body, numerous internal injuries.

Jimmy's chest is smashed by the pressure of the steering column. His head is almost entirely severed from his body.

He has been killed instantly.

Sanford Roth and Bill Hickman reach the scene and recognize at once that Jimmy is dead. Roth's instincts as a news-magazine photographer—he and Jimmy met when Roth was assigned by Colliers Magazine *to shoot the cast members of* Giant—*go to work. Roth begins taking pictures, but later will resolve never to show them publicly.*

Craig Tepper, heading home to Bakersfield after a day watching the speed trials at Bonneville Flats, stops to see what's going on. He hears someone shout-ing "It's James Dean, the actor," and "Get him out of there, careful! He's bad off. Don't be rough with him, for Christ's sake!"

An ambulance arrives. Jimmy is still breathing and crying softly for help as he's lifted inside. The ambu-lance races fifteen miles to Paso Robles War Memorial Hospital.

Jimmy is pronounced dead on arrival.

Jake and Belinda Lowy tell California Highway Pa-trol investigators they were passed on the highway by the Porsche Spyder less than a minute before the crash. The Spyder was doing a hundred or better. Jake Lowy, noticing the Ford getting ready to make a left in front of the Spyder, knows he's about to observe a col-lision and tells his wife, "Watch that!"

Lowy tells the CHP, "I got out to have myself a closer look. Not much more than a jigsaw puzzle be-hind the wheel. Dead as a doorknob, that poor man. My stomach did a dance so bad awful, it was all I could do to get behind my Chevy before throwing up, not to embarrass myself."

Ralph Alvin, on his way to Los Angeles from the Salinas wine country, the "Pastures of Heaven" made famous by Nobel laureate Steinbeck, explains how he watched from across the highway as spectators eased someone out of the wreckage and, too loudly anxious to wait for an ambulance, hurried the injured party into a car and sped off.

"The car says on it 'Little Bastard,' and all the while I'm thinking to myself, 'Poor bastard,'" he tells the CHP, the press, and anyone else who'll listen.

Before heading off to pick up Stevie for dinner, I tracked down LAPD Det. Lt. Jimmy Steiger.

Jimmy and I grew up in the business together, him working for the law, me covering it and, on more than a few occasions, covering and saving the other's exposed ass; the other's life on three occasions, but we have never kept a count that says "You owe me." That kind of friendship is for fools.

If he were a better politician, Jimmy would be an assistant chief of police by now, maybe even the chief, but he only knows how to play by the rules—bending them every so often for me, of course—so he's been stranded for years at Parker Center, checking in and out of problem divisions, watching hotshot cops who know less push past him.

Jimmy's direct number call-forwarded me to a pet hospital on North Main, somewhere between Olvera Street and Chinatown.

"Is it your ulcer acting up again?" I said.

"Very funny," Jimmy said, not sounding amused. "It's Sherlock, and he's not so good right now." His voice choked. Sherlock was one of Jimmy and Margie's three dogs, all of them rescued from the pound: a black, hairy mutt the size of a Sherman tank, with large, sad eyes that are always begging for snacks and love, in that order—clearly Jimmy's favorite.

"Tell me."

"We noticed he wasn't acting right, not for two or three days, so I brought him on over here earlier in the day. The vet sees right away he's got yellow jaundice and keeps him for x-rays, blood tests, the whole nine yards. . . . I come back to hear, well— You ever hear about this immune-mediated hemolytic anemia?" I told him I hadn't. "His whole immune system is for shit, is what it means, pard. Sherlock is sicker'n a—"

Steiger couldn't come up with a word, so I said, "dog," and we both laughed.

"You and your college education," Jimmy decided,

sounding better for the relief. "I'm waiting to learn if they're keeping him here for the night, and then we'll see what we'll see."

"Any prognosis?"

"If he's still with us in the morning, we'll see what we'll see."

"How's Margie?"

"She's holding up better than me, on the outside, anyway."

"The kids?" The Steigers have six, including one less than a year old.

"We didn't let on to them it might be serious, so it won't matter unless I walk in without him."

"What are you going to tell them?"

"Whatever lie works best, of course."

"They'll see it on your face, Jimmy, hear it in your voice. You can't fool kids."

"Daddy will do the best he can." His voice broke again. He coughed his throat clear and said, "Enough with that. I know you didn't call about Sherlock. If it's about what you asked for last time, it's handled, pard. All taken care of."

"I figured as much when I didn't hear otherwise the last day or two. Also has to do with this James Dean business, but something else."

"What now?"

"It can wait, tomorrow or the next day, Jimmy. You have something more important on your mind now."

"Spill it and let me decide," he said, sounding almost relieved to have the diversion. "Hold a min."

I heard muffled dog noises in the background.

Jimmy again, "You can't believe how many pooches and those other—cats . . . dogs and cats are out here waiting for the next available vet. You'd think it's my HMO. Hold a min. Got a three-legged shepherd sniffing at my ankle like it should be his, poor guy. . . .

Nice doggie, Nice doggie. . . . Okay, go on. . . . He's found somebody else's thigh he prefers."

I told Steiger what I was after.

He said, "Pard, it sounds like you are really buying more and more into the idea Dean's still alive and it was him killed Mercouri, played blow up the post office, and washed it down with a misfire at that one-eyed friend of ours in the toga."

"It's a cassock, and it's not that at all. What I question is the eyeball-witness stuff at the scene, stories that contradict one another, and all the bad history that's been written—based on it—for the last forty-five years."

"My vet's coming back. . . . I'll see what I can see and let you know in the a.m.," Jimmy said, abruptly ending the conversation.

Stevie didn't want to go out for dinner as much as she needed company, so we ordered in a large vegetarian pizza from Palermo's on Vermont and washed it down with a few brews, stretched out on opposite ends of an overstuffed couch, watching old Carole Lombard movies on cable TV.

My shoes were off. As comfortable as I dared get without risking the usual stirrings her presence inspired.

She was wearing a halter and shorts outfit meant for a five-year-old, her hair running wild around her face, absent any makeup, but no less beautiful, and I was glad we were no longer husband and wife, or for certain we would be in bed by now, missing the wacky comic genius of Lombard, a knack Stevie also had and rarely was given the chance to display on *Bedrooms and Board Rooms*.

Stevie reminded me of Lombard in other ways.

Her feisty attitude, for certain. How on the set it was

evident she was adored by most of the cast and all of the crew. Her ability to share a dirty joke, although a particularly rowdy punch line could have Stevie shielding her embarrassment behind infectious laughter. Her swearing came mainly to make a point or in the heat of anger, like a lot of people, when the moment was slightly beyond control.

"*The Thin Man,* who's playing Godfrey the butler there, honey," she said, indicating the TV screen.

"William Powell."

"Well, duh, and thank you so very much, Exalted Movie Trivia Person, like I didn't know. . . . Not my question. Were Lombard and Powell still married when they filmed *My Man Godfrey?* That's my question."

"No, Lombard was married to—"

"Gable."

"Why did you ask if you knew?"

"It was a *when* question, Exalted Movie Trivia Person, not a *who* question. I knew the *who* of it."

"Powell and Lombard were already divorced by the time they made *Godfrey* over at Universal, but you'd never know it from the chemistry they're oozing."

"A lot like us."

"More than you know."

"Meaning?"

"They got married eight months after they met. There was—" I closed my eyes and thought about it "—a difference of sixteen years in their ages. They divorced after two years, but stayed friends."

"Then nothing at all like I and you, honey." Stevie eased into a sitting position and wedged herself into a corner of the couch, her arms clasped around her long legs, her chin resting on her knees. "Only an eight-year difference between us, not sixteen. Together seven years, not for two. And, we're still *better* than friends."

"Granted and granted, but what do you consider *better than friends?* Lovers? We're not lovers anymore."

"Sure, we are," she said. "We just do not make love." Her eyes dodged mine and rose to the ceiling beams. "Of course, sometimes there are exceptions to every rule."

"Can you give it a name?"

Stevie thought about it and said, *"Us.* How does that work as a name for you?"

This time it was me who looked away. There was a gleam in her eyes I didn't mind observing but was afraid to interpret.

She changed the subject. "When you were talking to Jimmy Steiger, you tell him about the picture your art person at the paper made from my description?"

"Still not yet."

"Why not yet?"

"One James Dean at a time is enough."

"Before you said it's because I was hallucinating and, like, my memory sucks."

"That, too."

"I know what I saw, honey. He's what I saw."

"Like you also knew the license-plate number?"

"Rat!" She tossed her head back and finished the last of her Heineken and threw the bottle at me. I caught it midair.

"Refill? Right!" I rose from the couch and headed for the kitchen, ignoring her complaints that I should have more faith.

"Just wait, you'll see," she called at my back. "You'll owe me some apology one of these days and take my word for it, I intend to collect."

I was back in a minute with the brews. They'd be our fourth for the night and I was feeling a little wobbly on my legs.

Stevie patted a spot for me next to her.

I handed over her Heineken and eased down.

She leaned over and kissed my cheek.

"I know you only want the best for me, honey," she said, and touched the place on my left index finger that once housed a wedding band. "It's just that I'm so, oh, you know, over this brain warp I'm going through."

She couldn't bring herself to say "scared" or "frightened," words she'd never admit to keeping in her personal lexicon, but I saw the fear lurking deep behind her frozen stare.

"Your memory, it'll get better. You heard the doctor. Traumatic stress. Nothing permanent. Happens all the time."

"I know that," she said. Read the print on the beer bottle. "But what if it doesn't, honey? What if this is it, as good as it'll ever be?"

It had to be the beer talking. Stevie is stronger than that. I put an index finger to her lips to quiet her.

She inched it aside, leaned forward to reach the *Bedrooms and Board Rooms* script on the coffee table, and plopped it onto my lap.

"Tomorrow's sides. Including two scenes and four and a half pages of stupid dialogue for me. Only four and a half scrawny little pages. . . . Got delivered with my call time for tomorrow, about an hour before I phoned you.

"That whole hour I worked at it, honey, trying to memorize four scrawny little pages. It used to take me five minutes. Ten max. Now—nothing! Nada. Zip. Zero. Screw it, Neil! I had to call the production office and tell them to write around me again. It's not getting better, honey. It's getting worse. I'm getting worse, honey. Worse."

She was in my arms, clutching for comfort, tears wetting my shirt.

I stroked Stevie's cheek, ran my hand through her hair and combed it behind her ear with my fingers, pressed my lips gently against the heat of her broad forehead, kept repeating over and over how everything would be fine, give it time, until—

Stevie's sobbing ebbed. Her body no longer heaved spasmodically against my chest. The rhythm of her breathing told me she was asleep.

I held her, resisting any move that might startle her awake, and thought about the quirks of life and the word *Us* as a name for Stevie and me.

Us.

Just the two of us.

The beer was working its magic. My eyes struggled to stay open, but the beer won. When they opened to the new morning, we were still on the couch, Stevie still asleep in my arms.

My watch said a little past ten. I stretched for the portable phone on the table, trying not to jostle her, and tapped in my home number.

Of the dozen or so calls, there was the standard early-morning demand from Augie to let him hear from me at once, under penalty of instant excommunication Augie-style, but not the one I was anxious for from Jimmy Steiger.

The caller recorded a little after seven was the most interesting. The most frightening.

A voice I didn't recognize, angry and deliberate, vowing, "For what you went and wrote today, you are going to die, mister. . . ."

What I "went and wrote today"?

Of course.

The Dean column had run today.

It had produced the results I'd hoped for—smoked out the bad guy—but the degree of steam I heard hissing in his throat was not supposed to be there. The revised column angle should have generated a kinder, gentler connection.

As careful and calculating as I thought I'd been,

clearly, somehow, I had mismanaged a word or thought.

I eased free of Stevie and settled her into a fresh position on the couch without waking her past a few words of unintelligible protest, padded noiselessly across the room, and inched open the front door.

A brisk chill hit me in the face, along with the fresh canyon smells of morning.

The home edition of the *Daily* was waiting down the drive, in her mailbox.

I tucked the portable phone under my arm, opened the paper to my column.

The wrong one.

They'd run the wrong one.

It was the first take, the column that spared no adjective in tearing apart the myth of James Dean.

The column that served as an invitation for Nico Mercouri's killer to come after me.

And, it was no accident the wrong column had run.

I knew instinctively what had happened.

The Spider Woman was up to her usual tricks.

8

I dialed her direct and through the switchboard, every ten minutes, always with the same result: the Spider Woman would not take my calls. Veronica Langtry's secretary pleaded meetings, appointments, conferences, long distance calls, overseas calls, and I ran out of patience before he ran out of excuses.

My voice rose with my temper, and so did Stevie's. I told her what had happened and tossed the paper at her. She didn't have to read more than the first few paragraphs before she turned to me with a sour look on her face.

"What's the woman trying to do, honey? Get you killed?"

"Cheaper than the pay-out on my profit-sharing and retirement benefits."

"You sure do know how to attract the bitches into your life," she said, then realized what she had said. "In your professional life, of course."

"Of course."

I tried Langtry again. She had left her office briefly to greet a bunch of Brownies and Girl Scouts who were touring the plant, Kevin, her secretary, reported, but Ms. Langtry knew I'd called and wanted me to know she would call me back.

"Kevin, you're saying that with a straight face?"

"If I were, it'd be the only straight thing about me," Kevin said, giggling. He loved exaggerating, flaunting his flame. "Only doing my yob, Mr. G."

I remembered Kevin had no love for his boss. She had tried to have him fired her first week on the job, but his threat of a sexual discrimination suit put a quick end to that. His unflappable loyalty subsequently made them the odd couple of the *Daily*.

"It was more difficult for her at first than for yours truly," Kevin once explained to me. "Spidey could not stand knowing I probably looked better in a dress than she did."

I'd always figured it for a draw, mainly because Kevin had youth on his side.

A few minutes before noon, Stevie and I trooped into Langtry's outer office. It had been redecorated since I was last here to do battle with the boss lady, that time over printing a column I'd done suggesting the city's money would be better spent developing better means of protecting our schoolchildren from armed gunmen with a gripe against society than to rebuild the Coliseum in order to be awarded a new National Football League franchise.

She argued that bringing a football team to L.A. was a priority of the paper. Keeping kids safe was one of mine, I said. She wouldn't budge. I went over her head and almost lost mine in the process, before we hit a compromise that let her save face and me the idea that children matter more than touchdowns.

The office had lost its austere wood paneling and stuffed-leather look and now resembled something decorated by someone angling for a six-page spread in *Architectural Digest*'s "Cedric Gibbons Meets H. G. Wells So Far Out It's In" issue. Barely comfortable in a discomfiting way.

Kevin looked up from behind his marble slab desk, flashed his perfectly-pruned teeth at us, and declared in what passed for French, "*Quel non surprise,* Mr. G., except, of course, for the vision of loveliness at your side."

He rose from his swivel chair, hurried around the desk and, aware of my roving eyes, advised with back of the hand confidentiality, "Spidey's darling nephew, an aspiring decorator. He, you should excuse the expression, blew into town with delusions of adequacy. . . . But what have we here?" Kevin took Stevie's hand and made a courtly bow before air-kissing it.

"The one, the only Stephanie Marriner, as I live and pant," he sighed dramatically. "Before you go, you must autograph my heart."

"You're Kevin," Stevie said, touching his cheek with her palm. "On the way over, I heard the most wonderful things about you from Neil."

"The man is an absolute saint," Kevin decided at once, lacing his fingers at his chest and honoring me with a regal smile of approval, "but, I fear he's wasted one of his rare journeys downtown to the *Daily*'s hallowed halls."

I said, "She's gone?"

"Not exactly, Mr. G., not like Garland is gone." He made a fist and coughed into one end. "Spidey is merely not here." He darted an index finger at the pile carpeting.

"And if I were to check her office?"

"Maybe there, but, of course, I'd have to call building security if you so much as attempt to force your way by me and try her door." He turned an imaginary knob. "Her unlocked door?"

His memory was as sharp as his wit. Whatever his loyalty to Langtry, he knew he owed me payback for making an arrest warrant go away a few years ago.

Stevie also picked up on the cue and gave Kevin the excuse he was lobbying for: "I feel a migraine coming on, sweetie pie. You think you could find me a couple of aspirin somewhere?"

He scanned her figure and said, "Anything for you, you silken creature, you." Took her by the hand and led her off with a sideways caution to me, "Don't you go and do something I wouldn't, just because this might take us about five or ten minutes, Mr. G."

"Fifteen would be my guess," I called after him. He answered with a wave and, five seconds after they had disappeared into the corridor, I pushed open the door to Veronica Langtry's office and stepped inside.

The click of the lock caught her attention, but she didn't look away from her desktop monitor in wondering, coldly, "What took you so long, Gulliver? I expected you hours ago."

Langtry neither ducked my accusation nor denied responsibility for switching the Dean columns. "It was a better piece, stronger, more dynamic, and I elected to go with it," she said with the calm, Southern simplicity that betrayed her Texas prairie origins.

I took a deep breath, trying to keep my temper. "It also happened to be in my personal slop file, Ronnie, and that's a place where you shouldn't be snooping."

"Really? I don't recall that rule, Gulliver. One of yours?" Her fingers slipped absentmindedly through her hair, cut short and dyed the color of Indian ink. "I like my rules better."

"Call it good manners, then."

"I would call it bad management," Langtry said, eyes coldly examining me for someplace to sink the next knife. "The *Daily*'s columnist plus the *Daily*'s computer system equals the *Daily*'s property, so thank you for your input. You'll find the door where you left it."

"Yep, there all right."

I settled into one of the guest chairs and locked on to her tight, emotionless face, looking for signs of life inside amazing blue eyes that would have been capable of stirring real passion and thoughts of sexual adventures if they belonged to a real person. She rose from the high-backed executive chair and moved into a half-sitting, half-standing position by the side of the desk.

Langtry was a going-on-forty ambiguity, a woman who professed to be all business betrayed by a caretaker's concern for surface appearance. Flattering make-up painted her face the way a Renoir might. Her tall, lanky build in an outfit put together from the most expensive pages of a Neiman Marcus catalog. Camel-colored cashmere tweed jacket adorned with hunters pockets and handmade buttons over a rich brown turtleneck. Brown leather pants. Matching cap-toe calfskin boots with an eccentric heel.

I pulled my eyes back to her face and said, "You should have discussed the column with me first."

"Heavens! Not doing so, an impeachable offense?" Langtry investigated me like I was the ranking member of the Senate Stupidity Committee. She wove her arms together and made a career of thinking. Finally, "I tell you what, Gulliver. If it's some consolation, I promise you we won't run that Dean column again."

"Your generosity puts me at a loss for words."

"If ever I can find the way, I'll thrill to make that a permanent gift on behalf of the *Daily*." A guileful smile stretched across her face. "But, until that time—"

"You'll stay out of my slop file."

"I think·you've hit on something," Langtry said, ignoring my statement. "This Dean business . . . Clancy's Post Office Poltergeist. Now your column, Gulliver . . . The public is mindful of Dean again, and it could be sumptuously good for circulation, grand for newsstand sales. . . . I want you to stay with it. Give me a series on Dean. Cover his life, his death, anything in between that smacks of glamour and keeps the copy desk busy fixing your assaults on spelling and the rules of grammar."

The Spider Woman cocked an eyebrow and waited for me to respond.

I wasn't about to tell her she'd done me a favor by giving me license to move with a freer hand and on the expense account in a direction I was already heading.

"The idea stinks," I said, out of arbitrariness and to feed her sense of power. "James Dean's already been done to death. He's a dead issue. What you're asking for, I'd be like a gravedigger covering old ground."

Langtry listened like she was taking notes and, when I was through attacking her news sense, she paused in thought before announcing, "You're right, absolutely right, Gulliver. I stand corrected."

It wasn't the reaction I expected or wanted.

Where was her usual stern rebuff, the exercise of authority, the need for Langtry to have the final word? Her word.

The Spider Woman wrinkled her mouth into a power sneer and said, "Do it anyway."

I tried to look upset.

She said, "Only, Gulliver, try to write it better than

you were talking it just now. Goodness! Playing with
your words like some adolescent boy who's just discovered his twanger."

Before I could spring some nifty retort on her,
Kevin bounded into the room, declaring, "It's all
right, Ms. Langtry! I've called Security! They're on
their way!"

*He thought it might be someone from the church, mak-
ing sure he'd be there for choir practice. He never
missed choir practice, but someone always called anyway, because that was the system, same as they always
answered him with a "How wonderful," when he said
he would, like it was the biggest thrill they'd get all
week.*

*He was surprised to hear Eddie's voice coming over
the phone.*

*"Hello, boy. Something new to tell me about Augie
Fowler, I'm betting."*

"Sorry, not that," Eddie said. "Not yet, anyway."

*"Not more about the girl in the park, and I wish you
hadn't done that, you know?"*

*"I know. I know. Well, she noticed and told me so, so
what was I supposed to do?"*

*"Nothing? That would of been a good idea. What if
they caught you, Eddie? You know how upset that
would of made me."*

*"I apologized once already. I said I'll try and do
better next time, didn't I?"*

*"Come on, now. Don't lose your temper. Just try
and see to it there isn't no next time, okay?"*

"Yeah. Fine."

"Try to stay away from the park."

"Fine, I said."

"So, what is it, Eddie? What's on the fire?"

"The column guy who was at the post office that day and wrote about it?"

He didn't like the tone creeping into Eddie's voice. "Yeah. So, what about him?"

"He wrote something again today and I thought I should read it to you."

"Go ahead."

Eddie read the column slowly, stumbling over most of the longer words and needing his help sounding out some of the others.

"Brief candle, is that so?" he said when Eddie was done, hardly happy with what he had just heard. Gave it some thought before deciding, "I think we have to make this column writer Neil Gulliver a brief candle himself, out of respect for the dead, don't you agree?"

"Why I called you. Yeah, I do. In fact, I already told him so."

"You already told him so?"

"Too mad to wait on calling you, so I went and called him and got it off my chest. Told it like it is and how it's going to be, him dead and all."

"Eddie, Eddie. So impetuous, sometimes I don't know what our good Lord had in His mind when He created you, but you have good intentions, so it's okay anymore. You go ahead and, with my blessing, you go send that Neil Gulliver to meet his maker."

"I will, for sure, and maybe sooner than it'll be over for Augie Fowler."

Augie wandered into the kitchen to fix himself a fresh pot of coffee, the way he liked it, strong, thick as a redwood, and was surprised to discover Jared Gallagher doing more than the lunch dishes.

Jared was hanging up the wall phone.

He should not have been.

Augie reminded him, "You know, it's not allowed, the telephone. Our Order's rules prohibit a candidate from communicating with the outside world during his period of evaluation without my express permission or permission from a senior brother."

Jared answered his stern look with appropriate contriteness, and offered the back of an envelope on which he'd jotted some notes, explaining, "I was here finishing up the dishes and the phone started ringing and ringing, so I snapped it up. It was someone wanting to get this message to you, Brother Kalman."

Augie didn't remember hearing any phones ringing and he normally would have, but it was possible. He thought he recalled the snap of a ring in the last half hour or so, as if a call had been snatched up by someone, but it might have been more. At the time, Brother Ian had been bellowing about his need for more budget for landscaping and also to repair serious rut holes in the access road and the parking areas brought on by the last unseasonal downpours. And, the brothers tended to ignore the phones and anything else that might remind them of whatever personal dread had drawn them into the Order of the Spiritual Brothers of the Rhyming Heart in the first place.

The caller had been Neil, to say he was driving up to the Salinas Valley today. Probably taking Stevie along. Maybe for a couple days. If Augie needed him for any reason, leave word on his machine or call the *Daily*. They would know where to find him.

Augie grumbled, stuffed the envelope in a pocket, wondered, "He say anything else, Jared?"

Jared thought about it for a moment, then pushed his glasses back against the bridge of his nose, shook his head.

"Only for me to have myself a good day," he said, stepping over to the sink, where he slouched over the suds pool and began fishing out dishes and moving them into the king-sized dishwasher. He seemed to make an effort to keep his back to Augie.

Was the kid this shy? Augie wondered to himself, or trying hard not to be studied, as if aware Augie thought he knew him from someplace?

Meanwhile, Augie snarled over Neil's plans. He'd had a fresh thought about Nick Adams that came to him in a nightmare last night. An old thought, really, a puny little thought he had put out of his mind, about an incident that occurred in 1955, when he was in Marfa, Texas, filming his bit in *Giant*. It also involved Sal Mineo and, maybe, here was a better, quicker way to ID and locate the third man at Nick's house the night Nick died.

He'd intended to drag Neil with him later today, once business at the Order was out of the way, but that was not going to happen, was it? The Salinas Valley. It didn't take a genius to figure out Neil had it in mind to do some backtracking on Jimmy Dean. This morning's column was one sign of that. Putting himself into the line of fire, damn fool, probably off more urging from Stevie about catching Nico's killer and sending him past the edge of the earth.

It's not the kind of column Augie Fowler would have written, Augie Fowler being too damn smart for that. Of course, it was, Augie corrected himself. It was exactly the kind of column he'd have written—violating a cardinal rule of journalism by injecting himself into the story. Why he felt the way he did about Neil. The son he never had and blah-blah-blah, the fool. The damn stupid fool.

Augie put down the empty coffee pot on the stove and yanked the receiver from the holder. Tapped out Neil's number. The machine answered on the first ring.

He snapped an order for Neil to call him before setting off on his trip to Salinas or anywhere past the L.A. city limits, then tried Stevie's number.

Got her answering service.

Left his name, the private number, and a message to have Neil call him.

Called the *Daily* and left the same message with Maggie on the switchboard and, for good measure, Andy Collins on the Metro desk.

Augie caught Jared stealing a look at him, his face wishing Brother Kalman were somewhere other than five feet away from him. The face familiar, maybe recognizable inside the mustache and the whiskers? Jared's voice, also ringing silent bells.

"Jared, I have to run some errands later. You'll come along. I'll welcome the company." Also, kiddo, he told himself, a chance to dig deeper into you.

Jared finger-wiped his lips and looked around for some invisible companion, showing reluctance to answer, where any other candidate for the brotherhood would likely have jumped at the chance to spend isolation time with the founding father, whose vote was the deciding word on who of them could stay.

"That sure would be fine," Jared said.

"Excellent. Finish up here and—"

"Only I can't, Brother Kalman. I mean, thank you and all, but I shouldn't." His eyes swept the floor tiles. "I already told Brother Brent how I'd help him out in the garage today? I'm good under the hood with cars, and—"

Augie stopped him with a ref's time-out signal and said with finality, "I'll explain to Brother Brent."

Jared almost said something, then shrugged his shoulders. Then, changed his mind again.

"Could I maybe ask you a favor, though, Brother Kalman? I know how it's against the rules, but my mother, she was ailing something fierce last time we talked, and so I'd like to call her up and see?"

Augie tried not to show it, but the request brightened his spirit, because it shed light on Jared's inner character. Jared hadn't provided many clues before now. "Of course," he said, first making it seem like he'd wrestled with the concept of a rule being broken. "Go on and make your call."

Jared thanked him, wiped his hands dry on his apron and stepped back to the wall phone, removed it from the holder, then hesitated.

Augie recognized that Jared needed privacy. He gave him a finger salute off his forehead and retreated, but stopped just past the door and cocked an ear, to catch a piece of the conversation.

"This here's Jared Gallagher? My mama, can she come to the phone?" After about a minute. "Hey, mama, how goes? This here is your son—Jared Gallagher?"

Augie smiled. Started down the corridor. Abruptly realized he had forgotten to make fresh coffee. Swiveled on his sandals. Headed back into the kitchen.

Jared noticed him at once and lowered his voice, then stopped speaking entirely and hung up the phone.

Augie wasn't certain, but he thought he'd heard Jared use Neil's name.

I became aware of the Porsche following us when Stevie and I one-stopped in Newhall for a late lunch, but it wasn't until making the series of maneuvers routing us onto Highway 33 from the Interstate 5 that I was certain the sports car was on our tail, a '96 or '97 silver and black Twin Turbo capable of leaving Stevie's Jeep in its dust, yet it had hung back two or three car lengths from the time I first noticed it, outside Thousand Oaks.

I had opted for a quick getaway once we left the Spider Woman, before Langtry might feel my enthusiasm and, maybe, change her mind. I also wanted to come as close as I could to duplicating Dean's death drive, to give anything I wrote an added dash of verisimilitude.

Stevie was adamant about making the trip with me and I was up for her company. First, we drove back to her place, where she threw together an overnight bag and got on the phone to *Bedrooms and Board Rooms,* to say her memory was getting worse, not better, and it would be a couple or three days before they could expect her again, slammed down the receiver frowning, complaining how they almost sounded relieved by the news.

She trailed me over to my condo in Westwood and waited while I parked the Jag, hurried upstairs, dumped fresh socks, underwear, and shaving gear into my travel bag, and conveniently forgot to take the beeper and cell phone Langtry insisted I carry as part of the deal, knowing how I hate being connected electronically to anyone anywhere full time.

We could have picked up the 405 off Wilshire and been on our way north in a matter of minutes, but I wanted to start where Dean had started, so I went east on surface streets to Vine in Hollywood, to about where Competition Motors had been, and imagined Dean boyish and giddy as he climbed into the Porsche and took it for a few test spins, showing off a little for his father, Winton, and his uncle, Charles Nolan.

I slowed passing the intersection of Vine and Fountain, where the Hollywood Ranch Market had been, where Dean and his relatives had walked for coffee and doughnuts while his mechanic, Rolf Wutherich, cleaned up and changed clothes for the drive to Salinas. It was a strip mall now, in a city that sometimes seemed to me a collection of strip malls connected by shopping centers, gas stations, and fast-food franchises, like the El Pollo Loco on the corner.

The dashboard clock read one-thirty. I took that as a positive sign. It was one-thirty when Dean sped off, with Roth and Hickman right behind him in the Ford wagon, towing the trailer.

I gloated about this to Stevie as I used Sunset, then Los Feliz, to get to the Interstate 5.

"That explains why you've been running yellows and posted reds," she said. "Obviously, you have it in your mind to end the trip the same as James Dean."

"Were you always a back-seat driver, even sitting in the front seat?" I said.

"Were you always a stubborn so-and-so?" she said. "You just can't stand to give in, especially when you know I'm right, right?"

"Hard to say. You're right so infrequently." I pushed down on the gas pedal. "Please stop telling me what to do, okay?"

"Wasn't that once my line?" she shot back.

I answered the wisecrack by flooring the pedal; watched the speedometer crack seventy on its way to eighty. I pushed the Jeep as I imagined Dean had pushed the Spyder and was hauled over for speeding at the Grapevine, where Stevie was polite enough not to say "I told you so," letting her cackle say it for her.

We were stopped about three-thirty, still on the Dean timetable, about a half hour after leaving Top's Diner in Newhall, where I ordered a glass of milk, which I never drink, because Mother Nature meant it for calves, but I was playing the Dean role, while Stevie, playing the Wutherich role, had a Diet Coke instead of the iced coffee she really wanted.

It wasn't the same diner Dean and Wutherich had pulled into, not Tip's, although that's what we thought at first, and Top's clearly cultivated the mistake. The narrow diner, a long counter augmented by twelve tables along the opposite wall, was decorated in James Dean: mounted posters of his three movies, framed movie stills, and yellowed front pages from local newspapers that ran the crash story under bold-faced headlines five inches tall.

"It looks to me like you must get a lot of James Dean fans stopping here," I said to the fry cook, a chain-smoking Asian in his sixties, who somehow kept a growing length of tobacco ash from falling into his soup pot.

He wiped his hands on his apron, dropped the butt into the sink, and lit a fresh Marlboro while explaining, "I get some, Taps gets more, you should see there."

"But the diner where James Dean stopped for his milk. *Tips.* How about there?"

He shook his head. "I'm never hearing of no place called that. Only here and Taps, my brother place, only the two."

"You never heard of Tips?"

"Only the kind get left behind by customer who realize a man gotta make a living," he said, showing off an almost toothless mouth, letting me see he expected us to be in that category.

The CHP officer who pulled us over was wearing mirrored sunglasses and his one-ton stomach over his belt. His face was red, freckled with cancer spots, and a drop of sweat hung precariously from his nose, put there by a midafternoon sun burning through the clouds at eighty-five or ninety degrees.

He chewed a green toothpick, dispensing the usual motions and admonishments and, after handing me the ticket and my license, leaned over the window to advise somberly, "You ever hear of James Dean? The actor, I mean, not that sausage guy?" Stevie grunted a surprise noise. I couldn't manage even that, too marked by the coincidence to answer. "He did some crazy driving around here and went on to get hisself killed the same day, so you watch it now, okay?"

"Okay," Stevie and I guaranteed in unison, our voices popping the word unnaturally.

The CHP officer hedged his withdrawal from the window, using the extra seconds to examine Stevie, as if he might know her if she were not wearing one of her typical disguises—oversized shades and a floppy straw hat possibly inspired by Ray Bolger's scarecrow in *The Wizard of Oz*—shook the idea and some sweat beads away, retreated with a fingertip salute.

Saluting back, I became aware of cars slowing as they passed, reading the scene, and feeling sorry for the driver, me, the way it happens on public roads all over the world.

The standout was a silver and black Porsche Twin Turbo that hesitated longer than the other cars and, about fifty feet later, gunned the engine and sped away. I wrote it off, like the officer's comment, as coincidence, either that or figure James Dean's ghost had settled here instead of back home in Fairmount, Indiana.

Except—

The Porsche should have been miles ahead of us by the time we reached Highway 46, what had been Route 466 in 1955, only—

It wasn't.

I spotted it behind us moments after I angled the Jeep off the 33 into Blackwell's Corner and pulled up to a gas station pump. It drifted into the lot and stopped maybe thirty yards away.

I sensed the driver making us before he eased the Porsche into a graceful arc and passed under a directional sign to a parking area by the James Dean Memorial General Store and Last Stop Dinette.

As it rolled out of sight, I asked Stevie, "You mind pumping while I make a call?"

"Punch the time clock with mommy dearest?"

She meant Langtry.

I nodded the lie.

I planned to call Jimmy Steiger and see if he had anything new for me yet, maybe something to check out while we were up here. Tell Stevie that and she'd start in on me again about the composite photo of a young James Dean that resulted from her description of the getaway driver. She'd been harping about it constantly since we left Los Angeles.

I pulled a credit card from my wallet, handed it over. Got out of the Jeep. Stretched my legs and headed for the Memorial General Store and Last Stop Dinette, wondering if my curiosity was strong enough to try putting a face to the driver of the Porsche.

I hadn't gotten a good look before, couldn't even tell if it was a male or female behind the wheel, although there was still plenty of daylight savings time left to the day. It may have been my imagination, but I thought I saw the driver purposely turn away from me.

I checked my watch. Five thirty-five, hardly more than a half hour behind Dean's arrival time at Blackwell's Corner. The new 65 mph speed limit had been good to Stevie and me.

It should have been better for the Twin Turbo, I thought, but at once ordered myself not to invent problems where none existed. The driver could have stopped somewhere else first, could have had a flat tire, could have . . . There are lots of Porsches on the road. . . .

Accept coincidence for what it is, *coincidence,* I demanded of myself, and—

—veered from the entrance to the general store, in the direction of the parking area.

If I'd thought to turn around for any reason, I might have noticed the two men creeping up on Stevie from the other side of the building.

9

Stevie thought Neil was returning, until she felt what was unmistakably the edge of a blade against her neck and heard a voice unmistakably dangerous warn her not to do anything stupid.

"Like scream or yell out," the voice explained, as if she might have trouble defining the word.

"Or turn around?" she volunteered, releasing the squeeze handle on the gas pump. She knew that seeing a face would increase her jeopardy.

She'd been in this kind of situation before—oh, how well she remembered—and she'd made the mistake of too obviously trying to learn a face. She was younger then, too young to know all the rules of survival, believing everyone could be her friend if she worked to make it so, wanting so dearly to be the friend of everyone.

Something she still yearned to achieve, the way she imagined an addict needs his morning fix, but nowadays with more caution than she had shown on *that* day, never so many years ago that it didn't feel like yesterday whenever she thought about it.

"That, too, slit!" A second voice, higher, drier, equally dangerous, and the barrel of a gun jammed into her side. "If you're trying to be clever with us, don't be. It never works out so good for the girls who try to be clever with us."

Two of them.

At least.

There was only one the other time, when she was still asleep in her cocoon of loneliness, a shy, pudgy, and awkward preteen the other kids shunned, who often sat on her playground bench—this bench—after school, talking to imaginary friends who understood her dreams and ambitions, encouraged her in the secret language they shared when she talked about becoming a movie star some day.

"Of course, you will, Stephanie."

"A big, big movie star, Stevie."

"So famous and popular everyone will want to know you and be your friend, Stevie."

"Big, big, like even Marilyn Monroe was, Stevie."

So agreeable they always were, Zelda and Daisy and Jordan, Rammy and Rocker, telling her what she wanted to hear, but saying it like they believed it, too, as much as she believed it, helping her to blow up the balloon of dreams the real neighborhood kids only looked to puncture.

"You're a pretty little girl."

A man's voice.

A real voice.

Not one of them, not Zel or the others, although he sounded as old as Mr. Rocky, as old as she supposed her father would be today, if he was still alive.

A sudden presence on the bench, her bench.

"Do you have a name, pretty little girl?"

She knew better than to answer.

Her mama taught her that, over and over, always made her say it back to her before she left in the morning for work at Mr. Rosenbaum's pharmacy.

"Could be the president of the United States, only you don't answer," Mama said. Mama said, *"You don't ever say anything. Mind your business and get on your way as fast as your two feet can carry you, honey."*

"Snap to, slit. You hear what I'm saying to you 'bout being clever?"

Stevie took a silent swallow of air, closed her eyes, pressed down hard on her back molars, told herself not to panic.

"My bag is on the seat. My wallet. Credit cards. About six or seven hundred dollars in cash. Take what you want, take the whole bag, and just go."

Handling it better, she thought, than that little girl on the park bench had handled it, the little girl who never heard anybody real call her "pretty."

The kids, if they bothered to notice her, called her "Freak Face," because of all her freckles, and "Blimp," because of her weight, and other cruel names she refused to say to this day.

"Thank you a lot, but I don't think so, that I'm pretty, I mean."

"Pretty as a picture. In fact, I'd like to take your picture. How would you like that? Would you like me to take your picture?"

Nobody before had ever wanted her picture, except Mama, and that was in a four-for-a-quarter photo machine at Ocean Park.

She felt his leg pushing against hers. Trying to make it seem accidental, but it wasn't. Not accidental, not accidental at all.

"No, thanks. Gotta go home. Mama waiting for me. Already late."

She got up and adjusted her skirt, got as far as the

street before he was on her, the smile out of his voice as he slapped a hand over her mouth, clamped an arm around her waist, lifted her off the ground like she was a sack of feathers, saying not to fight him or he'd kill her for sure instead of only taking pictures, thinking she'd believe him like she was some dope or something.

Where was somebody to help?

Late, near closing and there weren't that many people left on the playground, but didn't Coach or anyone see what was happening to her?

I am not invisible! she screamed inside herself. *I am not invisible! I am not invisible!*

She began crying. The man banged a fist against the side of her head and told her over and over to shut up, the words gargling in his throat as he carried her over to his car, tossed her into the back, followed her inside, and in a minute had her roped like a calf ready for branding.

First Voice said, "You listening to her? *Take the whole bag and go*. Instructions and directions she's giving to us in the same sentence."

"Neither of which I for one need," Second Voice allowed. "I want instructions and directions, I already got an old lady for that, my own slit."

"So why don't you just be smart on yourself and shut up?" First Voice instructed her, shaving an inch down her neck.

And Second Voice probed her spine with the gun barrel, ran it down her spine and kept going until he got to the spot he was searching for and shoved the bore hard into her jeans.

"Great ass," he said. "Wouldn't mind a piece for myself." He made a purring sound. It went with the *too much truth* Stevie heard in his voice.

She flinched as a hand pressed down on her left boob.

"You really got a great pair of knockers there," First Voice said. "She got a great pair of knockers there," he repeated, in case his friend had missed the review.

"Goes with the great ass," Second Voice said.

"They real?"

When she didn't answer, he jabbed her neck with the blade, lightly, but with enough pressure to puncture her skin. Stevie felt a sliver of wetness running down her neck.

"They're real," she said, her breath clogging her throat. She swallowed hard to empty it, aware she could not let these perverts know she was afraid. The knowledge would only make them more dangerous.

The man in the long ago had known she was afraid, beyond her tears. He knew it by her quaking and the way her unformed body tossed relentlessly against his weight, until all strength left her. By the way she'd obeyed when he told her how he wanted her to pose for his pictures in the final violent minutes before he put a map of welts and bruises on her that stayed for months, and warned her before he pushed her from his car and sped away:

"I saw how you were looking so hard at me, why I give you something to remember me by. It's a warning. You forget what you saw, you hear me? You go and forget what I look like. Everything about me. Don't say a word to anyone ever or I come back and give you a whole lot worse than the beating you just got. You get that? You understand?"

She understood, almost as well as she understood what had to be done now. She had to forget about the past, focus on extricating herself from this situation, and—

Something else.

She had to get them away from the Jeep before Neil got back.

Neil saw this, realized what was happening here, he

would go nuts, do something foolish, something that got him gutted or his head blown off by these morons.

She thought, keep your cool, girl. Pull out all the stops and do some of your best acting. The solution's in your purse.

You're still packing the .32.

Get to it. Get your hands on it.

Use it.

Answer force with equal force.

Where had she learned that solution?

Oh, yeah.

Power Squad 9, the Showtime movie she made with Lance DeLario, Tori Chin, and Sir John Gielgud. How they won the war for freedom, answering the enemy's force with equal force. And then some. Especially in the karate scenes where she could show off everything she'd learned from that guy, Barry Someoneorother, who had once studied with Chuck Norris.

Okay, credit where credit is due.

Also from Neil.

He taught her how to use a gun, did not let up until she proved to his satisfaction she had a marksman's eye. With his friend Jimmy Steiger's help, ran her through the Police Academy course until he was sure she wouldn't hesitate to use a weapon in a life-endangering situation.

She remembered asking Neil, "What if I can't be sure, honey?"

"Take the odds," Neil said. "Better to be in the wrong than in a body bag."

He had to do it once, and it saved his life and it changed his life. He became a different person when he made the leap from covering murders to committing one, but told her when he finally brought himself to talk about it, "I'd do it again, and so will you if you ever have to."

First Voice moved his shaggy-haired head to her shoulder, lapped her neck with his tongue. It felt large, coarse, with a surface pimpled like a dill pickle, and his breath smelled like he had eaten used gym socks for lunch. His body odor was worse.

As if this were her old improv acting class with Tracy Roberts, she threw a character into the situation, a chick who liked her sex as much as the guys. Don't resist, Stevie, she told herself. No, not Stevie. A name that fits the part. "Raven." Good enough. Raven. Play into them and get out of it what you need, Raven, not what they want.

Get them away from the Jeep before Neil gets back and get your hands on Stevie Marriner's .32.

Stevie told First Voice, "You give good tongue," putting enough spin on her words to let the creep know she might be interested in more than tongue.

First Voice licked her neck again. Squeezed a boob. Ran his hand down her. Slipped his fingers into the pocket between her thighs.

"I'd be more receptive if we had some privacy," Stevie said, whispering the words. "Too much diesel in the air here. Too much traffic. Too many sightseers for what I have in mind, don't you think so too?"

She turned her hand so that her palm touched his leg, ran it across, and patted his crotch. He moaned into her ear, and his mouth emitted an invisible cloud of stink.

Second Voice stroked her with the gun barrel.

"Where can we go?" Stevie panted. "I could use a little bone-jumping from both of you."

"Man, have we found ourselves one hot babe here," First Voice said.

Second Voice grunted and wheezed and grunted some more.

They were buying her. Raven.

Stevie asked, "You up for some fancy Lewinskying, big guy?" Second Voice groaned. "So am I, so quit with your teasing me and let's find someplace."

First Voice made tongue lapping noises and said, "In the Jeep."

"No. My man's due back any minute. He's packing and he's the crazy type, strip-mining LSD, you follow?"

"Screw him!"

"No me. Screw me, baby. The station has to have a can. Lock ourselves in and party."

"And your man, he come searching?"

"He knows I don't need him to find the roll of toilet paper. C'mon, baby, don't let me lose the light."

Second Voice made half a noise and pushed himself against Stevie.

She pushed back.

"Yeah, baby, it's my kind of dip stick you got yourself there," she cooed seductively.

Figured now was the moment to try to finesse the .32 in her bag.

All this time, Stevie had been locked in a three-quarter crouch. She took a chance and began rising slowly. Receiving no objection, she shrugged off a few kinks in her shoulders and her back, one-stepped away and turned to face the two men.

They were in their twenties, dressed like home boys who were mostly at home on a farm, lumberjack shirts inside coveralls, thick-soled work shoes. A bush of blond hair on First Voice and scalp showing under Second Voice's trucker cap. Their faces were ordinary and, under two-day growths, betrayed hard lives, cheap living; their eyes the truth of the hunting knife and the pistol. Robbery was not a new concept to them, probably not rape, either.

Through her nostrils, she sucked up the gasoline and oil fumes, grease spiraling from the dinette's exhaust stacks, froze an inviting smile on her face, the tip of her tongue suspended like the stem of an apple, stepped off in the direction of the restrooms.

Motioned them to follow her.

Halted suddenly.

Promenaded and started back to the Jeep, passing between them with only a glance at their instantly curious faces.

Second Voice seized her by the collar.

She looked at him over her shoulder and said, "I need to get my bag, hot stuff."

He showed her the pistol and said, "What you need is what I got for you in my pants, so start marching."

"Got my condoms in my bag," she said, pleasantly, thinking, And my .32, you moron. "You wouldn't want to go and risk us joining the epidemic, would you?"

"Forget it!" Second Voice said harshly. "I don't believe in cock socks. Only thing I want you to get right now is my engine running."

First Voice said, "The same time you're guiding my missile to outer space," and cackled at his cleverness.

Second Voice twisted her around, gave her a hard shove toward the restrooms.

Stevie stumbled, then held her ground. "No glove, no love, handsome. You're going to do me, you'll have to do me here."

Second Voice surveyed the area, checked to see if they were being observed. A few cars rolling in and out. A covey of cigarette talkers outside by the dinette entrance. An overweight woman in hips and a halter, taking no note of them, walking her pretend dog, watching the golden ball of fluff pee on the tire of a camper.

"Let her have it," First Voice urged, "then we'll let her have it." Stevie knew by his tone he only meant to humor her until they got to the can. "Besides, what'd she say about her wallet and all the cash? Six, seven hundred? No sense leaving it here, where someone might go and steal it, is there?" His laughter came in short bursts.

"Go on and get her bag," Second Voice ordered, "but don't you make any bets over me and her cock socks."

First Voice was back in half a minute, her bag strapped over his right shoulder, complaining in a light-hearted way how it weighed as much as a pig in a pie.

"I'll carry it," Stevie said, reaching.

"Least I can do," he said, and found that funny.

He pushed her hand aside and led the way to the cans, cursing three quarters of the way there, when he saw a man hurrying into one of them like his body was about to explode.

Stevie had a different reason for cursing.

She recognized the man:

Neil.

Neil was one of those people who went into the bathroom with reading material, a newspaper, a volume of the *Encyclopedia Britannica,* and didn't emerge until he'd worked his way from cover to cover.

Don't be in any hurry now, honey, she thought. I don't need you walking out until I get my hands on the .32.

First Voice tried the other door. It swung open and he flipped on the light, poked his head inside. "Looks like the ladies' crapper for us," he said. He flipped off the light, stepped aside, and bowed, inviting her, "Ladies first."

"My bag, sweetie?" Stevie held out a hand.

First Voice checked with Second Voice, who gave a little shrug of indifference.

First Voice handed it over.

Stevie smiled, pinned him with an erotic look as she dipped into the bag, scrounging for the weapon.

Found it.

Gripped it.

Said a short prayer, getting ready to use the .32 if the two morons gave her no other choice.

Before she had the chance, the other door opened.

Neil appeared. Aiming a Glock at them. Using the doorjamb as a shield. Shouting instructions: "Freeze, and don't you mud toads do anything as dumb as you look!"

With a gymnast's speed and grace, Second Voice moved behind Stevie. Put the pistol to her temple. Pulled back the hammer. First Voice ducked behind him and had his blade at her throat as Second Voice announced, "Drop it or she goes down."

"Who the piss cares? I want your money and you got any drugs, I want them, too, or it's dead-brain time, you follow? She dies and you die. You, too, balloon nose."

"I'm getting it fixed one day," First Voice said, deeply offended.

"You and your friend should live so long," Neil said. He asked Second Voice, "What's it going to be, pond scum?"

Neither of them saw Stevie removing the .32 from the bag. She displayed it briefly for Neil, who shook his head like a nervous twitch, told her with his eyes not to do anything foolish.

"Man, we're busted," Second Voice said. "We were just trying to score for ourselves."

"Where? In there? The First National Bank of Piss and Turds?"

"Thought we'd screw around with the chick first."

"It was her idea," First Voice offered.

Second Voice wondered, "Maybe you want to join the fun and games? Two's company, three's a party."

First Voice said hopefully, "She said she got six, seven hundred dollars in her bag. We can split that, too."

"I'm not the sharing kind," Neil said. "Not my women, my stash, anything else."

"Take her all, then. You're welcome to the slit."

"I can buy her kind of dime-bag chick on almost any street corner in Hollywood. Money's what I dig. Dig?"

"What you and us got then is a standoff?" Second Voice asked logically.

"Only if you insist on hanging around."

"And if we split?"

"Have a nice life and no hard feelings."

"Except," Second Voice said, "why is it I think you're the slit's main squeeze and not so ready for me to make grave hash of her?" He said it like he'd just won the lottery.

"I'm nobody's pimp," Neil said grimly. "Go ahead, test the theory, man. When you wake up dead you'll know the answer for certain."

"Please, Jerry," First Voice said. "Let's just us split, okay?"

Stevie read on Neil's face and in his eyes that Second Voice didn't believe him.

Her mind raced through her options.

She had no options.

Second Voice would squeeze the trigger before she could somehow break free, swing around, and use her .32 on him and the other moron.

Second Voice finished deliberating and said, "We got here first. We leave with the bag."

Neil took equal time to think about it. "Fair is fair," he decided. He nodded at Stevie and told her, "Hand them the bag, Miss Tits."

Stevie scowled at him, hesitated, then extended her arm, letting the bag hang like a piñata.

First Voice snatched the bag from her, turned, and fled toward the gas pumps. Second Voice pushed her at Neil as Neil stepped out from the john, then quickly wheeled around and chased after his buddy.

Neil caught Stevie with his free hand and pulled her close while he raised the Glock and fired into the air. The shot startled First Voice into dropping the bag.

Neil demanded, "Tell me you're okay, babe. Tell me you're okay."

"I'm okay," she said, clutching him, "and don't you ever again dare call me Miss Tits. And— Jesus! Those two morons are stealing the Jeep!"

As the Jeep tore away from the pumps, a Porsche Twin Turbo materialized from somewhere and screeched to a stop in front of them.

"They're in the Jeep!" Neil called at the open passenger window. He kissed Stevie on the cheek. Told her to wait for him in the dinette. Hopped into the Porsche.

The driver gunned the engine, gunned it three more times, and roared off after the Jeep.

Stevie propped herself against the wall, using her hands as a mask to cover all of her face, except for her eyes, and struggled to catch her breath.

Said a little prayer of thanks.

After a few minutes, went looking for her bag. Found it. Collected a few items that had fallen out when it hit the ground. Headed for the dinette wondering about the Porsche. Where it had come from. What it meant.

Stevie bought an espresso and wandered about the dinette and through the general store examining the James Dean artifacts on the walls—substantially more than she and Neil had seen earlier today at Top's Diner in Newhall—and the souvenirs in the gift areas.

She was careful to hide her identity under her hat and sunglasses from the dozens of James Dean curiosity hunters sharing thoughts in hushed tones, like pilgrims at a sacred shrine.

They were taking pictures, loading up shopping baskets with postcards and posters, T-shirts and sweat-shirts, hardcover biographies, as well as paperbacks and picture books, coffee mugs imbedded with various versions of the famous face, beach towels, party nap-kins, watches, snowballs, even lithographs of Dean's beloved beige-and-brown Siamese cat, Marcus, a gift from Elizabeth Taylor he had left behind in the care of an old girlfriend.

Stevie didn't want to be recognized.

Were she recognized, she'd be nice, of course; ac-cessible. She was incapable of disappointing her fans. She'd sign autographs for them. Stand still and smile for the photos. It's how stars were supposed to behave. How it was in the days of the studio system, when they understood the fans made the stars, not the other way around.

She was still shaky, her mind not quite through playing out alternative endings to the experience she had just gone through.

What if Neil hadn't shown up and she got the gun and she had to use it? Could she? Could Neil? Could he have dropped the two morons he was still chasing?

Yes, she decided.

She could have and he could have.

And she shuddered at the truth.

She had been roaming for about twenty or twenty-five minutes when, around six-thirty, while examining the small boxes of packaged dirt from the crash site, under an immense photo wall mural of the site taken within hours of the crash, Stevie began to decipher the jumble of voices that was breaking through the store like surfers' waves, reporting in disbelief the news all over local radio:

There had been another crash at the dangerous Y

intersection of 46 and 41, east of Cholame. A Porsche Twin Turbo and a Jeep. No information yet on anyone involved in the collision, their conditions or their identification.

Stevie didn't have to be told to be certain who one of them was.

I remembered shouting, "Hit the brakes!" but when was that?

How long ago, and where was now?

Where was I now?

If this was Heaven, why did I feel like Hell?

My eyes felt glued shut. I fought to open them, but the lids would not cooperate past a slit of blurred vision.

My throat resisted the struggle to make three words understood inside the gargling sound I knew was me fighting to communicate with the undecipherable image of colors and lights hovering over me like a Calder mobile.

I tried again: "Where am I?"

Only, it sounded more like "Whirmmuh?"

"Whirmmuh?" I said.

An answer from a voice I knew, spilling down on me from my Disneyland of confusion:

"What's that, honey? What are you trying to say?"

"Whadhppn? Whirmmuh?"

"I don't understand, honey. Say it again, okay? Are you hurting or what? Can you tell me?" A hand clasping mine. Dry. Smooth. Tight. Trembling.

A sun moving closer to my face, bringing with it a warm rain. A sweet fragrance. "Tell me that you're okay, honey? Can you tell me?" A gentle touch to my cheek.

Stevie? It sounded like Stevie.

Her voice. Her touch.

"Strvey? Im guh—"

Then, a different, heavier voice. Harder: "Can't you tell he's Swacked City from the pain killers they been feeding him?" Also familiar. "We should split out of here and let him be for now."

"Please feel free to follow your own advice, and don't let any speed bumps slow you down. I and Neil will do ultra-absolutely splendid without you."

"You don't have to get snippy with me, lady."

The other voice:

DeSantis.

That's who.

"DeZnt," I called, with almost all the energy I was able to muster before falling back down the black hole, wondering if this was how Alice felt and would I see her at the bottom.

And the White Rabbit.

The White Rabbit, not to forget about the White—

"Rvrt?" I heard myself calling. "Whrryurvrt?"

Stevie turned from Neil and looked up at Det. Lt. Ned DeSantis, who was hovering over her shoulder. *"Not* get snippy with you? And end a great tradition? Should I remind you all over again, lieutenant, that you're not my favorite person in the world?"

"Like I care?"

"Caring would be a human emotion."

"I suppose a lot of people love putting up with your star crap, is that what it is? If that's what it is, don't look my way. The only bitches I clean up after walk on all fours."

"Exactly what I'd expect from a Cro-Magnon, but what it is is— You almost killed him."

"Miss Marriner, again you are starting to sound like I went and did it on purpose to our mutual friend."

"You were driving. You were behind the wheel."

DeSantis contemplated her smugly and said, "You

seem to forget we were trying to catch some guys who might of killed you, the both of you, if it wasn't I come along at the right time."

Noises, emanating from Neil, who might or might not have been enough awake to hear and understand, turning a moan into a sigh.

Stevie momentarily diverted the special grimace she always kept reserved for DeSantis, to squeeze Neil's hand again and wonder, "Honey, I'm here. I'm not leaving. So, anything you need, you just tell Stevie, okay?"

"How about he needs a little peace and quiet, maybe? Like you could shut off the TV set?"

"I just so happened to have turned it to one of his favorite programs."

"The eleven o'clock news?" DeSantis snorted. "You know what? I'll bet you the program is going to be on again tomorrow night. And, tomorrow night, Gulliver might even be alert enough to know it and give a rat's patootie."

"You offering your patootie?"

DeSantis looked at Stevie like the custodian had missed her when he cleaned the room. She returned the shot, not wanting to give in to his glower, but got tired of the game after another minute, pushed back her visitor's chair from the hospital bed, rose and wheeled around to confront him nose to neck.

What was it about DeSantis she couldn't stand?

It was a question whenever they came together, a sometime unavoidable circumstance since that ugly business about Black Jack Sheridan, Jeremy Brighton, all the rest of it at the Motion Picture Retirement Estates, had turned him into another one of Neil's LAPD buddies, this loud, coarse, crude, arrogant, ambitious, largely unappealing cop.

She knew, of course.

It was the closeness she resented.

Neil wasn't hers anymore, not since the divorce, and the divorce had been her choice, but she never liked to think he was anyone else's either.

It was selfish of her and she was working on it.

Admitting to selfishness was half the cure, her shrink had told her.

Fine, fine, fine, but they were still trying to identify the sickness.

Jealousy, yes, but more than jealousy.

What else? What more?

"How about a truce, DeSantis?" His eyes searched Stevie for hidden weapons as she stepped back and held out her hand. He took it cautiously. "Nothing permanent, okay? We're not going to bond and wind up splitting the cost of a six-pack or sitting on the fifty-yard line at the Rose Bowl cheering for UCLA or anything like that."

"I'm a baseball guy myself," DeSantis said. He released her hand and raised a victory fist. "Go Big Blue!"

"Neil hasn't much cared about the Dodgers since they traded away that catcher . . . Pizza."

"Piazza."

"Yeah, him . . . except for the home run guys, Mark McGwire and that precious Sammy Sosa . . . Bottom line, we're basketball people. The Lakers."

"Most of the time I can't stand basketball."

Stevie liked DeSantis better already.

"I desperately need a smoke," he said. "You think we could move this truce somewhere outside?" He noticed her hesitation. "Neil's lost to the world. He'll never know and I promise not to tell."

Seeing no trickery in his hard brown eyes, Stevie turned and stepped back to the bed, found the call button, signaled for the nurse.

"I don't want Neil to be alone while we're gone," she said. She adjusted Neil's covers and told him, "I'll be right back, honey. Doing a favor for your friend, DeSantis. Outside for just a couple of minutes."

Neil answered, startling her.

"Whrryurvrt!" he said, maybe a word inside the jam of growls and wheezes congesting his speech.

I heard new, unfamiliar noises, like crepe soles scraping along a floor, thighs rubbing against one another, heavy breathing pushing in and out and getting closer. Not at all as before Stevie and DeSantis left a minute ago.

Two minutes ago?

Three?

Four?

There was no way of telling time on the floor of my black hole, stranded alone, abandoned to the unknown. No White Rabbit lamenting his lateness, no Alice to comfort me with her own curiosity. This is when fear of the unknown attacks as swiftly as a common cold and I became frightened without my shield of knowledge.

"Whrayuh? Whirmmuh?"

"Shhhh, Mr. Gulliver. Shhhh." I didn't know the voice quieting me and the fingers pushing confirmation on my lips were cold and carried a foreign odor. "Give me a chance and you won't feel a thing."

The fingers worked their way past my teeth, pried my mouth open, ignored the noises I made that were meant to put a stop to this, whatever *this* was.

"Nuhduhnstp! Stp!"

"Don't fight. Relax your throat. There's that's a good boy." Humming an unfamiliar tune. "Swallow like a good boy."

A new voice, across the continent: "Who are you and what do you think you're doing?" Sounding as alarmed as the noises signaling for help in my mind.

"You're the night nurse?"

"No, I only dress like this in case the casting director from *E.R.* drops by to discover me." Closer now, whispering indignantly. "And you still haven't answered my questions."

"Don't take that tone with me."

The night nurse said, "Will your hearing improve if I leave now and come back with our security people?"

"I wouldn't advise it."

I would, I would, I thought, trying to turn the thought into words that wouldn't come.

The light on the floor of my hole was dimming.

One of the doors here—was it the one Alice went through, chasing the White Rabbit?—disappeared, leaving me no choice but the other one, the one marked "Enter" or "Do Not Enter." I couldn't tell for certain.

The words were in Greek and I don't know how to read Greek, but I knew I didn't want to go through the door without Stevie and DeSantis.

"Strvey! DeZnt! Strvey! DeZnt!"

I heard myself calling for them and wondered if they could hear me, if anyone else could hear me.

Help me.

10

Stevie and DeSantis had settled on opposite ends of a weathered wooden bench in the enclosed patio adjacent to the main entrance of Paso Robles War Memorial Hospital, where she listened intently to DeSantis's explanation of how the crash happened after DeSantis took several heavy drags from the Camel she'd lit for him after he tried and failed doing it for himself.

His left arm was in a heavy cast that ran from his fingers to midway past his elbow and trapped inside a sling, making it difficult for him to juggle between the cigarette pack and the old-fashioned box of wooden matches in his jacket pocket.

He was limping a little, favoring the left leg, and his face looked like he had climbed into the ring with the old Mike Tyson—deeper gulfs under his high cheeks and fresh, crimson cherry pits salting the acne scars that gave character and a strangely handsome quality to his face—but the emergency room doctors had released him after reviewing the full battery of tests they'd ordered run.

Neil, on the other hand, had no broken bones and hardly any cuts and bruises, only a mild concussion and the pains associated with various organs that were jostled like a tossed green salad, so the doctors had filled him full of sedatives and were holding him for overnight observation as a precautionary measure.

What they were telling her anyway.

Neil seemed worse than the doctors made it sound, and that one nurse who got her autograph let it slip she'd seen emergency room patients surprise everyone and go from doing great to the grave in minutes.

"Look, like me he's a Workout Wally and six years younger, so those are plusses," DeSantis had said, trying to reassure her. "Write us down as one lucky pair of aging baby boomers. More lucky than the two jerk-offs what swiped your Jeep."

Stevie acted like she agreed that was all there was to it and, getting him back on the subject, said, "So, there you were on their bumper . . ."

"Exactly," DeSantis said. "Once we caught up, and that was almost the minute we left the gas station, no way the Jeep was going to put any distance between us. They hit top speed and stayed there, though, and I told Neil the way it was going we were candidates for starring in a live high-speed chase on Channels Two, Four, Five, Seven, and Eleven.

"Neil says for me to try and maneuver in front of them, slow them down and to a stop that way.

"I say, 'What if they decided to play bumper cars with us?'

"He says, 'We'll go to Plan B if that's the case.'

"I say, 'What's Plan B?'

"He says he don't know yet, although he will know by the time we find out if Plan A works.

"It's not so easy to begin with. There's a shitload of traffic out there, both directions, a lot of stop and go false starts. Meanwhile, the Jeep is playing a game of its own, slamming down on the brakes or putting pedal to the metal. More than a few times I'm close to slamming into its backside or getting rear-ended myself, but about half a mile from where the 466 and the 41 come together, I see my chance coming. I got the clearance I need to stream around the Jeep.

"I get in front of it and I slow down. The Jeep slows down. Only for a second. Then it speeds up. I gotta speed up to avoid making it Cream of Porsche time.

"The Jeep uses the moment to sweep around me, honking while it passes only an inch from trading paint jobs, and comes up in front of me again.

"That's where I realize Neil is yelling for me to hit the brakes. Not because of the Jeep. Because we are a hundred yards or less from the Y intersection, where the mother of all two-tons has started to turn and is making a wall across our lane.

"The wheel man in the Jeep comes down hard on the brakes. I do likewise, certain that my foot will go through the floor boards and be dragging on the asphalt any second. The Jeep smashes into the side of the trailer, bounces off, and does a series of rolls across the road, down and dirty, and comes to a stop all over the damn roadway, busted up in more parts than the old Soviet Union.

"My Porsche tailspins, whirls like a merry-go-round, and just misses its own home-plate slide into the two-ton, angling past that mother, flying over a drainage ditch, and somehow landing on all fours in an open field, hard enough to do damage, but we must have had some saint looking over us, Neil and me, not like them two punks who came at you at Blackwell's Corner." He shook his head. "I woke up here in the hospital, a little worse off than you see me now. Neil, too." He shaped a perfect smoke ring and watched as it sailed up and away to the three-quarter moon standing sentry in the warm night air. "Now, you know as much as me."

Stevie said, "I don't think so."

He sent her a questioning look.

"Who were they, DeSantis? Why did they come after me?"

"The usual reasons, money and sex. Cop who took my statement said they were two of the homegrown punks who like to make Blackwell's Corner a target. Lot of one-stops because of the James Dean thing, lookie-loos who usually take off without bothering to file a report, glad to still be breathing. He expects the autopsy to show they were high on crack, same as when they got busted the last time, when they lucked out with a goodie two-shoes judge, who let them off with a lecture and community service. . . . That do it?"

"No. I don't know what you're doing here. Tell me that, but don't tell me it was a coincidence."

DeSantis laughed. He ground what was left of the Camel under his heel and said, "Sure, but it will cost you another light."

She obliged, wondering, "Hasn't anyone convinced you yet that smoking causes cancer?"

"Couldn't be any worse than the women I inhale," he said, at once seeming to regret the comment, shrugging, forcing a smile onto his face as replacement for whatever memory had plastered it with a drop-dead frown. He fired a long stream of smoke from a corner of his mouth, parked the Camel there, and reported, "I was following him and you, of course. To protect and to serve, that's me."

Stevie tried to hide her confusion, but DeSantis spotted it.

"S'okay, Neil didn't know it neither. . . . It was Jimmy's idea, Jimmy Steiger. Neil asked him to check out a thing or two on this James Dean business, some other stuff, and Jimmy, he phoned up and passed about fifty cents of the buck to me. Also, he wanted me to keep an eye on our boy."

" 'Keep an eye' . . . that meant *following* him?"

"No." A jet stream of smoke, butt inspection. "It meant keep an eye. So, I was digging away, learning some of the answers Neil wanted could be up north, had no plans for coming up here myself, until I got this call today from Friar Tuck."

"Augie Fowler?"

"The one and same mad monk himself, carrying on like an off-course SCUD missile, telling me Neil could be in danger over this column of his he wrote about Dean, and how I had to prove my friendship by protecting our buddy's butt, *Pronto,* amigo, like I'm the U.S. Cavalry.

"He figured out from some phone message Neil left that he was heading up here and probably on the same route Dean drove. Like I've said on more than one occasion, Friar Tuck probably sniffs the old glue pot much too much, but he ain't stupid. I put out a fast all-points and got a read on your Jeep about an hour and a half later.

"No way for me to play catch-up in my wheels, so I did a fast-favor borrow from Grand Prix Motors in Studio City and had the Porsche licking your tail before Neil was much outta Thousand Oaks. No sense sounding alarms, so I hung back, but Eagle Eyes made me early and came after me once I low-geared behind you into Blackwell's Corner.

"He was shoveling out his piss-and-vinegar pissed-off attitude to me about anyone, especially me, playing his babysitter when we spotted your problem with the two future statistics. We threw together a fast plan, not bright, but expedient, I handed over my spare Glock, and—you know the rest."

He eyed Stevie for some indication. She did have questions, but her attention had been diverted by—

Something.

She wasn't certain what.

"DeSantis, I swear I hear Neil calling for me. Calling out my name."

DeSantis studied her for sanity. Shook his head.

"You'd hafta have twenty-twenty hearing, because there's no way any voice could carry through them hospital walls into your ears," he assured her.

Stevie held out a hand to silence him. Listened intently, certain she was hearing something. Neil. She was hearing Neil. Neil in danger and calling for her.

Her bag was on her lap. She located the .32 and, passing the bag to DeSantis, jumped to her feet, ordering, "Hold on to this. Neil needs help. He's in trouble."

"What the—? Hey! Wait up, dammit!"

DeSantis rose awkwardly, putting too much weight on his left foot. It buckled under him and he dropped back hard onto the bench and was still calling after her to wait for him as Stevie darted through the hospital's automatic doors and up the corridor to Neil's room, jostling a green-clad janitor pushing a mop, causing him to bang against his mop bucket, which overturned, sending a sudsy water stream and a series of curses after her.

The door to Neil's room was closed. She stopped, got a firm two-handed grip on the .32, took a deep breath before shouldering the door open. Barged inside and into a wide-legged stance, the .32 pointing at the broad backside of the man bent over the bed, shouting—

"Freeze! My gun is loaded and I'm not afraid to use it!"

He froze and after a moment floated his arms out from his body, showing he was unarmed, except for the large hypodermic syringe in his right hand.

At the same time, someone shrieked from a part of the room outside her peripheral vision. Keeping her sight trained on the man, Stevie ordered, "Whoever you are, move over to where I can see you! Closer to the bed. No tricks!"

"Dear God, is this some kind of prank?" the man asked, angrily. "What in the name of hell is this? Who in the hell are you?"

Stevie demanded, "You first! Who in the hell are you?"

Before he could respond, the shrieker answered, "She's Stephanie Marriner, the star of the soap *Bedrooms and Board Rooms*. Mr. Gulliver there is her ex."

The shrieker was the night nurse, who stepped over to the side of the bed opposite the man, a nervous smile popping on and off her face, eyes the size of half dollars darting back and forth between the man and Stevie.

"Oh, for Christ's sake," the man said, turning around to face Stevie, arms akimbo. "I've heard you actors are all crazy, and this certainly helps prove it." His appearance matched his kettle-drum voice, oversized everywhere, including inside his two-thousand-dollar silk suit.

The nurse said, "This here is Dr. Beisell, Ms. Marriner. I didn't know him either, but he is taking Dr. Rudd's rounds tonight. Dr. Rudd got himself stuck in San Francisco, Dr. Beisell said, so he phoned to Dr. Beisell and—"

"And it's really none of her business, nurse. It's really none of your business, Miss Marrim."

"Marriner," the nurse corrected him.

"Marriner," Stevie corrected him, less politely.

"Marriner. None of your business, Miss Marriner. Now, I plan to turn around again, so that I can administer this sedative to Mr. Gulliver." He held up the hypodermic for inspection. "If you have any objection, shoot me, but, please, not before I've taken care of my patient."

Flushing with embarrassment, Stevie lowered the .32 and started to apologize as—

DeSantis, panting between words and syllables, affecting a life-or-death tone, commanded, "Make one false move, shithead, and you are wallpaper!"

Stevie glanced over her shoulder. He was limping in from the doorway, his Glock resting on his arm cast, in a direct line with Dr. Beisell's chest.

"Take it nice and slow putting the needle down on the bed, asshole, or you are an immediate candidate for the past tense," DeSantis said, coughing and wheezing.

"Jesus Christ a'mighty!" the doctor shouted to the ceiling. "What goddam television show are *you* from?"

Sometime during the middle of the night, I woke up terrified. It wasn't from the nightmare where DeSantis couldn't stop the Porsche from plowing into the trailer. A dream never kills the dreamer, dreamers know that; not even the worst nightmare. Dreamers always live to dream again. I had flown from the car just before the crash happened, like the hero in an old Republic serial.

What terrified me occurred in the next dream and it involved Stevie. I'm stretched out in the middle of the road, counting the first stars twinkling out a greeting to me in some Morse Code of twilight, and she comes running to me, stretches out beside me, one arm under my head and the other making nice-nice up and down my body, and whispers to me in a voice like penicillin, "Everything is going to be just fine, daddy. You're going to be just fine here in your mama girl's arms."

That did it, the "mama girl" part. It was a term she had not used with me since the divorce. Up to then, it was the one she treasured most, next to "daddy," which she used interchangeably with "honey." And she, of course, was my "baby" then, my "babe" still.

It terrified me and I woke up, terrified that it wasn't the truth, and, of course, it wasn't.

It was only a dream.

A different kind of nightmare.

The kind of nightmare that lets you die a little every day that you're awake.

Only, I was certain that I was not by myself in the hospital bed. I was certain that Stevie was snuggling alongside me, fully clothed, her lips a breath away from mine, whispering gently, "Your mama girl's right here with you. Everything is going to be just fine, daddy. You're going to be just fine here in your mama girl's arms."

I was less certain that I was awake. Truly awake. Really awake. The drugs, I supposed, easing my pains while rolling me from one dream into the next. More likely, Neil, more likely.

And when I awoke the next morning, fully alert, only a few death-defying aches to remind me of what I had been through, Stevie was curled up asleep in an armchair near the foot of my bed, bathed in slats of light seeping past the window blinds.

I escalated the bed and studied her for I don't know how long, before DeSantis arrived ten steps behind his voice, bellowing, "You're absolutely not gonna believe the earful I just got about this James Dean business." He made a flamboyant gesture, working a dozen directions at once as he light-footed it to my bedside, favoring his left leg.

Stevie had been startled awake by his voice. She moved into a sitting position, her legs crossed yoga style, shook the sleeping-sand from her head while she interpreted his words, and inquired, "DeSantis, exactly what are you telling me?"

"Telling you? I'm telling him." He turned back to me. "Buddy boy, the hospital says it has no record of James Dean ever being admitted here."

About three hours later, after submitting to a brief interrogation by CHP investigators, I checked myself out of the hospital—ignoring recommendations that I stay under care for another day, but gratefully accepting a vial of thirty three-times-a-day-or-as-needed pain killers that allowed two refills—and headed for the office of hospital administrator Randall G. Webber with a barrel of questions, anxious to hear for myself what he had told DeSantis about James Dean.

DeSantis was off asking some questions of his own and making arrangements to have the Porsche released by the CHP for towing back to L.A. Stevie was with him, to pick up copies of the accident reports she'd need for her insurance claim. She'd gone reluctantly.

She had wanted to stick with me, arguing that the paperwork could wait and, besides, the Jeep was totaled and destined for a junkyard. I was adamant, reminding Stevie I conduct my best interviews without an audience.

"Tell that to Laura Dane," she demanded irately, bringing up a situation that would have failed without her, during a murder investigation starring Stevie as the prime suspect.

"You were acting that time, not in the audience," I

said, "but I'll certainly tell Laura if I see her again. Should I also give her your regards?"

She threw some silent rage at me before flouncing out of the hospital room a mile ahead of DeSantis, who hung behind to snicker and remark, "And here I was thinking you two lovebirds had played kiss and make up."

"What's that supposed to mean?"

"It means I know who has been sleeping in your bed, buddy boy . . . besides you, I mean." He winked grandly and took it with him out the door.

DeSantis's advisory was still playing tricks with my psyche as I was ushered into Randall Webber's office. I sensed at once the meeting wasn't likely to be productive, with or without Stevie.

It showed in the way he shifted uncomfortably in his executive chair, finger-beating gently on the desk top, like he was playing bongos, although my only sin seemed to be leading with a smile and attempting to get a handshake, both of which he ignored.

He was in his early twenties and his gaunt face was set off by a pair of suspicious eyes that never quite looked squarely at me, and by a perfect frown frozen on a small mouth that never moved when he spoke. He exhibited all the uncertainties of somebody with too much authority too early in his career, probably in a position that paid at least a third less than equal experience brought in the big city. And, he looked uncomfortable in his suit and tie, like he really belonged in a T-shirt with a funny cartoon on the front, to go with the row of teenage fuzz across his upper lip. I was ready to bet he had never been called by a nickname, not even the obvious "Randy" for "Randall."

He did a funny thing with his mouth and nose when I plopped down into one of the guest chairs without waiting to be invited and advised me, "Anything you ask, I probably already told your detective friend."

His voice reminded me of the sound one of those whistles makes piping some admiral aboard a ship, perfect for a room decorated in early war memorabilia befitting the name Paso Robles *War Memorial* Hospital. The one appropriate to the moment was an ornately framed poster on a wall full of posters from the World War II era that cautioned "Loose Lips Sink Ships."

I overacted astonishment. "Again? Detective De-Santis pass himself off as my friend again?" Disdainful turns of the head augmented by a deep sigh. "He does that a lot."

"That's supposed to be a joke, isn't it?"

"Just warming up."

"I don't have a lot of time."

"I don't have a lot of jokes."

"Thank you," he said.

I found his response sort of funny and grinned.

He didn't.

We stared in silence at one another for a minute or two, until he offered, "I told him, Detective DeSantis, that James Dean never was admitted to our hospital."

"Yes, the magic words that brought me here."

"Okay? Are we done now?"

"The old news stories I read say he was, that he was taken here straight from the scene of the accident and pronounced dead on arrival."

"But never admitted. Our records only deal with patients admitted to the hospital. Like you, Mr. Gulliver, and, by the way, you released yourself this morning over a strong recommendation to stay at least one more day. So—" He gave me a fish eye. "If your condition should happen to worsen, any thoughts you may have of a lawsuit won't hold water in a court of law."

"Same as my late uncle."

"Excuse me?"

"He was on trial for burglary. He had to go to the bathroom. By the time the judge noticed him waving for attention, it was too late."

"That's another joke."

"Not to the judge. He slapped my uncle with two to seven, with no time off for good behavior, but at least the prison doctor was able to correct my uncle's prostate problem."

"I see," Webber said, and looked at his watch.

I said, "So, even though your records don't show it, James Dean could have been brought here and pronounced DOA, just as the newspapers reported?"

"I suppose."

"Maybe you keep records besides admissions, like maybe staff physicians? Doctors on duty? Duty logs showing who did what to whom, say the doctor who was on duty when the ambulance arrived with Dean?"

"Do you know how long ago that was, sir?"

"Forty-five years ago?"

"Forty-five years ago," Webber said on the same beat, and watched his fingers practice a new melody on the immaculate surface of his bongo desk.

"Just a lucky guess." I flashed a smile from ear to ear, shrugged, flipped my palms upward. "Is there some statute of limitations on keeping records?"

"Anything before the last big quake, destroyed."

"How about a doctor or a nurse, an orderly, who might have been here that day—"

"—September the thirtieth, nineteen hundred and fifty-five." He spit out the date faster than a gunfighter, then found a spot across the room to stare at.

"Lucky guess?"

"You're not the first newspaper reporter to come here asking questions. . . . Nobody I know who was around except for—" He caught himself. Shook his head. Fixed his stare on the framed salon portrait photos on the wall to my left, most of them in sepia and cracked with age.

"Maybe one of your predecessors?" No response. "A name and an address or phone number and I'll be out of your way faster than you can say goodbye, Randy."

"Randall." He thought about it like I had asked him to define Einstein's theory of relativity. Finally, "I only know my grandfather, in that photograph." He pointed to a grander frame above the faux fireplace and at once I saw the resemblance, in the way grandpa's frown seemed set in concrete. "My grandfather, Garfield R. Webber, was the hospital administrator here at PRWMH when it happened."

"And he never propped little Randall on his knee and told him all about it or, maybe, said something to your daddy, who passed it along to you?"

"They never talked much about anything, he and my father. The way our family was."

"Like a lot of families, but maybe grandpa will talk to me."

"I don't think so."

"Let me find out for myself." I settled back in the chair, locked my hands in my lap, illustrating that I intended to keep him company until he satisfied me.

Webber understood body language.

He pulled a slip of blank memo paper from a box next to his computer monitor and wrote a name and address in a small, precise, almost flowery hand, using an ink pen he retrieved from a cup holder full of ink pens.

He blew on it gently and, handing over the slip, said, "Don't say I didn't warn you."

I'm sure it was my imagination, but I thought I saw Webber try to smile.

Within the hour, after reaching the address he'd

given me, I would understand both Webber's warning and his smile. By then I had a greater concern:

Augie was missing.

I learned about his disappearance while waiting for Stevie and DeSantis to return.

I'd found a lobby phone and called home to check messages. The standard assortment included six from Augie, and he sounded more and more anxious with each call. First came his to-be-expected complaints about my taking off for Salinas without inviting his counsel or having the courtesy to invite him along. Then, irritation that he had not heard from me. Next, an advisory he was heading off to chase down an interesting lead about the Jimmy Dean affair without me, suggesting we might be closer to finding our third man than we knew.

Next, with a whispered urgency and a shortness of breath, informing me the Dean situation was far more dangerous than anyone had imagined.

Then, about eight last night, frantic, with a demand to hear from me the minute I got this message, no matter what the time.

Sounding like the old days.

More than a trace of the sauce?

I disconnected to the buzz and tapped out the *Daily*'s credit card number followed by Augie's private number. No answer.

I switched to the main number for the Order of the Spiritual Brothers of the Rhyming Heart and the phone was answered on the first ring by an unfamiliar voice. I identified myself and was put through to Brother Saul, who greeted me pleasantly enough, but there was an underlying concern in his voice.

"He's not here," Brother Saul said. "We haven't

heard from him since last night, and that's most unusual. He rarely stays away like this, without telling me where he's off to." He gave a false laugh. "But you best of all know our Brother Kalman. . . . I expect he'll be showing up any time, as if nothing were unusual, telling us about some new discovery he's made or some revelation not to be believed."

"What time did he call, Saul?"

"Seven or seven-thirty, perhaps."

"He say where he was?"

"No."

"Anything?"

"Only that he and young Jared Gallagher might be a while and, if you called in, to have you leave a number he could reach you at."

"Jared Gallagher? What's a Jared Gallagher?"

"One of our newest candidates, a bright, sturdy young man who came to us from the streets this week and is not afraid of work. Brother Kalman took a special interest in him, probably because Jared seems to be a rules breaker, same as Brother Kalman. Same as you, too, Neil."

"So, wherever he is, at least, Brother Kalman is not alone."

"Not in the least and, as I always say, safety in numbers. Otherwise, I'd be a mite fearful of where Brother Kalman is keeping himself."

But for Augie's last phone messages, I might have agreed with Brother Saul.

"He'll be fine," I said, sounding as upbeat as I could to give him a measure of comfort, and hurried to end the conversation without adding to his worries, then tapped in my credit card code and Jimmy Steiger's number at Parker Center.

He had taken the day off. I tried the house next, got Jimmy's machine and, while leaving a detailed message, glanced past the lobby view windows and saw

Stevie pulling up to the hospital entrance behind the wheel of a Jeep with new registration and a paper plate taped to the windshield.

"I saw I was going to have time on my hands once De-Santis got to doing his thing with the CHP," Stevie said. "Besides, since we were going to need something to get back to L.A. in, it made sense to buy the new Cherokee instead of waiting." She shifted her eyes off the road momentarily to shoot me a look that pleaded for agreement.

"As easy as stopping in for a supersized Big Mac instead of waiting for dinner," I said, not sure why I felt irritated, unless it was because she usually made her major purchases only after consulting with me.

Stevie must have known.

"I got a terrific price," she said. "What'd you expect me to do, drive around in a rent-a-wreck? What if I was seen? You know how fast it would be on *Entertainment Tonight* or in the *Enquirer*? Coming on top of me being so missing from the show right now, what do you think people would be thinking and saying?"

"Stephanie Marriner is unusually psychotic?"

"Ha. Ha. Ha."

"Babe, I know this will be impossible for you to accept, although it won't be the first time you've heard it from me, but—the world does not revolve around you."

Stevie sniggered and said, "Friendly Frank would disagree with you."

"Friendly Frank being—?"

"The owner of the Friendly Frank Auto Bank, the number one new and used Jeep dealer in northern San Luis Obispo County."

"Of course number one. Never let it be said you take number two from anyone."

"Ha. Ha. Ha . . . He recognized me immediately. He's a fan. Right away, he lopped twenty percent off the sales sticker, and that was even before he asked for my autograph and to take a picture with me and his pet bulldog, Edsel."

"Edsel also a fan?"

She ignored the question and, on top of the stop sign, hit the brakes hard enough to smell.

The street I'd told her to watch for had crept up on us.

"Left or right?" Stevie asked, angrily spitting out the question, her way of letting me know she wanted the subject of the Jeep dropped.

I checked the map the hospital receptionist had drawn on the back of an admissions form and told her. She signaled a left, although there were no other cars at the intersection, and took the turn at a noisy, rubber-burning five hundred miles an hour.

The address I had inquired about was right behind Mission San Miguel Arcangel, the receptionist said, adding a look of curiosity that begged a question she had thought about twice before asking. "You know it's not your usual tourist stop, not one of our wonderful wineries?"

"We're not your usual tourists," I said amiably.

"Of course not," the receptionist said, unable to move her hungry eyes off Stevie.

The rest of the drive took about fifteen minutes.

There isn't much to Paso Robles, an agricultural community that clings as much to its Old West traditions as to the grape vineyards that began taking shape after a mid-1800s tourist boom created by the discovery of hot springs reputed to have magical therapeutic qualities. Even outlaws like Jesse James and members of the Dalton Gang stopped for a soak while outrunning posses, or so the legend goes.

I did a column about Paso Robles about two years ago, after coming up here to the springs for myself,

hoping they'd ease the back pain that returned every
cold season, sort of like the swallows at Capistrano,
only this was the place where Georgie Adamo's stray
bullet almost killed me; came within six inches of
putting me into a wheelchair for life. The waters
helped and they could have kept helping if I'd chosen
to spend every winter in Paso Robles. Alas, not the
kind of condition that goes well with steady employ-
ment in Los Angeles.

Stevie skimmed past Mission San Miguel Arcangel
and, barely a minute later, dime-stopped and backed
up the Jeep about fifty yards.

"If this is it, your hospital administrator sure picked
a funny place."

"Can't be it," I said, comparing the address on the
memo paper to the address on the engraved metal
plaque affixed eye-level to the brick wall enclosing
All-Eternity Memorial Park.

It was the same address and suggested why I had
caught a flash of anemic smile on Randall G. Webber's
iron-plated face.

"Let me guess," Stevie said. "We've hit a dead end."

11

DeSantis was sitting on the brick wall outside the CHP substation, splitting his attention between the Camel he was holding like a baton and a young woman also ignoring the Surgeon General's warning, who seemed to be hanging on his every word. She was a knockout, a brunette with big eyes and a body built for comfort, who made her business outfit look like it cost her a hundred dollars more than her monthly paycheck.

He saw us pull up and hopped off the pony wall, demolished the butt under his heel and, guiding her by an elbow, brought her to the Jeep for introductions. She field-stripped her cigarette along the way.

"Audrey Mae, like I was telling you, this here is my old and close friend for years, Stephanie Marriner, who you know from *Bedrooms and Board Rooms.*" His face, framed in the open driver's window, begged Stevie's confirmation. "She's a fan, Stevie, and I said how happy it would make you to do me the favor of giving her a personal autograph."

I could only see the back of Stevie's head, so I couldn't see her expression as she responded, directing it to Audrey Mae. It was a golden opportunity for her to turn her least favorite of my friends into a boy soprano, but I knew how she would handle the moment.

She treats her fans like they're the stars and doing her a favor by asking. And, she believes it. More than a hundred times, I've heard her complain about the behavior of some actress who'd caught the brass ring and was now behaving in the pages of *People* like it was gold and she was here forever.

"I would be flattered and honored," Stevie said. Audrey Mae pressed a splayed hand to her ample chest, her honey face breaking into an expression I thought was owned by lottery winners. "Besides, I can not ever-ever deny this wonderful man anything he asks, can I, Neddie?"

"Thank you, sweetheart," he said, sounding a lot like Humphrey Bogart. He pushed at her a pen and slim-line steno pad he pulled from somewhere.

"You're welcome as ever and always, sweetheart," Stevie said, doing a Bacall sort of thing.

"Oh, you kids," I said, keeping a straight face. "And, by the by, Audrey Mae, my name is Neil Gulliver."

"Hello, yeah. Lieutenant DeSantis told me. You write a newspaper column or something like that." Her voice was a lot like Cher's modified with three lumps of sugar.

"Something like that."

Up close Audrey Mae was a decade older than the early twenties I had first made her to be. The lines hiding under a ton of cosmetics added interest to her look without disrupting her appeal, and I saw why DeSantis was attracted to her.

Why Audrey Mae was attracted to DeSantis, and it flew off her like a laser beam, was another one of life's darkest mysteries. DeSantis had somehow turned into this mousetrap maybe without even knowing, that's how hard he appeared to be trying to impress her.

"In Los Angeles," Audrey Mae said.

"City of the Angels," I agreed.

"I write, too," she said. "I just finished a new play that I think the Paso Robles Players are going to do next season at the Community Playhouse, as soon as they get it to read."

She nodded enthusiastically and angled around Stevie for a better look at me.

"It's about the Hearst Castle up there in the Santa Lucias," DeSantis offered. "It's got a ghost and everything, a lot of movie stars, and that publisher guy you once told me was that Orson Welles guy in that movie, what's it?"

"Citizen Kane."

He gave it some thought. "Yeah. That one."

Audrey Mae said, "I call it *The Ghost in the Castle.*"

"A wonderful title," I said, trying to share her enthusiasm without revealing how many other writers I have seen who never get beyond their dream.

"The Paso Robles Community Playhouse, my boss is going to personally take it to the executive director, who he knows like almost best friends."

"Bosses are good for that."

"She works for the police locals," DeSantis said.

"Chief records clerk," Audrey Mae said proudly.

"Audrey Mae's been helping out today," DeSantis said. "Not just chauffeuring me, either."

"Service with a smile," she said, smiling.

DeSantis said, "I told her you'd love to read it sometime, Gulliver." He bit down on his back molars, his look daring me to disagree.

"I'd be flattered and honored," I said, trying to sound like Stevie.

"I'll see that he does," Stevie said, squeezing my thigh, letting me know she meant it even if I didn't.

I did, though, and not only because of DeSantis. It's a payback thing, a way to say thanks to the people who took the time to encourage me when I was flying blind into what I wanted to be a career, sure of my goal, less sure of my gift, if you can call it that.

Audrey Mae's face brightened again and she showed her enthusiasm by hugging DeSantis. She pressed against his cast and it made him wince, but he otherwise took it like a shy kindergarten kid, may even have blushed under his olive complexion, stepping back fast after she released her hold.

DeSantis said, "You got my card, right?" Audrey Mae patted a jacket pocket. "You saw my home number is on it, so call anytime, remember?"

"Aye, aye, lieutenant," Audrey Mae said perkily, saluting DeSantis, who took a step toward her, then changed his mind, opened the rear driver's-side door and climbed awkwardly inside.

He dropped his window and returned Audrey Mae's goodbye waves as Stevie sped off, at the same time telling us, "Nice kid, and she tried hard to be helpful, but . . ."

He let the thought hang there.

After another moment, I said, "But she wasn't."

"She was not," DeSantis agreed, "but she turned me on to someone who was."

DeSantis settled himself across the seat and shut his eyes to the passing scenery, Mama Nature's best under a sky of brilliant smog-free blue, ruptured occasionally by a roadside community stretching a few parallel blocks, mainly gas stations and the ubiquitous fast-food pit stops, while he described his day.

"Like I began telling you at Blackwell's Corner, Gulliver, before them two maggot pies went after Stevie, I thought I could do us some good when I was up here, better than I was doing for Steiger and you working the horn from L.A. . . . Wrong!" His head turned left and right. "First, I was getting the same shut mouths or contradictions.

"I got it fresh from that hospital guy, Webber, but thought I could do better in person with the CHP, only they had nothing for me but more jazz riffs, like they gave me over the horn. Old records were long gone to the depths of their HQ in Sacramento, they said, what wasn't destroyed by the earthquake, same as the hospital said; none of them knowing, they said, anyone who might still be around from that day.

"I taxied over to the locals, thinking I could do better there, but everyone was gone except Audrey Mae, gone to some all-day seminar to hear some guru in blue tell them how to become better cops and human beings without putting their cop asses on the line for some psycho boner who's got a beef against the world.

"We hit it off and, after I told her what I was after, she rummages through the files. Nothing there. She hit the computer. Came up with another goose egg. It begins to look like the Dean thing never happened up here. . . . Star, what say you be decent enough to let me light up?"

DeSantis already was moving a Camel from the pack to his mouth.

"Don't you dare," Stevie said into her rear-view.

"If I promise to blow it all out the window?"

"Negative, DeSantis. I've already done my favor of the day for you."

"Yeah, so good, too. You may be a real actress after all." He mouthed the cigarette back into the pack, put it beside him on the seat, and continued, "Just then, in walks one of Paso Robles's former finest, so antique he could of been working a beat here before anyone thought to plant a grape seed up here. His spine so bent out of shape, poor guy, he can't even stand up straight. He walks like a human hook.

"Mel Snowbacher's his name. He likes Audrey Mae and he likes to gab, so she asks him if he happened to be around when the actor James Dean got creamed.

"Mel says, 'Yeah.'

"She says, 'My friend Ned here is also a police officer, a detective louie down in Los Angeles, and he is trying to find out which story is true.'

"'You mean, the rumor that Dean walked away from the crash?' He says that, Mel. Just like that. Like it ain't the first time and, turns out, it ain't. Only he don't want to talk about it, he says, and his scrawny face shows me he thinks he's already said too much.

"Audrey Mae sees it, too, and she descends on Mel like a moth to a flame, telling him she'd like to hear what he has to say and how we'll be circumspect and confidential and he buys it, probably because she's stroking the back of his neck, the few hairs on his head, and pretending not to notice his bony hand massaging her tush.

"Turns out Mel used to be asked that a lot back then, less so over the years.

"He says to me, 'I wasn't there in no official capacity, mind you. It was a CHP matter, but I got radioed to check it out, lend support if need be, and so I got there about two minutes behind the ambulance.

"'First, I thought I saw this Dean fella, what was left of him anyway, being moved to it, but I couldn't get a good look. Then, some guy comes over and asks me who it is they're carting away.

"'I know it's not the guy who was with Dean, because he's over there in the ditch, hurtin' like a sum'bitch. And it ain't the guy was steering the other car, the Ford Sedan, Turnupseed—who could ever forget a name like that—because he's over there lookin' like he don't even need a Band-Aid.

" 'I respond it can't be none else but this actor Dean, from what I know. He tells me it can't be Dean, because he saw a couple fellas taking Dean from the wreckage of the Porsche into a car and hightailing it away.'

"I say, 'Mel, you telling me it wasn't Dean who bought it in the Porsche and was DOA by the time they got him to the hospital, or before?'

"He says, 'I'm telling you what I seen and heard and remember. You don't need me to do no speculating for you.' "

I drew a deep breath, felt my heart charging over what DeSantis had told us. It supported the statement I had come across from one of the eyeball witnesses, Alvin, Ralph Alvin. It meant James Dean could still be alive, forty-five years later, could be the "Post Office Poltergeist," Nico Mercouri's killer.

Nico called out his name before he was murdered.

Augie said later it could have been Dean.

Now, Mel Snowbacher, repeating what Ralph Alvin had said at the scene, that someone had been pulled from the Porsche, the Little Bastard, by spectators and driven away in a car, not the ambulance.

Corroboration.

Or, maybe, not.

Maybe this old cop, Mel Snowbacher, had talked to Alvin and it was a case of gossip feeding on itself.

I said, "Find a place to turn around, Stevie. I want to go back. I want to talk to Mel Snowbacher myself."

"Ain't going to happen," DeSantis declared. "I promised Mel I wouldn't tell a soul what I just told you two, and I happen to be a man who keeps his promises."

"Gimme a break, DeSantis, you've already told us, so that's that."

"Not if Mel doesn't know it," he snapped back.

"We've gotten a lot of stonewalling about Dean. He's our first crack."

"Well, I just cemented it over, and you give me your promise you won't double back on me."

I made like I was giving it deep thought, heaved a sigh, and said, "You have my word."

"Thank you," DeSantis said.

Stevie reached over to squeeze my thigh and said, "Mine, too."

She was snickering under her breath, aware that I was again using the newspaperman's whammy Augie had taught me about giving your word, but keeping promises.

DeSantis had promised the man on his terms; now, he had my word on my terms.

Hopefully, I'd be able to explain the concept to his satisfaction if I had to go back to Paso Robles, seek out Mel Snowbacher. After all, what's a little deception between friends?

Back in town, Stevie and I got DeSantis safely deposited home before she dropped me at my condo, having fought off my insistence that she could use the company after what she'd been through, giving me one of the "Stop treating me like a child" looks she uses to put a period to our arguments.

Within minutes, I was confronting the likelihood that someone had broken into my unit and was lurking inside.

The Heathcliffe Arms has the kind of security you find at most condominiums: ineffective. Getting beyond the front entrance takes a key or a buzz-through and there's a guard directly inside the door to deal with strangers and suspicious faces, provided he hasn't wandered from his desk to steal a smoke somewhere, snag some shuteye or—wonder of wonders—check out a real problem.

Anyone with a little ingenuity or patience can slip inside simply by waiting for the guard to leave and a resident with a key to arrive.

Or, by monitoring any one of the four entrances to the underground garages and ducking in behind a driver who knows the code that raises the gate.

Having achieved building entry, breaking into a unit becomes a matter of try and try again. Most standard locks are simple to bypass, and dead bolts add a challenge, less so the sliding patio doors on units facing the central courtyard that homeowners often keep open or unlocked.

The big surprise is that we've had few break-ins over the years. Some car break-ins and thefts, a burglary now and again, and occasional acts of vandalism, but True Crime—a category I reserve for murder and various forms of life-threatening mayhem—seems to ignore us for the taller, classier high-rise condos in the millions-of-dollars range that stretch on both sides of the Wilshire corridor between Westwood and Beverly Hills.

Unless it was the sound of True Crime I thought I heard, a sense coming at me through the thick mahogany door to my unit that there was a physical presence moving through the rooms as I plugged the key into the lock, a Granite 287 double-reverse bolt built to defeat all but the craftiest of pick experts.

I inched away.

Did a quiet turn that put my back against the wall to the left of the door while I took stock.

My place is on the third floor, out of the way, so chances are it was targeted. It's an interior unit and faces the street. Anyone trying for my narrow patio would first have had to scale a flat wall, using pole climbers. Not likely and, besides—

It was only now beginning to turn dark, so his entry would have come in daylight, increasing the odds of his being observed by the heavy foot and vehicular traffic on Veteran Avenue.

Unless—

He managed to break in sometime last night, when I was chasing shadows in Paso Robles War Memorial Hospital.

I flashed on my James Dean column and heard the voice on the answering machine yesterday, assuring me—

"For what you went and wrote today, you are going to die, mister. . . ."

I pictured the caller patiently waiting for me to come through the door.

What then, Gulliver?

Ready, aim, fire?

The phone threat was genuine enough, and there's never a shortage of nut cases in L.A., all looking to make a headline, and—

I heard it again.

Through the door. A noise. A shuffle. A presence. Someone searching through the spy hole.

The voice rang in my head again:

"For what you went and wrote today, you are going to die, mister."

Now what, Gulliver?

Hidden inside one of the dozen shelf boxes in my bedroom closet is my Beretta 92f semiautomatic. I keep it loaded with sixteen rounds of 147-grain hollow points, for emergencies, although this emergency was a little closer to home than I like.

Could I fast talk this fugitive from a Wes Craven movie into giving me the minute or two or three I'd need to fetch it?

My chest was constricted. It was hard to get out a breath. My temples began throbbing. I moved my fingers to a vein that felt like it was channeling crude oil to my brain. My knees signaled that they were ready to collapse under the weight of my body.

My eyes fled up and down the hall, searching for an easy answer, which, of course, was obvious: Get thee the hell from here, Gulliver. Downstairs to the lobby. Grab the guard's phone and 911 for the cops.

The door opened before I managed a first step.

"Quick!" Augie ordered. Sounding desperate.

He grabbed my shirt and pulled me inside. Pushed the door closed and hastily double-locked it, including the interior no-fault catch of the Granite 287. Threw the slant lock for good measure. Gave the door knob a few twists and a pull.

"Were you followed?" he wanted to know, his good eye the size of a saucer, its thick eyebrow eating into his hairline. He read properly the look written on my face. "It is no joke, amigo. No joke whatsoever."

It was then I saw Augie was holding my Beretta at rest, the muzzle pointing to the ceiling.

"I smelled you standing outside in the hall," he said ominously. He looked at the Beretta like he was trying to give it a name. "A good thing, too, I know your scent by heart, or I would have put one into you the minute you came through the door."

He stepped quickly down the entry hall, urging me to follow him, and with a dancer's grace made a sharp right turn into the living room, where I was momentarily blinded by my floor lamps.

He'd moved them and adjusted the shades so that anyone coming into the room was spotlighted, but would not be able to see him. He'd see them first. He also had moved my armchair so that it sat in front of the couch, facing the hallway: clearly his command post. The pillow and the tossed blanket told me he'd used the couch for a bed, but it was positioned so that it made a barricade Augie could hide behind.

He settled into the chair, tossing his legs over one arm, adjusting his cassock, positioning the Beretta on his lap, and assured me, "All's well for the moment, kiddo. Relax, grab a cold one, make yourself at home."

"I am at home," I said, trying hard not to let my fear convert to anger.

"So you are, so you are, and about time, amigo."

A grin began to break across his leathery face, adding to the lines, creases, and crevices that gave Augie the look of a street map in the Thomas Guide. More than a hint of booze on his breath.

"Augie, what's going on here?"

"I thought you'd never ask," he said, but there was nothing cheerful in the way he said it. "First, go get yourself comfortable, then we'll reason together about my friend, Jimmy Dean. And Nick Adams. And Sal Mineo. And the Big Bad Wolf I've been expecting at your door."

His face became a mask that gave nothing away.

12

By the time I had pulled a brew from the fridge, finished half the can in a swallow, and calmed down enough to confront him dispassionately, Augie had Sinatra singing in the background. I recognized the cut, an obscure Rodgers and Hart song titled "Glad To Be Unhappy," from *In the Wee Small Hours,* one of the Chairman's albums of the memorable Capitol years.

Settling onto a stool at the counter between the kitchen and the living room, I asked, "Since when are you a Sinatra fan?"

Augie stepped from the turntable, which now had a half dozen records stacked on the drop spindle, and heading to the armchair said, "That voice, always. The man and some of his cronies, only rarely. I had my fill of mobsters and wannabes on the crime beat, a long time before that, too, when I was still trying to catch a break in show business."

He eased down, repositioned the Beretta on his lap,

pulled out the hip flask filled with brandy that he keeps in a pocket of his cassock, and took a healthy swig. I was surprised. Augie never owns up to carrying the flask and I've rarely seen him use it since he quit serious career drinking for what he's described to me as occasional albeit sincere reprieves from total sobriety.

He used the back of his hand as a towel across his mouth and smiled blissfully. Produced a major-league Cuban from another pocket. Pledged he would not light it. Took a deep dry suck before asking, "You ready to listen? Or, you prefer reporting first on your latest exploits?"

"Before anything—You talk to Brother Saul yet? Does he know where you are? He's worried about you."

"When was this?"

"Early this afternoon, when I called from Paso Robles. Returning your calls."

"How nice of you," he said sarcastically. "How long after I needed you? Ten, twelve hours? More? I could have been at death's door for all you knew."

"Soon as I heard your messages. Before that, I had a little crisis of my own."

I told Augie about the attack on Stevie, the car chase, the crash.

He tried disguising his concern with a few jokes, throwaway lines, but I saw it on his face before he changed the subject back to Brother Saul.

"This afternoon, you said?" I nodded. "He should have known by then, long before then. I'd sent someone to tell Brother Saul last night. Even before I called you for the last time."

"Jared Gallagher? Saul told me he wasn't overly concerned, because you were out with someone named Jared Gallagher?"

"Yes. Whom I sent back to the Order." He looked now like his mind was sifting some truths from a set of evidence, so I helped myself to another Heineken from the fridge and relaxed with Old Blue Eyes, who was putting his personal stamp on Ellington's "I Got It Bad and That Ain't Good."

Finally, Augie said, "I didn't want to keep him with me, so it became a test. See if he'd actually go back to the Order and pass on the message to Brother Saul I was here." He studied the cigar like he was reading a thermometer. "Why aren't I surprised Jared didn't?"

"You tell me."

He raised his shoulders. "A strange duck, kiddo. No need to quote chapter and verse. He made me nervous and then worried over some of his actions, so I kept him close to me, kept the good eye open. You remember the old saying about how to handle enemies. . . Keep them where you can see them?"

"This Jared's an enemy?"

"Maybe too strong a word. So far. But he lurks. He makes calls he shouldn't be making. . . . I'd swear I heard Jared drop your name in a long distance he supposedly was having with his mother."

"My name? How'd he know my name?"

"Shah!" His crossing guard's arm went up. "Your name. You called yesterday, left word you were going up to Salinas. Jared took the message."

"Could have been, I suppose. I didn't recognize the voice."

"Did you say anything about Jimmy or just that you were going to Salinas?"

"Just Salinas. Nothing else he had to know and I figured you'd understand the why of the trip once you got the message."

"Correct, but maybe he did, too?"

"Why would he?"

"For the same reason he didn't go back to the Order? Another old saying, amigo. If they're not part of the solution, maybe they're part of the problem."

"And what might that problem be?"

Another shrug. "Not everyone loves me, you know."

"Frequently including your friends."

He pointed an admonishing finger at me as a sly smile lit his face. "They did, I'd start to wonder where I went wrong," he said. "But this one, Jared Gallagher . . . He looked familiar to me the first time I laid eyes . . . soon as I remember the face I'll have the rest of it."

Augie described Jared in the kind of detail that always punctuated the copy that made him the *Daily*'s Number One reporter in his day, as if it might lead me to the ID eluding him, but it set off no bells.

"Just another puzzle to be solved in time," he murmured confidently, adding as his mood darkened again, "assuming we live that long."

"How about long enough to tell me about this Big Bad Wolf of yours?"

"Could be yours, too," Augie said. "But who's afraid of the Big Bad Wolf, right, amigo?" He swallowed a slug of brandy, then took another mouthful and swished it around before letting it slide down his throat. "I suppose me, for one, so listen close and judge for yourself. . . . You remember hearing from Manny Gelman about the third man, the guy with Jimmy the night Jimmy killed Nick Adams . . . ?"

The way Augie told the story, there was not much to Marfa, Texas, back in 1955, when director George Stevens filmed *Giant* there. Getting to the tiny town took a two-plane hop, a jet into Dallas and then a puddle jumper into Midland; followed by a three-hour drive through a hot, flat landscape ringed by distant mountains, alternately desert brown and green, the "Big Bend Country" of Presidio County.

Marfa seemed little more than a hole cut from the

base of the mountains, a population of barely twenty-five hundred Texans trying to be solemn in the presence of movie stars in life as large to them as the monumental figures they seemed on a movie screen.

Elizabeth Taylor.

Rock Hudson.

James Dean.

Of the three, it was Jimmy who in a short period of time had won over everyone, become the favorite because of his accessibility, his boyish charm, a down-home Indiana sensibility that came closer to matching their own than the ingrained Hollywood veneer of Taylor and Hudson that seemed to put an invisible wall between them and the townsfolk.

"There was calculation to it," Augie said. "Jimmy was always going out of his way to win more converts to the cause, the cause of his fame and his stardom, his intention to become as big a star, bigger, than his two idols, Marlon Brando and Montgomery Clift.

"I got to hanging around with him and that's how I saw it day after day. And, if you wonder why me—because I was older. I wasn't competition and I posed no threat. A bit player who was going nowhere except back to Los Angeles when the shoot finished. I had been around, could talk show-business history to him, and that also was an attraction.

"He had this great thirst for knowledge the easy way, like a *Readers' Digest* condensed book was sufficient to his needs, and I could give it to him that way, easy as I ultimately came to fit a two-thousand-word story into a three-hundred-word hole on page one.

"This particular evening, the shoot wrapped, he invites me to join him and Sal Mineo over to the Marfa Inn. Sal has a small part in *Giant* and he's been dogging after Jimmy like some Juliet to her Romeo, I've heard, ever since they did *Rebel Without a Cause* together.

"The inn is a couple blocks from the courthouse, on

North Austin Street, a converted two-story Victorian-era home filled with historical relics of the earliest settlers and old religious artifacts that look like they belong in a church, or were stolen from one. The lobby and public rooms have the kind of smells time can't erode, like time itself, and you could almost see Jimmy breathing in the atmosphere, immersing himself in it as we moved inside, like it'd help him do a better job in front of the camera, turn the actor he was into the Jett Rink character he was playing.

"Waiting for us there is none other than Jimmy's other *Rebel* buddy, Nick Adams. He's come to Marfa to hang out for a few days with Jimmy and, I get his whisper later, maybe get noticed by George Stevens and pick up a job. Nick was that kind of ambitious kid, but Jimmy didn't figure him for competition and never hesitated to tell him so.

"Besides, Nick so obviously idolized Jimmy that Jimmy knew he could count on Nick to kiss his ring or kiss his ass, whichever he felt like ordering. Nick never seemed to care. He acted like it was Jimmy's way of joking around, like he didn't see the truth burning in Jimmy's blue eyes, but he wasn't a good enough actor to entirely hide what he saw or the sting he felt every time Jimmy turned vicious.

"Anyway, Nick hasn't made the trip to Marfa by himself. He's brought along company, some actor buddy who has tied onto Nick the way Nick has tied onto Jimmy. His name is Chip Kiley, and he resembles a cross between the two of them. About five eight or nine, in the one-fifty, one-sixty pound range. Blond hair, although it could have been a bottle job. Rich milk-chocolate eyes. A slouch when he stood, a loping hunch-shouldered kind of walk, almost like he had been studying Jimmy's mannerisms.

"After a few rounds in a dining room off the bar that we have to ourselves, all of us pretty high by then on our specialties, Sal starts laughing and kidding about how the three of them—Jimmy, Nick, and Chip—look enough alike to be brothers. Or, maybe, the Andrews Sisters.

"The crack gets a rise from Jimmy, not over the sex angle, but because he hates being compared to anyone. He tears into Sal, telling him he is nothing but a closet faggot whose career will be over once the public sees he can't hold his wrists straight.

"Sal gets so upset, the tears running down his cheeks, he stumbles into a corner and pukes all over an elaborately carved angel. Jimmy finds this hilarious and shouts it to the world, rocking on the balls of his boots, that hyena laugh of his bouncing off the walls. Nick feels sorry for Sal. He suggests good-naturedly that Jimmy might want to go over and say something nice to the kid. At once, Jimmy isn't laughing. Now, he's taking offense at Nick.

" 'Who the fuck are you and where the fuck do you get off telling me what to do?' he yells. Nick realizes his mistake and tries to back off. It's too late. Jimmy ain't buying.

"Jimmy, well into his cups, glues his face onto Nick's and orders him, 'Go home. Pack your gear and get the fuck out of here. Right now! Tonight! You understand?' I am telling you, amigo, he could have been rehearsing his drunk scene from the movie, except this was no act. Nick appeals to him. Jimmy still ain't buying. The two of them lock onto a stare for another minute, then Nick escapes Jimmy's eyes, takes half a step back, and surrenders with a 'You got me' kind of arm gesture.

"He asks Sal if Sal needs some help getting back to his room. Jimmy tells him Sal is fine, he's staying and isn't that right, Sal?

"Sal finishes wiping vomit residue from his mouth and says, yeah, thanks, Nick, but he's fine. Now, Nick

says to Chip Kiley, 'Come on, Chip, we're going.'
Chip gets up and starts to fall in behind Nick.

"Jimmy catches Chip by the shoulder, orders him,
'Not you. You stay.'

"I see Chip's been around Hollywood long enough
to know a pecker from a pecking order, because there
isn't even a pause before he says so long to Nick and
tells him to have a safe trip home. Something about
this makes Nick start to laugh and he's still laughing as
he passes out of the room."

Augie paused for another shot of brandy. He saw I
was impatient to know where the story was leading, although I already had a pretty good idea.

He said, "Next morning, I don't have a call, but I
wander on over to the set anyway. It's either that or go
off somewhere and study the tumbling tumbleweed.

"They're lining up the next shot and who do I see in
front of the camera? It's Chip Kiley, of course.
Jimmy's pulled a tantrum string and, while George
Stevens's made it plain who's the boss and won't give
in to Jimmy's demand that Chip become his stand-in,
there's been a rapprochement of sorts, because Chip
has become the stand-in for Jimmy's stand-in. And he
becomes Jimmy's shadow, too. I never see one without
the other, right up to the day I'm released and head for
home.

"It stayed that way, I heard later from friends I made
during the shoot. Jimmy and Chip became inseparable.
Not like Siamese twins inseparable, more like a star
and his gofer, with Chip always a step away, ready and
anxious to satisfy any of Jimmy's whims."

Here I interrupted Augie.

"And Chip Kiley was the alleged third man that
night at Nick Adams's house, when Dean allegedly
murdered Nick."

He sat on my words a few seconds, then mocking
me said, "It's allegedly possible." He offered me the

flask. I declined by indicating I wasn't finished with the Heineken. He offered "Cheers!" and helped himself, brushed his lips dry with an index finger, and said, "Decidedly possible, if you buy into the theory that Jimmy did not die in the crash and was still alive at the time of Nick's—" his eyebrow went up "—*alleged* accidental death a dozen years later, but why speculate, I asked myself, after my memory all of this came back to me the other night . . . why speculate when there's the possibility of finding out for certain."

"From Chip Kiley."

"The thought, yes, but SAG had lost any trace of him years and years ago. They told me when I phoned, and I didn't fare better with the other guilds. SAG was able to give me the name and a number for his last agent of record and I gave him a call. Harry Chalk.

"I knew him from the old days, when he handled a lot of stars for Major Artists Corporation and it took him a month to return a call—when he bothered—but MAC hadn't existed for years and I suspected Harry had fallen on soft times when he personally answered on the first ring with a brisk, 'Harry Chalk, The Harry Chalk Agency,' like it was an accident that he picked up, the caller taking him away from an important meeting.

"Harry pretended to remember me and was affable in the small-talk department until I mentioned Chip Kiley and explained why I was calling, then his memory left for the moon. He didn't remember Chip Kiley. Come to think of it, he didn't remember me. I got the feeling that, another minute, he wouldn't remember himself.

"Instead of another minute, Harry hung up.

"I called him back, only this time he let the phone ring, so I decided to pay a personal visit to Mr. Harry Chalk.

"I phoned you expecting you'd go with me, amigo, but as it turns out you were already Salinas bound, so I took Jared instead, figured to let Jared drive the Rolls while I studied him, working more on the ID puzzle close range.

"Harry Chalk's office turns out to be a cramped cubicle in the twin towers at Century City, where a slot in the underground parking garage—where I leave Jared to wait for me—probably costs twice as much a month as a space in the second-floor suite and central reception area he shares with a dozen or more companies. The directory says Harry is down corridor C, room C-7, between a PI lawyer and a Juicey Juicey distributor.

"The name on the brass plaque reads Harry Chalk Talent International, which I figure means Harry subscribes to *U.S. News & World Report*. Underneath is a hand-printed sign that says Enter, so I knock for courtesy and waltz in.

"Across the ten by twelve space, staring out the window at a hospital across Avenue of the Stars, is Harry, or who I presume to be Harry, since it's just him and me. He's the one in the motorized wheelchair, his back to me, and I call out his name.

"Without turning around, he says, 'Leave the pizza on the table. And I hope for your sake this time you didn't forget the extra mushrooms.' As if to emphasize the threat, he lets out this tremendous gas explosion. Or, putting it in simpler terms, he fills the room with a king-sized fart.

"At once the stench is something dreadful and I know that Harry has had more than his share of mushrooms in the course of a lifetime, which—as he spins the wheelchair around and faces me—I judge to be some eighty-odd years.

"Harry's been helped a lot by surgery, his face tighter than a tomb. No bags. No beetle brow. His thin lips stretched beyond movement, explaining why his shout was not much more than the murmur I'd heard earlier over the phone.

"His eyes are giant green marbles behind a pair of thick lenses encased in black horn-rimmed specs like Lew Wasserman always favored, and as ferocious as the new fart he chooses to share with me. He's wearing an expensive suit with out-of-style lapels, probably something he'd picked up at Carroll & Co., when that was the place the stars shopped in Beverly Hills. His legs are covered with a blue cashmere lap blanket that quits above a pair of gleaming wing tips.

" 'You are not the pizza man,' Harry says. He gives me a good up and down and says, 'The building doesn't allow solicitations, not even for religious orders, so if you please . . .' And he urges me out by raising his chin. With another fart for inspiration.

"Cupping my palm to my nose and pretending I have an itch, inhaling my skin for survival, I tell Harry who I am. He repeats my name, losing it in a belch as big as his farts, and thinks about it. He belches again after another few moments, layering in another fart, and I see by the way he recoils in the chair he's remembered.

" 'I have nothing to tell you, sir,' he says, 'so do me the courtesy of leaving at once.' Belch. Fart. I tell him I have just a few questions about Chip Kiley and then he'll be rid of me. Meanwhile, I'm thinking about picking up one of his Salvation Army chairs and shattering the window with it, anything to get some fresh air in there.

"Just then, the phone rings.

"Harry has this contraption on his head, an ear and mouthpiece like a telephone operator's, the mouthpiece up like an antenna. He moves it down in front of his mouth and presses a button on the wheelchair control panel, gives out with that busy 'Harry Chalk, The Harry Chalk Agency.' He wiggles in the chair like he is muffling the next fart, for which I made a mental memo to extend our dear Lord an extra thank-you at the Order's next devotional.

"I watch as the network of blue veins under his stretched, snow-white skin starts to pulsate and grow and bring a blood-red color to his face. Whatever he's hearing over the phone is not happy-time news. He grunts a lot and says 'Yes' almost as often, tosses in a few belches, places a hand over his heart like he is either about to say the Pledge of Allegiance or is making certain it's working, and shoots an index finger at his desk before telling me, 'He wants to talk to you. Use the phone on the desk. Line one, where the light is lit.'

"Curious, amigo, since nobody knows I'm here but Jared. I move over to Harry's desk and click onto line one of two and while I'm identifying myself and asking who this is, Harry points at his pee pee and sails past me, opens up the door, and navigates out.

"I don't have a chance to stop him, because I am trapped by a voice that sounds like it's wrapped in a layer or two of cellophane, and what it's advising me already has me as agitated as Harry had become.

"The voice is saying how Harry called him before to tell him about my call, and he thought I might be stupid enough to show up here. I was a marked man anyway, only now it was going to be sooner than later and, if I didn't leave Harry alone now, right now, this minute, he also would be a dead man in the next twenty-four hours.

"You remember how it can be in a tight situation like that, kiddo? You're out of breath, then out of words, then your mind garbles reality, and when you finally think of something to say it's something stupid.

"I said, 'Who is this?'

"I get an earful of silence, like the voice cannot believe the question. Then he announces, 'I'm the Big Bad Wolf and I'm coming to blow your house down.'

"You know what? I believe him. But I'm determined not to leave there empty-handed. I want an answer or an address for Chip Kiley out of Harry.

"I find the john, only there's no Harry there.

"I test inhale. No familiar Harry Chalk smell to prove Harry even one-stopped on his way to wherever he's gone to hide.

"The rest you can figure, amigo. I had Jared drop me off at the Heathcliffe Arms. Sent him back to the Order with the message for Brother Saul. Used the duplicate set of keys you handed me years ago, remember? In case of an emergency? Went straight to the closet and found the Nike box where you hide the Beretta, and . . ."

Augie's voice petered out and I saw at once how reliving the experience had drained him.

It would have been different fifteen years ago, even ten years ago, when these kinds of threats came often and bounced off Augie like bullets off Superman. Maybe the panic came from his cozying up to another old acquaintance, all that brandy.

I'd already made up my mind that, with or without Augie, I was going to Century City tomorrow for a sit-down with Harry Chalk, a little heart-to-heart about Chip Kiley. Anyone or anything that could shed light on the risen James Dean, who had become as impossible to keep in his grave as Count Dracula.

This was nothing I had to share with Augie until the morning. No reason to say anything that might keep him from the good night's sleep he so obviously needed. I said instead, "You think a call to Brother Saul is overdue? Let everyone know where you are?"

Augie was momentarily distracted by Sinatra. A new album had dropped onto the turntable, and I knew from the opening bars of the first cut that it was *A Swingin' Affair,* and Francis Albert was about to slide

into Cole Porter's "Night and Day." He also knew, began leading Nelson Riddle's orchestra with his cigar.

I repeated the question.

"Make it for me, you mind?" he said, cueing Frank
on the next line. I hand-signaled my okay, bounced off
the bar stool, and headed around the counter for the
phone on the kitchen wall.

"Ask if Jared's back, okay?" Augie called across the
room.

"You also want to tell me how to spell my name?"

He ignored my sarcasm. "The answer is probably a
negative, and I wouldn't be surprised if he's in Tijuana
by now, selling off my Rolls for parts to some junk
dealer."

Before I could answer, the call connected to the Order of the Spiritual Brothers of the Rhyming Heart and
a minute later I had been transferred to Brother Saul.

The concern I heard in his tentative greeting melted
into a deep sigh of relief when I announced I was with
Brother Kalman now and white-lied how he'd been
fine all along and there never was anything to worry
about.

"Probably not until sometime tomorrow," I said, answering Saul's question about when he might expect
Augie to return. "Brother Kalman is spending the
night here at my place with me. We have some errands
to run tomorrow."

Something hit my back. Augie had thrown his cigar
at me, to get my attention.

His face accused me of forgetting to ask Brother
Saul about Jared. I hadn't, and did so, hung up after a
few more incidental exchanges, and told him, "Still no
sign."

Augie was now conducting the orchestra with the
Beretta. He stopped long enough to make a face and
tell me, "Definitely Tijuana. Any street guy falls into a

Rolls, he doesn't have to touch the leather to know the trade-in value. T-Town for sure is where he's gone, amigo."

He studied the exterior of the Heathcliffe Arms from a spot across Veteran Avenue, leaning against one of the shade trees lining the parkway and smoking a cigarette like he was some housebroken husband no longer allowed to satisfy his nicotine craving inside his own domain, the collar of his windbreaker turned up against a cool breeze that had become chillier in the last hour.

The moon swept out from behind a bank of black clouds threatening rain, casting a half light on his face and, instinctively, he adjusted his position to take refuge in the shadows.

It was unlikely that either Augie Fowler or Neil Gulliver suspected he was this near, this close to killing them, so the possibilities of either one taking a look out the window and spotting him was remote, but always better to be cautious than to take unnecessary chances and find himself nabbed by the law and demanding his rights.

Jimmy was A-OK correct about that. The woman up in Griffith Park, she was fun, but she could of been a mistake, his undoing if someone had come along and seen them. So, no more visits to the observatory and no more kicks until he got the important business out of the way. That was top priority, man. No more screwing around until Fowler and Gulliver were added to Jimmy's scorecard, and what a scorecard it already was.

He reflected on some of the names: Nick Adams, Natalie Wood, and Sal Mineo. They were the big-timers, he supposed, where Fowler and Gulliver would be a step down, somewhere below Nico Mercouri even, along with—

That woman.

The old girlfriend.

He knew her name, but couldn't think of it now, the same way there were other names that meant nothing to him. After all, he wasn't even a gleam before some of them were gone.

Certainly not Elizabeth Taylor.

No way to ever forget Elizabeth Taylor.

"Lucky Liz," Jimmy was always calling her.

Well, pretty soon her luck would be running out, he'd see to that. Lucky Liz's number was coming up. She was Jimmy's dessert, the frosting on the cake.

But, first, Fowler and Gulliver.

He had cased the building after Fowler got there yesterday, even been inside. Twice. No trick to inching in through the front entrance behind someone with a key, or by way of the garage, where the gates took their own sweet time closing.

He located Gulliver's apartment, gave a serious think to taking care of them there. Make it look like a breaking-and-entering gone sour.

But that came with too many unnecessary risks, Jimmy said, like not knowing what waited for him on the other side of Gulliver's door, especially since he had given both of them cause to understand they weren't long for Mother Earth. Right, Jimmy, fine.

Fine. Fine. Fine.

They had to come outside eventually. Hopefully on foot, not in Gulliver's old beat-up Jag, where he'd, maybe, have to fast-like psych out the way they were heading, jump into his own wheels, and hope not to lose them having to do a sharp U on Veteran.

He took a last drag, wet-fingered the tip and field-stripped the butt, clutched the windbreaker's collar to his neck, all the while watching shadows play inside the drawn blinds of Gulliver's apartment.

Wondered the big "What If." What if, maybe, they used one of the back exits on Kelton? Jesus! He'd lose them for sure. So, maybe, wouldn't it be easier to just go ahead and get it over and done with inside there?

13

My internal habit clock roused me sometime after six, the constant hum in my ear emanating from the minitower on my desk, where I had fallen asleep once my eyes gave out and my brain went dead after three or four hours of research at the computer. By then I'd added to my store of knowledge about James Dean and his crowd and I knew who I wanted to see next. It was not Harry Chalk or Chip Kiley or anyone in Paso Robles.

It was Lionel Ray Williams, the convicted killer of Sal Mineo.

Adding what I learned to what I already knew, I'd become increasingly convinced that through the years there were far too many curious deaths associated with Dean to be written off as coincidental.

No question Sal and Nico were murdered, but there were questions about the deaths of Nick Adams and Natalie Wood that never were put to rest and were being challenged now by Augie's stories, especially the one about Nick Adams that had been corroborated by a retired coroner.

Overnight, my own list had grown longer than that.

I studied it on the monitor and shook my head as I had many times already, every time I found a new name to add and caught myself repeating, often aloud, that there was some connective tissue, some fabric of truth, possibly some universal motive tying all the deaths together.

If I could find that common thread, maybe—

Better than maybe—

I could find the killer of Nico Mercouri.

And, yes, however far-fetched it appeared, truth in what Augie believed, that, yes—

James Dean was alive.

A movie icon turned murderer.

Maybe Lionel Ray Williams, a murderer very much alive, could tell me how they fit together or if, in fact, they did, assuming I could get Lionel Ray Williams to talk.

Augie was asleep in the armchair, the Beretta cradled in his lap, his even breathing interrupted by an occasional snort or an unintelligible word or phrase, in one position since the brandy had overcome his anxieties and closed his eyes in the middle of a rambling discourse on the evils of evil.

I snapped off the computer, got up, and quietly padded into the bedroom—taking care not to disturb Augie—relieved myself, and climbed into my jogging outfit, Nikes, and Lakers cap, gearing up for my morning run around UCLA and the ritual one-stop at my Westwood Village diner for a caffeine fix and toasted bagel among the usual faces at the usual seats wearing the usual expressions that said "Do Not Disturb."

I paused at the security desk in the lobby long enough to check out the headlines on the two copies of the *Daily* always waiting for me. Verified that the Dean story still held a chunk of page one of the Metro section, even though Clancy McPhillip's galloping prose was a rehash of the known and had nothing new to share with the readership. Did a set of knee bends before following a fellow homeowner and a golden retriever better groomed than she was outside and up Veteran Avenue.

The gray sky was overcast, as flat and formless as the painted backdrop in a B movie, the chill in the air colder than usual.

I tracked my route on automatic pilot and played over in my mind the clear vision I had of the list of the "James Dean Dead" on the monitor.

In the light of morning, some names seemed almost irrelevant, as if my decision to add them was caused by an increasingly tired, wandering imagination, like one of his early girlfriends, Beverly Wills.

The daughter of a popular movie and radio comedienne, Joan Davis, she ultimately rejected Dean and a decade later was killed in a house fire that had absolutely no business happening. That was in 1963. Wills was twenty-nine and coming into her own celebrity as a comedienne, in movies such as *Some Like It Hot, The Ladies' Man,* and *Son of Flubber.*

Was this any more curious than the death of movie star Pier Angeli, the beauty frequently portrayed as Dean's true love, whose domineering mother destroyed their romance and forced her to marry the singer Vic Damone?

Years later, a twice-divorced mother of two, but supposedly still agonizing over Dean, Pier turned to drugs and in 1971, at the age of thirty-nine, committed suicide by swallowing a fatal dose of phenobarbital.

Or, was Pier's suicide no more or less a suicide than Nick Adams's overdose?

I also had question marks alongside the deaths of

Nicholas Ray, the director of *Rebel Without a Cause,*
and David Weisbart, who produced the movie.

Questionable circumstances, both, for someone in a
questioning mode and inclined to put aside the dozens
of personal and business acquaintances of Dean who
were still alive and well or, clearly, had died natural
deaths.

I also had questions about the late Sanford Roth,
Dean's photographer pal who'd followed behind The
Little Bastard in the white Ford station wagon, toting
the Spyder trailer, taking pictures of Dean he later
vowed he'd never make public.

So far as I was able to determine, he never did.

Were those photos still in existence? Or, was it more
likely Roth destroyed them out of some sense of grief
and loyalty?

I also had questions about Rolf Wutherich, the
twenty-eight-year-old Porsche mechanic in the seat
next to Dean, who survived the crash of the Spyder.

The *Daily*'s files showed that he had returned to
Germany after recovering from his injuries, became a
rally driver for Porsche and one of those incidental
celebrities whose fame springs from others, something
of a precursor to Princess Di's bodyguard, President
Clinton's self-declaring groupies.

A year after the crash, Wutherich sued the Dean estate, claiming he suffered physical and mental injuries
caused by Dean's "negligence, carelessness, reckless-
ness, and willful misconduct." The court threw out the
suit on a technicality, ruling he had filed it too late.

The clips grew sparse after that, an occasional mention in a graph on a back page of the main news section, hole plugs, usually reporting that the Dean crash
survivor had divorced another wife or taken a new
bride.

He went through four of them and went after one

with a knife, in a frenzied attack that put him away for a time in a psychiatric hospital.

There was a larger mention in early '81 about a book deal he had signed to finally tell his version of the death of movie icon James Dean and describing his plans to come to the states to begin work on it.

The story was bigger shortly afterward, in July.

It reported on Wutherich's death, ironically in an automobile accident.

He had been drinking in a bar in Kupferzell, his hometown, and apparently had one too many for the road on a rainy night. Wutherich climbed into his car and sped off on the rain-slicked streets.

Within minutes, he lost control and crashed into a house. More irony: like Jimmy Dean, he was pinned in the wreckage.

Doctors struggled to revive him. Failed.

Wutherich, at fifty-three, was dead.

And I, at two in the morning, was staring at the photo of a typically Teutonic, boyishly handsome face, dark curly hair and bushy eyebrows, an uncertain hint of a smile that seemed to need permission to explode—Rolf Wutherich a few weeks after the Dean crash—and trying to absorb a new set of doubts raised by circumstance.

Was it an accident?

Even drunk, wouldn't Wutherich have known better than to speed on wet streets he knew well?

Even drunk, wouldn't years of authority behind a wheel, reflexes that didn't need direction, have kept him in control of his car? I wondered if it was a Porsche. The story didn't say. And, I wondered if it really had been an accident. Or someone's way—whose way?—of keeping him from writing a book that, a quarter century later, revealed—

What?

What about James Dean and the crash?

James Dean: Wanted Dead or Alive.

Mind games. Mind games.

My mind out of control until I crashed and woke up knowing Lionel Ray Williams could be the closest living link to truths buried by time.

Only it didn't work out that way.

Not at first.

First I had to find him.

I gulped down the last of my coffee and bagel and fifteen minutes later was back at the Heathcliffe Arms.

The guard on duty, missing from his station when I left, was pretending to study the bank of monitors that take up most of the desktop with their roaming views of the garages and various points of building entry.

He must have seen me coming from the corner of an eye, because only moments before I had noticed through the plate glass door panels that he was focused on the portable TV under the counter that all the guards use whenever they feel safe from the prying eyes of homeowners. It's usually tuned soundlessly to ESPN.

"Hey, Earlier," I said, knuckle-knocking on the counter top. "What's shakin', bro?"

Earlier Bogus looked up, feigned surprise, and broke into a gargantuan smile rising to greet me by name. He was a large man in his mid-thirties, with deeply pitted skin the color of rich coffee beans and large, round eyes that signaled a temperament as gentle as his voice.

We swapped the latest hand jive and, spotting the stack of books by the wall behind his swivel chair, I asked him, "How's school coming, Earlier?"

The question pleased him.

"Another A my last test, Mr. Gulliver, and I plan to off the next one and the test after that, as well. Like I'm always telling you, I plan on being the first one in my family to earn a high-school diploma. Afterward, my CPA."

"Like I'm always telling you, Earlier—I believe you will. I could always breeze through any class that used words to create pictures, but I hit a wall with algebra or geometry or anything tougher than two plus two. From what I see, you have a special gift for numbers."

"Used to run 'em once upon a time," he said, not entirely kidding.

"Better this way. Just keep at it."

"I appreciate your good thoughts, Mr. Gulliver. Your words of encouragement take on special meaning when I remember how old I am and count the years I wasted before straightening out my life."

His head bounced to the beat of his words and he played with his tie and the brass buttons on his uniform, a bad fit he had inherited last year after Early, his younger half-brother, enlisted in the Marines and Earlier took over the post. Frayed cuffs rested well above his wrists and the strain on the buttons was evident.

He snapped his fingers, like he'd just remembered something. "He find you, Mr. Gulliver?"

"Did who find me?"

"Fella came looking. It couldn't have been more than five or six minutes after I came back from my rounds and saw you racing out the door behind Miss Hartounian and Sunshine from 36E. He was looking to enter with Mr. Okuna from 12C, like they were friends, but nobody gets past me where I don't have a name to go with the face.

"This fella tells me he's your friend and here to meet with you. Has an appointment, he says. I tell him you just ran off on your morning jog. He wants to wait inside, but I tell him it's against our condo rules. I tell him he can wait for you outside there, over by the buzzer bench."

I swiveled my head to the glassed-in entry I had just passed through.

The only person seated on the cushioned bench across from the directory wall and intercom was a kid in tennis shorts and a Bruin sweatshirt, Reeboks with blue tassels, his sunburned legs stretched and crossed at the ankles, intent on the tennis racket he was balancing on his index finger.

"Unh unh," Earlier said, shaking his head. "He sat there maybe a minute, your friend, his face all tight like he can't figure the last word in this week's *National Star* puzzle, then jumped up like the seat was too hot for his bottom and left like he don't want to be late catching his bus."

"What did my friend look like?"

Earlier eyed me strangely, his fat cheeks almost colliding with his eyebrows. "You don't know what he looks like, this fella who——?"

At once he realized it was none of his business and described the man. He had a good eye for detail, good enough to draw a word picture close to the one Stevie had given Ron Pipes at the *Daily*—

A young James Dean.

I sucked in air as adrenaline surged through my body. Just because my visitor left didn't mean he had not found another way into the building. The Heathcliffe, like every other condo in town, was no impenetrable fortress.

I grabbed the desk phone, connected to my place, and under my breath demanded Augie answer as the phone rang and rang. After the ninth or tenth ring, I pushed the phone at Earlier.

"Don't hang up," I instructed. "Someone answers

and it's Augie—Brother Kalman—you tell him . . . You know his voice?"

"Hear it often enough."

"Tell him I'm on my way up and not to answer the door for anyone else."

Earlier saw the panic on my face. "What if it isn't the good bro who answers, Mr. Gulliver?"

"Nine-one-one," I said, calling out the three numbers I never had problems with, already halfway across the lobby to the stairwell.

I took the steps two at a time, the landings in a giant hop, and raced up the third floor corridor like I was Indiana Jones five steps in front of the giant boulder.

My apartment door was open—

Augie standing in the doorway.

The fingers of his gun hand locked onto the Beretta—

His other hand gripping the bath towel draped around the ample midsection of his otherwise naked body, water matting the mattress of hair on his chest and what hair there was on his head, his feet in a modest puddle.

He was not wearing his eye patch and the blind socket looked more disturbed than his good eye while he hissed out a warning at me, "Better be a worthy explanation for this, kiddo. You know there's nothing I hate more than being yanked from my morning tub."

Stevie woke up knowing how to find James Dean.

The answer had come in another dream, at first less a nightmare than a romantic fantasy, printed in large block letters on the gift card accompanying a dozen long-stemmed red roses from—

Who?

She didn't understand, not right away.

A series of letters and numbers, the letters first, no signature on the card.

She asked the delivery man if he knew who the bouquet was from, if he understood the meaning of the card, and he began laughing. A high, familiar cackling sound that caused her to look up at him. His face was hidden inside a fog curtain.

She pushed the curtain aside with her hands and saw James Dean smirking at her as if Stevie were the only one not privy to some gigantic joke.

Dean began to retreat, running backward, making funny faces and weird signs at her, taunting her, daring her to catch him. She chased after him, demanding he take back the roses. "They're not mine," Dean called at her before the next steps moved him back into the dense fog, leaving behind his pointed laughter. They now sounded like notes on a musical scale.

The scale grew larger and turned into a marquee, the notes into the same letters and numbers she had seen on the gift card, glowing so brilliantly she had to shield her eyes from the light.

Determined to catch him, Stevie ran faster, stumbled, tripped, fell, and—

Woke up—

Holding on to her dream—

Repeating the letters and numbers aloud.

Stevie snapped on her night table lamp, tossed aside the covers, leaped from the bed, and scrambled after a pad and pencil.

Repeating, repeating.

She hurriedly jotted them down before she forgot them, then moved across the bedroom to the window and drew back the thick curtains to let in the bright light of late morning.

She glanced at the clock radio and saw it was almost noon. She grunted a laugh. Worn down by the pile of recent events and the long trip, she had finally managed to get a good night's sleep. She probed lightly under one eye, then the other, and was unable to feel the bag puffs she'd seen building there yesterday.

Stevie smiled grandly, turned her attention back to the row of numbers and block letters, contemplated them squinting against the light, and almost at once understood what she was staring at—

The license plate number on the black Honda James Dean had used to escape the post office the day he murdered her dear Nico Mercouri.

Below the row, she wrote down the earlier line-up that had sent her and Neil on a wild goose chase to that unpleasant Rawlings person who thought he was on *Candid Camera*.

The difference now was the position of the seven and the nine.

This time the nine came first.

This time, she was certain, the license-plate number would lead to James Dean.

The phone was on the night table. She crossed over to it and dialed Neil on the private number.

Got no answer.

A second try. Again no answer.

The general number gave Stevie his machine and she left a message that vaguely referred to "good news" and told him to call her at once.

She wondered if she should be concerned.

She hadn't heard from him and, knowing Neil as well as she did, it would have been more in keeping with his character for him to have phoned before splitting, if only to see how she was. He certainly did it often enough when there wasn't anything special disturbing her life, except maybe his calling to campaign against a new boyfriend who might measure up to her standards but not to his. On those occasions he could be a real pain in the ass, but at least he was her pain in the ass, and Stevie wondered why all of a sud-

den she was missing him as much as she needed to
know Neil was okay?

Stevie moved to the dresser mirror and double-
checked her eyes. Smiled. The dark semicircles and
the bags were gone. She examined the lines dressing the
outer edges and the quotation marks by her lips. The
light crease marks ranging across her forehead and in
the valley between her brows.

Not so bad for her age, including her real age, she
decided. Did a half turn to check her profile. Threw
back her shoulders to accentuate her boobs under the
silk pink baby dolls she didn't remember putting on
last night, that's how burned out she'd been by the
time she got home from dropping Neil off at his place,
as hard as Neil had tried to convince her to stick with
him, or let him stick with her, because she needed—

What?

Consolation? Protection?

Like she was still some kid who couldn't handle
herself, not the woman Neil had helped her to become
after he saw her and rescued her from herself and her
garden of self-doubts, showed her pretty wasn't an excuse not to be smart, especially when she knew she
had the desire and the mind to be both.

He saw that, Neil. Saw through her enough, got to
her, watched her grow up, eventually away from him,
when he lost his own way in a swamp of betting, booz-
ing, and other bad habits she had tried unsuccessfully
to rescue him from.

"Nobody's perfect," he told her.

"Nobody has to be, honey."

*"Look at the lousy job of packing you're doing.
Proves it. Proves my point."*

"Leaving you is lousier, but it's the way it has to be."

"Don't I get a vote?"

"Not this time. Maybe next time."

"When'll that be?"

"When you grow up, honey. When you're old enough to vote."

"Hold on a minute, lady! When I first laid eyes on you, you were the teenager, you remember? Not me."

"No, you were a child, but that's something I had to learn for myself. In some departments, I've been a slow learner. That was one of them, honey."

They'd been married seven years the day she left.

Add another seven.

Fourteen years ago, fourteen-plus years ago that was.

Fourteen-plus years later and—

Neil always ready to vote.

Stevie still too wise to call the election.

Meanwhile, for all he had done for her, what had she done for Neil?

Bought him his condo.

Guilt.

Brought him through the worst of his years.

Gratitude.

Stuck around.

Greed.

She had never stopped needing him, and that she didn't have to say. He was too smart, Neil, not to know it by himself.

So was she, because she knew it, knew that some parts of your life you never throw away, even if you can.

Smart of you, Stevie, she congratulated herself. That's using your head.

A wink at her reflection in the mirror.

A thumbs up.

To most people Stephanie Marriner was only the "Sex Queen of the Soaps," but it was her mind that got her where she was and it was her mind that would keep her there.

She knew that, too.

They didn't have to know that, the people who never saw past her looks, labeled her a sex object, and spoke within hearing distance like English was a foreign language to her.

Better her secret.

Her secret weapon.

Who told her the story when she was just starting out, upset that all the reviews talked about her looks and not her acting ability, and Army Archerd's column in *Daily Variety* the first to tout her as the next Sex Queen of the Soaps?

Augie Fowler.

Undecipherable Augie Fowler, listening patiently to her complaint, already understanding without being told that she was smart enough to still be around after time and gravity had done their worst to her.

He'd once known an actress named Marie McDonald, Augie told her.

"Tall and beautiful and blonde, like you," Augie said. "Worked her way up from B movies in the forties to a string of A pictures, always playing off her nickname, 'The Body.' The way Lana Turner started out as 'The Sweater Girl' and Ann Sheridan was 'The Oomph Girl,' she was always Marie The Body McDonald, like it was part of her name.

"We got into conversation at the cast party end of the shoot for *Living in a Big Way*, where she costarred with Gene Kelly, and I asked her straight out, 'Marie, does it ever bother you being called The Body?'

" 'Never, Augie, darling,' she shoots right back at me. 'I would never have gotten as far as I have being called Marie The Brain McDonald.' "

Stevie stared at her reflection.

Mirror, mirror, on the wall . . .

She grinned, congratulating herself on holding Mama Nature to a standstill.

From the physical evidence, Stephanie Marriner would remain the unchallenged Sex Queen of the Soaps for a few more years, unless she found an escape route from the soap jungle, landed on a prime-time series or a juicy movie role that finally let her graduate to the big screen.

Why not?

It happened for Meg Ryan. For Sharon Stone.

For Gwyneth, who went on to win a Best Actress Oscar for *Shakespeare in Love*.

For Marisa Tomei—Marisa Tomei!—who went on to win a Best Supporting Actress Oscar for—

The phone rang, startling Stevie.

She got it on the second ring and shouted Neil's name into the mouthpiece.

Only it wasn't Neil.

It was Darwin Armateaux, one of the new *Bedrooms and Board Rooms* associate producers. Mid-twenties. Tall, dark, and serious. Attractive without being good-looking behind a pair of horn rims and a lazy-shaver's beard. A high-strung voice that competed with chalk on a blackboard whenever he got excited. He'd made secret eyes at her a few times, but never more than that.

Darwin had been hired a year ago as one of the show's dialogue writers and instantly gave the words bite, a sharpness they'd been lacking. When he asked for a raise, they gave him a promotion instead. Not really a promotion. A title. Made him one of eight or nine associate producers.

She had lost count. Titles were a bargain to the show, to the writer as good, maybe better, than more money.

To give him more money meant shelling out more to the Writers Guild, where a title gave the writer a stronger identity, a stronger shot at making it to a real producer's job, although everybody in the industry knew how the phony credits system worked.

"Dar, darling! What's up, sweetie?"

In a tentative voice, Darwin wondered where she was.

The question puzzled her. "How many guesses you need, Dar?"

An awkward silence, then somberly, "You know you were on the call sheet for this morning?"

"No such thing."

"Such thing," Darwin said, and seemed embarrassed to be contradicting her. "With the script dropped off last night. If you check, you'll see—"

"Script? I didn't get any script."

"And your sides, put at your door, like always, the messenger said, between the screen door and the door whenever you don't answer the doorbell or your phone."

The door, like always. She'd meant to lock the driveway gate. Keep anybody from getting as close as the front door. Forgot to? Or just didn't remember to? Memory lapse? The old brain cells still not kicking in on cue?

"Stay with me, Dar, baby. I'm heading there now."

Stevie hummed tunelessly into the portable phone as she hurried from the bedroom and raced across the living room.

Threw back the locks.

Opened the front door.

A large brown manila envelope fell forward.

"Stevie?"

"Still here, Dar," she said, stooping to pick up the envelope. The address label carried the *Bedrooms and Board Rooms* logo. "Hold on another minute."

Stevie opened the envelope, pulled out the sides containing her lines—five pages containing three scraggly lines—for the segment taping this afternoon, according to the call sheet anchored to the top of the script with an oversized paper clip.

She sighed in exasperation. How exhausted was she last night to miss hearing the doorbell and the phone?

What other calls did she miss before she woke from her dream.

A call from Neil?

"It's was here, Dar, sorry. I slept through all the noise. Overslept."

"Yeah. Shit happens."

Something was troubling Darwin. She heard it in his voice. "Besides, they know my memory is still holier than the Holy Grail and I wouldn't be up for anything for two, three days. Probably the rest of the week."

In fact, Stevie's memory had not been troubling her much. Dar didn't have to know that.

"Yeah," he said. Fell into a silence disturbed by labored breathing.

"Dar, sweetie, what's this call really about?" Stevie said, sensing it had to be more than the script or the sides, her not being on the set.

"They're thinking seriously about dumping you, Stevie, I thought you ought to know," he finally blurted out.

Now it was her turn to be silent, except for the noise her heart made bouncing around her chest.

"They were confident you wouldn't show," Darwin said, "They had me reworking the dialogue for Karen Walls, even before they sent off the messenger. They're building up a case against you, for their lawyers to use whenever they decide it's the right timing to break your contract."

"Why, Dar?"

"Beats me. Your guess is as good as mine. Hold on . . ." Conversation distant and jumbled behind a hand held over the mouthpiece. "Gotta split, Stevie," he said hurriedly. "Karen needs help with everything over two syllables. Take care, okay? I cannot believe all the double-dealing around here."

The dial tone replaced his voice.

Stevie told herself she wasn't going to worry about it now and, while worrying about it anyway, dialed the *Daily,* identified herself to the switchboard operator, asked who was on the Metro desk and, relieved to learn it was Litrov, asked to be connected. He was on in a moment, identifying himself by name. After a minute of old-friends conversation, she told him what she needed.

"The plate sounds familiar, Stevie. Didn't I run it once already for Neil?"

"Not exactly. He transposed the numbers somehow, but this time he got it right and asked me to call it in for him."

"It's for Neil then?"

"Yes," she lied. "You need to hear it from him, hold on and I'll drag his sorry butt out of the shower."

Litrov told Stevie not to bother, said to give him ten or fifteen minutes.

Waiting for the callback, she tried to figure out why the show would be even remotely interested in getting rid of her.

She was still its number one draw and right now *Bedrooms and Board Rooms*—as much as the fact insulted her emotions—was riding its highest ratings in months because of the print and broadcast coverage tied to Nico's murder and her brush with the killer.

It wasn't her memory problem.

Everyone understood her memory would get back to normal in time. Even she understood that.

What then?

A smile slid onto her face.

Karen Walls! Of course Karen Walls.

The Eve Harrington of *Bedrooms and Board Rooms.*

This was all about Eve. All about Karen.

Since joining the soap last year, her character, the vamp secretary available on demand to anyone with a platinum American Express card, had shot up in importance and camera time, the same way Karen had planted her two-inch nails into the show's exec producer, Jack Arbogast.

Well, Karen Eve Harrington Walls, we'll have to see about this, won't we? You are certainly not the first to try swiping the crown away from Stephanie Marriner, and you won't be the last, either. Only the latest.

The phone rang and she snapped it up.

It was Litrov with the name and address.

At once Stevie forgot about Karen Walls. Less than an hour later, she was on her way to investigate the owner of a black Honda whose license plate number was the same as the one she had captured in her dream.

Edward Grizzard was his name.

The address was about twenty minutes away, in the area around Western and Wilshire.

14

Salvatore Mineo, Jr., was stabbed to death the night of February 12, 1976, outside his inexpensive West Hollywood apartment, in an area of the homosexual paradise known as "Boys Town," where darkness routinely brought out assorted street-corner hustlers, hookers, and pimps, drug merchants and their customers, and other known species of criminal creepy crawlers.

Sal, thirty-seven at the time, was returning from a rehearsal of the stage play *P.S. Your Cat is Dead*, which was opening the end of the month in L.A. after a successful run in San Francisco, Keir Dullea of *2001: A Space Odyssey* fame in one of the starring roles.

It was about ten when Sal parked his Chevette in the open-faced carport facing the street beneath the two-story building on Holloway Drive, according to statements of neighbors, who told police they heard a man screaming out, "No! My God! No!"

One of the neighbors said he raced outside and found Sal in a heap on the concrete floor of the carport. His chest was pooled in blood and it was clear he'd been stabbed several times.

In fact, a heavy blade had pierced his heart.

Sal was dead before paramedics arrived.

Other witnesses saw a man race from the murder scene. They described him as a white man who jumped into a small yellow car and sped away.

Lionel Ray Williams, the nineteen-year-old pizza delivery man ultimately tried and convicted of killing Sal Mineo and shipped off to state prison for fifty-one years, was black.

"And that's the reason we're heading downtown to the Criminal Court Building?" Augie said, fidgeting after a more comfortable position in the passenger seat of my Jag. "To verify Williams was black? I covered the story and saw he was black, amigo. Check out the trial clips. He'll still be black there."

"I checked," I said. "It's what none of the clips said that I wanted to ask Williams about."

"The white man in the small yellow car."

"The white man in the small yellow car."

Augie thought it over.

"It was late, it was dark, and it happened in a flash, kiddo. The man who fled could have been black the same way the yellow car could have been red or green or polka-dotted."

"The man who fled the scene was white and the car was yellow to too many of the eyeball witnesses who quoted to the cops, Augie."

"Maybe he was yellow and the car was white, and he was someone who also happened on the crime and did not want to get involved."

"Unless he already was involved, and not *instead* of Lionel Ray Williams. In addition."

"An accomplice."

"Give the man a cigar."

"Thank you very much," he said, fishing a half-smoked Cuban from the same cassock pocket where, before we left my apartment, when he thought I wouldn't notice, he'd slipped my Beretta.

"Not in the Jag, Augie. You know the rule."

He grumbled something under his breath about re-formed smokers being worse than reformed drunks and announced, "Why I agreed to make the trip with you I'll never know."

"Because I finally got it into your thick head that you can't spend the rest of your life hiding from a death threat delivered over the telephone."

Augie bit down on the unlit cigar, flexed his jaw muscles, and said, "You thinking it was something you said sold me on the idea? Think again, kiddo." Indignant. Every word flying into the windshield.

"A foolish guess on my part," I said.

"I smell insincerity, but nevertheless you're apology is accepted." He stashed the stogie. "Now, change the subject."

Before I could, Augie turned on the radio, tuned as always to my favorite music station, and the air at once filled with an unmistakable performance of "It Don't Mean a Thing (If It Ain't Got That Swing)."

"Ella and the Duke. It's the live album they did for Norman Granz at the Cote D'Azur," I announced. "Their International Festival of Jazz concert in '66. On Verve."

"Thanks for the education," he said. Turned his gaze past the window to the streets in a neighborhood full of signs in Spanish; storefronts and sidewalk vendors that also spoke to the shift in population and culture returning Los Angeles to its Hispanic roots.

He was silent the rest of the way, leaving me to ponder his state over Ella and Duke's master class in the international language of jazz.

If not the threat on his life, maybe something in the Williams files he didn't want to confront?

That didn't make sense, but ultimately it was the best I could do.

I'd found ways to convince myself his problem was as simple and foolish as that by the time we got downtown, Ella and Duke just about through leaving an ownership certificate on "The More I See You."

My original plan was to pull a prison location on Lionel Ray Williams and go calling, only that wasn't to be. Williams had been paroled three years ago, after putting in thirty-five years on the fifty-one–year term handed down by Judge Bonnie Lee Martin once the jury said guilty on eleven of the twelve counts the state tried him on.

The jury made it murder two on the Mineo killing, because the cops were able to link him to the murder weapon and get Williams to confess after picking Williams up on one of the robberies three years after Mineo's death.

The other ten street crimes were first-degree armed robberies, where Williams had carried and sometimes used various weapons on his victims, including pistols and hammers.

Judge Martin called for Williams to serve the terms consecutively, which might have put an older person behind bars for the rest of his life, but Williams was back on the street in his late fifties.

And I'd been unable to get a bead on his address. I'd spent a chunk of the morning calling around, but nobody could tell me where to find him.

Williams wasn't exactly lost.

Misplaced, maybe.

I'd become equally frustrated trying to draw out any information beyond what I'd gathered from the newspaper files. The *Daily* had little and the *Times* on-demand service less about the Mineo murder. The best the *Times* could come up with was a 1992 summary of sensational deaths in L.A., where Sal was a bare-bones paragraph alongside the infamous Black Dahlia, Elizabeth Short; screen legend Lana Turner's mobster boyfriend, Johnny Stompanato, who was knifed by the actress's fourteen-year-old daughter; *Playboy* "Playmate of the Year" Dorothy Stratten, who was raped and murdered by her jealous husband; Hillside Strangler victims; and even a walk down Hollywood's memory lane with actress Thelma Todd, whose mysterious death was called suicide by some, a murder by others.

Nobody I reached at Parker Center, the DA's office, Superior Court, or the Department of Corrections could help me out on the question of the white man in the yellow car or any other aspect of the case.

It was too old.

History.

Most of them never heard of Sal Mineo, or had a vague memory of him from "That movie with whoozis, you know the movie I mean?" Half the time they meant *Rebel Without a Cause,* the rest of the time *Exodus,* and I stopped counting how many female clerks sighed over how gorgeous Paul Newman was in that one. "Gaw-jus, Neil, absolutely gaw-jus."

Records had been converted to the computer, but not that far back. Not yet, anyway, and maybe never. Did I know how much the process was costing in time and money? I did not. I did not care, either. I visualized the files I was interested in lost inside decaying packing cases under tons of dust in a warehouse somewhere, next to a sled named "Rosebud." *If* the files still existed. More than wheat gets shredded nowadays.

A Corrections clerk who sounded trapped inside a tight girdle apologized for not being able to give me a read on Lionel Ray Williams over the phone. Against policy, she said. I needed to apply for Forms 2,000 through 7,000,000, submit them in triplicate, and try holding my breath under water for a month or two, something like that.

I could do better going through the *Daily,* later, if it was necessary, but—

I caught a different kind of break first.

An old contact at the County Courthouse mentioned I might be able to find data about the trial in the Hall of Records archives.

If so, I figured, there might be something useful about the white man in the yellow car. The possibility was worth the gas downtown so, for the time being, I pushed the hunt for Lionel Ray Williams onto a back burner.

Following Gulliver's Jag at a cautious distance as it worked the streets downtown, Eddie congratulated himself on his astuteness. That damned nigger guard made him have a second thought about finishing off the two of them there in the building. He'd taken a good look at Eddie and might blab enough description to the cops to put them on his tail. Not find him, of course. He was always too careful for that to happen. But no reason to take chances and invite a slip-up.

So, he'd figured, What the hell, move the action round to the rear of the building, and that's exactly what he did for the payoff.

He moved the car round back to a parking space across the street, between the two garage entrances,

*and settled behind the wheel for however long the wait
would take for them to pull out in Gulliver's Jag or that
show-off red Rolls of Fowler's. Tail them in the Cougar
he had boosted yesterday and, for extra safety, given
out-of-state plates switched with another street car. No
cop who checked the Cougar against a theft report
would think twice about stopping him after noticing the
plates didn't match up. If they were bright enough to do
that, they wouldn't be cops. He cackled at his joke and
thought, Clever boy you are, Mr. Grizzard. Clever boy.*

*The Jag crossed Temple on Hill, Eddie a cautious four
car lengths behind it, half-hidden behind an RMV.
Without signaling it made a sudden U-turn halfway
down the long block, heading south again, and he spit
the word "shit" at the window, fearing he had been
spotted, although that made no sense. He had been extra careful, done nothing to give them a look at him or
call attention to the Cougar.*

*Eddie pedaled hard on the gas, sailed past the Jag
preparing to speed off and forget about Fowler and
Gulliver for the time being, catch up with them later at
Gulliver's apartment.*

*In the rearview he saw the Jag maneuver into a slot
along a construction fence, by a busted meter, between
a Ford Mustang and a BMW. They had not made him,
only found free street parking. He laughed at Fowler
and Gulliver for the cheap SOBs they were.*

*His problem became finding his own parking space
before he lost them.*

*Eddie traveled another twenty yards, slowed to let
some traffic shoot by, executed a turnaround, and
inched back up Hill, slamming down on the brakes
when he noticed a spot about to open. The Toyota
pulled out and he glided in.*

Through the window he saw Fowler and Gulliver,

jaywalking across the street, reach the intersection as the light turned against them.

Luck was still running with him. He grinned like a kid in a burger commercial.

Eddie bounced out of the Cougar without bothering to lock it. Pat-checked himself for the switchblade in his windbreaker and his .38 where it belonged, jammed down his jeans on his hip, inside his belt.

There was an hour left on the parking meter. He dropped in two quarters to bring it up to the two-hour max, waited for a break in the traffic, and charged across Hill Street, answering the honking horns of a few drivers with the universal finger.

Fowler and Gulliver were crossing Temple.

Eddie hop-skip-skidded to a slower pace, watched them as they headed up the steps into the Criminal Court Building. Gulliver looked like he almost had to force the older man in the silly outfit inside. Eddie wondered what in the name of sweet Jesus hell that was all about.

Augie grew increasingly tense the closer we got to the Criminal Court Building.

By the time we passed through the doors, he was sweating, the water settled in the furrows in his brow, not quite ready to overflow. A similar line of beads had formed below his generous nose, the veins reflecting all the years he was romanced by booze.

Maybe also the latest flirtation.

Augie's steps didn't falter, he carried himself as erect and overbearing as ever, but there was a twitch in his speech that didn't belong there.

Any more than he wanted to be here.

"There is nothing in those records that we can't find quicker somehow else, amigo." Augie said it more than once and in various ways. More carryover from the call he took at Harry Chalk's office, the death threat that put him into hiding at my place? Was that it?

This behavior was not typical.

When he balked at the entrance, I pushed open a door with one hand, propelled him inside with the other. Pointed to an unoccupied slab bench against a wall across from the elevators.

Augie seemed relieved by the opportunity to sit. His body froze in one position, his spine pencil-straight, his fingers locked on his lap, squeezing so hard that his hands turned pink from the pressure. His good eye wandered up and down the corridor like a lost explorer.

I settled next to him and said quietly, "Okay, chief, what's it all about? What's going on with you?"

"You know."

"No."

His body rose another four or five inches as he angled away from me, chin rising defiantly and challenge settling in his eye.

"You do."

"I don't."

"Of course, you do. Don't play reporter games with me of all people, kiddo. Especially not the games I invented and chose to teach you out of charitable sympathy."

"Any game going on here, Augie, it's yours."

He mopped at his forehead with a hand, used the index finger of his other hand to swipe away the moisture on his upper lip and the mist gathering in the eye.

I told him what I'd observed about his behavior and said, "So, what is there about the Williams court files you're afraid I'll find?"

The question seemed to throw Augie.

A smile flickered on his mouth and settled into a smirk. "You really believe that's it, the files?" he said, shaking his head. "Not as simple as that, kid."

Augie sounded sorry for himself. He lost the smirk.

His mouth pulled back into a slash of resignation familiar to me, signaling circumstances beyond his control and conclusions over which he had no authority, unwelcome events that made Augie Fowler as ordinary a mortal as the next man, and, as his good eye bore hard into mine—

I recognized what he was going through.

Felt foolish for not figuring it out sooner.

I said softly, "Wimpy Angleman."

Augie pressed the palm of his hand over my mouth, all I needed to understand my assumption was correct.

After another moment or two, he removed it and said, "I haven't been in this building since the bombing, amigo. I haven't been anywhere near this building." His voice was as quiet as a graveyard chorus.

He gripped his hands in his lap, took a heavy breath, and yawned it away. I couldn't be sure if the wet streaks running under his eye were formed by his rampaging sweat. My guess was otherwise.

"I didn't know that, Augie."

"Why should you?"

"You never mentioned it."

"Why should I?"

"His death, Wimpy's, it wasn't your fault, that I know. So will you one of these days."

"Leave it, kid."

"You have to—"

"I said leave it." The words fairly hissed. "And try to remember who you're talking to next time you even think about talking to me that way."

"I'm sorry, Augie. I apologize." He brushed my words off with a gesture. "Look, you're uncomfortable with this, go back to the car and wait for me. I'll get through what I need to do as fast as I can and—"

"I'm already here," he said, snorting his nose clear and swallowing. Augie rose, toweled his face with a hand, used both of them to tug his cassock straight, gave me a few pats on the cheek. "Long overdue," he said. "I've thought about it, tried it by myself once or twice over the years since. Flopped, so maybe you're doing me a favor."

Before I could answer, he swiveled around and strode forward to the building wall directory to check on exactly where we were heading, moved on to an information desk, and returned a minute or two later to report we had missed the direct route, two elevators rising like isolated monoliths outside and behind the Criminal Court building.

We took an indoor elevator to the basement and followed the green and red directional floor arrows down and around empty corridors that echoed with our movements. My Nikes, Augie's sandals tripping along the hard cement. The rustle of his chocolate-colored cassock. His labored breathing increasing in density as the arrows carried on endlessly, past locked doors, around fork lifts and flats brimming with supply cartons. Fork lifts. Wooden crates. Scattered piles of green plastic sacks of discard.

It was a route the Phantom of the Opera would have approved. We wondered along the way if we might bump into him, a gag that eased the tension of the preceding minutes, which Augie tried to wash away with a rat-a-tat string of memories about happier times covering crime for the *Daily,* a reverie I didn't try to match, just as Augie in the past always listened quietly, his expression awash in understanding, while I blathered on and on about my own private beasts and demons.

The longest corridor moved us underneath Hill Street and into the belly of the Hall of Records.

The final two turns in the labyrinth brought us to the department we sought.

In the large reception area that could have been a

classroom or a study hall, fifteen or twenty people were spread out along three rows of abutted library tables like students taking a test. They poured through files and took notes while another half dozen waited quietly for the files they'd ordered, in chairs closer to the counter separating us from endless rows of ceiling-high metal shelves crammed with green filing boxes.

I filled out separate request cards for each of the three file numbers my courthouse contact had given me and drew a puzzled look from a tired clerk practicing slow motion, who clamped her hands onto her invisible breasts and looked to the ceiling for divine guidance before she decided, "These ones go back farther than me down here." She ran the numbers through her computer and smiled. "Exactly!"

The twenty-year-old court files I wanted had not yet been converted to the county's computer system. They were still on microfiche and not here in the archives.

For a moment I thought it had been a wasted trip and Augie already was muttering the same thing, when the clerk asked for identification and, satisfied I was the photo on my driver's license, pushed a Take-a-Number tab across the counter and gave me directions to another archive storage cavern, a basement level below this one, like a stewardess talking about flotation cushions.

This time we found the correct elevator and, down one floor, followed a set of passageways to a smaller room with fewer people waiting in a cramped reception area for their turn at one of a half-dozen microfiche viewers.

Our numbered tab keyed to the ordered files and fifteen minutes later I was running through files on the first roll of film with Augie staring at the screen over my shoulder.

I slowed down approaching the earliest files on Lionel Ray Williams, convicted killer of Salvatore Mineo, Jr.

Stopped at the key number.

Gave the files a fast survey and knew at once they were of no use to us.

They dealt with a crime two years before Sal's murder, grand theft and receiving stolen property, and Williams hauled back into court for violation of parole.

We had slightly better luck with the next two rolls of film.

They contained the files on Williams's trial for murder and the dozen 211s charged against him, all the surface details, the jury's verdict after four days of deliberation, Judge Martin's sentence, even the defendant's motion for a new trial, denied, but—

Not what I had hoped to find, not what brought me downtown in the first place.

Nothing about a white man in a yellow car.

"Certainly there is," Augie said after I shared my newest frustration. He ordered, "Check back through the pages," thumping the screen with an index finger as thick as one of his choice Cubans.

"What am I looking for?"

"Slower this time. Pay more attention. You were running too fast before. You'll know it when you see it, what I mean."

I rotated the viewing dial slowly, this time not entirely intent on finding something that said "white man" or "yellow car," and—

Saw what Augie meant.

Rather, what wasn't there for anyone to see.

Upon motion of the district attorney's office, the transcript of the grand jury proceedings that led to Lionel Ray Williams's indictment had been sealed by court order.

"There's something in the grand jury transcript about the man and the car, is that what you're telling me?"

"Review some more, again," Augie said, ignoring my question, coaching over my back. "You're going too fast. Slower . . . I said, slower. Don't be in such a hurry. Pretend you're still a reporter who knows how to dig for details."

I might have been insulted by the remark, except it had the sting of truth. Writing a feature column isn't the same as trafficking in news. It's mostly the bare facts dressed in a costume, meant to entertain, not necessarily to inform, and—

There it was, what Augie was talking about.

I'd missed it the first time, but he hadn't.

A witness list.

The grand jury transcript had been sealed, but not so the list of witnesses who took the stand in Judge Martin's courtroom to testify against Lionel Ray Williams.

There were a number and closeted among them was one I knew well enough to have spotted by myself, if I had been more careful—

Chip Kiley.

Chip Kiley, the link between James Dean and Nick Adams and Sal Mineo and—

More than that?

If Chip Kiley was the third man at Nick Adams's home the night he was murdered, was he also the white man in the yellow car the night Sal was murdered?

I announced the discovery to Augie and rotated my seat around, looked up at him to wonder what he made of it, and saw—

Augie wasn't wearing his glasses.

Without them, there was no way he could have read the screen.

Augie knew what there was to be found before we came here.

15

The construction project on Hill Street had shut down lanes in both directions and traffic was sparse as we crossed to the Jag on a diagonal, me squinting against the afternoon sun and urging Augie to conversation while Augie pretended I wasn't on his heel and hummed a tune that might be recognizable hummed by someone who knew how to hum.

I dug out my keys and started to unlock the door when Augie, who had been moving around the front of the car to the passenger side, let out a short, strident howl.

I jerked my head around to see the problem.

Augie was gripping his left upper arm, just below where a knife handle protruded, but only until a kid I took to be a mugger yanked it free and reared up his arm high to strike Augie again.

The next thrust caught Augie somewhere on his back, which he had turned as a shield against the mugger. The mugger drew out the blade, raised his hand for another strike.

As the blade started down, Augie sent a backhand into space. It caught the mugger on the wrist, causing him to lose his grip. The knife sailed against the construction fence and clattered onto the sidewalk.

Augie, growling violently and shouting profanity I hadn't heard him use since he turned into Brother Kalman, lunged at the mugger and smothered him in a bear hug.

The mugger needed several moments to break free.

By that time I'd come around to the sidewalk to help subdue him.

I reached out. He twirled and kicked me in the gut in a swift, single motion. I slammed backward against the Jag and instantly felt a river of pain course through my body.

Augie once more had him in a grip, but there was no power in his left arm. The mugger shifted loose easily. Retreated backwards five or six steps and, when he stopped, had pulled a gun from somewhere.

Was aiming it in an unsteady singlehanded grip at us.

Demanding Augie stop in his tracks.

Augie stopped, flung an adrenaline-filled laugh at the mugger, and challenged him contemptuously, "Why, you little worm? To give you a better target?"

The mugger danced into a shooter's stance and slapped his other hand onto the .38, took tight aim as Augie advanced on him sneering, "You don't have the guts, dickhead."

"Your guts and they'll be spilling all over the ground," the mugger snarled, and—

Squeezed the trigger.

The shot hit Augie high and pushed him back. He made an *oomphing* noise, not quite a cry, and did a half-gainer on his way down.

The mugger turned his gun on me as I shouted out

Augie's name and stepped toward him as he hit the
ground, startled to see there was an armed man behind
Augie, also in a shooter's stance, his weapon aimed at
the mugger.

Two shots rang out simultaneously.

One was louder than the other. I froze, certain I was
dead or about to be, and looked up at the sky for what
came next. A pathway in the clouds. A bright light at
the end of the tunnel.

There was only darkness, until I realized I had my
eyes closed. I opened them to find the shooter who had
been standing behind Augie was now lifeless on the
ground behind Augie's own immobile body.

The mugger was up the block jumping behind the
wheel of a Mercury Cougar and seconds later he had
pulled out from the curb into a sharp, screeching U-
turn toward Sunset, too fast and far away for me to
catch the plate. It looked out-of-state; only that.

I dropped to one knee beside Augie and felt his neck
for a pulse, then did the same on the shooter. He was in
his late twenties or early thirties and dressed in jeans
and a beige turtleneck under a light-brown sports coat
that was growing a bloodstain already the size of a
pancake. His right hand clutched his weapon, a short-
barreled .38 police special pulled from the empty slot
holster on his hip. His shades were askew and his
ocean blue eyes stared back at me uncertainly.

Instinctively, I knew who the shooter was.

Two cars and a U-Haul had stopped, drawn by the
gunfire. I ran into the street and banged on the window
of the nearest vehicle, a Mercedes, and before the window was all the way down was questioning if the driver
had a cell phone, yelling each word between deep
swallows.

He did. Pulling past my blind panic, I realized he
was on it. I commanded him to disconnect and call

911. "Tell them two men down," I yelled. "Shot. Tell them one's a cop. Tell them officer down."

Stevie slowed passing the duplex, then speeded up and rolled around the block again, double-parked across the street with the motor running long enough to prove again to herself no black Honda was parked in the driveway. A few on the block, but none with the telltale license-plate number.

Maybe Edward Grizzard was at work?

Possible.

Stevie checked her Rolex. Almost two-thirty. She didn't relish hanging here all day, waiting to find out. It was just as likely he had ditched the car, figuring someone might have made the plate and could use it to track him.

Was Grizzard that clever?

And how much smarter was she, she wondered, to be giving serious consideration to confronting an accessory to murder? Alone, no less. Neil wasn't around. She'd tried him twice more before leaving the house, only got the machine; damn him anyway, making her worry like this.

She briefly considered phoning DeSantis, actually started to dial his number, quickly disconnected, realizing she did not want to embarrass herself if the address led to another dead end, especially not with him. DeSantis would never let her live it down.

Besides, wasn't it still a secret from the cops, her ID of the driver? Hadn't she and Neil kept secret the computer composite based on her description to Ron Pipes at the *Daily*? Or, did Neil have a bigger secret, that he told DeSantis about the composite? Jimmy Steiger, more likely.

She dipped into her purse for the cell phone and

tried Neil again. Got the machine again. Got worried about him all over again. Squeezed her eyes and her mind trying to make a psychic connection. Call me, Neil. You call me at once, you hear? Studied the duplex, a relic of the thirties in a jumble of apartment buildings: in desperate need of a paint job and patches on the wood shingle roof, pinned on three sides by high-rises that kept the place in a constant state of shadows. Sometime in the past, an owner had made a mistake, either refusing to sell to a developer or holding out for a better price.

Stevie decided to go back home, try again later. Get hold of Neil. Give him hell. Get him to come back here with her. Maybe, instead, show up unexpectedly at *Bedrooms and Board Rooms,* have it out with the producers over this Karen Walls business Dar Armateaux had confided to her. She did not need reinforcements for that. The Sex Queen of the Soaps had battled with those bozos before and always come out smelling like bubble bath. Haven't you, Stevie? Stevie asked herself, her self-doubt as usual lagging a step and a half behind her self-confidence.

Half a block ahead, a Grand Prix pulled away from the curb. She took it as an omen, a parking spot on a block that was bumper-to-bumper cars on both sides of the street.

About three minutes later, Stevie stood on Edward Grizzard's porch, knocking on his door, the one closest to a narrow driveway that ended about twenty yards back at an open, empty one-car garage. The penciled slip in the name slot of the empty mailbox told her she had the right place.

No answer.

She knocked harder.

Still unable to rouse anyone, Stevie moved closer to the opaque windowpane in the door and used her hand as a sun shield connecting the glass to her forehead.

From what she could make out inside, no one was home.

Stevie stepped back and was turning to leave when she noticed a folded paper stuck in the door jam. Printed on the front in a precise script was the name "Chip Kiley."

She looked around to see if anyone was watching her. No one. She eased the paper from its perch, checked again over her shoulders before opening the paper. It had been folded in quarters.

The message inside, in the same hand, said, "If you come by and see this, I'm still out taking care of our business, so either come again later on or make yourself at home. The door's unlocked. Beer in the fridge. Save one for me so we can celebrate proper. Eddie."

Stevie gave the old-fashioned cut-glass knob a full turn and pushed on the door. It glided open and she hurried inside, closing the door behind her. She refolded the note and looked around for someplace to put it, where she'd remember to replace it when she was ready to leave.

Of course. Back in the door jamb.

The side of the door inside the house.

Stevie draped the strap of her tote bag over her head, so the strap hung over her chest with the bag under her left arm. It was a trick she'd learned a long time ago, to discourage the grab-and-run snatchers. Here it gave her faster access to her .32 Colt, not that she expected to need it.

A fast look around, that's all she wanted.

See what there was to see, find what there was to find, if anything, and get out. Find something tying Edward Grizzard to her suspicions, no, her *belief* that he had been James Dean's accomplice, and come back later with the cops.

The place was clean and well-kept, old furniture that emitted a musty odor that seemed to fit the lived-in look. A strong hint of what Stevie recognized as pot layered on the drapes.

The kitchen behind the dining room was oversized. Plenty of cupboard space. A gas stove that might have been made before Sears met Roebuck. Except for a few dishes in the sink, neat and orderly. In the fridge, as advertised, a six-pack of beer, two cans missing. Linoleum well-scrubbed and glistening, a cousin to the spotless rugs and highly polished wood floors elsewhere.

Up the hallway, a small bathroom, nothing out of place. Shower curtain drawn across the tub. The tub, clean. A modest water rumble from the toilet. A leak to be looked at before it became a major problem? Towels tidily folded and stacked on a wooden shelf next to the medicine cabinet. Nothing in the cabinet that did not belong. Shaving stuff. Six kinds of aftershave and cologne. A cuticle cutter. A bottle of aspirin, double-strength. Brown vials with labels from a RiteAid, with capsules and pills for allergies and asthma, the labels made out to Edward Grizzard.

Behind the next door, a small bedroom.

A queen-sized bed, made; a colorful quilt covered with a dozen or more pillows in various sizes and shapes. A six-drawer dresser, clothing neatly organized and arranged. A small closet. Everything on metal hangers. Three sports coats. Three pair of matching and contrasting trousers. A lot of pressed jeans and casual jackets. A number of caps on the shelf, in a neat row face forward, advertising rock-and-roll stars, Stevie supposed, because most of the names were unfamiliar to her. She knew the Stones tongue symbol, of course. Sir Elton. The Eagles. Springsteen.

Back in the hallway, reaching for the next door handle, she found herself wondering if Edward Grizzard was the clean freak or if there was a cleaning person. If the latter, maybe Grizzard would give her the name and address before the cops carted him off to jail. Her cleaning person was her sixth in the last eight months, since Consuelo went back to Brazil, and as bad as the others, possibly a little worse. The place seemed dustier after Maria finished, as if she brought a fresh supply of dust with her.

Stevie pushed open the door and was startled by what she saw. This may have been the master bedroom at one time, but now it was a shrine—

To James Dean.

Where the walls elsewhere were practically bare, except for an amorphous framed picture or a doodad, hardly an inch was uncovered here.

Impeccably arranged, clearly showing an artistic eye at work, were photos of Dean, posters of Dean, posters of Dean movies, stills from Dean movies, rarer stills from his early Broadway and TV appearances, oddities like sheet music covers, songs about him with Dean's picture on them, one, "The Ballad of James Dean," memorializing his death. Two Dean lithographs by Andy Warhol were hung side by side on the wall opposite the door, even more opulently framed than the posters and pictures.

On a pedestal in one corner was a bronze copy of the Dean bust Stevie remembered from outside the Griffith Park Observatory, when she was filming that network movie for ABC, *Revenge of the Park Monsters*. Smaller bronzes that appeared to be the work of the same artist strategically placed elsewhere.

A bookshelf was filled with biographies of Dean, volume upon volume, the biographies of costars that would not have been complete without some reference to Dean. The index boxes contained old magazines with Dean on the cover, hundreds of them from overseas.

The brilliant track lighting overhead had all of its spotlight boxes trained to give everything in the room an equal prominence, as if proclaiming no aspect of James Dean's life or career took a back seat to any other aspect.

Stevie wandered the room like a museum visitor, counterclockwise around the plush armchair on a swivel base in the middle of the room. Seeing. Touching. Feeling.

Her reaction constantly moved from simple amazement to an almost dumbfounding disbelief.

So engrossed she didn't hear any of the sounds that might have told her someone had entered the house or that he was standing behind her, until a dry wheeze of a lung-clearing cough startled her into spinning around.

She knew it was Edward Grizzard staring back at her with volcanic eyes, because—

His was the face in the computer photo made by Ron Pipes from her description.

He was the boyish James Dean in all the photos in this room.

Except, unlike the photos, he was for real and he had a gun aimed straight at her.

Old habits die hard.

After listening to the motorist put in the 911 call, I swiped away his cell phone and, stepping away from his protests, I tapped in the direct number to the Metro desk, at the same time directing other motorists who'd come out of their cars to gawk to be useful—a jacket, anything, to make sure the victims on the ground were warm.

TV news may have the monopoly on fast-breaking stories, but for the second time in less than two weeks it didn't have what I had, a first-person eyewitness account of a shooting.

Litrov answered with his name and, while I took another distressed look at Augie and the cop, uncertain if either or both were still alive, I briefed him on what had happened.

He quickly linked me to McCracken on rewrite, who pumped my dictation into the computer while Litrov watched the story unfold on his monitor half a room away from him, jotting down facts and omissions that would need checking out once I signed off, like a positive ID on the cop.

There was plenty of time for a remake of page one of tomorrow's first edition, the evening bulldog that gets shipped to the farthest reaches of the *Daily*'s circulation, places like Long Beach, San Pete, Vegas, and Frisco.

When I finished, Litrov came back on the line to tell me a photog was five minutes away and to wonder about Augie.

The sound of approaching ambulances grew louder above the normal Civic Center din. I capped an ear against the deafening noise of two news choppers already circling overhead and shouted into the cell phone, "Augie's not so good. Pulse was failing, so it's either plasma or prayer."

"You holding up okay?"

"Hell, no."

"I'll call up his obit and see if it needs any freshening, also have ready our best piece of art on him."

"Gee, that makes me feel better already."

Litrov ignored my sarcasm. "The one when he took those Press Club honors?"

"Only if you retouch his bloodshot eyes. Better to go with something Brother Kalman-ish."

"I think a suit and tie for the send-off, Neil, instead of the costume."

"Then stop thinking, Al. Just go with something Brother Kalman-ish, okay?"

"Okay, okay," Litrov said, a scarred veteran of knowing when not to argue with me.

"Thank you. . . . You need me for anything else?"

"No, I— Oh, wait. A question. Did the ID and address on that license plate number work out for you?"

The question caught me short. "Say that again?"

Litrov thought I had hadn't heard him because of the choppers and raised his voice. "The plate Stevie called in, I said. I said, did the ID and address work out?"

He read my silence correctly. "She scammed me? Why would she scam me like that?"

I took a deep breath, because I was pretty sure I knew why. The driver of the black Honda. Somehow she'd come up with another plate number.

"Al, you still have the name and address?"

"Yeah. Hold on." It took him a minute and I had my pen out. "Hey, Neil. A computer screwing up the works. Give me a number I can call you back in five."

I didn't know the number.

The owner of the cell phone was out of his car and hounding me from a foot away. I asked him for the cell number. He scowled and suggested I shove it where the sun don't shine.

I told Litrov I'd call him, disconnected, and told the driver to shut up. Please. To please shut up. I had another call to make.

Stevie's service picked up on the second ring.

No call-ins from her.

No messages left behind for me.

No idea where she was.

I twitched a smile at the cell owner and raised an index finger to signal one more call. He was a big guy, beefy, and had a genuine case of road rage building on his saggy-jawed face.

Afraid he was about to yank the phone, I faked a forward pass with it. The old kid's trick. As he pirouetted to see where it would hit, I fled in the opposite direction and was safely locked inside the Jag before he could reach me.

I tapped in my private number.

Lots of messages from Stevie on the machine.

Three of them confirmed she had a fresh lead on the driver of the Honda, a name and an address on two of them, but both times she neglected to give me either. Her final message advised me she was heading off to check him out, complained it was my fault she had to go there alone. She didn't explain how it was my fault or where there was.

My heart was doing a rumba.

She had said to try her on her cell phone.

I tapped in the number.

All circuits busy.

The cell phone owner was shouting at me through the side window and pounding on the glass.

I tapped in the Metro number, got a busy signal, waited thirty seconds and tried again. Another busy signal.

I tried Stevie's cell phone again.

All circuits busy.

The cell owner was wrapped around the windshield, looking uglier, spittle dressing the corners of his mouth.

I hit the redial button.

Litrov answered with his name, verified it was me, and gave me the name and address he had earlier given to Stevie. I scribbled them onto the back of a gas receipt sitting in the drink cup well.

Grizzard. Edward.

A street I didn't know.

"Somewhere over in the Wilshire district," he said. "You carrying your Thomas?"

"Hold on." I opened the glove and got lucky. The map book was there. I checked the street index and flipped to the page and grid. A few blocks northwest of the Wiltern Theater, on the hem of Korea Town.

The cell phone owner was getting ready to kick a souvenir dent into my fender. I pushed open the door and jumped out, slapped the cell shut and straight-armed it at him with a warning that offset my fake smile.

He knew the look. His foot dropped to the ground. "Thanks," he said, contritely, and dropped the cell into a shirt pocket.

"You're welcome," I said, turned and raced over to Augie and the cop. Under their jacket blankets, neither showed any signs of life.

The ambulances were just arriving.

I settled onto my knees beside Augie.

Felt for a pulse. Ants do better.

Fumbled around until I found the cassock pocket in which he'd put my Beretta and slipped it into my jacket pocket.

Whispered in his ear, "Gotta see an ex about a man, but I'll be back, kiddo. Hang in there." I thought I saw his eyes flicker, the edges of his mouth do a little dance. It may have been my imagination. I leaned over and kissed him on the forehead. Too cold. Too cold.

16

It took me twenty minutes of city driving to get to the
address, slowed down by construction sites that cut off
lanes on sections of Wilshire Boulevard streets that
rise and dip like a shallow roller coaster. Apartment
high-rises almost buried the old duplex and I might
have driven past it, but I saw Stevie's Jeep parked up
the block, then something that made my heart stop—

A Cougar parked in the driveway.

The creep who shot Augie and the cop got away in a
Cougar, same color or close, but too fast for me to
catch a number, only that the plate was out of state—

Like this one.

I shook it off as coincidence.

There had to be hundreds of Cougars with out-of-
state plates around.

The street looked like a parking lot and I didn't have
time to be smart, so I pulled into the driveway behind
the car.

Checked the Cougar's hood.

Still warm.

Approaching the porch, I patted my pocket for the Beretta and tried to slow down the million thoughts racing through my mind. The best way inside? What would I find in there? Stevie? The mugger? Stevie with the mugger? Stevie alive or dead?

Stevie harmed in any way and, even if it were my last act, I'd have him on the Dead Man's Express.

I turned the knob, gave the door a gentle push. Locked. I retreated silently down the steps and around to the rear of the duplex, my heart and my head pounding like a drum duet by Gene Krupa and Buddy Rich.

The service porch door was locked.

I retraced my steps, methodically checking out the windows. All locked. Do a 911, was it down to that? Was there enough time to get a couple squad cars here on silent alarm to get Stevie out of harm's way, or was it already too late for that? Get them how, Neil? Where's your cell phone? At the apartment, of course, in the desk drawer with the pager, still your way of telling the Spider Woman what you think about her old demand you keep them both with you at all times during working hours, as if you were a dog who barked on command. I made a mental note to move them to the trunk. I'd still be making my point, only my way. Yeah, Neil, so what did that mean now? Here? For Stevie?

I rounded the corner to find her standing on the front porch, hugging herself tightly against a chill that wasn't in the air, but I saw it in her stare, fixed across the street and past the apartments, as if she were looking for flying saucers.

The door was open behind Stevie. I took out the Beretta and, hanging my arm by my side with the gun behind my thigh, approached her cautiously.

My Nike caught in one of the sprinkler heads on the

perfectly manicured lawn and made enough of a noise to get her attention.

Stevie turned in my direction, in slow motion, saw who it was, and smiled gratefully. "Hi, daddy," she said, her voice as flat as a coin. "You hear me thinking about you? I left messages, too. A lot."

My eyes alternated between Stevie and the door.

"You okay, babe?" I asked calmly, trying not to betray my uneasiness. I took another two steps toward her.

"Not really, daddy, but better now that you're here." I moved the Beretta, hoping she'd notice, and send me a clue. She noticed and shifted her head left and right. Animated a hitchhiker's thumb over her shoulder. "Go on in and see for yourself."

"You're all right?"

"Yes, come on," she said, holding out her hand for me to take, and led me inside. I kept the gun ready, not happy that she was between me and whomever might be waiting with his own weapon.

Stevie guided me down a hallway to a room at the back. The door was open and she stood aside and ushered me in with a "you go first" gesture.

Nothing about her spoke to danger.

Nevertheless, I signaled her out of the way and, after Stevie had stepped back, twirled around and into the doorway with my elbows locked, the Beretta ready to shoot anything that moved.

Staring back at me were a pair of Warhol lithos of Dean and, in the next moment, I thought I could be back at Top's Diner in Newhall, only this was more than a James Dean museum. It was the Louvre of James Dean museums.

My eyes swept the room as I stepped inside.

The body was just to my left, invisible from the doorway. Sitting on the floor, the period at the end of an exclamation point made by his blood as he slid down a wall he must have been using for support. More blood stained his shirt and the floor. His chin rested on his chest. His eyes were open and seemed to be looking at a poster of *Giant*. He held a gun in his right hand, and I supposed it was the one he had used in the past hour.

Everything had happened too fast then for me to get a real look at him, but that was no problem now.

He might be the mugger. Might be Edward Grizzard.

He most certainly was the reincarnation of James Dean, and as dead as Dean had ever been.

"You do this, Stevie?"

"What?" Her mind seemed to be wandering.

"Him," I said, using the Beretta as a pointer.

She shook her head. "He said he was going to kill me. Aimed the gun. I believed him. No way I could get yours out of my bag before he fired. I closed my eyes and said a prayer. . . . Nothing happened. I don't know for how long. So, I peeked and he was sliding down the wall, watching me watch him as he slid down to where he is. He could of killed me and I was not ready to die, daddy. I. Was. Not. Ready. To. Die."

Stevie, stripped bare of her braggadocio, seemed about to wilt. Her tears were flowing freely. I stepped to her. Took her in my arms. Reassured her. It wasn't enough. She pressed tighter, clung to me like a life preserver and pushed her perfect lips against mine, hard, harder, making noises that were little sighs and cries at the same time.

I felt no passion, only her need to be rescued, protected, and I didn't mind; I always relished whatever brought us together. I minded that there was no permanence to our togetherness and maybe never would be again. Maybe? I offered a sign to the truth my mind would never accept. Take whatever you can get, Neil. Take whatever you can get.

We stood like that for about five minutes before I guided her into the lone armchair sitting in the middle of the room like one of those leather loge seats they used to offer at a higher price in the old movie theaters.

My baby needed to be out of here, but there were things I had to do first.

I went over to the body and carefully felt for a wallet. He was carrying it in the inside zipper pocket of his windbreaker. Sixty dollars in fresh twenties, the kind that roll out of an ATM. Plastic flip holders filled mostly with photos. Two credit cards, American Express and Visa. A valid California driver's license, expiring in two years. A little black telephone book tucked inside a card slot, full of names and addresses.

Impulsively, I dropped the little black book and a couple other items into my jacket pocket before replacing the wallet.

Stevie's handbag was on the floor where she must have been standing when Grizzard surprised her. I picked it up and dug out her cell phone.

The call to the Metro desk sailed right through the system this time.

Litrov answered with his name.

"Can we still make the bulldog, Al?"

"Oh, hi, Neil. Tight, but maybe. First street for sure. What's up? You find that address okay?"

I gave him a quick summary and heard him humming laughter by my third sentence, as close as Litrov ever came to shouting "Stop the presses!" He was too reserved for that, a professorial type who looked a lot like Michael Douglas and dressed the part, always in a fresh starched shirt and tie he never wore open at the collar.

"Hold it there until I plug in rewrite," he said. "I'm also going to voice you onto the main frame, so talk it slow and clear, Gully."

"One other thing, Al."

"If it's another corpse, please save it for the home edition." Litrov was beginning to sound like Michael Douglas.

"A piece of computer art Ron Pipes did for me last week. Call it up. It's something you'll want to use."

"Minute." He was back in two. "James Dean? What don't I get?"

"That's the face that goes with the body on the floor here."

He thought about it. "This story tie to our Post Office Poltergeist?"

"Too early to say," I said, lying.

"The guy you were checking out? Grizzard?"

"Yes and no," I said.

"What's that supposed to mean?"

"Means you might want to hold off on a positive ID until you hear it from the cops," I said, not exactly lying again.

The faxed copy of the newspaper story wasn't the best. It didn't have to be for Jimmy to understand Eddie was dead, killed by a police officer while in the act of attempted robbery. Somehow managed to flee the scene and drag himself home to die.

The story didn't identify Eddie. It said the cops were in the process of determining that, but Jimmy knew for certain. The fax copy was good enough for him to recognize Eddie in the photograph.

He had watched the photograph come through and knew at once what the story would say, even before he read the headline or the details through eyes racked by sorrow. Eddie had committed some foolish error and it had cost him his life.

Jimmy went about his business the rest of the day, applying his usual grins and smiles, pretending noth-

ing had happened to destroy his peace and contentment, a large part of what little life was left to him.

He mourned Eddie in his heart, where Eddie always
had been and would stay forever. When he was where
no one could see him, he let himself be consumed by
the anger he felt toward that Neil Gulliver.

The cops thought the shooting had to do with a
mugging, but Jimmy knew better, better than the cops
and better than Gulliver, whose tawdry little story portrayed Eddie as just another John Doe good-for-
nothing whose luck had run out.

As if that rotten column he wrote about James Dean
had not been enough to add his death to the list. He
had to go and pick on Eddie, too.

Well, Neil Gulliver, Jimmy said to a sky brimming
with rain clouds, Eddie is dead, but the death warrant
on you is still alive.

Jimmy took consolation in the fact Augie Fowler
and the cop were also dead.

At least, Eddie went out two for one.

When Jimmy took care of Neil Gulliver personally,
it would be three for one, and it would not end there.

There was a lot of other unfinished business.

Chip Kiley called after dinner, while Jimmy was banging out his anger and sorrow on the bongo, to check on
him and also to be certain he had received the fax.
Jimmy thanked him for his concern and they spoke a
while about what had to be done, especially about
Gulliver.

"He's the spit on Eddie's soul, Chipper, and we
have to wipe him clean away, send him to the same
hell as Augie Fowler."

"About that, Jimmy. Not dead, Augie. Leastwise, not
yet. Him and the cop, too, both still hanging on by a
thread. I heard it on the six o'clock, another reason

I'm calling. Heard it was the cop's bullet that got Ed-die. Only repeating it because you'll hear about it soon enough."

The news struck him like a mule kick in the head. His throat went dry. It took a minute before he could speak again. *"Then I'm on my way there, first plane out. Not going to let Eddie go unavenged."*

"Bad idea, Jimmy."

"I'm listening."

"Think about it. Cops still hot on the Mercouri thing and sooner or later bound to identify Eddie, probably connect him to it. Eddie's memorial room will point them in the right direction. After that, who knows what else is out there can lead straight to you."

"And also to you, Chipper?"

"Sure, me, too, Jimmy, but not the point."

They went round and round a while longer, but Jimmy recognized Chip's reasoning was correct and finally told him so.

Chip sighed audibly into the phone.

Jimmy said, *"Maybe it won't be tomorrow, Chipper, but I'm not giving you any lifetime guarantees."*

"The one I already he got from you is good enough for me, Jimmy." Like he meant it, and of course he did, while already he was thinking how he'd want to check plane schedules first thing in the morning.

Go for that Saturday overnight discount and save himself a bundle on top of his discount. Couple more trips and he'd be flying for nothing on his Frequent Flyer miles.

Three days after the shooting, I got a call from Harry Chalk. His voice meant nothing to me, sounding like a cider-vinegar dressing, sweet with a touch of tartness, but his name caught my full attention. I hadn't had a chance to chase after him, yet here he was on the office number, onto me, and my first thought was, No coincidence. I didn't want Chalk to know that, so I played my end like I knew him only by his reputation. He fell right in with it.

"Where do you know from talent agents?" he said, suspiciously, maybe thinking I was putting him on, the way a lot of old people mistrust anyone who's younger by more than five or ten years.

"Student of the movies," I said, "and I've met a lot of show business people over the years. Interviewed a lot of them for my column."

"Like who?"

You know how it is sometimes when a question is put to you that you'd normally have no trouble answering? Your mind goes blank. His question threw me off balance. I tried covering by telling Chalk, "People you know, but of course you knew everyone in your time."

"They all knew me and be advised, Mr. Gulliver, that it's still my time until I decide otherwise," Chalk snapped, conjuring up memories of Norma Desmond. He caught himself and said, "But this call isn't about me. Go on and name some names."

I made thinking noises for about twenty seconds and then the memory pipe mercifully unplugged. I gave him a name. Three or four more. Another couple. Stopped, figuring my credentials were established.

Chalk had yeah-yeahed me after each of the names. He stepped into the break to declare proudly, "Shtupped her, Laura Dane. Couple others you mention, a laundry list, you want to know the truth. She was a hooker before she was a star, you know that?" I pretended I didn't. He lowered his voice and dropped some history like it was a state secret, then confessed, "Most of them gone from the business, not like me, but all my calls still go through. Quite a stud once upon a . . . still get it up without Viagra, if you catch my drift. Not all the time, but enough."

I threw out several other names, took a chance and dropped Chip Kiley into the mix, to test his reaction. If Chalk thought I was after something, he didn't let on.

"Mick, still a client. And Chip. Loyal. Both of them. Know if there's anyone keeps their best interests in mind, it's Harry Chalk. Why the phone's always ringing here and a shame I can't take on more clients than I do. Time is money, though, and I tell most of them, If I don't have the time, neither of us can make a dime . . . which is why I called you, Neil. All right I call you Neil?"

"Sure."

"Feel like I know you, Neil, reading your column often enough over the years. Call me Harry. You have a way with words, Neil. Clean and crisp as a winter's night. Easy to swallow, like the finest bubbly. Dom Perignon. Cristal." He carried on like this a bit longer, buttering me up, for what I didn't know, plying his trade with the same kind of skill a veteran boxer needs to outfox his younger, quicker opponent. "So, let me get to the point, Neil."

"Okay, Harry."

"Neil, I truly believe we can make some beautiful moola together, a few dimes for me, but ninety cents on the dollar for you. Lots and lots of dollars here, Neil, yours for the plucking—with me under the money tree showing you where the best branches are."

I couldn't believe what I was hearing. "Harry, you want to be my agent?"

He did a ta-dum. "You won't be my first writer client, but you can wind up richer, more famous than the rest of them combined."

"If you've been reading my column, why now, why all of a sudden?"

"Not so all of a sudden at all, just that now you have struck a commercial mother lode. I would be lying if I didn't say so and if you haven't already heard it from some other agent it only shows to go you how here, like always, I, Harry Chalk, am ahead of the field."

"What am I missing, Harry?"

"You creative talents," he said mockingly. "All alike. Never see the potential in the outer limits of their creativity. . . . Your stories since Tuesday? They got all the elements it takes for Boffoville on the big screen, and that's even before we pretty up the package with an A-list director like Bobby Wise—he was the film editor on *Kane,* you know that?—and openers like a Travolta or Tommy Hanks, although I hear Travolta is booked the next four years, so it probably would mean Tommy, but I don't want to trap you into thinking I can do an automatic with Tommy, you know?"

"I can't see Tom Hanks as a murderer," I said, playing along, wondering where Chalk was heading with the conversation.

"Of course not," he said, implying by his tone how clever I was to understand that. "Tommy Hanks is our Neil Gulliver."

I moved the phone away from my face. It was all I could do to keep from laughing. "I don't think I heard you correctly, Harry."

"You most certainly did, and— Minute, Neil. My other line." I could almost picture him counting off the beats. "A callback from Jimmy Cameron I've been waiting on, Neil. Big, big, big, so look— How about us finishing this later? Meet somewhere for a drink or coffee?"

I had been looking for an opening that would let me move the conversation to the same idea. As much or more than figuring I could get to Chip Kiley through him, I had something to shove under Chalk's face that might be the key to the entire Dean puzzle, a more direct route to Dean than even Kiley.

"Name it, Harry," I said.

Lupe's Golden Enchilada was a take-out joint too small to qualify as a hole in the wall, a half block east of Hollywood and Vine, across from the Pantages Theater, currently between shows, its iron gate pulled across the entrance to keep the walking wounded from using it as an overnight refuge. I arrived about twenty minutes late for our seven-thirty meeting, caught in a freeway snarl on the drive from the County-USC Med Center, and parked the Jag in the metered pay lot behind the Red Line subway station on Argyle, at the end of the block.

I cut across the street-level plaza smiling at the décor at this stop, as camp as a drag queen's wardrobe. Replicas of the old Brown Derby restaurant, the roof of the Chinese Theater, and a white stretch limo sat on top of the pedestrian shelters. A yellow brick road of tile started a twist down a stairway to the mezzanine level. The station's roof lined with actual reels of 35-millimeter film, painted blue. In all, the reality of the unreal, near a crossroads that once marked the film capital of the world and now was the center of an area that needed a miracle to go with the Chamber of Commerce's revitalization efforts.

A warm breeze from the east had washed the sky clean and the exposed full moon worked like a spotlight on the dirt and debris of the building facades, the sidewalk, and the gutter.

I was feeling great about Augie. He was still under heavy sedation but had been taken off the hospital's "critical" list during the dinner rounds. He'd roused a few times without opening his eyes, and I had made my customary threats about what would happen to him if Augie let me down and died, before slipping out, stopping to whisper a couple words of encouragement at the cop in the next ICU bed, who was laboring for his life under a mess of support systems.

I stood in Lupe's doorway acclimating my eyes to the gloomy interior lighting that made it impossible to recognize anyone sitting at a dozen or so tables taking up all the limited space across from the order counter.

The smell of Mexican dishes saturated in grease permeated the air, reminding me I hadn't eaten dinner and touching off my taste buds. A desire for a chicken and bean burrito. A bowl of chili topped with fresh-cut onions and tomatoes, a dollop of shredded cheese. A bottle of ice-cold *cerveza* to wash it all down.

"Neil, that you?" Harry Chalk's sweet and sour voice came at me from behind. I twisted at the waist to see him standing half in and half out the street. Looking at least ten years younger than his age. Sparse white hair on a withered, weatherbeaten face pushed back and falling just below the collar of his gray silk turtleneck sweater. Blue tinted lenses obscuring his eyes. Blue jeans tapered and tailored to further show off a remarkably fit physique on a frame about five-six or five-seven. A thick black wool jacket draped over the crook of his right arm, which he pressed against his chest like he was saluting the flag.

Only, if he was Harry Chalk, what was he doing on his feet? Where was his motorized wheelchair? Where was any of the Harry Chalk Augie described to me only days ago?

For certain, he wasn't here with me now at Lupe's Golden Enchilada, but I was pretty certain I knew who was. I grinned back at him like I didn't know any different and called him by name.

"Harry!"

"Didn't mean to be tardy, Neil, sorry," he said, extending his left arm for a Hollywood handshake.

Showing two rows of too-perfect teeth permanently stained yellow from too much nicotine. "Traffic coming in over the Pass."

"You live in the valley, Harry?" I said to make pleasant conversation.

"Brentwood, but my office it's there. I moved to the valley when the industry did, all but Columbia or Sony or whatever they call the place now. To me it'll always be Metro, of course. Metro-Goldwyn-Mayer." Saying it like I might not have known. "They used to brag about 'More Stars Than in Heaven,' and a load of them were signed to me. . . . You hungry?"

Before I could answer, he nudged me aside and had a look inside, deciding, "Too busy, no privacy. They make a hell of a tamale, but maybe we should go somewhere else for our chat. Somewhere with a little more elbow room. . . . A great Sizzler is about a mile from here, at Western, what do you say?" His bushy white eyebrows humped above his glasses.

Chalk was trying not to sound as suspicious as he sounded, and I figured to myself he had more in mind for me than an all-you-can-eat buffet.

"Sure, Harry, why not?" I said, thinking how to best handle the situation, throwing my best Steve McQueen side-of-the-mouth grin at him.

He said, "Where you parked? I'm next door, right on over there." Pointing. "Behind the Taft Building."

"MTA lot."

"Play piggyback with our cars or, say, how would it be, the subway? Get off at Western and hike the block up for the exercise. Especially after we're done chowing down, too, the way I always pack it in at the Sizzler."

I turned a "why not?" palm up, knowing to go down into the subway with him this time of night was about as smart as a stroll through South Central.

We moved out to the sidewalk and Chalk slipped

into his jacket while we fell into a side-by-side step and, picking this as my Moment of Truth, I snapped my fingers wondering, "Hey, Harry! Maybe better than you and me taking the subway . . . maybe we both can fit in your wheelchair, ride down in that?"

He stopped short, looking over his shoulder at me, and burst out laughing like he'd just heard the joke of the year, until he recognized in my expression that I knew who he wasn't.

I said, "Who are you really, Harry? Chip Kiley? That's my first guess."

It must have been the right one.

He hesitated on a thought, then knocked me aside using both hands and took off down Hollywood Boulevard in the direction of the subway.

17

Chip Kiley was quicker on his feet than anyone his age had a right to be.

I needed barely an instant to regain my balance and chase after him, but he was already ten yards ahead of me. He reached the subway station's yellow brick road, stopped sharply, and in one motion wheeled around and pulled a handgun from his jacket. Got off a quick shot that passed my ear, near enough for me to hear it above the blast; hit something behind me that shattered like storefront glass.

I froze and the world went slow motion as Kiley adjusted himself sideways and took a sharpshooter's aim at me. I dove for the pavement and did a body roll. His second shot flew harmlessly overhead and more glass shattered.

He repositioned and took more careful aim.

I cursed myself for leaving my Beretta in the trunk of the Jag. Who knew? Did another body roll as the third shot thwapped into the cement where I had just been and threw out a gray dust cloud.

A pedestrian shelter five feet away was my only bet. I leaped to my feet and aimed for it.

Kiley's next shot sailed by me into the shelter pole, which I hit running, blind with desperation.

I managed to do a quick wheel to safety in front of his fifth shot, greeting a side of the pole he couldn't see, like an old lover. Tried to reason myself out of the situation before Kiley shot any of my ideas full of holes, me along with them.

It got too quiet all of a sudden and I dared a peek. I saw a flash of Kiley's back disappearing down the yellow brick road. Finished catching my breath.

Once again abandoning basic common sense and good judgment, I took off after him. My squeaky Nikes answered the echoes of his racing steps, until I stumbled. Tripped. Did a body-banging twist and slide down fifteen or twenty steps to the mezzanine.

Allowed a moment to groan and verify nothing was broken, then amazed myself with how quickly I sprang up and resumed the chase through winding corridors decorated with hand-painted wall tile tributes to Hollywood history, past a dozen or so commuters heading out, all of them eyeing me with apprehension.

Otherwise, the subway was eerily empty.

Chip Kiley nowhere in sight.

Ahead, a train readying to leave.

A uniformed station guard holding up a post, his face buried in a paperback.

I leaped on board the rear compartment seconds before the doors slid shut and cut off the guard's angry "Hey, you!" shouts. The compartment was empty. Something made me glance out a window as the train began moving. It was a pinpoint of light from one of the overheads bouncing off a gun barrel.

Kiley was standing on the platform, giving me a look that said we'd meet again.

I wasn't armed.

He was.

He knew where I'd parked my car, not that it was a Jag, but that would not prevent him from staking out the MTA lot and having another go at me later.

Deciding I'd been enough of a target tonight and it was somebody else's turn, I took the subway to Western and Hollywood Boulevard, where decorative granite tiles on the walls and floors of the station showed a camel's tooth, the toe of a prehistoric horse, a remnant of some mastodon, and other clues to creatures that supposedly roamed these streets before there were streets, before there was a here here.

Stevie lived about ten minutes away. I found a phone and called her. Told her about Kiley. What I had in mind. What to bring. She said give her a half hour. That meant forty-five minutes, if I got lucky.

Over the last few days, Stevie had pretty much shaken off the stupor that develops when you think you're staring down certain death, as it appeared she was when Edward Grizzard came home, before she saw that role being played by Grizzard himself.

At first she had seemed almost embarrassed by the way she had behaved when I found her, as if revealing any fragility at all was somehow sinful. It definitely was not how she had behaved at the post office, when she got almost too brave for her own good. At Blackwell's Corner, when she stared down the two cretins with robbery and rape on their minds. Not being able to fathom what caused the difference troubled her. She made noises like she wanted my opinion on one of our trips to the County-USC Med Center to see Augie.

"Obvious," I said. "Both of those times you had an audience to play to."

"Rat." Stevie punched my arm and pushed her lips into a pout. "Honey, I know you don't really believe that. Tell me."

"You won't like it."

"Try me."

"The mother instinct both times. With Nico. With me. You weren't thinking about yourself. This week, looking down that gun barrel, you had no one to protect and no one else to think about but yourself, so you could."

"That's it?"

"That's it."

Stevie went quiet, pretending like she was more interested in the passing scenery than in what I had said, for about five minutes, when I could almost see the bulb turn on in the cartoon balloon above her head.

"That was a compliment, wasn't it, honey?"

"Disguised as the truth," I said.

She touched a finger to her lip and pressed it against my cheek. "I love you, Neil."

"I love you, too."

"Don't ever let us get married again, okay?"

"What, and ruin a good thing?"

I waited for her at an all-night hamburger stand cater-corner from the station, wolfing down a half pound of grease on a bun and a side of deadly fries, in a cramped patio enclosed by iron bars, maybe to make the locals feel at home.

Street people, some of them pushing their life in shopping carts, strolled in all directions, heading from nowhere to nowhere, except for a few who had found decent doorways to settle in for the night.

Hookers wearing more skin than scanty shorts and halter tops were hanging out near the bus benches, except for the pair at the next picnic table, competing for a john who'd just moseyed in from the sex shop next door carrying videos and some magazines in a wrinkled brown grocery bag.

A table away from them were two uniforms, who belonged to the patrol car parked out front, both recent kindergarten graduates, one female, probably Korean, one male, Hispanic, ignoring everything but their coffees and each other, sliding fingertips at one another.

The horn honking made everyone else look up.

Stevie's Jeep Cherokee.

Stevie leaning out the window.

Motioning for me.

The hooks continued working subtle hand magic on the john, and gave her a high sign without missing a beat.

A bench bum in a Swiss-cheese sweater jumped up and shook an angry fist at her.

I sucked up the last two fries and moments later was fastening my seat belt and giving Stevie directions to Harry Chalk's home.

She leaned over and touched my face.

"Sure you're okay? You look like you've been cleaning up after the elephants."

"There's a reason for that. . . . Were you able to reach Jimmy Steiger?"

"At County Med, yeah. Jimmy said I and you should not worry about Augie. He's watching him personally for now and he'll trade off later when DeSantis gets back from Paso Robles. Also to thank you for asking, that Sherlock's getting better and stronger. Poor sweet little doggie . . . How come you didn't tell me DeSantis was going up to Paso Robles, honey?"

"It was when you still weren't in the mood for conversation."

"I knew it was only a matter of time, he couldn't resist seeing that Audrey Sue again. I knew it, I knew it." Unbridled glee, not for DeSantis, for the guess she assumed was correct.

"Her name is Audrey Mae."

"Audrey Mae, Audrey Sue. Same difference. Enough sparks were flying between them to torch Rome. . . . I think our street is coming up soon, right?"

"Right, only you'll turn left. Lockland. Another two blocks after the next signal." We were driving west on Melrose, just passing La Brea, an area with a heavy Jewish population, a synagogue on almost every block, store signs in Yiddish and Hebrew.

I remembered the street because it had come up once in a column I did about the area, quoting a rabbi who told me, "Given the people who live here, maybe better the street should be named Loxland?"

Lox, the Yiddish term for smoked salmon. A joke that could be taken as anti-Semitic coming from a gentile. I actually got a few pieces of hate mail—and one marriage proposal.

Chalk's place was in the middle of the block, a single-story Spanish villa with red tile roofing, garnished with several mangy palm trees and a tall oak tree that hid most of the outside view from a giant picture window. The lawn had been bricked over to create a parking lot and an old Plymouth van rigged with a motorized chair lift sat in front of the door. A security camera guarded the entrance.

I stopped behind the van, out of camera range, while Stevie moved to the front door and rang the bell. It sounded like mission chimes summoning Zorro. Any louder and the hunchback of Notre Dame also might have come.

A voice belonging to somebody unhappy about be-

ing disturbed blasted out of the squawk box over the
mail slot.

"Go away! We don't want any."

"Mr. Chalk?"

"Mr. Chalk is dead. Go away."

"Mr. Harry Chalk of the Harry Chalk Agency?"

"Six feet under."

"My name is Stephanie Marriner. I'm an actress,
and I need to see you." No response. "I have something for you, Mr. Chalk."

Stevie held up the manila envelope she had under
her arm for the security camera to see. I was counting
on his curiosity to get him to open the door for her.

"You actresses, all alike," he growled. "Almost
ten-thirty at night. If it's from Stevie Spielberg, okay,
or even Arnie Kopelson. Quentin Tarantella, whatever the boy's name. Otherwise, your picture and resume and you're looking for representation, you call
my office tomorrow to ask for an appointment. Drop
it off." Sounding like he was the busiest agent in
town.

"It's from Edward Grizzard."

No response, then, "What was your name again?"

"Stephanie Marriner."

A pause. "The one from *Bedrooms and Board
Rooms,* and all over the news this week? Almost got
killed, found a body, something like that. Something to
do with James Dean. That one?" Stevie told him yes.
"And before that, that post office murder, right? I tell
you, dearie, I was a friend of yours, I don't want to
stand too close to you anymore."

"Mr. Chalk, with his dying breath Edward Grizzard
begged me to bring you something. I have it here."

Nothing came through the squawk box for a minute,
like Chalk was thinking. Then, "Grizzard? The dead
man?" A moment. "I don't know this Edward Grizzard, dead or alive."

He hung up on Stevie. She kept her finger on the buzzer until he answered again.

"He's only dead, Mr. Chalk, and I gave my word I'd bring you the envelope. Deliver it to you personally."

A moment. "What's inside, not that I care?"

"He gave it to me sealed and said don't look."

"You're being nice for someone who the news said wanted to kill you before he died." Suspicion entering his voice. "Too nice, I think."

"I get bonus Pearly Gate points, you never hear of that?"

Chalk laughed, and there was another noise that sounded like he was passing gas. Stevie turned toward me, away from the camera, and made a face.

"Okay, Stephanie Marriner. Delivered. Slide the envelope under the door, or put it in the mailbox. Thank you. Good night and, by the way, you're as *shaneh* here as on TV, take my word for it, only do something about your clothes, what you wear, know what I mean? The real stars never used to go out in public like you are now."

"Oh? What's wrong with how I am now?" Getting agitated. Forgetting why we're here. No, wrong about that. Stevie is looking my way, giving me a wink. She's acting. Leading him on.

"You think Crawford ever went out in public like that? Lombard? Loretta Young? Hayworth? Monroe? Dietrich? Harlow? Taste and style and mystery. Made them what they became. Big, big stars. Real stars. Movie stars. Glamorous stars. Television came along, took it all away."

She looked fine to me in a tight black crewneck tunic over a snug pair of black Capris, strap sandals, her hair pushed up under a silly white cotton cap with a floppy brim, ever-present shades resting there like headlights. Only a dab of makeup, even that more than she ever really needed with her radiant complexion. Lip blush. Some eyeliner.

Stevie stared up into the monitor, posturing and showing off her boobs—a favorite trick whenever she was playing to the cameras—while giving a nod of agreement to everything Chalk had to say.

When he sounded done, she wondered, "Mr. Chalk, do you remember Barry Nagle?"

"Where do you come off knowing Barry Nagle?"

"He was my first director on *Bedrooms and Board Rooms* and I and him became great pals. He took me under his wing and was teaching me a lot, but he had to retire after he went blind and deaf the same weekend. Something genetic, I think."

Starting to invent.

I heard it in her voice.

"Barry, poor, poor Barry. One of my oldest and dearest friends. You see him anymore? You could send him my regards for me."

"Not since his funeral. Two years ago. Almost three." Embroidering. About to take it somewhere.

"Yes, of course," he said, like he'd forgotten, but it was clear Chalk was faking it. He made a whining noise and what could have been more gas passing. "I must have been out of the country, that was it."

"Barry used to praise you to the skies, telling me Harry Chalk was absolutely the best agent in town, knew what making stars was all about, and now, just listening to you talk about glamour and stuff—I know why, Mr. Chalk."

She turned to me and dabbed a stray hair into place to shield a wink from the camera.

A symphony settled in Chalk's voice. "Made a lot of them, absolutely. . . . May I inquire if you're happy with your present agency representation, dearie?"

Stevie showed off her million-dollar smile, how much it was insured for as a publicity gimmick after she'd spent about that much with the orthodontist.

"I am, but I know in this business it never hurts to listen."

Grand opera now. "Why don't you come in, bring along the envelope, and we can chat a bit. Minute. Listen for the buzz."

Stevie shot me a victory look and, upon entering, left the door open a crack.

A minute later, I followed her inside.

A minute after that, Harry Chalk was looking up and demanding to know, "Who are you?"

He had just rolled into the living room from the hallway and was locking the brakes on his wheelchair. Had on a tatty white cotton robe, a light floral green blanket over his legs. A remote control and a cell nesting on his lap. Pulled his thick horn rims forward and backward like he was trying to get a bead on me.

"I'm a friend of Augie Fowler, Mr. Chalk, come to finish the conversation he was having with you before you disappeared while someone on your phone was threatening his life."

He picked up the cell and poised a finger over the dialing pad. "Leave at once or I'll be forced to call the police. I have nine-eleven on automatic, and it also rings straight through to my security company. See the sign out front? Armed response. They shoot first, ask questions afterward." He saw I wasn't impressed. "You are one cocky son of a bitch, aren't you?!"

"It's been said. Anyone else in the house or do you get around by yourself?"

He put down the cell, held up the remote.

"My man Godfrey, ex–Green Beret. Stays out back, room over the garage. I signal him with this, he's Johnny-on-the-spot to get rid of you, so forewarned is forearmed. He is one big mother, twice your size, Godfrey, and very, very protective of me."

"Stevie." I pointed to her bag. She dipped into it and

pulled out the Colt .32, which she aimed at Chalk. "And Ms. Marriner is very, very protective of me."

"Touché," Chalk said, replacing the remote on his lap. He pronounced it "tushy," like he knew we had his ass in a ringer.

"Where were we? Oh, yes, we were about to finish the conversation Augie Fowler began with you, about how you pulled a David Copperfield after putting Augie on the phone with someone making a nasty threat that almost came true."

Chalk shook his head vigorously, the expression on his face suggesting I was wrong about that.

He looked away from me, to Stevie.

"You certainly fooled me, dearie, worming your way into my home with that cockamamie story of yours. You are one fine actress."

He was still selling her on Harry Chalk, and she took the compliment with a gracious nod and a tight smile, slipping me an elbow in the arm and relaxing her gun hand.

Chalk looked back at me. "You're that newspaper guy, Gulliver. I recognize you from those ads on the sides of the busses, so think about getting your facts straight, fella. I did not disappear. It was toilet time. My bowels don't have earthquake insurance. When I got back, it was your friend—" Stumbling around like he couldn't remember Augie's name. "What's his . . . ? Fowler? Foul ball? Foul-up? Yeah, Fowler. Dressed like he was practicing for Halloween. He was the one who disappeared on me. Get that?"

Chalk was clearly giving me a lot of crap and I let him know I knew.

"Augie told me he went looking for you and you were not in the toilet. . . . Who were you talking to on the phone when you handed it over to him, Mr. Chalk? Was it Edward Grizzard? Chip Kiley?"

He swatted away both ideas like pesky flies. "He

looked in the wrong can, Fowler. They had to add a new one for me, the wing over, because of my fiery chariot here. He went there, he would've seen my wheels under the door. Chip is my client and up for more parts than they got at the Pep Boys store. Edward Grizzard, like I only just said to this ravishing creature here—" Chalk's smile bespoke visions of ten percent "—the name means nothing to me."

I turned to Stevie, this time holding out a hand.

"The envelope, please."

As I undid the prongs and lifted the flap, Chalk said, "And the winner is . . ." but under his false humor he could not hide his nervousness over what I might be pulling out.

He had been dry-wiping his hands constantly and now started using them as if to verify body parts while a foul smell assaulted the living room like a surprise attack by terrorists.

Stevie looked like she was trying as hard as me not to breathe, pretend the smell away, while Chalk studied us accusingly, a sure sign he was guilty of creating it.

I pulled out a set of photos, copies I'd had made from the ones I took out of Edward Grizzard's wallet before calling the cops.

Chalk's eyebrows danced expectantly as I handed them over. Looking through them, his expression did bumps and grinds and the blue veins a dance of their own through the translucent skin of his face as he pondered one photo after another.

I said, "I especially like the one of you with Edward Grizzard kneeling beside you, your arm around his shoulder. The one of him with your client, Chip Kiley, is also very nice. Look like they were taken the same time, maybe the same day? A barbecue? The background's a little blurry, but it has that feeling."

Chalk looked up, his head almost resting on his shoulder, "Notice how the camera just loves him?" he asked Stevie, talking like it was none of my business. "You have the same quality, dearie, only bigger, more colossal, and you go and waste it on a soap." He probed her with a wise eye.

Stevie flinched separating the complaint from the compliment and I said, "Judging by the look on Grizzard's face, you might say the same thing about him loving Kiley."

I had Chalk's attention again. "Don't go there, fella. Couldn't be farther. Respect and admire him, maybe, but there it ends. Eddie's as straight as a Gillette. Was."

"And also a killer. If you're following the news, you know the police have tied him to a killing in Griffith Park, a woman jogger up by the observatory, by the knife he used on Augie. Maybe another five or six murders you'll be reading about by the time they're through running checks on the knife and his .38."

Chalk shrugged. "What's it to me, except maybe, I lock into the rights, a story that sounds primo for selling to HBO or Showtime?"

"What's ten percent of accessory to murder? I'd say you're looking at twenty-five to life minimum, and that just on the Griffith Park killing, Mr. Chalk. Not even what felonies are commissionable from Chip Kiley."

Playing to Stevie. "Twenty-five to life? I don't think he's taken a good look at me. The cops guarantee me twenty-five more years of living, happy to do it. I might even confess to a few crimes they guarantee that."

If he was fazed, he didn't let it show.

He pinched the tip of his nose with a thumb and forefinger, cupped his palm over his mouth like a gas mask, and settled the arm on top of the arm now draped across his chest. Said through his fingers, "I learned a long time ago never give away free anything has a value to someone else." His eyebrows reached for the top of his head.

Chalk doing what he did best, negotiating.

Stevie understood before I did.

She motioned me to be quiet, took a deep breath through her mouth. Moved in closer and settled at an angle beside the agent. Wondered in a flirtatious whisper, "Maybe you'll do it for me?"

He studied Stevie's eyes, with a side trip to her boob, and said, "Dearie, I'll be honest, level with you. I couldn't do it now, not even with a Viagra." Reached over to graze one of them.

She didn't flinch, and I knew she was into some game. Otherwise, Stevie would have cracked him a good one, like she would anyone else. "You know what I mean, silly."

"Tell me, dearie. Let me hear it from you."

"Answer all his questions about Edward Grizzard and Chip Kiley and I'm your client, how's that sound?" She dropped the .32 back in her bag.

"Whatever I know about Eddie and Chip in exchange for you, right?" Hooking his head toward me. "And, nothing ever gets said about me being an accessory— not that I was."

"Neil?" Stevie looked at me like a drill sergeant ordering the troops to fall in.

"Not only Eddie and Chip," I said. "There's a pile of history to review, going all the way back to James Dean. Nick Adams. Sal Mineo. Natalie Wood—"

"Some looker, Nat. Prettier as she got older. And she was afraid of the water, too, you know?"

"Pier Angeli—"

"A beauty. Such a tragedy."

"I want more than your opinion, Mr. Chalk."

"Yeah, sure. The opinions I just throw in are for nothing and maybe that's what they're worth." Chalk laughed and gave Stevie's cheek a pat. Comfortable with the way the conversation was going.

"A whole lot more," she said, opening her arms to the ceiling.

Chalk nodded agreement.

I stepped up to him and swiped the photos off his lap. Rummaged through them until I found one in particular and displayed it for him.

He leaned in closer to make it out. Pushed out a sigh. Said, "Prettier than the lot, wasn't she?" but not in a way that invited argument.

I said, "Also about her. About her and the others in the picture with her."

"Kit and kaboodle," Chalk said, a trace of a smile to go with the sheen of memory racing across his eyes like a new toy. Turning back to Stevie, a bigger smile for her.

She said, "You tell him what he wants to know and Stephanie Marriner is yours, baby. The Harry Chalk Agency's newest client."

"Can I trust you?"

"I trust you, you trust me."

Their eyes locked.

"Shake on it," Chalk said, extending his hand.

She snatched it between hers, brought it to the cleft in her chest, like a gift of gratitude.

"Better," Stevie said. "I give you my word."

She glanced at me.

We traded silent understanding of the game I now recognized she had been playing with Chalk: "You give your word, but a promise is something you keep." Stevie had just borrowed from me the lesson I'd learned from Augie Fowler.

A creaking floor behind us drew our attention.

The giant in the archway was rubbing sleep from his eyes with a hand the size of a ham, the one that wasn't holding the .45 aimed at us.

He was wearing jockey briefs decorated with small red hearts and a pair of unlaced purple, green, and gold

Air Jordans. Showing off muscles that had muscles. A small face perched on a neck the size of Rhode Island.

Ominous black eyes shifting between Stevie and me while he apologized to Chalk for his delay, explaining in a rush of words, his voice a growl of regret, how he'd fallen asleep in front of the TV and only a minute or two ago woke up to see the red light flashing.

"It's okay, Godfrey, false alarm."

Godfrey studied him to be certain. Satisfied, he uncocked the hammer and threw the safety.

"You can go back to bed, Godfrey. We're closing a deal here. I'll let you know."

Godfrey tossed Stevie and me warning looks, like he was memorizing our faces just in case, and retreated in front of another air attack by Chalk, who did his nose and mouth thing again and said, "So, fella, sit. You, too, my dear, and tell Uncle Harry where you'd like him to begin."

Stevie got up and moved over to the old davenport across from Chalk, its faded floral garden pattern covered in plastic, settled down with her feet tucked under her and motioned me over. I sat down and she moved closer, pressing a thigh tightly against mine, as Chalk proposed, "Cut right to the chase, maybe?"

I shook my head.

"Take it from the top. We have all night."

"Sure, all night," he said, smiling to his ears. "Who can sleep anyway, knowing what I know I can do for my new client here."

Two days later, we were heading for James Dean's hometown, Fairmount, Indiana, closing in on more answers and, if Harry Chalk was to be believed, maybe James Dean himself.

18

Getting to Fairmount called for a Continental flight to Indianapolis, followed by about an hour's drive north on the I-69 to the SR-26. After that, it was pretty much a straight shot into town, past open patches of land broken by the kinds of aging buildings you'd expect to see in a farm community of three thousand people.

In a way it reminded me of the Jeanne Crain and Walter Brennan forties movie that's always turning up on late-night cable, *Home in Indiana,* although the Twentieth Century Fox back lot and Technicolor couldn't compete with the real late-afternoon sky hanging overhead like a vivid dreamscape composed in alternately bold and subtle slashes of primary colors.

Downtown was the size of a shoebox, feeding off a Main Street that couldn't make up its mind whether it was a commercial or residential area, the two living side by side with only vague references to the passage

of time since the first farmers settled down here around
the turn of the last century. Business buildings stretched
for two streets, and then it was hit and miss leading into
rich farmland in all directions.

We drove around like tourists in our rented Ford
Mustang, past the weekly *Fairmount News,* the volun-
teer fire department, at least a dozen churches, including the Quaker meeting house where the memorial
service for Dean had been conducted back in '55 and
then almost annually, ever since his legions of fans
turned the city into a shrine, although he wasn't born
here and he left after eight years to pursue his dream.

Stevie called out, "There, honey!" and slapped my
shoulder.

I hit the brakes in front of a restored two-story farmhouse nestled on a stone foundation. A series of gabled
roofs sporting fresh red shingles. Three fireplaces. A
sign hanging above the broad stairway to the front
porch, almost too small to read in the sinking light:

HARMSTEAD'S FUNERAL HOME
THE BEST IN ETERNAL REST SINCE 1972

I realized I'd passed it twice before.

An elderly couple bundled against the weather in
overcoats with upturned collars and fur hats with ear-
muff attachments were leaving as we entered, the man
guiding the woman with a palm lightly supporting her
elbow as she took every small step with caution. I held
the front door open and got a nodding thanks from
both, while Stevie went off to find someone in charge.

She returned in a minute or two with a kid in a blue
physician's tunic, loose up top, exposing a bushel of
curly black hair spilling out over his V-neck T-shirt,
half the size of the black bushel piled on top of his
head. Looking barely out of his teens. A thin gold band
dripping from both nostrils. Another one in each of his

ears. Green surgical gloves. A smell emitting from him worse than Harry Chalk's gas. Formaldehyde. After another whiff, I gave the blue ribbon back to Harry.

"How many more times do I have to say this?" he wondered in a decided Hoosier twang, looking from Stevie to me. Sounding too irritated to be a front man here.

"Just once, Alexander," Stevie said reassuringly, pushing a finger into his chin dimple. He tried hiding how much he liked that. Another victim. She owned him.

Alexander hurriedly recited, "Yes, Mr. Edward Grizzard is here. Yes, I am preparing Mr. Grizzard now for his funeral or trying to except for all the interruptions. No, you can't view the deceased without authorization, and Mr. Harmstead or anyone to give it isn't here. Gone for the day and forgot to lock the door, or something. Won't be back until first thing in the morning." He shot Stevie a hopeful look. "Can I go back to work now?"

I held up a hand. "How many times have you said it before, Alexander?"

He looked at Stevie like he needed permission to answer. She smiled back at him and moved her head up and down a few times.

"Once," he said, "to the two in here just before you."

"The old couple?"

"Yeah."

"Who were they?"

"The Grizzards, I guess. Sweet people. Shame to see them so sad like this."

"You guess?"

"They never said, only that they wondered if they could view their grandson yet, so I supposed they were the Grizzards." Turning to Stevie. "Unless they were related to the deceased's mama, or there was divorce or something in the family, then they might not be the

Grizzards by name?" Starting to rattle off another possibility as—

I wheeled around and raced out the door, down the stairs, and out to the sidewalk, certain it was too late to catch them. It was. The street was empty in both directions and I had even helped them get away, holding open the door of the mortuary for James Dean and his wife.

There are no hotels in Fairmount, so we spent the night in a motel Alexander recommended, the Comfort Suites, located about twenty miles away in Marion, on Baldwin near the junction of the SR-9 and the SR-18, sharing a room in the city with as much claim to Dean as Fairmount. Where he was born and where his birthplace at Fourth and McClure is a major landmark, along with the site of the 1812 Battle of Mississinewa, the final battle between Indiana settlers and the Miami Indians. Population 32,000 plus, the big city in the middle of an agricultural region rich with corn, soybeans, and hogs.

I put down the tourist brochure I'd picked up at the reservations desk and was reciting from, called through the bathroom door at Stevie, "You hear any of that?" She'd been lounging in the tub for almost an hour.

I'd just wrapped up a run at my laptop.

Finishing and uploading a column to the *Daily*. E-mail, including one to the Spider Woman, reassuring her the trip here related to the Dean investigation, pointing out I'd been a good boy and had brought along the cell for immediate contact and, even though she had not demanded it, the beeper. Neglecting to say both were sitting unattended in my carry-on, but Langtry didn't have to know everything. It would only spoil her.

I got up from the round dining table meant to double as a desk and crossed to the door. Peeked in. Saw Stevie was up to her neck in bubble bath, eyes half shut and focusing on nothing in particular.

Walking in, I said, "You hear me?"

"About the Indians? What were Indians called the Miami Indians doing in Indiana and not in Florida?"

"A tribal thing," I said.

"What's that supposed to mean?"

"Why the state is called Indiana. It was created as a free state for Indian tribes everywhere and anywhere in the country, where the various nations could come, meet among themselves in guaranteed peace and tranquility."

"In other words, you don't have a clue."

"Not one."

I was under the covers when Stevie finally came out of the bathroom naked except for a towel turban on her head, hardly paying attention to the Turner Classic Movie I'd already seen three or four times, Cary Grant trying to win back Irene Dunne in *The Awful Truth*, because it had set my mind examining some of the awful truths Harry Chalk fed us, assuming they were truths, especially about James Dean and Pier Angeli, trying to convince us their romance was at the root of the murders and why we should think about going to Fairmount.

Chalk was still far from the chase, somewhere in the middle of obliging my request to take it from the top, describing and explaining or analyzing everything in detail beyond what you would expect from the memory of an eighty-something-year-old. About the crash of the Little Bastard. The deaths of Nick Adams, Sal Mineo, Natalie Wood, others I had come across in my research and some I had not. About Nico Mercouri.

The attempt on Augie's life. Why I had also made the death list.

"All hearsay," Chalk kept repeating, claiming he was showing off his story-pitching abilities as an agent so Stevie could further appreciate the genius now guiding her career. Heard it second hand or third hand, but it made for good dinner conversation, didn't it? It sounded more to me like he was distancing himself from the accessory charge I had threatened him with. Of course, he had my word on that, the same way he had Stevie's word on their deal, but Chalk was nothing if not cautious, an agent who understood deals are made to be broken and, quoting producer Samuel Goldwyn, how an oral contract isn't worth the paper it's written on. We laughed with him over that and tried not to let him see that the last laugh would be on him.

"You give your word, but a promise is something you keep."

"You know they were in love?" Chalk said. "Not a secret. Whatever else he was, whoever he'd be shtupping at any time, that beautiful *bambina* was the one true love of Jimmy Dean's life. And, to look in her eyes was to know Pier loved him intensely. Passionately. Eternally. He had become Anna Maria Pierangeli's whole world, Jimmy Dean had. . . . That was her real name, Pier Angeli, like her twin sister became Marisa Pavan. A little thing, maybe an inch over five feet. Maybe a hundred pounds drip-drying. And that face . . ." Chalk kissed the tips of his fingers and flung them away, Italian style. "Any A-list artist, Botticelli or Titian, a Raphael, definitely Leo Da Vinci, he'd have had a field day feasting on that *punim.*

"Newman introduced Jimmy and Pier, one night they were on the town with Joseph Wiseman, you remember him from *Viva Zapata!*? Joe and my dear client Michael Strong, they did a lot together those days. Like *Detective Story,* with Kirk? Anyway, Paulie making that bomb of a *Silver Chalice* at the time, over at Warner's, where Jimmy is doing *East of Eden*. Pier one of Paulie's costars. Did I already say Nat in it, too, Natalie Wood?

"Next thing you know, Jimmy and Pier are an item. Closer than Tracy and Hepburn. In the studio commissary at lunchtime, holding hands. Hanging out on each other's set, more hand-holding, smooching around corners and not really caring who notices, the way the gossip columnists did soon enough, Louella, Hedda, Sheila Graham, little Sid Skolsky, and, if it was supposed to be a secret, it isn't anymore.

"This being Hollywood, nobody really cared except to wonder what a sweet, virginal girl like Pier saw in him, a rude, uncouth show-off whose ego extended to his dick and who was not above peeing on a sound-stage wall if it got him more attention." Sending Stevie an aggressive smile. "Well, she was twenty-two, him a year older. Kids, what they were.

"Except, Pier's mother cared. A dominating woman of the old school. Devout Catholic. Jimmy not. She was not about to let her daughter marry out of her religion and not to the likes of him. Jimmy tried to get on mama's good side by switching from his usual torn jeans and scarred leather jacket to slacks and jacket, sometimes a tie, when he went over for a visit. Minded his manners. She wasn't impressed and finally she forbade Pier to see Jimmy anymore, so Pier took to lying, telling mama she was going out with a bunch of friends, never mentioning the bunch included him and the banana he had waiting for his Chiquita."

Chalk stopped to cough his throat clear, checked to see if Stevie and I got the joke. "They carried on like Romeo and Juliet for about three months, Jimmy calling her maw, because he heard that was what Gable had called Lombard. Pier calling him baby, who knows why? Like Bacall was to Bogey, maybe.

"She gives him a gold St. Christopher medal, you know the patron saint of travelers? He wears it around his neck, and he also has this gold and enamel locket he shows me one day I'm visiting clients on the *Eden* set and looking to drum up new business, you know how it is? Jimmy knows me better than I know him, and I feel the butter he's laying on me thick, in case I can do him good sometime down the road. He opens up the locket and says, 'You know what's that in there, Mr. Chalk? That is a lock of Pier Angeli's hair.' And looking like he can't believe what he's saying as the words come out, 'I have never loved any girl like I love her.' Like he's talking to the world. Heads turning.

"Next time I run into him, I'm having dinner at the Villa Capri with Mike Strong, Jimmy comes in alone and sees us, saunters over to say hello. Slides into my booth without an invitation and then he's showing the locket and the lock of hair to Mike, telling us how he's planning they get married soon. I look up from my spaghetti marinara and ask him how he got her mother's blessing, Mrs. Pierangeli. He laughs this crazy laugh like I'm the crazy one and puts a finger to his mouth to shush me. Swipes a slice of garlic bread and munches on a couple bites, checking this way and that for eavesdroppers. 'We're going to elope,' he says. Mike and I congratulate him. He says, 'Only Pier doesn't know it yet.' I ask him if he's planning to share the news with her, already wondering how many points I can get calling Hedda.

"He swipes a swallow of my dago red, sloshes it around in his mouth, and I'm certain by now he had one too many before he got here, before he stage whispers, 'She has got my kid in the oven, so she'll want to and the old lady won't be about to kibosh anything.' Realizes he's being loud and puts his finger to his lips again. I'm thinking no call to Hedda, not from me. I'm not into doing a Bergman on them for any amount of points. Harry Chalk's a star maker, not a career breaker." A solemn nod at Stevie.

"Around the same time, I bump into Jimmy and Pier at the *Star is Born* premiere at the Pantages, looking as loving as you can get. Who'd I have in it? Carson? Charlie Bickford? Someone . . . Jimmy takes me aside to announce he'll be on his way to New York any day to visit friends. He says 'visit friends' in a way that means in not so many words that Pier is going, too, and this is the big elopement.

"So my jaw is down there with all the others when I read in the columns, the trades, that Pier Angeli and the singer Vic Damone have announced their engagement. Catholic and used to date her, her sister, too, and Mrs. Pierangeli was crazy for Vic, probably anybody about this time except for Jimmy. Wham bam, like that, they're up the aisle at St. Timothy's in Hollywood, Vic and Pier.

"Night before the big nuptials, I'm having dinner again at Patsy's, this time with Francis Albert, who'd made the Villa a *primo* celebrity hangout singlehandedly. Jimmy is at a table with some pal or other, wearing his heart on his face. Staring into his meal like it's his last before the gas chamber. Shooting daggers at Damone, who's at his own table celebrating with buddies.

"Maybe Damone doesn't sense this, because he ups and walks over to Jimmy's table. It looks like he wants to shake hands. Jimmy gives Damone a pair of dropdead daggers and says, 'You're marrying Pier, but she's not yours, now or ever, and never will be.' That's all Damone needs to hear to take a swing at Jimmy and they start to go at it before the waiters race over to drag them apart and Jimmy makes a fast getaway."

Chalk held up a hand like he was taking an oath. "The truth, and more to it. I'm at Timothy's next a.m. for the ceremony, with five, six hundred others, in the

A section with Debbie Reynolds, Danny Thomas, Jack Benny and Mary, Annie Blyth, you know? And afterward, outside across the street, not invited, but sitting on his motorcycle like it's the best seat in the house. Jimmy. Looking like shit. Jeans and biker jacket. Eyes spitting hate as Pier and Vic on the top steps lay in a heavy kiss for the photographers. He guns his motor to make sure he's been noticed and races off. I go for a glimpse at the bride, wondering, but Pier's expression is as flat as a Roger Corman budget.

"That was the end of November '54. Pier and Vic, they had a son in August of '55. Split not long after that and by '58, '59 the marriage was history."

Chalk's eyes wandered through us, like yesterday was waiting outside.

Stevie took his pause as a cue to ask him, "Are you suggesting the child was James Dean's?" Looking at me in disbelief.

Chalk shrugged. "Do the math and it falls either way, dearie. I go for the version that floated around town, how abortion was forced on Pier by her mama the minute mama found out. Right before Pier broke up with Jimmy and Damone was back in the picture. Either way, abortion, Jimmy's kid, Damone's kid, it was the kind of hurt stuck to Jimmy like a magnet on metal."

"Why Pier's suicide might not have been suicide?" Stevie said, looking at me for an attitude.

I had my doubts and said so. "More likely Dean would have gone after Damone if he intended to go after anyone. He loved Pier too much to harm her."

Chalk nodded agreement, tapping a skinny finger to his temple, and urged, "Like I keep telling you, fella, save yourself a helluva lot of time by going to Fairmount. That's where you find the answers you want. A lot of them. Maybe all of them."

"And what else will I find, Mr. Chalk?"

"By now you should be comfortable in calling me Harry," he said.

Stevie removed her turban, checking out the movie while she used the towel to finish drying her hair, tossed it onto a chair, slipped into my twin instead of the empty, her skin warm and inviting where it pressed against me.

I'd started to drowse. Her voice brought me back from a conversation I was about to have with the woman in the photo I'd lifted from Eddie Grizzard's wallet, like it was a dry run for tomorrow.

"Not teasing and no pleasing, honey. It's just I don't feel like sleeping alone tonight. You know? A strange town? Always like this in a strange town." She fluffed her pillows and breezed her lips across my cheek, turned on her side facing me, settled an arm across my chest. In a minute she was asleep, her even breathing through her mouth sometimes ruptured by a short gasp.

Strange towns had something to do with the father who abandoned Stevie and her mother when Stevie was still a kid. Old enough to remember him, though not well enough or, maybe, too well.

All these years since meeting my baby and I still didn't know for certain. The occasional clue from her, from her mother, but it never seemed to open conversation to the bigger picture.

I teased her about it a few times and usually got the same answer: "There's a lot you don't know I could tell you, maybe when it's the right time, honey."

Sometimes we could read each other's mind, but not our memories.

I was still waiting for the right time.

Irene Dunne was explaining something about Cary

Grant to Ralph Bellamy. I listened for a moment, hoping I might hear something to explain Stevie and me. No help. I clicked off the TV and closed my eyes, hoping to resume my dream where I'd left off with Ada Montgomery.

The woman in the photo.

Ada Montgomery. The name Chalk swore he had no address for, only an understanding she lived somewhere in or near Fairmount.

Ada Montgomery. A name not in Eddie Grizzard's little black book or on the paperwork that sprang Eddie from the coroner's cooler, sending him on his way by air freight to Harmstead's Funeral Home. The Best in Eternal Rest Since 1972.

The name the coroner's office got for the one-way manifest was Grizzard, and I was betting the elderly woman Stevie and I saw leaving Harmstead's was Ada Montgomery by any name.

Eddie's grandmother.

And the elderly man with her?

Grandpa Grizzard?

And who else, Eddie? Who else?

"Who else, Ada?" I began our conversation. Asleep before I could hear her answer. And soon after that, seeing Stevie in my dream instead of Ada Montgomery.

19

The farmhouse was invisible from the highway, up a stretch of paved dirt road just wide enough for two cars and full of ruts and rock craters caused by a recent rain that had turned the irrigation channels three feet down on either side into ugly mud banks. Tall, weatherbeaten grass stretched out in all directions, lush greens blending with yellow and brown patches on the other side of white wooden rail fencing in dire need of post repairs and a fresh coat of paint.

No sense of what crops might have been grown here at one time, but now more a small, comfortable homestead on the outskirts of Fairmount, also in need of touch-up to the clapboard siding. Shingles to replace the dozens ripped off by windstorms. Somebody to look after shutters missing or hanging askew on the house and a barn about ten or fifteen yards away that had been converted into a guest house and garage. A gardener to nurse back to health uprooted bushes and strangled flowers now running indifferently around the property.

I parked the Mustang near the barn and, as Stevie and I headed for the house, the storm door swung open and a woman moved slowly, cautiously onto the narrow porch, using the door jamb for support and, with her free hand, signaling a greeting at us.

A matronly figure hunched against the breeze. A knit wool sweater over a simple print dress. A silk scarf wrapped around her neck and tossed over her shoulder in a single suggestion of style. Comfortable tennis shoes. Thick burnt-sienna hair combed straight and parted in the middle, falling to her shoulders. Glasses hanging from a shoestring chain. Hiding the wear and tear of time under enough make-up to cover the entire cast of *The Women*.

It was nearing noon and the dark clouds that had hung overhead most of the morning, threatening a full-scale rain to go with overnight drizzles and whistling winds that kept Stevie cuddled in my arms, were gone, replaced by a red sky that could mean anything.

The woman called out our names and said, "I hope you're hungry. I've made a nice light lunch for us. Nothing fancy. Homemade vegetable soup. Fresh-baked bread. A simple green salad. Coffee's ready, so just say the word." Moving aside so we could enter. "Come in, come in, and get rid of those coats. Nice fire burning in the fireplace and already comfy warm inside anymore."

Her voice soaring free as a songbird, giving all the words proper respect.

"I appreciate your seeing us, Mrs. Grizzard," I said, returning her smile.

"We don't get many visitors," she said, "so this is a treat, even though it has to be under such a terrible circumstance as my grandson's passing." Stevie had her coat off and was looking around the living room for a place to put it. "Just anywhere is fine, dear. Over the sofa, or I can hang it there, the guest closet—" pointing to a door "—you prefer."

I took the coat from Stevie, hung both hers and mine on closet hooks. Matching ankle-length, weatherproof Burberry trench coats in black. Double-breasted, cut full for extra boot room. Storm flaps on the shoulders for extra protection. D-rings on the belt for attaching equipment. A removable lining, so the coat can double as a robe. A thou apiece. Mine a present from Stevie three or four years ago, no holiday in sight, but Stevie may have felt guilty about spending that much on herself. Closet hooks because the bar was jammed tight with men's jackets and coats. Space on the shelf for her mink hat and my Lakers cap alongside an array of headgear. Two fur hats like those I'd seen on the couple leaving the mortuary last night.

"My son will be home shortly and I know he'll be so very pleased anyone should come out from Hollywood for the service, like this." She motioned us to take the couch across from the open hearth pouring out heat and the rich aroma of fresh burning logs and, after we assured her twice the coffee could wait, settled carefully across from us on the straight-backed cushioned seat.

"And Mr. Grizzard. Your husband?"

Eyes closing to the concept. The corners of her heavily painted lips doing a shadow dance. "Deceased, Miss Marriner. Oh, so many years ago." Her fingers doing tricks in her lap. "Just Jimmy Junior and me since then. A pair we are. His dear wife gone to Jesus in childbirth, so now it's only us to mourn for Eddie. . . ." Tears welling in her eyes as her words drifted off.

Stevie said, "I can tell you—he didn't suffer, Mrs. Grizzard."

She was lying, a sympathetic fib, trying to make the old woman feel better.

Mrs. Gizzard held out a hand between them, shook her head. "I know you were there in the room when Eddie . . ." Lost her voice. Tried again. "Know it wasn't you to blame. Heard on the TV. You were only there when he . . ." Moved her hand to her chest. Eyes closing, then opening again into a vague, unfocused stare.

She hadn't wanted to talk about it on the phone earlier, suggesting we wait, so her son, Jimmy Junior she called him, also could hear anything Stevie wanted to say, maybe ask questions.

I felt sorry for Mrs. Grizzard, the pain she had to be feeling. Glancing at Stevie, I saw something else on her face. Something disturbing her.

Stevie started to apologize, but the old woman cut her off with another gesture.

"We'll just wait for Jimmy Junior," she said.

"Sorry, of course . . . I understand," Stevie said, and maybe she did, more than me.

From being a woman.

Me, only from years as a newspaperman observing and interpreting the emotional merry-go-round of life.

For several minutes, we sat staring across the table at one another, the way uncertain strangers do, and made small talk between bursts of silence, smiles plastered on our faces, to go with the conversational inanities. Mrs. Grizzard sometimes appearing to investigate me harder than I surveyed her for evidence of the vivacious, fresh-faced starlet Ada Montgomery, who'd disappeared on the verge of stardom more than forty years ago.

Ada was a tall, slender brunette with hair that cascaded down her back, features on an oval face that were just enough off center to make her interesting as well as beautiful. A cat's purr for a voice, promising delivery on the intoxicating sparkle expelled by her every glance.

I noticed it when I saw her for the first time, playing a bit part in a Randolph Scott western that turned up on American Movie Classics as part of a salute to cowboy heroes. Made a point of finding out who Ada Montgomery was and verified my impression with Blockbuster rentals. Placed her in a category with Louise Brooks.

The End.

Until that photo in Eddie Grizzard's wallet.

And Harry Chalk confirming the ID, telling Stevie and me she was Eddie's grandmother. Insinuating James Dean was Eddie's grandfather and the reason behind Ada's sudden disappearance.

"Jimmy knocked her up," Chalk said. "He put a little bun in her oven. Found out. Shipped her off to Fairmount to stay with some of his people until the blessed event. By my calendar, Jimmy was a highway statistic before then and Ada never came back here. A toughluck shame. She had talent to spare, not just a looker. I heard secondhand how he pushed for her to get *The Searchers,* Jimmy, and got her tested for the part they gave to Natalie Wood after Ada dropped out of sight.

"Until then, she was the leading candidate, same as there'd been talk he was hungry to tackle the role went to Jeff Hunter, either because Jimmy wanted to do something with Duke or Pappy Ford. Some scuttlebutt says was because he needed to show up Jeff, who traveled in some of the same circles as Jimmy." He held out an invisible offering in his hands. "Take whatever story you like best."

"So much for his undying love for Pier Angeli," Stevie said.

"Getting even," I suggested.

Chalk agreed.

"Ada got Jimmy on the rebound. Looked a little like Pier and maybe that had something to do with it. Even say he knew he was drilling for fatherhood when he landed Ada. Showing Pier he didn't need the bun he had put in her oven or how he was getting even with her for letting mama talk her into the abortion. If none of the above's to your liking, add your own theory, or maybe Ada will tell you if you go to Fairmount and find her."

"James Dean, too, Mr. Chalk? Harry?"

"Certainly, why not, you believe in ghosts." He thought about it. "Listen, you run into him, send regards and tell Jimmy no hard feelings then or ever about him not signing with me."

Mrs. Grizzard wondered again, "Sure you wouldn't mind a coffee while we're waiting for Jimmy Junior? Don't know what's keeping him, although he didn't know to expect you. Was gone when Mr. Harmstead's assistant called up to say who you were and asked about you driving on over."

"A teacher, you said?" Infiltrating the opening she had handed me.

"English and drama," she said proudly. "Fairmount High, same as his father. Always makes it a point to have a hot meal at home at least twice a week, except when there's a play in rehearsal. One starting up next week. *Our Town.* A Fairmount favorite he's been doing every other year for—" She raised one finger after another and got to her thumb. Decided, "More years I got fingers."

She paused and I seized it as my opportunity to remark, as if it were common knowledge, "When you say his father, you mean James Dean."

Mrs. Grizzard's face said otherwise after a few tics of surprise and she filled the space between us with little lilts of laughter.

"My, oh, my, Mr. Gulliver. Granted Jimmy Dean is the town legend and the drama-class icon. His picture on a postage stamp, for mercy's sake. That festival and all the fuss come every September the thirtieth, the anniversary of his death, year after year, when his cult moves into town. Memorial services at Back Creek Friends Meeting, then over to Park Cemetery, the James Dean Memorial Park? To worship at his grave. What they all do, you know? Flowers and tons of pictures taken. Not only ordinary fans either anymore. You know who Martin Sheen is, the actor fella? He come one year. Not just him. Like Dennis Hopper a few years ago?"

"Was that a yes, Mrs. Grizzard?"

More laughter, tinged with indignation before she composed herself. Cupped her hands in her lap. Transferred a smile from me to Stevie and back again.

"Jimmy Junior's father was the late James Madison Grizzard, sir. A distant cousin on his mother's side to the fourth president of our United States?" Waiting for it to sink in. "Jimmy Senior was a classmate of Jimmy Dean's and they even raised a little Cain together those years at Fairmount High. Both took drama with the late and much loved Adeline Mart Nall and Jimmy Junior's always been proud about taking over drama from Miss Nall when she retired."

A different thought commanded her face.

"Is this what this visit is truly all about, Mr. Gulliver? Just another reporter trying to find a story and ready to make it up if he's got to? My sweet grandson only an excuse? That be the case, then you are intruding on my hospitality and maybe better you should leave now."

The fireplace did nothing to offset the cold rage burning in the looks she threw at us.

"Yes, an excuse," I said, sensing a breakthrough if I made her angry enough. "We're genuinely sorry for you, Mrs. Grizzard, and for Eddie's father, just as we're sorry for the families and friends of the young woman he killed."

The old woman rose on unsteady legs. "I'll thank you to leave. Now!" She pointed at the door. "Disrespect for that sweet child is something I won't tolerate from anyone." Tears welled in her eyes.

Stevie picked up her purse and started to rise, then plopped down again, pushed me back against the couch, and announced, "I don't think so, not until we learn what we came to learn."

"Trespassing!" Mrs. Grizzard screeched at her. Said it twice more. Fled the room, leaving unfathomable sound waves behind. Legs not as tired as they had been, swift enough to return before Stevie and I had finished trading questioning stares.

Pointing a shotgun at us, both barrels cocked, while moving deeper inside the room to a can't-miss spot behind her chair.

Using the crest of the seat back to offset the weight of the weapon. Her entire being radiating deadly determination.

"Maybe we should come back some other time," I said, turning to Stevie for confirmation. "Maybe we should come back some other time?"

"Maybe you two should of thought better than to come by in the first place," Mrs. Grizzard answered, menace audible in a voice suddenly devoid of lavender and lace.

Stevie seemed to be weighing the situation for options. She returned from somewhere else and said, "Are you really Ada Montgomery?"

Just like that.

Disarming Mrs. Grizzard, if not her shotgun.

"That's what we really came here to find out," Stevie said. "So, Neil?"

"So," I agreed, playing along, understanding a small piece of the truth when I hear it. Grinned my Steve McQueen grin.

Mrs. Grizzard's expression told us nothing. She held her finger steady on a trigger, working out something new in her mind. Then, "And it was such a lovely meal I'd prepared."

"Ada Montgomery?" Stevie, determined.

"The movie actress?" Me, making conversation to buy time, deliberating over my options. Thinking, somehow distract and disarm her.

"What about Ada Montgomery?" Mrs. Grizzard said.

I said, "Harry Chalk thought we'd find her here."

She defined the answer, deciding, "Harry always did talk much too much." A sprinkle of laughter to go with an angry memory. More subtle difference in her speech, not the midwest; something else.

Moving her left arm in and out until she found the range to read her wristwatch.

Clucking almost to herself: "Don't know what's keeping Jimmy Junior."

To us: "Jimmy Junior, usually very punctual."

Another new thought at Stevie: "You any good at following directions?"

Stevie gave her a disarming smile and said, "None of my directors have ever complained," adding as a pointed afterthought, "Miss Ada Montgomery."

The old woman flattered Stevie's foolhardiness with a flutter of eyelids. Adjusted the gun barrels another inch in her direction.

"Listen to me closely now," she said. "Kitchen is over there." The beginnings of a wattle disappearing as she pointed with her chin. "A pitcher of fresh lemon-ade in the fridge. Glasses in the big cabinet left of the sink, on the first shelf. Fill three for us. A serving tray, the cabinet across, left of the stove. It should not take you more than I need to count to twenty. Be back by twenty or I promise I will be telling the police how I shot him first; saw he had broken in, grabbed for my shot . . . Boom!"

Stevie, arguing: "We didn't come here meaning you any harm, Miss Montgomery."

"One . . . Two . . . Three . . ." Slowly. Deliberately.

Stevie looked at me with panic-flooded eyes.

Jumped from the couch and fled for the kitchen.

Was back with the serving tray shaking in her hands by Mrs. Grizzard's wickedly pronounced "nineteen."

The old woman directed me to clear space on the table. Motioned Stevie to take her seat again after she'd put down the tray .

"Drink up," she ordered us. "I make it with fresh lemons and just enough sugar to take away the tart-ness. Not so sweet you mistake it for anything else. Better that way. Refreshing."

"On second thought, that coffee sounds good," I said.

Mrs. Grizzard withered me with a frown, like she was reading my mind. Like she thought I was thinking some silly thought, like her lemonade was spiked with something besides sugar. Like I was taking real life and reducing it to a dime novel. Ridiculous of her, as ridicu-lous as having to come to Fairmount, Indiana, to have an old woman poke a loaded shotgun at my future.

A new voice filled the void.

"My, my, what have we here?"

Reflexively, I turned around to look.

Discovered James Dean looking back at us.

* * *

He was not the James Dean Stevie and I saw strike down Nico Mercouri. Not old enough, but older than the Dean who turned out to be Eddie Grizzard. This reincarnation was somewhere in between, in his mid-to-late-forties, wearing a catalog blue pinstripe faded from years of dry cleaning and a blue shirt with a button-down collar, a wide tie open at the collar that would have worked better with a brown suit, brown shoes in desperate need of a shine, but there was no mistaking the resemblance. James Dean, and—

He wasn't alone.

A teenaged girl was with him, racked tightly by his side, his arm stretched behind her and clamped to her thick waist. Buxom, but a body otherwise hard to define in a loose blouse falling to hide her hips over baggy pants. Doc Martens. Pounds of hair done up in corn rows piled on her head. Too much makeup. A ring running through the left side of her lower lip. Another through the hole drilled in a clump of cheek on the other side of her butterball face.

Her curious brown eyes growing big as boulders when she lowered them and saw the shotgun. Raised them to Jimmy Junior, inquiringly, and received a few reassuring pats on the hip.

She smiled coyly, as if sending a confidential message to herself, and took an *at ease* position while he freed himself to cross to the wall table and set down the pile of books he was carrying under his other arm.

Mrs. Grizzard called to him, "Jimmy, where have you been? These people, here under false pretenses, saying they were friends of our Eddie's from Los Angeles. Tracked us from the funeral home. One a reporter digging dirt like a pig farmer. Invaded our home."

Jimmy Junior.

If he was the son of someone named James Madison

Grizzard Senior, where did he get off looking like
James Byron Dean?

The question answered itself.

Spoke to the true identity of Mrs. Grizzard as well as
anything she might have confessed to Stevie and me.

Jimmy Junior's eyes roamed us, showing suspicion
short of alarm, his mind visibly analyzing the scene like
a director trying to decide where the camera belonged.

"He called our Eddie a killer!" Mrs. Grizzard interrupted. "Looking to make more headlines is all what
brought them here. Even to asking if James Dean was
your father. Her there trying to say I was someone other'n me."

The girl brought a palm to her mouth to stifle a
giggle.

A smile traveled across Jimmy Junior's face and exploded into laughter.

"And this here is Monica Lewinsky," he said, and
now the teenager's laugh grew larger than his. "Oh,
mother, be reasonable and put the shot away. These
folks mean us no harm."

Mrs. Grizzard gave him a disapproving look.

Jimmy Junior closed his eyes and shook his head.

Pulled a pair of horn rims from his hanky pocket
and fit them to his face.

Studied us for a moment.

"You'll have to forgive my mother. She hasn't been
herself since we learned about my darling son's
death."

He choked on the words. Bit his lip.

At her again: "Mother, please? Please go ahead and
put the shot back?"

Mrs. Grizzard momentarily pondered the request.
Snorted at us and stomped out, a slow shuffle actually, as disdainful and proud as her sloped back
allowed.

* * *

In the kitchen, Mrs. Grizzard carefully replaced the shotgun on the wall rack inside the door connecting to the dining room, crossed to the cabinet where the liquor bottles were kept, moved them around until she located the bottle of Jack Daniels, and took a swig straight from its narrow mouth.

Ran a finger across her mouth.

Took another swig.

Not that the old nerves needed any steadying.

Just that she needed a couple of booster shots for getting the work done later.

She'd forgotten Jimmy Junior planned on bringing another one of his cuties home this afternoon, until after the invitation was made to Gulliver and the actress, but no harm, Jimmy assured her when she reached him.

"Let's take care of them while we can," he said. "Not really a good idea having them run around town asking questions that could come back to haunt us anymore."

"What do you suppose?"

"Lemonade, same as we do with the girls. Then, the usual for the girl, and a surprise for that pair."

She took another nip and returned the bottle of Jack Daniels to the shelf.

Walked back to the rack, only this time went for the .38 police special instead of the shotgun.

Parked against the wall and, while waiting for Jimmy Junior's signal, thought about the providence that had brought Gulliver and Marriner to their doorstep.

Jimmy Junior turned to the girl and said, "Go on over and pull up a seat, there next to my mother's, Joanna."

Joanna did as she was told. Noticed the glass of lemonade on the table and wondered about it.

"Help yourself," Jimmy Junior said. "Mother won't mind at all. She always makes a fresh pitcher or two when I invite over my students anymore for rehearsals." He angled a hand to the side of his mouth and called, "Mother, we're needing two more glasses for the lemonade when you come on back." Then to us: "I teach drama over at the high school. Mr. Thornton Wilder's *Our Town* is again this semester, and Joanna here hopes to play Emily. I'm using the lunch hour to do some boning up with her . . . her lines." His words came with a wink of dubious meaning that Stevie also noticed.

Joanna gave a celebrity nod, raised her glass and toasted, "Chinny chin cheers!" Brought the glass as far as her mouth before settling it on her thigh. "So there's two of us in the room, Ms. Marriner."

"You know me?"

"Know you?" Looking like the question had been an insult. "I worship you. My girlfriends and me, we tape your show every day. We wait for the weekend and we make a party of seeing them all at once, skipping over the duddy commercials that way." Screwing one side of her mouth into a cheek. "You haven't been around much lately. Bummer. That actress trying to make out she's you?"

"Karen Walls."

"Her. About as sexy as skin on a potato. You can almost see the actors making puke lips before they have to kiss her. You will be back soon, won't you? Or, me and my friends, we can send letters and E-mail complaining the way we did once before, for taking away *Melrose Place*."

"Of course, I will," Stevie said, reassuringly, and took an absent-minded sip from her lemonade, her look at once analyzing the taste; running her tongue in and out past her lips.

Joanna followed suit and also noticed. "It is a little sour, but—" Holding the glass high again. "Chinny chin cheers!" This time draining half the glass.

Stevie hesitated, then "Chinny chin cheers," and took another sip. Wrinkled her nose and returned the glass to the table while Joanna finished the rest of hers in a single gulp.

Jimmy Junior inquired, "You don't like lemonade, Mr. Gulliver?"

"The truth? Pink or otherwise, Mr. Grizzard," I said, placing my glass on the table, struck with wondering how he knew my name. Didn't Mrs. Grizzard say the call from the mortuary came after he'd left for school this morning?

"About the same for me, but I drink it to humor mother," he said, making small talk. "Her herbal teas also leave a lot to be desired." Another wink.

Joanna coughed hard into a fist and said, "I don't suppose I could have your autograph, Ms. Marriner."

"Stevie, and certainly you can. How sweet of you to ask me, Joanna." Looking around. "Do you have something I can write on?"

"This should do the trick," Jimmy Junior said, pulling a spiral note pad and a pencil stub from a pocket, explaining as he handed it over to Stevie, "I use it for cast notes."

Joanna watched adoringly while Stevie scribbled away and carefully pulled the sheet from the pad. Leaned over to hand it to Joanna. Had it snatched away by Jimmy Junior before it reached Joanna's outstretched hand.

He regarded the inscription aloud, "To Joanna, Much love from Candy and Dandy Lyons, who you know better as your friend Stephanie Marriner."

Hearing the question in his voice, Stevie said innocently, "It sounds like Mr. Grizzard is not the fan of *Bedrooms and Board Rooms* that you are, Joanna."

Joanna's eyes and mind seemed to be wandering, and it took her a moment to react. "She was wonderful in both roles last year, Mr. Grizzard. Every year she gets to play a character besides herself and she is great all the time. Twice so as the Lyons twins . . . Karen Walls, she can't hold a candle to you, to be perfectly honest and all."

Stevie put her fingers to her lips and blew the kiss to Joanna.

Jimmy Junior handed over the autograph to Joanna, who folded the paper to fit her blouse pocket and started to thank Stevie, but quit midsentence. Rose suddenly and, a bit unsteady on her feet, announced, "I need to go to the little girls' room. Right now soon." Eyes desperate. Hands moving to mouth and chest.

"Up the hall and left to the second door," Jimmy Junior said, pointing.

Joanna stumbled off.

Jimmy Junior called out, "Mother, what's keeping you?" To us: "Happens a lot more than you think, they're trying mother's lemonade for the first time."

I didn't have a chance for a question before Mrs. Grizzard emerged from wherever she'd been, this time aiming what looked like a snub-nosed .38 at us.

"Joanna, another sickie, mother."

"How about them?"

"She took a little, Gulliver nothing."

"Okay, then, the both of you, drink up and do it now," Mrs. Grizzard said. "No more games."

20

Stevie woke up, startled by—

Nothing.

The absence of anything beyond a pounding in her head. Distressed eyes. Dry throat. Muscles aching. Wanting to hug herself against the bone-chilling coldness. A vague recollection of passing out and the anxious conversation of Mrs. Grizzard and Jimmy Junior, arguing loudly, until their voices melted into a blackness different from the dark she was unable to penetrate now.

She couldn't get her arms to travel away from her body. Her legs, either. Strapped to a chair here, wherever here was. Her pulse began to race at the nasty tricks being played on her by her mind, reminding her why she was afraid of the dark more than almost anything else in her life, all these years later, a consuming fear she could never summon enough intelligence to void, one that had cost her years of therapy and thousands of dollars.

After they were married, Neil teased her about the need for the nightlight that gave her as much security as her old baby blanket, until she finally told him to shut up. She needed it and that was that. No reason he needed to know why. Anybody needed to know. Just know that she needed it; that would have to do.

His teasing stopped immediately.

He had that knack with her, understanding about her even what he couldn't understand. She had yet to find anyone else with that gift.

Sweat, running down her forehead. Preying on her eyes. Stinging. Flop sweat, only now *fear* sweat. Yes, she was. She would be even if there were light. There had been something about Mrs. Grizzard that sent the message to her, almost from the moment she saw her. Before the shotgun. Too much about her not ringing right.

Especially how she didn't want to talk about her grandson, her dear Eddie. Wanted to wait for Jimmy Junior. Any mother would want to know immediately, now, at once, a victim of grief demanding to know more and more about her lost child.

A grandmother, too.

Would want it piled on—the pain, the suffering, the agony of detail—in order to assume a different kind of death for herself, a tragedy beyond simple mourning.

Neil may have seen it, or maybe not. Neil was the best at judging people, but not in her class when it came to judging actors. Mrs. Grizzard struck her as someone who was playing a role, not really inhabiting the character. No Actors Studio consistency in the performance.

If she was Ada Montgomery, maybe Jimmy Dean had done her a giant favor by knocking her up and out of the business.

"Neil?" Struggling to make the word happen.

She remembered him slumping over, head falling

against her shoulder, just before her own world faded to black.

"Honey, you here? . . . Neil?" She would have known if he was. Felt him.

Another thought: "Joanna?"

Where was the girl last time she saw—? Oh, yeah. Sick. Stumbling to a bathroom.

Wondering where she was now. Here, with her, with Neil? Back at school where—if she was a big enough fan of *Bedrooms and Board Rooms*—maybe she had understood what the autograph meant, remembered what being Candy or Dandy Lyons meant. Smart enough to call the cops.

The cops. Could be on their way here now.

Here?

Would they know where here was?

"Joanna? . . . Neil?"

A snigger from four or five feet away.

Not Neil, but someone, and she realized one of the vague sounds she'd been hearing was quiet breathing. Not Neil, because she'd have recognized, known; nothing quiet about Neil's breathing when he slept. Always tiny splinters of noise. His deviated septum.

"Joanna?"

Again. Louder than the first snigger.

Definitely not Neil.

Stevie knew she was going to pass out again if someone didn't say something, and soon. Her fingers were freezing, probably because of the tight rope or whatever, and she wiggled them for circulation. Her toes. Pulled in stale air by her mouth and felt her chest press against the constraints.

"Mrs. Grizzard? Mr. Grizzard?"

"Which? You only have one more guess. Make the third one the charm."

The voice startled Stevie, sent a shiver through her.

Familiar in an unfamiliar way, the surprise so sudden and strong she could not be certain if she'd heard a man or a woman.

She found her voice.

"What if I guess wrong?"

"You won't have to worry about guessing right."

Not Mr. or Mrs. Grizzard, neither of them, but male. Definitely male. Studied. Hiding a regional accent?

"If I don't guess at all."

A beat. "You won't have to worry about guessing right." His words taking on a fresh colorations; an actor toying with her.

Unable to concentrate on the game in the dark. She needed some light more than she needed anything else right now, and she told him so.

"You mean, 'Let there be light?'" Amusing himself at her expense. "That was God's command, wasn't it? 'Let there be light!' He commands. 'And the darkness rolls up on one side and the light was shining on the other.' Something like that. By James Weldon Johnson. Learned it in school. Used to know it by heart. Letter perfect, but that was so very long ago."

The snap of a switch.

Sudden brightness illuminated the room. Startled Stevie's eyes shut. Rainbows running in circles inside her lids.

Her eyes open again, acclimating, and—

"Mrs. Grizzard!" she called out in astonishment.

"And I'm willing to bet you'd of guessed wrong," Mrs. Grizzard said, finally sounding like herself. A laugh that raged like a Malibu fire.

She was sitting across the narrow room, five or six feet away, her back to an old-fashioned pedestal vanity with an elegant dressing glass that had an array of photos stuck in the framework, a number of Western Union messages taped to the yellowing glass. The tabletop was hidden under a mess of make-up tubes and jars. A flowing hairpiece out of a Shakespearean play sat like a crown on an otherwise naked mannequin.

Her arms rested across her chest, hands clamped on her breasts. Legs spread in an unseemly fashion, the hem of her dress pulled up over her knees, exposing a pair of red silk panties.

The burst of light that had temporarily blinded Stevie came from an overhead bulb, maybe a hundred watter. Most of the space she could make out was bathed in shadows.

The walls were of brick. Lots of shelves filled with varieties of canned goods. Bottled water. Batteries. Flashlights everywhere. Two bunk beds, neatly made; tight corners like Neil had once showed her how to make. Several radios. A television set. A clothing rack, packed tight. A chest of drawers. A kitchen table and three chairs. A pile of books and magazines on the table; other piles scattered around the room. A small fridge. An extra large washbasin. A *shoji* screen that cut off one end of the room, maybe ten or twelve feet from her.

"Cozy, huh?" Mrs. Grizzard said, when Stevie's survey caught up with her. "A bomb shelter left over from after the war, when everyone was afraid the Russians would begin dropping their A-bombs and H-bombs on us any minute, so later, when we knew we were safe as summer tomatoes, it got turned into a tornado shelter and still is anymore."

"Where's Neil?"

The old woman checked her watch.

"If we're keeping to the schedule, right where he belongs, in Hell. Down in Hell getting the guided tour they have for newcomers. You join him soon enough, Jimmy Junior gets back and finishes up with you." She cackled. "Has this thing for actresses, Jimmy does. A TV star like you . . . like a rich, creamy dessert, cherry on the top, for someone has to usually satisfy his appetite with deep-dish apple pie from the high school."

Mrs. Grizzard eyed her smugly. "Oh, and by the way—" Picked up a paper from the dresser and held it out for Stevie to see. "Whatever it was you were trying to say to Joanna by your autograph? I'm not that dumb, you know?"

She crumpled the paper into a ball and tossed it away.

Stevie's body convulsed involuntarily against the hemp ropes holding her to the chair.

Complications. Almost wishing he'd picked another day to invite Joanna over. Stupid girl. Bad enough vomiting her guts all over the bathroom and then the hallway runner, but in the car after that, making her the new puke queen of Fairmount High. No, wait, he told himself, the title still belongs to what's her name? Miss Skinny? From two semesters ago. Built like a pencil, but a pretty face, big eyes, big lustful eyes, a mouth that knew what to do when the Rohypnol kicked in and her mind went blank, but not her body, and oh so good until all that puking, pouring out of her like one of those soft yogurts over at Gentry's ice cream parlor. An A student up to then, on and off the stage. A shame she had to go and get him so messy, turning his chest into a lunch counter when she upchucked that stuff, got him so mad he had to . . .

Well, nobody lives forever.

He was careful with that one, like he should have been today with Joanna. Nobody saw them leaving campus, so it was easy to stay in the clear after her folks reported her missing. A runaway, the police finally decided, with a little direction from him. Talked about running off to New York and becoming a Broadway star, the way James Dean once did. Anything to do with James Dean was believable around here, and why not? Only one James Dean ever left Fairmount and went on to become a movie legend for all time.

But Joanna, using her mouth the usual way first, telling friends where she was going. Not her daddy, so that was good. Wouldn't have mattered if it was only them when he got her to the farm. The Rohypnol would have cooked her prime for his appetite and, later, back at school, no memory of any of it. Wonderful drug that, Rohypnol. Convincing her like any one of the others before her how she passed out and maybe she ate something she should not have and that's why.

He laughed at his unintentional joke, the part about eating something she should not have.

But Joanna puked it all up, and that was that.

Complication Number One.

Saw Gulliver and Marriner.

Complication Number Two.

Changing everything.

Joanna would have to go, like Miss Skinny had to go, and the others, a lot of them Eddie's doing, a habit he never could break, even after he got to Los Angeles, where it didn't take any Rohypnol or any GHB, to get it on. Just a look and a line. That's how James Dean explained it to his friends. Just a look and a line.

Later, the police come calling, easy to explain how Gulliver and Marriner visited to pay their respects about Eddie. The funeral home would back up that part of the story. Lunch, and then gone, apologizing for not being able to stay for the services. Needing to get back to Los Angeles. Offering to give Joanna a lift back to Fairmount High.

Last they saw of the three of them.

By then, no evidence to prove otherwise anymore.

If the bodies, the car, got discovered later on, still nothing to point to them.

Meanwhile, Complication Number Three:

Who to play Emily now?

*Joanna didn't look the part best, but she was sure
the best actress in this year's drama class. All the more
the shame of what had to be.*

Up ahead, the pull-off leading to the old hole.

More mud than water this time of year.

Nobody around this time of day.

Just a few more minutes, and then—

Glub, glub, glub.

Goodbye to both.

Goodbye. So long. Auf Wiedersehen. Adieu.

That brought back a recurring thought.

Next year. Maybe it was time to try a musical?

I opened my eyes to darkness, no idea where I was or
for how long.

Movement. Vibration. The smell of gas. In a car?
Trunk? Trying to order my mind clear of whatever
they had used to spike the lemonade.

On my left side. Fetal position.

No room to move much. Not alone here.

Someone pressing against my backside.

Not Stevie. I would have known.

Another smell, and I remembered the girl, Joanna,
throwing up again and again. All over herself. The rug.
Who else? What else?

Not Stevie.

Joanna.

"Joanna?"

A moan. A plea. "No more, all right?"

"Joanna, you okay, kid?"

"Please. No more?" Whimpering. Like she was talking to herself. "It really hurt, Mr. Grizzard. You really
hurt me something awful."

Bastard.

Son of a bitch.

Remembered something else. "Joanna, this is Neil Gulliver. Stevie Marriner's friend. Listen to me, Joanna. Can you move at all?"

"He made me touch it."

"I know, but listen to me, Joanna—"

"I'm so dirty now. So very dirty."

"Joanna, listen, please. It's going to be all right, but now I want you to listen to me, okay? Listen carefully."

Noise passing for an answer.

"I want you to feel around with your hands. Can you? Can you move your hands?"

"Uh huh. A little. Don't let him hurt me again?"

"He won't, Joanna, so listen. . . ." I prayed to God we'd been put in the trunk of the rented Mustang. "If you can, feel for a travel bag. Somewhere behind you. A corner, if you can reach that far. Inside the travel bag and shaped like a small football." Where I'd parked it after we landed and got the car.

"Uh huh."

"Uh huh yes, you can reach that far, or uh huh yes, you found it?"

"Uh huh both." The noises of pain more audible than her voice.

I patiently instructed her to pass the package over to me. She pushed it over my body and it dropped to the base of the trunk.

A stretch to get my hands on it. Pull it closer. Work open the covering of heavy-duty aluminum foil.

Happy now that I had listened to Jimmy Steiger when I saw him at the hospital.

"Better safe than sorry," Jimmy said.

How I happened to fly to Fairmount with my pal the police lieutenant's .45 semiautomatic in my travel bag, inside a sweater and wrapped in layers of heavy-duty aluminum foil picked up at my neighborhood 7-Eleven.

Amazing how the most sophisticated, advanced technology designed to stop terrorists, mad bombers, and other bad guys can be thwarted by something as simple as aluminum foil that the metal detectors can't penetrate.

Joanna pushed her quaking body closer against mine, draped her arm under mine and tied it to my chest, clinging for comfort.

I reassured her we were going to be fine.

Trying to convince myself as well as Joanna.

"What are you going to do?"

I told her about the .45 and how, the minute the car stopped, I intended to blow away the trunk lock, kick open the lid, and go for the driver.

"You stay where you are," I cautioned her. "Out of the way until I tell you it's all right to come out."

"What if it's not all right?"

Just then the car rolled to a stop.

Her question was about to answer itself.

I freed myself from Joanna and felt around until I found the lock mechanism.

Aimed the .45.

Fired twice.

Two screams in chorus as the trunk lid flew open.

I made a body-banging exit, the adrenaline rush hiding any pain as I scrambled to my feet, pivoted around to charge the driver's seat, and—

Tripped over Jimmy Junior.

On his back, vertical to the Mustang, arms out like he was auditioning for a crucifixion.

Eyes and mouth wide open in surprise.

And in death.

The first scream had been Joanna's, the second one his. He must have been about to open the trunk when I fired. One or both shots had gutted his groin. The lid must have clipped him underneath his chin on its way up, because his head was almost ripped from his body.

If there was such a thing as the ugliest way to die, he'd qualified for the championship finals.

Joanna screamed again, on spec.

I helped her from the trunk and tried to shield her from a good look, but she resisted the effort, pushing me aside and stepping over to the corpse.

Studying it in morbid fascination.

Nodding her head, slowly at first, then faster and faster.

Mouthing words not meant to be heard by anyone but herself.

I covered Jimmy Junior's head with my jacket and led Joanna to the car and into the front passenger seat.

Common sense told me to go straight to the cops, but I was too frantic about Stevie for that. I had to get back to the farmhouse and find her.

Joanna babbled the whole way, tottering on the edge of hysteria, dumping tears and either pounding a fist on the window or both fists on the dash, panicked about how her parents would take the news.

"And they really, truly liked him, Mr. Grizzard," she wailed more than once, as if that were a consideration. "I probably won't even get to be Emily anymore," as if that mattered.

Making no sense half the time.

Making too much sense the other half, like when she asked, "Are you really certain he's dead for sure? I don't want him alive anymore, Mr. Grizzard, never again, after what he did to me."

"I'm positive, Joanna."

A smile temporarily broke through her anguish and then, as if ashamed for the thought, Joanna buried her face in her hands and gasped out a string of crying noises that sounded as painful as death itself.

"I don't know what you think you know about Ada Montgomery, but she was the one true love of Jimmy's life," Mrs. Grizzard started, making more idle conversation, this time bowing to Stevie's earlier curiosity about Ada. "One. True. Love." Putting the words in capital letters. Making each pay off like a punch line.

The old woman pushed up from her slouch to occupy the seat at the vanity like a throne, her expression turned resolute, her eyes softening at the memory.

"I know how people think it was Pier," she said, "and I'm not saying there were not other girls in Jimmy's life, but they were just flings. Diversions. Starlets the studio publicity people put with him for the gossip columns and the movie magazines. No more than that." Head bobbing anxiously. Eyes narrowing into unhappy slits and a pair of vertical furrows deepening between her eyebrows.

Stevie answered Mrs. Grizzard's challenging stare with one of her own. She was listening, but her mind was on freeing herself and escaping before Jimmy Junior returned.

The old woman said, "I could give you all their names, the whole catalog anymore, going back to New York, when Jimmy was there in the beginning and starting out like a house afire."

"More than names if, God help you, what you said about Neil is true," Stevie shot back. "If you did anything to harm him, I swear—"

"Harm him? Does death count anymore?"

A gargle of laughter rose from her throat as Mrs. Grizzard raised the eyeglasses hanging around her neck and inspected Stevie like a scientist examining a specimen. "I don't see that you're in a position to make threats I have to take so seriously, Stevie." Checked her watch. "But you go on ahead, it gives you pleasure in what time's remaining to you." Resumed where she'd left off, like they were next-door neighbors trading gossip over the backyard fence.

"Jimmy told me all about them; everything. Like Christine from the Actors Studio. Dizzy. Barbara.

Then in Los Angeles." Counting off on her fingers: "Terry Moore. Natalie Wood. Steffi Sidney. Lili Kardell. Beverly Wills. Ursula Andress; that affair lasted about a month. Maila Nurmi, the one who played Vampira on television? Pier." Scoffing. "How there was never one like Pier, before or after? Well, there was Ada Montgomery, Stevie, there was Ada Montgomery before *and* after.

"He was coming into Googie's all the time, the all-night coffee shop next door to Schwab's. Sunset, the corner of Crescent Heights? Across from the old Garden of Allah? Not there any more neither. A record store and some movie theaters, a gym, one of them Spago restaurants you're always reading about, but then a regular hangout for people in the movie business, and Jimmy was already making noise, while poor old Ada was making ends meet as a counter girl. That's where it started, across the counter. Giving him lip as good as he gave." Her gaze drifting out of the room. "He liked that a lot, needing someone to help him keep his feet planted on the ground, he said. Then more than lip, a whole lot more."

Reflecting momentarily, sharing a secret or two with herself.

"Maybe Pier did matter to Jimmy for a while. You see where it got him, though? Back into the arms of sweet, kind, loving, caring Ada, who gave up her own career, just when it started to take off, to come on here to Fairmount to have his child. James Grizzard Senior, a good man, a good friend, married to make it right for Jimmy, give the boy a proper name. Jimmy Senior grew to love Ada the same way she eventually came to love him, although never as much as she always loved James Byron Dean. . . . Now, do you want to know another secret?"

Stevie waited the old woman out.

"Jimmy Junior gets back, then we'll have our fun,

Jimmy Junior and you and me, so I can share the secret with you, because you won't be taking the news away from here. . . . No, I am not Ada Montgomery, Stevie. . . . Ada Montgomery died a long time ago . . . and so did Mrs. James Grizzard, Sr."

The sound of a buzzer bounced around the walls.

The old woman regarded it with uncertainty.

She checked her watch.

Laundered Stevie with a false smile.

"Don't you go anywhere," she said, on the way to disappearing behind the *shoji* screen, her laughter trailing after her.

Another moment and the light went out, leaving Stevie alone and in the dark again.

21

I parked the Mustang about a hundred yards away from the farmhouse, had Joanna move behind the wheel, and gently commanded her to switch on the ignition and get out of there at the first sign of trouble.

Approached the farmhouse cautiously.

The front door was unlocked.

Took my time moving inside.

A door squeak, a floorboard bending under a stray step. Other than that the place was quiet. Too quiet. Empty quiet. Even smelled quiet.

No sign of Stevie or Mrs. Grizzard.

Our trench coats still in the closet.

The three lemonade glasses still sitting empty on the coffee table.

The fire in the fireplace barely burning, begging for more fuel.

I worked the rooms tactfully, holding Steiger's .45 tight against my chest, barrel pointing to the ceiling, shooting position and ready to fire given provocation. The "ask questions later" attitude that even the most sincere gun-control advocates have been known to adopt after surviving some weapon-toting human health hazard.

A foul odor in the hallway.

Evidence Mrs. Grizzard hadn't bothered to clean up after Joanna.

In the kitchen, Mrs. Grizzard's cozy lunch still waiting to be served. The vegetable soup in a large kettle on the old four-burner, the kettle cold to the touch. The loaf of bread, sliced, sitting in a platter on the counter, next to a crystal bowl filled with three or four types of lettuce. Sliced tomatoes and cucumber. Diced carrots. What looked like jicama. Salad sprouts. Croutons.

I realized how hungry I was. It had been about eight hours since Stevie and I had breakfast on the run, motel room coffee, a sweet roll from the vending machine heated in the microwave.

Hungry, but no appetite.

My stomach on the verge of a nervous breakdown over Stevie.

A gun rack on the wall, where some families might hang a framed, hand-embroidered homily. The shotgun racked above a couple rifles. Two empty slots. One I supposed for the .38 Mrs. Grizzard had turned on us. The other probably for something Jimmy Junior was carrying.

The rest of the house checked out empty.

Leaving the basement.

I hit the light switch inside the door and took the steep wooden stairs slowly, leading with a two-handed grip on the .45.

A dead end, until I pushed aside a heavy blanket hanging like a dusty tapestry from the only wall not full of shelves lined with jars of canned preserves or storage boxes. It covered the entrance to a passageway

about eight feet high and the width of a candidate for
Weight Watchers. Wood beams had been strutted into
the walls about every ten feet and there was a similar
kind of support system holding up the dirt roof. A
switch that turned on a row of overhead bulbs.

Someone had gone to a lot of trouble.

I followed the underground corridor to where it
ended about fifteen or twenty yards later, by my reck-
oning somewhere below the barn, at a steel-reinforced
door built inside a steel frame, not another blanket.

I took the grip handle and gave it a shove.

Locked.

I retraced my steps, faster now, and a minute or two
later was hustling with zigzag caution across the ten or
fifteen yards to the barn. The side door led me into the
garage area.

Farm equipment that looked like it hadn't been used
in years. An old pick-up sitting on blocks. A late-
model Cad and, in an area by itself—

—a Porsche Spyder 550 two-door convertible.

Vintage 1955, but looking like it had rolled out of
the dealer's showroom a few hours ago. Silver with
dark blue tail stripes. The racing number 130 painted
in black on the hood and the doors. A '55 California
plate with the license number 2Z77767 yellow on
black.

And scripted in huge red letters across the rear
cowling—

—"*Little Bastard.*"

The wreckage of the Porsche had been purchased a
short time after the fatal crash by some guy who sold
off the parts at prices equivalent to what death souvenirs of JFK, Jackie, and Princess Di sold for decades
later. Pieces began to disappear, bit by bit. After the
chassis dropped out of sight in 1985, the Porsche existed only in photos.

"The genuine article, Gulliver, and I can't begin to describe what we went through over the years to put the Little Bastard back in one piece."

It was as if the voice drifting through the half open door to my right knew what I was thinking, and I knew whose voice it was.

Chip Kiley moved away from the door as I stepped through and, indifferent to the .45, turned his back on me and nonchalantly crossed over to the TV console. He snapped it off and said, "I knew you and I would meet up again, but I didn't figure it to be back in Indiana. I should of known better, huh, pal?"

He looked healthy enough to finish back-to-back marathons, wearing contractor jeans, a hooded sweatshirt, and a garish red, green, blue, orange, yellow, purple, and gold horizontally striped T-shirt under a canvas cargo shirt, and old-fashioned ankle-high tennis shoes.

This side of the old barn had been converted into spacious residential quarters. A combination living room, library, and den, with a kitchen and dining area off to one corner. A handmade stairway twisting to a bedroom loft that ran the length of the structure and at least a third of the width. Rustic furniture that worked well in the setting and had a comfortable, lived-in feeling.

Kiley pointed out a casual chair for me and chose a high-backed wooden rocker for himself.

I shook my head, moved into a shooter's stance, and demanded, "Where's Stevie?" It was as close as I could come to small talk.

"I was just about to ask you the same thing about Jimmy Junior." Kiley crossed his legs at the ankles, locked his fingers behind his head. Suggested calmly,

"You can put the gun away, really you can. I'm not a danger to you. . . . Not yet. Not right away, anyway."

He managed a big grin that under other conditions might have been infectious. He was comfortable and letting me understand he controlled the situation.

I kept the .45 on him anyway. Shook my head and repeated, "Where's Stevie?"

"She's where you can't find her and, unless you put that gun down and answer me about Jimmy Junior, she's going to be dead, dead, dead. Do I make myself understood, pal?"

There was no pretense here, no tough guy act he was assuming for my benefit, making his casualness all the more disquieting.

I said, "Loud and clear, pal," spitting out the words. I threw the safety on the .45 and shoved it inside my pants, at the hip. Kiley didn't seem to mind that I was keeping it.

"So, where were we? Oh, yes . . . You're here, and I saw her, too, from out the window, Jimmy Junior's new girl toy. You left her in the car. I don't suppose you also left Jimmy Junior out there in the car?"

There was no upside to lying about that.

Too easy for Kiley to check.

I said, "We left him back at the mud pond. All trussed up and—" A look at my watch. "By now the police probably have him in custody. Booking him for attempted murder and raping a minor, and you and I know that's only for starters, don't we?"

That was a lie with an upside, one Kiley wouldn't be eager to call the cops about.

I said, "Your turn. Stevie."

Kiley's wave-off said "Not yet."

"How did you and the girl toy get out from the trunk of the car?"

I shook my head. "Your turn. Stevie."

He tried to outwait me. When that didn't work, his

face squeezed tighter and his brows crawled over his angry squint.

"The cops don't have him, Jimmy Junior. That's horse shit, isn't it, Gulliver? The cops had Jimmy Junior, you would of brought them back here with you or just you would be here now, the kid off somewhere with the cops to give a statement. . . . Where's Jimmy Junior? What did you do with him? And God help you, you don't have an answer that makes me smile."

I tried staying calm in the wake of his ebbing patience. "A trade, Jimmy Junior for Stevie," I said, my face locking into what I hoped was an impenetrable stare, hoping I was more convincing now than when I tried running a bluff at the old Saturday night poker games at the *Daily*.

Kiley tilted his head and studied me with growing malevolence before his eyes drifted from their corners and stared past my shoulder to ask, "You hear any of it?"

A glance told me Mrs. Grizzard had joined us. She was framed in the doorway to the garage, her .38 trained at me.

"Seems like old times, Mrs. Grizzard," I said.

She ignored me to answer Kiley.

"Heard enough to know what's crossing my mind about Jimmy Junior. I don't like none of it."

"Me, neither," Kiley acknowledged.

He unwound from the rocking chair, tugged his clothes straight, pushed back the long strands of white hair that drooped in front of his sagging earlobes, and eyed me with glittering malice. Moved on me with a cat's grace and whacked his open palm onto my cheek. Caught the other cheek with his knuckles on the return.

The connects tore at my neck muscles. My hands automatically moved up to protect my face, too late to do any good. My eyes struggled for focus.

Kiley pulled the .45 out of my pants. Brought the

barrel down on my shoulder blade with enough force to make me cry out. I angled forward, locked my knees to keep from falling.

He jammed the gun into my belly, pushed his face close enough for me to smell his breath, and fairly hissed, "No trade, you lying turd. On a two-to-one vote."

"Democracy in action," I said, struggling to get the words past an uncooperative throat, not sure if I was being a first-class smart ass to prove something to him or to myself. "Jimmy Junior for Stevie. Straight trade. Last time I make the offer."

Mrs. Grizzard padded over and showed me what she thought of the offer by banging my ear with the side of her .38. Turned to Kiley and said, "The girl in the car, she'll know about Jimmy Junior."

"I'll go on out and get her in," he said, nodding agreement. "She's never seen me before. I'll feed her some crock about being a neighbor who happened on by. Horrified by what's gone on. Sent by Gulliver to fetch her."

Mrs. Grizzard waved off the suggestion. "Not a good time to be introducing any strangers. Better me the one to go."

Kiley said, "You and Gulliver, both. He leads the way to say all's fine and dandy. The Marriner woman waiting inside."

Mrs. Grizzard decided after a moment, "Just him will do. He'll go on down to the car and say what he got to to bring her back here, me all the while keeping an eye on him. You go keep the Marriner woman company and I'll bring them." Waving the .38 in my face, she said, "Let's us get a move on, and no funny tricks, you know what's good for you anymore."

* * *

The sudden light jarred Stevie awake. She turned in the direction of the *shoji* screen, accustoming her eyes, expecting to see Mrs. Grizzard, not a man she'd never seen before. She knew at once why he looked familiar. He matched Neil's description of Chip Kiley.

"Chip Kiley, right?"

He nodded an acknowledgement.

"Where's Neil?"

No answer.

"I said, 'Where's Neil?'"

"Your boyfriend will be along in a few minutes."

Forcing a smile she did not believe for a minute. Putting the tip of his index finger below her chin. Pushing her face up. Leaning over for a closer look.

"You're a lot prettier in person than on the TV, exactly the way Jimmy Junior was telling us."

"He's my ex-husband, not my boyfriend, and I'd be better looking if I wasn't tied to this chair."

"I bet so," he said, planting a kiss on Stevie's forehead. Stepped back from her and over to the dressing table, where he settled onto the seat Mrs. Grizzard had occupied. Checked his face in the mirror. Smiled at what he saw. Patted down his eyebrows and finger brushed at the wrinkle quotes on the sides of his mouth before he turned around to face her again. "So! How can we amuse ourselves until your—" Stretching the word a foot. "—boyyyfreennnd joins us?"

Stevie knew from the look in his eyes, before he covered them with the blue-tinted shades he had draped from the zip collar of the hooded sweatshirt that looked like it once belonged to the Unabomber, she had nothing to lose.

"Tell me about James Dean," she said. "Is he dead or alive?"

"The answer to that question is worth a lot more than you can afford, bright eyes."

"I'm paying with my life, aren't I?"

"She's smart, too, folks," Kiley said, addressing the air in the bomb shelter. "Let's us give the lovely lady a great big hand." Extended both arms straight out between them. Applauded vigorously. "A pretty price it is you'll be paying. Don't you just love it?"

Amusing himself at her expense.

Stevie spotted a scissors on the dressing table.

If she got free and got to the scissors, she—

"Okay, Chip, pass on James Dean. Tell me instead about Mrs. Grizzard."

Kiley weighed his answer.

Finally, "Mrs. Grizzard has my heart." Moved a hand to his heart. "She's a very special gal."

"Seeing how she's dead, I can understand."

Her comment sucked the cheery expression off his face. After another moment, "Exactly what is that supposed to mean?"

"What it means. What she told me herself. She told me Mrs. James Grizzard, Sr., died a long time ago. . . ." A beat. "Also Ada Montgomery."

Ada's name caught Kiley at the start of a snort and set off a king-sized coughing fit.

When it ended and he had wiped the spittle from his mouth and dried his hand on his pants, he said, "Who?" Fiddled nervously with something or other dangling from a thin silver neck chain inside his shirts.

"Don't do a dumb act with me, Chip. I'm talking about Jimmy Junior's mommy—by any name."

"Both dead: for years," Kiley said forlornly. He looked genuinely wounded by the knowledge. "How I came to be here . . . For Jimmy."

"Live Jimmy or dead Jimmy?" Stevie asked, pleased with herself for bringing him around again to the question. "I know he's alive—Dean. I was there at the Hollywood post office the day he murdered Nico Mercouri in cold blood. The SOB stood there and he watched my dear friend die. I swore he's going to pay for it."

"Not!"

Kiley rushed her, punched her face hard. A sharp crack and a burst of pain. He had broken her nose, she was sure of it. A trickle tickling down and over her lip, into her mouth. Blood. Broken for sure.

Stevie wasn't going to let him know her pain.

She used an Actors Studio trick, drew from memory a happy experience. Rambling through Griffith Park with her imaginary friends. Zelda and Jordan. Daisy. Rammy. Rocker. The merry-go-round. The zoo. Smiling at the mind pictures.

Smiling at Kiley as he backed off back into the chair.

"Are you always this brave after you tie up your women, you sad excuse for a degenerate?" What the hell. If they were going to kill her, him and Grandma Moses, she had nothing to lose. "Untie me and try that trick again, Chip—I'll have you spitting out your gonads for cherry pits."

Kiley smirked. Mimicked her words: "I'll have you spitting out your gonads for cherry pits." Told her, "You hear a difference? You got the emotion, but not the pitch, not entirely the right inflection. Work on it and bring it back to class next week." Overacted his amazement. "Oh, I forgot—*No next week for you, girl.*"

Stevie admitted to herself he was right, better with it than she had been, the creep.

He said, "Jimmy Junior, a fan of yours, although I don't know why, excepting maybe he couldn't see past your looks to what a miserable actress you are." A beat. "Jimmy Junior should of taken care of you when he had the chance, that day at the post office."

"Jimmy Junior?"

"Must be real surprise popping on your face like pimples. Too good to be acting. Yeah, was Jimmy Junior. A fine actor. In his blood, you could say." Kiley looked at her like his next meal. "Sure, why not?" He seemed to be addressing himself and Stevie at the same time. "Let's us talk about real acting while there's still time left. . . ."

Stevie knew to shut up and let him speak, more a mumble into his chest, and tried not to be obvious whenever her eyes drifted back to the scissors, waiting for another opening that would let her challenge Kiley again about the rope binding her to the chair.

When I got to the Mustang, Joanna had a tentative smile and a question mark for an expression. I signaled her to stay in the car, using my body to shield my hands from Mrs. Grizzard, who was on the porch, the .38 gripped behind her back. Then, for Mrs. Grizzard to see, I signaled Joanna to roll down the window.

I braced my palms on the frame and half leaning into the car told her, "No matter what I do or say, don't get out of the car, Joanna. First sign of trouble, I want you to drive off, get away from here, same as I told you before. Understand?"

Joanna nodded, then shook her head.

"What's going on, Mr. Gulliver?"

I explained the situation to her.

She screwed her face into a puzzle.

Her fearful look returned.

"Oh Lord, oh Lord, oh Lord."

"Stay calm, Joanna. When I turn to leave you, start the engine. I'll tell Mrs. Grizzard you want to see Stevie or you're going to the police. Let's see what that does."

"Oh Lord, oh Lord, oh Lord. I really don't have to go to tell the police, Mr. Gulliver."

I said anxiously, "Joanna, why do I think you're about to tell me something I don't want to hear?"

"Look in my hand."

She shifted her eyes downward, turned over her hand to reveal a cell phone.

It looked like mine.

"Your cell phone," she said. "I remembered it was in your bag in the trunk. Felt it when you had me going for your gun. I got it and stuck it in my pocket before we left Muddy Waters, you know? Just in case?"

I knew what she was going to say next.

Shuddered.

Shuddered again when she said it.

"Just before you came out on the porch with her? I called up the police at 911 and told them what happened and to hurry up on over," she said. "I didn't know about Stevie, didn't think, I wasn't thinking, or I never . . ."

Tears pooled in her eyes.

I reached over, patted her on the arm, reassured Joanna I knew she had meant no harm. Told myself I had to get Stevie out of there before any cops showed up and the old woman and Kiley proved they were crazy enough to make war. Felt an old ulcer stirring and shooting pains growing like the economy.

"Joanna, listen hard and don't ask why. . . . After I walk away, call 911 again and tell them not to hurry up on over."

"What if it's too late?"

"First things first," I said, trying to make new sense of the situation, For now, it was the best answer I could give her.

I told Mrs. Grizzard, "Joanna says she has to see Stevie first, see that Stevie's all right, or she's leaving and going straight to the cops."

"Didn't you say Stevie's right now sitting in the

front parlor over a nice cup of hot cocoa and wants her to join us there?"

"Joanna wouldn't buy it, Mrs. Grizzard. She knows what Jimmy Junior did to her and she believes you were part of it, because you didn't try to stop him."

"You sure it wasn't that you went and yapped off to her against my wishes?"

"I gave you my word, didn't I?"

"Like I was supposed to believe you?" She made a clucking sound. "You must think I am one dumb bunny anymore to buy that line of chalk. Like I'm supposed to haul her up here, the Marriner woman, and give you a chance to get away with the both of them? What kind of fool you take me for?"

"What are my choices?"

"Except for needing to get the girl, I'd soon as kill you now as later, so you watch your smart mouth. You go and get that girl here, or I hate to tell you what will happen."

New rain clouds were playing against a darkening sky and half bathing us in late-afternoon shadows as I left the farmhouse porch for the Mustang a second time.

Joanna lowered the window and I asked, "What did the cops say when you called back?"

"Oh Lord, oh Lord, oh Lord." Choking on grief, she said, "They told me that it's too late and my daddy's already on the way."

"Your daddy?"

"The chief of police? They said he said to tell me if I called again to not get out from the car and just keep my head low." More tears. "I'm sorry, Mr. Gulliver, I really am. Really. Truly."

I reached in and gave her shoulder a reassuring pat while I tried to sort out the fuzz balls of confusion, one circulating in my head, the other one eating through my stomach en route to my guts.

"Mr. Gulliver?"

"Yes, Joanna?"

"Either of the calls, I didn't say anything about what Mr. Grizzard done to me. You won't tell my daddy, will you? You won't?"

"Not a word," I said.

Joanna tried for a smile, came close.

I answered her with the best one I could muster, turned and headed back for the porch. Told the old woman, "Joanna's thinking it over."

"Thinking it over?"

"Considering it."

"For how long?"

"A while, I suppose?"

"Too long," Mrs. Grizzard said. "I'm not liking this, I'm not liking this at all." Began tapping nervously on the porch floor with her tennis shoe, first one foot and then the other.

"Okay," she said. "You go on back to her and you tell her to wait a minute and I'm going to get Stevie for her to see. You make sure she don't go drive off anywhere and you come on back here.

"And don't you give a thought to making trouble. Either of you is gone when we get back, any trouble in the making, any tricks, we'll have the Marriner woman dressed up to go off like the Fourth of July. Boom. Like that."

22

Kiley told Stevie proudly, like they deserved the Medal of Valor, "We had our reasons. Not one of them serial-killer things, if that's what you're thinking, bright eyes. Not one of us a Ted Bundy."

"Bad enough being you," she said.

He smiled slyly. "The team of Jimmy and Chip at the start, on a crusade to keep the memory of James Dean alive and forever burning bright. Later on, Jimmy Junior came to find out accidentally what was going on and wanted to make a contribution of his own to pop's memory. In time, he was proud to share the torch with Eddie."

"And it was him, Jimmy Junior, who murdered Nico Mercouri?"

"Wasting so much of his talent here in Fairmount, that boy. Even so, someone to make his daddy proud. A first-rate genius with the make-up. Put it on here and there, work on the hair, age himself, you couldn't tell it wasn't the genuine article if you didn't already know. Even a master with explosives, as it turns out."

"Why did you kill Nick Adams?"

That smile again. "His was a suicide as I recall, but if it was our doing, it was because he used friendship with Jimmy to advance his own career. Dubbed Jimmy's voice in *Giant* after the tragedy and right away thought that gave him the same talent. Years went by and Nick never once ever showed any true remorse over the loss of a friend."

"So you killed him, for that?"

"Suicide, I already said." He suppressed a smile.

"Sal Mineo, then. Tell, me about him."

Kiley rolled his eyes. Shrugged.

"Somehow beautiful little Salvatore learned things he shouldn't have," he said. "That and he went on to become a star, but don't I recollect someone found guilty and sent to prison over that one?"

"You tell me, Chip," Stevie challenged. "You were there."

"I was there?"

"An eyewitness. You testified at the trial."

"Yes, that's right. How true," Kiley said, and then he told her the rest about the night Sal Mineo died.

Proudly. An addict shooting up and savoring the instant gratification. Never entirely committing to guilt while taking pleasure in taunting her with the uncertainty.

Stevie threw more names at him.

He dismissed each in a dramatically embellished paragraph or two, even Nico.

Even Augie Fowler.

"Both of them, Nico and Augie, they dropped from sight or they would have been visited sooner," Kiley said.

"Visited," his word.

"Nico, when he traded in his obscurity for stardom

on your soap opera, he became a candidate. Then it was only a case of finding the right opportunity. The ceremony at the post office was the perfect time. What it did for James Dean was distinguish his ceremony from the earlier ceremonies for Elvis. For Marilyn. It'll be remembered a long, long time. Give posterity one more way to immortalize him."

His eyes ate into hers, searching for agreement.

She flashed back contempt.

"Well, one got what he deserved, Nico. The other one, Augie, he will soon enough. He would of before now, if Eddie hadn't been foolish to try what he did, but we all can make mistakes, so long as we profit from them. Mine I went and made with Gulliver, but I won't be repeating it any day soon. Or, with you, either."

Stevie's chill turned into a tremor.

Kiley let her see her reaction amused him.

She took several deep breaths to calm down.

Gave him a defiant smile.

"You're crazy, Chip, you know that?"

"By whose standards? What I do for James Dean I do for the love of James Dean. Anyone can die for love. How many can kill for love? Killing for love is not so crazy to me, bright eyes. To me it's simply beautiful."

This time she showed him nothing. "What took so long with Augie Fowler?"

"We were getting to him when he disappeared. Just seemed to up and vanish from the newspaper, from everywhere it seemed, until he showed up on the news dressed up like a Robin Hood movie."

"Why not someone like Rock Hudson?"

"Who says?" A wink.

"Elizabeth Taylor."

A real smile now. "Ah, sweet Elizabeth. You may not know it but Elizabeth gave him his cat, Marcus, for a present." His eyes glistening. "A beautiful Siamese, beige and brown. He loved that cat. Gave it to his friend Janette to take care of the morning he was readying to drive off in the Little Bastard." Pausing to reflect. "He loved her for her generosity, so how could he? Until Elizabeth seemed to forget about him anymore, showing more for the likes of a Michael Jackson. Freaky boys. So don't be too certain she's not back on the list right now."

"The way Natalie Wood was on this list?"

Another genuine smile.

"Nat went on and became a big, big star, big as Jimmy would of been. You think you could know how much that would of hurt Jimmy if he wasn't beyond being hurt? Natalie Wood getting what should of been rightfully Jimmy's."

Kiley's voice trailed off.

"Augie Fowler told Neil Gulliver he saw Dean with Natalie years later, long after he was dead. The night she died. Or, you going to tell me that also was Jimmy Junior?"

His eyes retreated to memory before Kiley pulled them tight and checked out the ceiling. Did a silent count on his fingers. Shook his head.

"Jimmy was old enough and had enough practice by then, but there were some special circumstances—"

And Kiley stopped, distracted by the sound of the metal door at the far side of the room gliding open.

Mrs. Grizzard.

Announcing in a voice crackling with bother as she stepped through the door, "We have to show the little brat the Marriner woman to reel her in."

They moved outside her hearing and rumbled back and forth like they were weighing pros and cons. This went on for several minutes before Kiley threw up his hands and muttered something about killing everyone, getting it over with.

Walked to one of the open shelves.

Dug something out of a cardboard carton.

Held it out for Stevie to see.

A hand grenade.

Nodding, he said, "You might remember seeing one of them at the post office. This baby's going to be hooked to the back of your pants. You listening close?"

"I'd prefer something from Tiffany's."

Did she always have a smart mouth, Stevie asked herself, or was it something she learned from Neil? Maybe, something she picked up in the divorce? No, she had taken nothing from Neil, besides herself. Genetic. It was genetic. Mama also has a smart mouth. Funny, Stevie thought, how in a moment like this her mind had turned to her mama.

So, mama, what do we do now?

Kiley gave her a cold stare and continued, "My finger will be on the pin all the time we're upstairs to collect Gulliver and the schoolgirl. One false move from you, anyone, and in ten seconds you will be in more parts than you could of possibly acted in your whole lifetime."

"That's a good one," Mrs. Grizzard said, amused by Kiley's remark, scoring him a point in the air with her index finger. Asked him, "What you got to untie her ropes with?"

"Scissors," Kiley said, pointing to the dressing table.

The old woman walked over and found them, stepped around behind Stevie and decided after she had fiddled for a minute, "Not doing the trick anymore. Rope too thick and can't work it into any the knots."

Kiley opened one of the drawers, rummaged around,

came up with a pocket knife. "Swiss Army," he said. "Could finally cut down an oak you had all the time in the world."

He traded Mrs. Grizzard and put the scissors back on the table while she went back to work on the ropes. This time successfully. Strands fell away from Stevie and to the floor and Stevie suddenly felt as if someone had turned the handle that restored circulation to her limbs.

"Get up and over," Kiley commanded, dangling the grenade by the pin like a Christmas tree ornament.

She stood, but her legs refused to cooperate.

She stumbled forward, falling into Kiley's arms.

He settled her onto the dresser table seat and told her, "Sit a minute till you get your sea legs back."

It took three or four minutes before she was able to get up, Mrs. Grizzard grumbling all that time and Kiley urging patience, assuring her, "Gulliver isn't about to let anything happen as long as we got her, same as vice versa. Don't you know true love when you see it?"

Mrs. Grizzard gave him a wounded look. "You of all people should be ashamed of yourself for even letting those words pass through your lips."

Kiley said, "You're right and I apologize."

Without hesitation, he took the old woman in his arms and planted a hard, lingering kiss on her thin mouth, showing more passion than people that age are given credit for by people half that age.

Stevie used these moments to grab the scissors and stash them inside her jeans.

I was holding up a wall inside the porch, waiting for Mrs. Grizzard to get back with Stevie, watching drizzle kick up specks of dirt as it hit the ground, when the storm door creaked a warning they'd arrived.

The old woman ambled out first. Stevie was next,

and my smile at seeing her slid from my face after I got a good look at hers. Her nose was swollen. It had been broken somehow, proof revealed in the two black eyes that reminded me of a raccoon. Dried threads of blood making a path over her mouth.

She spotted my angry need to damage someone, used her eyes and a small head shake to signal she was okay and don't do anything foolish.

Kiley was tight behind her, one hand gripping her waist, the other nudging her outside. He ordered, "Move up front with her, Gulliver."

Once I did, he gave Stevie the same instruction. We stood side by side on the lip of the porch, like a bride and groom, Kiley behind Stevie and Mrs. Grizzard behind me, her .38 jammed into the small of my back.

Kiley inched his mouth to Stevie's ear and told her, "Smile and wave for the girl to come join us."

Stevie did as she was told.

When nothing happened, Kiley said, "Do it again and make a bigger smile."

This time, Joanna cut the motor, slid out of the car, and stood behind the driver's door, hesitating for a moment before she waved at Stevie to come to the Mustang. It was one of the things we had planned in the time I had with Joanna before the old woman returned—

Trying to get Stevie to safety as a first order of business.

Explaining I stood a better chance of taking care of myself without Stevie to worry about.

Mrs. Grizzard decided, "The girl's too clever by half anymore."

"Well, bright eyes can't go down there without me and, anyway, I don't think it's the best idea," Kiley said.

Stevie answered my unspoken question.

"Mickey Moron has a live grenade clipped to my belt, honey. His bony finger's on the pin."

The news drained the color from my face and set my heart pounding like a Hitchcock kettle drum.

Mrs. Grizzard poked me with the .38 and ordered, "Go talk to the girl again."

"Maybe I just toss the grenade at the damn brat and that'll be that," Kiley said, almost like he meant it.

The old woman thought so, too. "Please. Baseball was never your best sport," she said.

"I wasn't so bad tossing a basketball," he said, snappishly, then to Stevie, "I lettered in three sports." Proudly, like that had happened the day before yesterday.

"Maybe this will do it," Mrs. Grizzard said, and squeezed in between Stevie and me.

Nothing hiding her from Joanna now, as she threw her free arm across Stevie's shoulders. Laughed and waved and smiled and told her, "You, too. Wave again and let her see what good friends we are."

The last of her words were drowned by my shouts of, "No, don't!," whipping my arms like a semaphore at the cops I knew had to be there by now—

Kiley ranting, "What the hell!?" and—

The sound of a gun burst—

A second or two in front of the bullet striking Mrs. Grizzard in the chest.

She lurched forward, off the porch and onto the ground, pulling Stevie with her.

The motion separated Stevie from the pin.

Live grenade.

I dove off the porch.

Fought to free the grenade clip from her belt, mentally counting off the seconds.

Eight.

Seven.

Six.

Got it. Got it. Got it.

Scrambled to my feet and pitched the grenade high

and away from the house, in the opposite direction from the Mustang.

One.

Zero.

The grenade hit the ground, and—

Nothing.

A dud. It was a dud grenade.

An explosion—

Sending a crater's worth of dirt and grass and rock in all directions.

Not a dud grenade.

Moaning after Jesus, calling his name like he was the paramedic she needed, Mrs. Grizzard rolled over. Facing me. Pointing the .38 at me, her aim couched by her elbow in the ground like a divot. Cursing me with her eyes.

Before she could get off her shot, Stevie jammed a scissors into the old woman's forearm, bringing it down like a dagger.

Mrs. Grizzard called for Jesus again and lost her grip on the gun, about the same time another bullet struck her and appeared to take off a large chunk of her head, her hair sailing three and four feet onto the porch while the impact pushed her on her side and into an awkward position only a corpse could tolerate.

I turned to look in the direction the shot came from, knowing what I would see.

A rifleman was stagger-stepping sideways toward us, his weapon still aimed for use, from the jungle of tall weed grass about thirty-five yards away, where he had been hiding, waiting to get off his clear shots at Mrs. Grizzard and—

Kiley!

He wasn't on the porch.

He wasn't anywhere.

Except gone.

The rifleman shouted, "Gulliver, you and her get down, stay down! The other one's still loose!"

We dropped on command and I pulled Stevie closer to me, protecting her with my body.

The rifleman called to Joanna, "Baby doe, I want you to hide down behind the door till I say so!"

Joanna, too terrified to be coherent, raced to reach the rifleman, calling, "Daddy! Daddy!" Locking her father in an embrace, her arms barely encompassing his hefty midsection.

He moved his trigger hand from the hunting rifle to her shoulder and moved her behind him, quickly got his finger back on the trigger, and worked his head around like a searchlight. Protected from the light rain shower by his long-brimmed trucker's cap and Ray-Bans.

"The other one must be back in the house, so you two stay down there on the ground!" he barked.

He was wrong.

That instant, as if on cue, we heard a noise like wheels turning. From the direction of the barn. The garage door rising. A motor gunning, and then—

Out charged the Little Bastard.

Chip Kiley behind the wheel.

Down the dirt road and gone.

A million miles an hour, maybe faster.

Joanna's daddy wheeled, set, and got off some shots, maybe popped a few raindrops, but that was all.

He cursed himself, cradled the rifle, and clicked on the two-way hooked to his belt. Called in a description of the Spyder and some commands on the microphone attached to an epaulet on his police chief's uniform. Ordered Joanna back to the car, then moved on Mrs. Grizzard.

Got down beside her, a knee and one foot on the ground, one arm resting on his leg, while he verified she was dead. Complimenting himself on his aim, then—

"All damned to Hell!" He looked over to us, his face full of disbelief. "You know this?" Rose and dusted himself off. Shook his head and poked half a smile inside his chubby cheek. "Damnedest thing ever. Come see."

I walked over.

"I'll be damned!" I said, more amazed than the chief had been.

Stevie, sitting cross legged on the ground, said, "What is it I'm the only one not damned about?"

"Mrs. Grizzard is a guy," I said.

"That's some joke?"

"An old guy," I said, "but definitely a guy."

Stevie strutted her eyebrows and bug-eyed at no one in particular.

"I'll be damned," she decided.

"Any idea who, or what, that's all about?" the police chief asked.

Stevie and I looked at each other like we both could answer his question.

The *who* of it, anyway.

The chief had just shot and killed James Dean.

He and the Porsche were invisible to the world by the time the all-points bulletins were being broadcast and police and the sheriffs were setting up roadblocks along all the main roads leading in and out of Fairmount.

It would take a minor miracle to find him.

Unless the cops knew where to look.

They didn't. He was confident of that.

About two miles outside Marion was a rarely used dirt road off the highway that led to a block of squatters' shanties, a "Hooverville" abandoned in the mid-thirties, a few years after Franklin D. Roosevelt was elected president for the first of four terms and began curing the nation of a depression that gave birth to the country's first generation of homeless.

It was the road he had followed to safety, using speed and a Blue Angel's caution.

Jimmy and his school pals had stumbled into the compound as teens. It became their secret playground.

Over the years he went there a few times with a date, for the occasional rarely memorable sexual scrimmage, but more often alone, to work on his part in the Fairmount High School stage play where no one could see him practicing his lines out loud and enjoying the sound of his own voice reciting the words from Mooncalf Medford.

The Monkey's Paw.

An Apple from Coles County, *his favorite play, because Miss Nall, his drama teacher and his inspiration, had given him the starring role.*

Those years, the young Jimmy quietly dreamed of the day he'd be a famous actor, cheered by the critics as the new Clift, the new Brando.

Or, better—

The first James Dean.

James the First.

King James.

And Jimmy would bellow at the sky words by Keats he had learned in class: "I would sooner fail than not be among the greatest."

And he had made it, hadn't he, but—

At what price?

An early death in trade for immortality.

Oh, Jimmy, Jimmy.

Would you really have wanted it any different?

What value in being a broken and disillusioned, busted-faced, fall-down drunk, and finally forgotten Clift?

What glory in a godfather grown old and fat and a

squandered talent, remembered for the past and given no hope for the future?

But James Dean—

Ever the rebel with a cause.

Eternity his Eden.

A giant to be mourned forever.

Proof: his beautiful face on a postage stamp.

The shanty town had stayed an important part of Jimmy's memory and, years later, back in Fairmount, after sweet Ada was gone and it became safer for him to step out, he and the others fixed it up, made it their bolt hole—

A hideout for the three of them to head for, it ever came to that.

Where Jimmy Junior had quickly made it one more place to enjoy in relative security the delights extracted from his doped-up, drugged-out students, his father used it to get back a piece of his life.

Jimmy frequently went there by himself, at night, navigating the eccentric dirt road like it was a stretch of Indianapolis Speedway and somehow managing to avoid so much as a minor scratch on the restored Porsche Spyder.

He parked the car in the shanty they had turned into a garage—working weekends over a three-month period, careful not to show outward signs of their handiwork—and covered it against dust and the elements, then moved on to the shanty they had made over into living quarters.

It didn't offer much by way of comfort, but there were three reasonably comfortable foldaway beds and enough canned goods and bottled water to make do on an emergency basis.

He kept a spare make-up kit there and the wardrobe closet was stocked with costumes Jimmy Junior had "borrowed" from the drama department's stockpile.

Backed by a Mag Lite and, sometimes, a traveling

moon, Jimmy would follow the old, forgotten footpaths into Marion, where there was less chance than twenty miles away in Fairmount of anyone penetrating his disguise.

He'd put in some time at a bar, never the same one too often, share local talk and—whenever he thought someone was eyeing him too closely, maybe even ready to ask a wrong question—he'd slap a couple bills and a healthy tip on the counter and sing his goodnights out the door.

Every so often, on especially melancholy nights, maybe a brew too many under his belt, Jimmy headed back to the shanty by way of Fourth and McClure, 320 East Fourth Street. Where he was born. The old Seven Gables Apartments his folks had left behind when he was a year old and they moved to Fairmount. Jimmy never knew what drew him there, only that it gave him some form of comfort being there.

Comfort.

No comfort now, not for me, he thought.

Everyone gone, but me.

I'm the last one left.

No comfort in that, only memories of the past and a place to prepare for the future and finish the work that was now more important to him than ever.

The deaths of Neil Gulliver and Stevie Marriner.

Everyone else on the list could wait.

It also was important that Gulliver and Marriner know it was coming. He wanted them to understand the power of fear before he took his revenge for the two deaths they had caused today.

Damn them!

Damn them!

23

Stevie and Neil finished with the police and the medics and, back at the motel in Marion, fell quickly into bed, where she matched him in a frantic, devouring, almost irresponsible kind of lovemaking. Not the first time they let their emotions pass for conversation, knowing what the words would be if words had been needed.

When they were done, equally exhausted, but still clinging to one another like orphans in a storm, she sensed Neil had to say something to her and urged, "Don't."

"I just—"

"I know."

"You, too? Tell me that much?"

"Can't live with him, can't live without him," she told him, her eyes fixed on the shadows on the walls, afraid to look at him now, fearing he would see it in her eyes and take it as a sign of—

See *what*, Stevie?

Take *what*, Stevie?

The part she still didn't have clear in her mind, except that she'd fought too hard, for too many years, for her freedom, the right to be independent, answer to no one but herself, come and go as she pleased, be who she was and whomever she chose to be.

Now. Tomorrow.

Whatever. Whenever.

Neil said, "Maybe you, us could try? Take a shot? Maybe we—?"

"Same old question, same old answer, honey."

"Tell me maybe someday—"

Stevie's hand covered his mouth before he could finish the thought he never stopped playing over and over with her, like it was one of the well-worn jazz records in his collection.

"Maybe someday. Now be a good boy and give me back my half."

"Half is better than none," Neil said, trying to lighten the moment, his way of always letting her know he understood.

Understood, yes. Believed, no.

Anymore than he believed Ingrid Bergman flew off with Paul Henreid, as he'd tell her whenever a moment like this erupted from common need.

"Besides, babe, I only came here for the waters," he said with a stiff-lipped lisp.

She forced a laugh, too.

Neil rolled to his side of the bed, tucked two pillows under his head, clicked on the TV. Switched the channels until he found CNN, already filled with stories about the farmhouse.

Late breaking news.

Live and on tape.

Tape only of them.

More of her than Neil.

File stuff from when Blackie Sheridan was killed and she faced a murder charge and the media fallout lasted for months.

Today they'd gotten away too fast, covered their tracks so the media could not find them before, with luck, they were on a plane heading back to Los Angeles.

Stevie Marriner adding celebrity and the kind of notoriety that automatically turns a murder story into an international event. How the Sex Queen of the Soaps escaped death at the hands of—

Like that.

Worth it, Stevie?

Public adoration feeding your constant need to be loved, that was one thing.

This wasn't that one thing, though.

Was it, Stevie?

Is it, Stevie?

More tape.

The police chief, Joanna clinging to his side, talking about his daughter's kidnapping by Jimmy Junior. His death. Her rescue. Joanna's eyes revealing truths she would carry with her through the rest of her life.

Neil had told her what Jimmy Junior did to the girl. If he hadn't, she would have seen it in those eyes. For how long had she seen it in her own eyes?

More tape.

Police Chief Murphy Phillips explaining without explaining about Mrs. Grizzard, acknowledging she was a he. Not mentioning James Dean by name or otherwise speculating on an ID.

The coroner wasn't due back for another three days from a forensics conference in Hilton Head, South Carolina, he said, and the victim's fingerprints were on their way to the FBI in Washington.

"When we know something you'll know," the chief said without conviction, staring anxiously into the camera.

Stevie turned on her side, facing Neil, tapped his chest for attention.

"I should have known Mrs. Grizzard was a man," she declared. "Should have seen it."

"You'd have needed X-ray vision to see through all that padding, the wig, the facial goo," he said. "And besides, you are talking James Dean here, dead or alive a killer of an actor."

"He lost it more than a few times, honey. In his voice, the way it rambled sometimes. Something in the way he walked. The way he sat there with his legs crossed when they had me a prisoner down in that bomb shelter."

The recollection brought her hand to the bandage on her nose. She patted it lightly.

Neil reached over and stroked her cheek and her hair, reminded her, "The doctor said you'll be as good as new in another week."

"I'll be the judge of that," she said, angling away from his touch, making a joke where she felt no humor.

"In any event, still better looking than James Dean after he survived the crash, and who knows what kind of reconstructive surgery."

"You're not a woman," she said.

"Neither was James Dean, not then," Neil said.

"You know what I mean."

"Most of the time."

She said, "Unbelievable, isn't it. James Dean alive and hiding out in Fairmount all those years, in the converted barn. Able to come out of hiding only after the real Mrs. Grizzard, Ada Montgomery, died."

"Good a theory as any," Neil said. "Dean dressing up and taking on Ada's identity when he went out in public, or when Jimmy Junior or Eddie were bringing someone home."

"You think we'll ever know if Jimmy Senior's wife really was Ada, or whatever happened to her?"

"Dead by any name. The chief has his men going over the farmhouse like a hurricane, looking for some of the poor kids who were murdered by Jimmy Junior or Eddie. Maybe they'll find her remains."

"Not after what Kiley had to say, how it was her, Ada, not Pier Angeli, who was James Dean's one true last and everlasting love. I bet Ada is resting in eternal peace somewhere nice that's not Fairmount."

"Let's ask Kiley when we find him," Neil said.

"You think we will?"

"As Casey Stengel, the old Yankees manager, used to say, 'It isn't over 'til it's over.' "

"Last time, you told me Yogi Berra said that."

"They both did, to each other."

It was nearing noon when I woke up.

Stevie was still asleep, her body half in, half out of the covers, steady breathing broken by the noises she always made whenever her sinuses were acting up. The air conditioning kicking around the dust, what was doing it to her.

The TV had been on all night, the big story still out of Fairmount. Comments over footage from earlier in the morning. The police chief announcing his guys had found the bodies of three young women reported missing over the past few years, two of them Fairmount High drama students. One victim discovered in the farmhouse basement, the two others on property behind the barn. The search for more bodies was ongoing, the chief told the camera and the world.

I kissed my fingers and touched them to Stevie's shoulder before easing out of bed.

Used the phone in the bathroom to call the *Daily* and see how they'd played the first-person piece I'd phoned in yesterday.

Page one.

SEX QUEEN OF SOAPS SAVED FROM CERTAIN DEATH.

A typical Spider Woman headline, more accurate than usual for her.

What surprised me was how Langtry had held back on anything identifying the late "Mrs. Grizzard" as James Dean.

I had Litrov transfer me to her office, and Kevin pushed me through in about five minutes.

She heard out my complaint and said in her slow, seductive Southern drawl, "Give me something solid to run with, Gulliver. Blood match. DNA. Prints. Hearsay and your wild-eyed speculation aren't good enough on this one."

"What happened? I left town for a few days and missed the scruples epidemic?" I said, but I was already talking to a disconnect.

The business-class flight attendant remembered me only because I was with Stevie. Another fan of *Bedrooms and Board Rooms,* telling her how much he missed her on the show and sneaking her a glass of champagne from first class just before takeoff.

"A call for you," he said, pointing to the phone mounted on the back of the seat in front of me. A smile for Stevie before retreating with her empty glass.

"Probably the Spider Woman," I said, moving the phone to my ear, but Stevie's expression went sour a flash after she saw the change in mine, even before I cupped the mouthpiece and whispered Chip Kiley's name.

He was doing his Harry Chalk impression, wishing us a bon voyage in the insane tone Milosevic probably used ranting about the ethnic Albanians.

"Didn't want you to think I'm forgetting about you and your whore," he said. "The both of you, responsible for two deaths, people I cared for, truly loved. Your turn next. Ridding the earth of you both, and it can't be soon enough to suit me."

That was it.

Click, and then the captain speaking about two minutes later, telling us the flight was being diverted back to Indianapolis.

Airport police and ground personnel were waiting on the tarp, and the passengers were hurried off a landing strip otherwise cleared of equipment, planes, and any other people. A couple hundred yards away, fire engines ready to roll.

"Figure it's a bomb threat," I told Stevie, too low to be heard by anyone else on the people-mover taking us to the terminal.

"You don't think . . ."

"Kiley? Why not? Except—"

I snapped my fingers.

Maybe no bomb. Just a threat.

Kiley had somehow tracked us to Indianapolis and the flight. This was his ingenious way of getting us back to the airport. He was lurking somewhere near, waiting for us to become clear targets.

I told Stevie to stay put.

I hopped from the tram as it slowed to ease around a corner and ran after anyone who looked like he belonged to a badge. It was a guy halfway through a thick sandwich, blue suit and a military spit shine as bright as his tie, with a matching earpiece to the mike pinned to his lapel.

He was the resident Fed in charge and his name was Michael Jordan, like the basketball great, but not him, he advised, probably in case his Caucasian features and a thick mop of neatly groomed auburn hair had fooled me.

I spit out the story and didn't get the argument I was half expecting.

He hustled me to a security suite on the ground level of the building.

Five minutes later Stevie was there, too, along with Michael Jordan and his reassurances that guards were stationed outside and no one could reach us without proper ID and authorization.

An all-clear was flashed about an hour later.

The jet had been swept and double-checked clean.

No bomb.

Stevie and I were guided to the plane through a series of personnel corridors, wrapped inside a rectangle of guards, pausing at the boarding steps long enough for her to sign autographs for some of the guys who'd missed her in the security suite.

The flight to LA was uneventful, but uneasy for us, despite Jordan's certainty there was no way anyone new could have slipped by the re-entry process and be on board.

"He could take another flight and be waiting for us on the other end," Stevie said.

"There's another way to look at it," I said. "We get there first and can be waiting for him."

She didn't think my remark was funny.

Neither did I.

Clairvoyant, maybe.

The next morning, I got off to an early start on the day. Checking my phone messages, a machine-full in the time I was away.

Returning most of the calls that meant something, like Ned DeSantis, telling me he was still in Paso Robles, hot onto something. Too early to say what, he said, but my guess was the girl, Audrey Mae, the luscious clerk-playwright. No answer at the number he left.

Deleting the other calls, most from boiler room

pitchmen with offers too good to resist, mispronouncing my name like it was a job requirement.

Batting out a couple meaningless columns to stay on top of my deadlines, think pieces that didn't take much thought. Like, would *Death of a Salesman* have invaded the American psyche the way it has if Arthur Miller had opened it with Willy calling, "Honey, I'm home"?

Getting back to my normal routine with a morning jog into the Village. Coffee and contentment at my favorite short-order counter. A brief, barbed exchange of words with the Spider Woman, a flare-up but no fire after she repeated how there'd be nothing printed about James Dean until I had something more substantial than my appetite for secondhand guesswork.

Secondhand because what I knew or thought I knew had come from people the boss lady disparaged as secondary sources, peremptorily dismissing Augie, his coroner friend, Manny Gelman, Harry Chalk, Stevie, even Chip Kiley, because what Kiley revealed he'd said to Stevie, not to me.

It didn't sound like Langtry.

As late as last week she had me hustling to make the Dean story play for headlines and circulation. She was 180 degrees away from there now, and the word "cover-up" struck me. I could hear Augie explaining why the Nick Adams story never got told. He had said, "Favors, kiddo." He had said, "The way of the world."

Was the Spider Woman covering up?

Somebody still out there caring about Dean, who had enough clout to get to the people who could get to the people who could tell her to put the lid on me and keep it tight?

There's a small prayer chapel at the County-USC Med Center, tucked away in a corner off the main entrance.

That's where I found Augie Fowler, meditating in the last row. He moved in from his aisle seat and patted it for me after I tapped him on the shoulder and he saw who it was.

I started to say something.

He silenced me with a hand gesture.

Here and there were other people, in couples or alone, a family down front, a few stray kids, some praying and others sitting in a motionless calm. They were the ones I figured for family members who had been going about their business in front of a call they hadn't expected. The cops. Something about an accident or an incident. A loved one at County and maybe they should be here, too. The reality not yet entirely sunk in. Pondering why a calamity had struck them instead of a winning lottery ticket. Innocent victims of civilization's downside.

When he was through praying and we were back in the ward he shared with a couple dozen others, Augie said, "You could've saved yourself the trip. I'm homeward bound in a day or two." Determined not to let me see how pleased he was I'd bothered.

"I wanted to see how the other half lives after the other half somehow manages to defy the odds and stay alive."

"Miraculously," Augie snapped.

"Eight-to-five, maybe, but not a hundred-to-one."

He slid under the sheets, elevated the bed a few pegs and adjusted his pillows, took a swig from the glass of green something on the bed table, and thought about it while I settled back in the visitor chair and pretzeled my arms over my chest, stretched my legs.

"I saw God, kiddo. What were the odds on that?"

"In your case, a million-to-one, seeing as how up to now I've had the impression Brother Kalman figured that was his own role in life."

"In life, but not across the way," Augie said.

I'd been teasing, but I saw he was serious.

"He spoke to me," Augie said, somberly. "I can't tell you what He said. It was just between Him and me, He said. Except, He told me Claire sent her love and so did Wimpy. . . ." His eyes getting a little wet. "He spoke to me and then He sent me back. . . . I'll be a better man for it."

"Augie, you weren't bad going in."

"I wasn't so good, either, amigo, not as much as I should have been. All those years. Those wasted years."

"Did those years teach you anything?"

He hunched up his shoulders. "Only that you can know it all and nothing at the same time."

A stretch of silence, until he aimed an accusing finger at me and said, "You knew who the cop was, the one who almost got himself killed saving our sorry asses."

He answered before I could.

"Jared. Jared Gallagher. Why he seemed familiar to me when he showed up at the Order. Cop smell. They all leave the Police Academy with it."

I said, "I checked on my way here. He's off life support and better than fifty-fifty now."

"So, you did know." He snarled under this breath. Then, "Jared. He was there to save us, downtown, out by the Hall of Records, because of you, right?"

"I was worried about you, for your safety, same way you were worried, so I called Jimmy Steiger. I asked Jimmy to put a watch on you. Jared Gallagher got the call."

"You know, you could have asked me if I wanted a watch."

"You would have said no, you stubborn old coot."

"I would have said yes, amigo. Stubborn, but not *stupido*." He made a jeering noise. "Like I'm so out of it I don't know they're still around? Steiger rotating them, but after a while they look alike anyway, even when I'm high on the pain killers."

"Around for the duration, Augie. When Chip Kiley goes down, the shields go away. Not until."

I brought him up to speed, including everything that hadn't made it into the news, the hearsay and second-hand stuff.

"Something I don't know, Augie. What was it that got you on Dean's greatest hits list that Kiley didn't tell Stevie? To do with Natalie Wood, right?"

"Don't go and bet the ranch on it," he said.

Made like he was debating how much to tell me.

"It was Pier, not Nat. When Pier swallowed her pride and sailed off into the black beyond, I wrote how their relationship was blown out of proportion, how Pier and Jimmy were never as close as the James Dean mythology mongers made out. My guess, anyway."

He sent his eyes back to the TV screen, making me wonder if it really was his guess, or even the right guess.

"And what I told you about the Spider Woman, how I can't stop smelling a cover-up?"

He had hopscotched over the subject earlier, but now he gave it new thought and said, "There's no statute of limitations on cover-ups, kiddo. Didn't I already teach you that? Didn't you get the idea for yourself the day we broke bread with Manny Gelman?"

"I also got the idea you played along. Did you?"

Augie closed his good eye to the concept before admitting, "You know the movie studios' PR powers-that-be liked me a lot, how much I liked them. Strickling. Mowry. Brand. Okay guys like that. Knew how to ask. Knew how to repay favors and debts."

"Not higher than the studios reached out to you?" I said, moving my hand to about four inches above my head.

"Those powers knew who to go to, go through, to

get my attention on Jimmy Dean, amigo. You think about it, you'll figure out how it paid me dividends down the road."

"And it never bothered you."

"Sure it bothered me, but I weighed the outcome, never the income. First made sure I could still live with myself."

"No way to get to Heaven, Augie."

"Been there, done that, remember?"

"And God, when He spoke to you, He had nothing to say to you about straying off the path?"

"Told you, He marked that confidential. Between Him and me. I can break my word, kiddo, but I've never in my life betrayed a confidence. God knows, I'm not about to start with Him."

24

Harry Chalk was already halfway through a pizza when Stevie and I arrived at Wolfgang Puck's in the Virgin Megastore complex at Sunset and Crescent Heights, easy to spot in the swarm of early-bird diners. He had positioned himself at a table for four close to the entrance, facing the door, so he could see and be seen by everybody coming and going. His Green Beret, Godfrey, was to Chalk's left, digging through the remains of a cheese-rich double pizza-burger and a plate of round fries that always reminded me of ringworms.

Chalk waved at us over a look usually reserved for old friends, patted the seat to his right, indicating he wanted Stevie there. That put me across from him, with my back to the entrance, never a favorite position.

Puck's aromatic smells were not quite enough to hide the agent's proclivity for spreading more gas than a Texaco tanker, now abetted by a designer pizza based on a mountain of mushrooms. He used a pinky nail to pick a shred from his back teeth and wiped it off on the napkin he wore around his neck.

"Neil, baby, news to tell you since you called, but first have I got news for this beautiful star here." Patting Stevie's forearm. "Why I had Godfrey tell you to bring her along with you, this glorious creature."

The waitress came to the table for our orders. A small dinner salad for Stevie, a Chinese chicken pizza for me. Chalk complimented us on our choices, observing, "Only the finest chickens Wolfy Puck imports from China," and if he was joking he didn't let on. After the waitress left, he told Stevie, "I got you the best deal in the world a client of mine could ever hope for."

Stevie shook her head.

"Didn't my lawyer call you?"

"That *shmendrick?* Yeah, some *dreck* about you not meaning to go with me, you already had an agent. I said to your lawyer *had* is right, how I already did the courteous thing and told the guy it was memoir-writing time between him and you."

"I don't think so."

"Of course you do, especially after you hear what I pulled off for you with those *momsers* who have the nerve to call themselves producers."

He bit into another slice of pizza and searched the nearby tables like he was looking for the source of the nose-curdling odor that had nothing to do with the food the waitresses were delivering to the tables around us.

Said, "First, I got you another two-year contract extension with perks like you wouldn't believe, not even Deidre Hall or Susan Lucci ever managed. Pay or play. Your weekly's only up ten per cent, but it jumps two points on any foreign. You get a piece of any future cassette sales, a producer credit after this year, and best of all—" Chalk stopped like he'd hit a speed bump. Showed his entry in the Cheshire Cat contest. Did a little musical trill. "This girl who was giving you garbage? This Wells?"

"Walls. Karen Walls."

"Her. Well, it's like a wall I got her marching up against, and then—" He shot a finger gun. "No uncertain terms. She goes or you go and, you know what? Well, I told you what already."

"And they agreed to all this?"

He rapped out a rim shot on the table.

"Not yet, I'm waiting for the final, but remember who Stephanie Marriner's agent is now." Thumping his chest. "Harry Chalk! I didn't become Harry Chalk a long, long time ago not knowing how to make the impossible happen."

Stevie's salad arrived. She picked a tiny piece of lettuce out of her salad and sucked it into her mouth, gave it an analytical chew as she retreated into herself, and I saw she was replaying all she'd just heard.

Chalk looked at me for some reaction.

I did the McQueen grin and said, "My turn now?"

He struck a sour face, and so did Godfrey.

"Baby, I have nothing to tell you is what I have to tell you," he told me, shrugging his shoulders, turning his hands to the wallpapered ceiling. Godfrey shrugged his shoulders and turned up his palms. It was like the two of them were joined at the gesture. "Since your first call, I have not been able to locate Chip Kiley for you. My client of whom we speak is missing. That's my news."

He made a sad clown face, and so did Godfrey.

"You know why I asked you to help find him, Mr. Chalk," I said. Pushed away the Chinese chicken pizza just set in front of me. My appetite gone.

"Me, too, Neil. Me, too. Great as Harry Chalk is with the impossible, miracles take longer." Godfrey joined him in the nod. "I tried all the numbers I have for Chip to no avail, leading me to believe that, contrary to what you think, he's not in town." Moved his head left and right, a beat ahead of Godfrey. "Chip was, he would not wait to hear from me before calling."

"You'll let me know?"

"Sure, of course, and something else? Across the street once was the world-famous Garden of Allah, you know that? A hotel built like it belonged on a back lot. Lot of writers lived there off and on, good as you. Dottie Parker. Bobby Benchley. Scottie Fitzgerald . . . actress who dreamed it up, maybe you heard of her—a little Russian chickie by the name of Alla Nazimova. A big, big star her day."

He gave me a sly wink.

"Ally shtupped Valentino. I shtupped her."

Godfrey winked, too.

The next morning, Stevie was lounging in the tub when she heard the two-tone bell signaling someone at the driveway entrance.

"Mailman, Ms. Marriner. Registered letter."

"Leave it in the box, okay?"

"Takes a signature."

"Who's it from, sweetie?"

"Lemme see," the mail guy said, in a flash citing the *Bedrooms and Board Rooms* production company.

Not the way a script gets delivered and not good news, she knew. In this business, good news always came on the phone. The bad news was delivered by mail or messenger.

Was this it? Had Harry Chalk managed to screw up her career? Was this a termination notice? Victory for Ms. Cunning, Karen Walls, the little—

Stevie shook her head in disbelief.

"Hold a sec," she told the voice on the other end of the squawk box.

She climbed from the tub, threw on a terrycloth robe. Checked her face in the mirror. Grimaced at the nose bandage. Plucked out one of those dark hairs always growing around her chin. Padded downstairs in her pink, bunny-eared slippers.

In the kitchen she checked the bank of security screens the surveillance company had installed after she moved in. The camera aimed on the mailbox showed the mail guy in his blue uniform, shifting back and forth on the balls of his feet, taking in the scenery. The registered letter in one hand, one of those electronic receipt boxes in his other.

The wide angle showed something else.

Showed something missing.

Stevie's adrenaline kicked in. She called at the squawk box, "Where's your truck?"

"What?"

Looking left and right over his shoulder and dead ahead. Spotting the camera lens poking out from its hiding place on the roof.

He said, "Just down the street, why? Even double-parking up here in the Oaks is a bitch."

Smiling like a screen test into the camera lens. The sun breaking through a cloud bank to send a glint of light bouncing off his blue shades.

"So's life," Stevie said, manipulating another one of the surveillance cameras.

Up the street: nothing.

Down the street: a classic Porsche Spyder. Two-door convertible. Black. Glistening like a fresh paint job. California plates she couldn't make.

Stevie tried to swallow and couldn't.

Almost strangled on her own breath.

Chip Kiley.

The SOB was back.

Standing at her mailbox.

The mail guy scanned his watch. Made a face. Held his wrist up for the camera. "I'm running late, see? Maybe you could please hurry up?"

Stevie got a grip on herself and said, "Another minute more, sweetie. You caught me in the tub. I'm making myself decent."

Punched in the code that signaled an emergency to her security patrol. The contract guaranteed armed response in under five minutes.

The mail guy checked his watch again. Gave his head one of those "some people" kinds of shakes.

Stevie looked anxiously from the monitor to the wall clock over the door leading to the breakfast nook.

A minute.

Four to go.

"Just one more minute," she told the squawk box.

"If you like, buzz me through the gate and I can walk it up to the door?"

"That's okay, sweetie. Thanks. Almost done."

Glanced at the bank of monitors.

Two security uniforms moving up from the C camera to the B camera, past the Porsche Spyder.

Handguns drawn.

Surprising the mail guy before he had a chance to do more than drop the electronic receipt box. Hitting the cement loud enough for her to hear.

His hands reaching for fruit flies.

Waving the letter at the security guys.

Telling them where to find his ID.

The security guy with the ponytail checking it out. Looking at the camera to advise her the mail guy was legit.

"Ask him about his truck," Stevie said, still not convinced.

The other security guy holstering his pistol and playing with his tie as he stepped up to take his turn in front of the camera. Adjusting his cap.

"Passed it on foot the way up, ma'am. Parked half a block below it, matter of fact. Parking around here, it's a real bitch."

The mail guy retrieved his electronic box.

Flushed with anger, he shouted, "You want this damn letter or you don't?"

Stevie apologized. Asked, "Can you sign for me?"

"Okay, that's authorization. You guys are witness she authorized it."

He signed somewhere on the box and pointed where he wanted them to sign as witnesses. Pushed the envelope at the guard with the ponytail.

Stalked off, turning a power fist salute into a middle finger display heading down the street, passing the Porsche as it gunned its motor four or five times and sped away.

The guard looked questioningly at the camera.

"The mailbox is fine for now," Stevie said, and thanked them; offered to write the company commending them for their prompt action.

"Just doing our job, ma'am," the guard with the ponytail said, like he was auditioning for the old *Dragnet* show.

He opened the mailbox and tossed in the letter.

And the mailbox blew up in his face.

I was trapped between a couple giant rigs on the Hollywood Freeway, in the middle of a bumper-to-bumper tie-up, when my cell phone rang. I retrieved it from the glove. Litrov on the desk, telling me a mail bomb had gone off at Stevie's place.

"Two security patrol guys almost got totaled, but

for the mailbox muting the blast and sending most of it in the opposite direction. Knocked the sails out of one of the guys and filled him with shrapnel."

"Stevie, Al. Tell me about Stevie."

"Wouldn't be me calling you if it was that kind of news, Gully. Uniforms on site said Stevie's shaken, but feisty. Thought it better you hear it from here first."

I said, "Pass her the word I'm on my way there, Al," clicked off and called the Heathcliffe.

Got Earlier Bogus at the guard's station.

"No, sir, no packages delivered for you."

I told Earlier not to accept any deliveries for anyone, clicked off before he had finished wondering why, called the Order of the Spiritual Brothers of the Rhyming Heart, and was put through to Brother Saul.

Same answer to my question.

Same instruction to Brother Saul.

The only phones in the wards at County General are at the nurse's station. Rather than alarm one of them and risk panic spreading throughout the hospital, I asked if it was possible to get Brother Kalman over to the phone.

It was and it wasn't, the voice on the other end said, her manner suggesting an exhausted nurse at the end of a long shift.

"He's in the chapel again," she explained. "He's been spending so much time there, we probably should make it easier on him, move him and his bed right in."

I humored her with a laugh and asked if there was a police officer outside the ward I could talk to.

"If he's not also at the chapel," she said. She put me on hold and returned a minute later to report, "He must be at the chapel also."

I had no choice. "Can you tell me if anyone has delivered a letter for Brother Kalman in the last hour or two?"

"I could tell you if I knew, so hold on." She put me on hold. "Yes, a beautiful get-well card to go with them others he's getting. Already taped on the wall. Why's that? You wanted to make sure he got your card?"

"Not exactly."

"Or, maybe the flowers are from you? They been sitting here waiting for the brother to get on back from saying his prayers again. Beautiful little basket, so you got good taste, I have to say so myself. Bright white and pink carnations. What's your name or the florist and I can see in the little card envelope if they's yours?"

"Don't touch the envelope! Leave it alone!"

"My, oh, my, some people. Forget how to be nice."

I'm not sure which of us hung up first.

I called 911.

Then, Harry Chalk.

"I swear, Neil, nothing besides what I told you before. You give Chip Kiley the blame, and I still say he would call me back he was in town. That right, Godfrey?" I pictured Godfrey hovering over the wheelchair, his head bobbing in syncopated rhythm with Chalk. "And you can pass on a message for me to our favorite love goddess. It looks like *Bedrooms and Board Rooms* is buying all our demands, so I'll really grind away on those *shmendricks* at the next go-round. Tell Stevie she ain't seen nothin' yet when it comes to Harry Chalk."

Harry hung up the phone and wheeled around with a gleeful expression, asking him how he had done, like a dog begging for a bone.

"Perfect," he said, throwing it to Harry. "You sure you never thought about being an actor? That's how good."

"Not as good an actor as you," Harry said, ever the agent, always earning his ten percent. "But I don't have to tell you that."

He was too honest to disagree. Gave Harry a nod and a two-finger salute off his forehead.

Harry said, "A call like that, enough to prove what I was trying to prove to you, how you need someone protecting your backside. Who better than Harry Chalk?"

He let Harry see he agreed.

Also the nursemaid.

It was the big guy keeping him from taking care of Harry now. Both of them. An edgy look to Godfrey, like he might have guessed what brought him here unannounced. The big guy excusing himself, coming back a minute later with that gun tucked inside his belt, just visible enough to send a warning message.

Harry had to be punished. For saying too much once too often, pointing Gulliver and Marriner in the direction of Fairmount.

Chances were good Harry would open his mouth too wide again sooner or later, say something he shouldn't, and that made him an unnecessary risk.

But why chance it now?

Godfrey armed, on guard that way.

The odds weren't working for him, but—

No hurry about Harry and Godfrey.

There were still others to deal with.

First the others.

Harry and Godfrey when it made better sense, when he had a chance to put the odds with him.

For now, Harry was right about it not hurting to have someone looking after his ass, even if it was only ten percent of the time.

*　*　*

Two days later, the message light was blinking when I got back from my morning run through Westwood. Lt. Ned DeSantis's cigarette-stained growl kicked in without a greeting from Paso Robles:

"Gulliver, it took some doing, me and Audrey Mae, but I cracked through the Berlin Wall up here and get this: I got us a new eyeball and better in old records we managed to excavate. Eyeball says it wasn't James Dean, repeat, was not, they pulled out of the wreckage.

"Dean wasn't even in the car, it happened. He was trailing behind in his other car, a '53 Ford wagon a pal of his was driving up after a late start that morning. Asshole buddy, you get my drift? That's who got pulled out from the Porsche Spyder, the buddy.

"Guy caught up with him at Blackwell's Corner and joined right into the party atmosphere with Lance Reventlow and the others. A couple of brews later, he was putting the arm on Dean to let him take the Porsche for a spin.

"Dean figures why not, and you know the P.S. Guy was Dean's stunt double, stand-in, something like that, on *Giant*. Looks like this was one stunt that didn't work out."

DeSantis promised more details when he got back to L.A. and hung up, leaving me to wonder what happened to Dean, why he went into hiding and played dead for forty-five years.

The chill of surprise wore off, and I dialed the police department in Fairmount, Indiana, identified myself, and a minute later was speaking with Chief Murphy Phillips.

"Was getting ready to call you, Mr. Gulliver," he said after an exchange of weather reports. "Prints got back only this morning from Washington and darned if they don't match Jimmy Dean anymore. The match is to a Kiley. Charles Chester Kiley. The coroner, though, isn't ready to go along with it yet, although he let it slip to me he couldn't make a match to Jimmy's old dental records."

I pumped him for as much as I could get, phone hooked to my ear while I knocked out notes and quotes on the computer, then I called downtown and had Kevin break into the Spider Woman's breakfast meeting.

"Marvelous," he cooed into the phone. "Spidey will absolutely hate this." Giggles. "Hold on."

He was back in less than thirty seconds.

"Sorry, Mister G. She said this time not before she's had her café au lait."

"Buzz her again and tell her I'm counting to ten and then I'm calling the *Times*."

Kevin roared and put me on hold again.

"Better be good, Gulliver," Langtry said when she picked up about four minutes later.

"How about *great,* as in circulation?"

I told her about DeSantis's call, my conversation with Murphy Phillips. Got a lot of silent contemplation in return, until I said, "That's it."

"So what are you telling me, Gulliver?"

"Still secondhand and still hearsay. Our little secret for now, but not after DeSantis gets back to town and leaks what he found out. You know his rep for being a glory hound, always bucking after the next promotion. So, call it, boss. Do we use it or lose it?"

"You're saying James Dean is alive."

"I'm saying it's clear rumors of his death in the Little Bastard were greatly exaggerated."

"This could backfire on us."

"That's what they said about Vietnam."

"Vietnam backfired on us."

"Not you and me. We were only kids."

"You have a perverted sense of humor, Gulliver."

"But a great news sense, Ronnie."

Langtry blew a breath storm into my ear and said, "It's still a pass."

My temper took over.

"Who are you covering up for, Ronnie?"

"I'm doing you a favor, Gulliver."

"That's not an answer."

"Be grateful for it, anyway."

"I'm taking the story to the *Times*."

"You'll get the same answer there, and anywhere else you try," she said. "So will DeSantis," she said, and left me listening to dead air.

He drove up to the observatory in Griffith Park again, to get out of his system the anger that had cost him his sleep for a second night, by studying the bust of James Dean and imagining Eddie here. Lovable, loving Eddie, good kid whatever his problems. Eddie relishing the company of his grandfather, taking pride whenever someone noticed his resemblance and drew him out to say something.

He moved a hand to his neck and pulled out the gold chain holding the gold St. Christopher medal she had given him, the gold and enamel charm which had held a lock of her hair over all these years. All these years and he'd never missed anyone more or forgiven anyone less. Said a hushed prayer for her, one of them he'd learned growing up.

"Excuse me?" A slender voice interrupting his reverie.

The woman was cute in a plain-faced way, cat's eyes and a prominent nose, a mouth hardly large enough to contain her teeth. Late thirties to early forties. Chubby in a sleeveless turtleneck that stretched across her boobs, hips hungry to break out of her Calvins.

He looked at her like he couldn't guess what came next.

"I suppose you get this question all the time," she said, "but I couldn't help noticing and, not meaning to stare or anything, you know who you look like?"

He shook his head. Smiled pleasantly. Wondered if they were real or implants. Swept the area with his eyes to get a sense if she was alone or with someone.

"Him," she said, pointing at the bust. "Like him. James Dean? I mean, you're older I know, but I see it, the eyes, so haunted and haunting at the same time. Even in the look you just gave me. The way your mouth tilts up at the corners when you smile. Yes! Like that just now again."

"Busted," he said, surrendering with his hands. Shyly, "I've heard it over the years."

"Go on!" She pushed out her lips questioningly, a sexy pout to go with eyes squinting after certainty. "That so, you mind telling me your name?"

He did.

She made a noise that had several heads turning as far away as the snack bar, where there already were a dozen or so people studying their morning newspapers over coffee and doughnuts. A photographer draped over a railing to capture moving shadows and light, the temporary moments in time all around him, with what looked like one of those new cameras that played back the pictures over a computer.

"I don't believe this," she said, rolling her eyes upward. Pushing her palms at the air. "I fly here all the way from Cleveland to finally get to see this place and where James once lived and all, so who do I meet?" Reaching a point of breathlessness. Filling her lungs. "His stand-in. It's like history coming alive for me. I read all about you in some of the biographies about James and now here you are, alive and in person."

"So, you were a fan of his?"

"Please!" she said, like the question had been an insult. "Am a fan. Since before and forever. James's number one fan! People can take their Leos and all the others who cannot ever hold a candle to James. . . ." Placed a hand over her boob where he'd just imagined his. "Would you mind if I asked you some questions?"

"Tell you what," he said. "Let's go over to the snack bar for a coffee and we'll talk a bit. How's that?"

"I'd be eternally grateful," she said, awash in the shock of disbelief, "but it has to be my treat."

When they were settled at one of the metal picnic-bench tables, he asked to be excused for a minute. A phone call he had to make.

At the phone bank, he dialed the number it had taken him weeks to get.

She answered herself on the first ring. Even with just a "Hello," he knew the voice at once. Aged, like a fine wine. Mellower, but as melodious as he remembered it from the first time he heard it on the set of Giant. A perfect voice for that perfect face.

"Hello? Hello?"

He didn't answer her.

He waited until she hung up, not wanting her to hear anything that would let her guess right, saving the big surprise for when he saw her again, and wandered back to the woman.

"So where were we?" he said, sliding onto the bench seat next to her, casually letting his hand fall on her thigh.

She threw him a curious look, but let it stay there, and asked, "What was James really like?"

"A lot like me," he said, waiting for her next question. He knew what that one was going to be, too. A request for him to explain.

She found a pack of smokes in her handbag and offered him one. He took two, lit both with his chrome Zippo, and moved one between her lips, visualizing how they'd feel sucking his dong instead of smoke.

She took a heavy drag, let the smoke drift out her

nose and from the corners of her mouth. After another moment said, "What's that mean, exactly, a lot like you?"

He moved. his hand inside around the curve of her thigh as he started the answer he always gave, and when she didn't react, take his hand and move it somewhere else, he knew for certain he had her.

I met Stevie at the *Bedrooms and Board Rooms* set just before the lunch break, and we retreated across Gower Gulch to her favorite sushi joint, where I broke the news about James Dean being alive.

Hard as she tried hiding it, I saw and felt her alarm. A shiver that not even a shot of saki could quell. I was feeling it, too.

"And it's really him, honey? Not Chip Kiley?"

"It's really someone."

"He'll still be after us, won't he?"

"By any name."

She studied the small porcelain vial, rolling it between her fingers, and after several moments said, "Stay with me today, daddy? Right now I don't think I can handle being alone."

"For as long as you like," I said, reaching over to make a dimple in her cheek.

She caught my finger to keep it there and smiled.

"That could be a long, long time," Stevie said.

"Got plenty of that," I said.

ACKNOWLEDGEMENTS

I'm indebted to a number of people who helped make *The James Dean Affair* happen, in particular: Natalia Aponte, my exceptional editor at Forge; other members of the Forge team, the class of the league—Linda Quinton, Jennifer Marcus, Kathleen Fogarty, Karen Lovell, Karla Zounek, Joe Bendel, Tom Espenschied, Jim Kramer, Paul Stevens, and, of course, the main man himself, Tom Doherty.

I also wish to thank my literary agent, Susan Crawford; Sandra Roberts, whose assistance with research and fact-checking was as invaluable to the author as the ongoing support she provides in the areas of public relations and publicity; "Mr. Memory," who still knows more than he's told; family members Deborah and David, Therese and Stephanie, Erin and Daniel, Judith Joy, Bertha and Ida, who are always in the front ranks of the cheering squad, alongside—my wife, Sandra, whose contributions extend far beyond the credit she receives for the photo on the jacket flap.

Drive safely.

Robert S. Levinson
January, 2000

Watch out for

The
JOHN LENNON
AFFAIR

A NEIL GULLIVER AND
STEVIE MARRINER NOVEL

by
Robert S. Levinson
Coming Soon from Forge Books!

The Chelsea on West Twenty-third between Seventh and Eighth was the only hotel in New York I knew by name and reputation. It was the place where rock stars on the rise and on the decline could create trouble and be ignored by the management, unlike the legendary "Riot House" on the Sunset Strip in LA, where the management was less tolerant and routinely called the cops whenever some bona fide rock star or a rolling clone tossed a TV set or the remains of room service, including the cart, onto the boulevard from his eight hundred dollar a day suite.

The bohemian landmark showed all of its seventy-five years and then some. There was something imposing about its street parade of balconied windows, something intimidating about the history I smelled inside, like Dylan tucked in a corner of his room writing "Sad Eyed Lady of the Lowlands."

I had to knock on the counter to get the attention of the desk clerk, who was following the news about John on a small-screen black-and-white TV on the shelf underneath the open-faced room-key cabinet.

He wheeled around on his stool with an expression that showed he was not happy about being disturbed. I put him in his early to mid-thirties, with penetrating black eyes he'd accented with a thick coat of mascara on his eyelashes and a slash under his lower lids. A tumbleweed of hair dyed black vying for attention with collagen-impregnated lips painted a rich shade of green. Clearly, no one had told him Halloween was last month.

I apologized for the interruption, and that seemed to satisfy him, but not his need to spray me with the kind of once-over that advertised its intention. A twice-over kind of once-over like he was looking for a place on me to plant a few bills and had just the place in mind. He gave me an immense smile of confirmation that showed off a mouthful of misshapen teeth and unredeemable decay.

I let him see I wasn't interested, but he flexed his muscles and did some shoulder exercises in case he hadn't read me right. Let me see what I was missing under his too-tight Freddie Mercury T-shirt that seemed ready to burst at the seams.

"I'm Neil Gulliver," I said. "Called you last night from LA and reserved a room?"

He shrugged his biceps and ducked under the counter, came up in a few seconds with a red-covered registry book that he laid on the front counter. Flipped open to a page marked with a pencil on a string.

His fingers, a garden of dirty, bitten nails, trailed downward until—

"Yeah. Here. Gulliver. Two nights, right?" His voice sounded more like a squeal, with a strong English inflection. "And only you for the bedsprings?"

"Maybe three. It depends. A single, yes."

"A bloody shame," he said, and made a clucking sound.

He took the pencil and wrote down something in the registry book before returning it beneath the counter, then moved a registration card in front of me. I took the pen he offered and began filling out the card.

"How you plan on squaring, Neil Gulliver what called us last night from Los Angeles?"

"Sorry?"

"Cash or plastic? You ain't known to the establishment, so the policy is no personal checks. Especially since you're also traveling light." He indicated my backpack and gym bag. "Too easy to disappear, a popular trick hereabouts on more'n one occasion, I might say, so no offense."

"No problem. None taken." I pulled out my billfold from a hip pocket, found the Visa card the *Sentinel* had issued to me, and passed it across the counter.

I knew I shouldn't be using it, given I'd been fired by Easy Ryder and was no longer on the *Sentinel* payroll, but I was owed a last check by the paper and told myself I'd watch it, make sure I didn't spend more than I was owed.

The clerk adjusted his tone again and wondered, "What band you with, mate?"

Making small talk while we did the paperwork.

I shook my head.

"I'm a writer."

He made a face that said that was less than he'd hoped for, but acceptable.

"Judging by your look, so much the clean-cut and proper lad, I'll guess middle-of-the-road. I'd wager you figure to become the next big pop sensation, right?"

"Not that kind of writer. Not a songwriter. A reporter, I meant. For a newspaper back in LA."

"Oh."

He was about to lose interest in me, until I pointed at the TV and said, "He's the reason I'm in New York."

He sat upright and studied me with renewed interest.

"Terrible about himself," the clerk said.

"Terrible," I agreed.

"Put my hands on the bloody bugger what done him, I'd give him a what-for to put him outside Heaven for eternity and a day . . . You can quote me, you're doing a write-up."

"No, I didn't come to work. To pay my last respects."

His eyes took a curious turn.

"You saying you knew him? You knew John Lennon?"

"Not as well as he knew us," I said.

He had to think about that, but quickly began nodding an emphatic *Yes*.

"So say we all, mate," he said. "So say we all."